TONY ABBOTT

★BOOK 2★

THE
SERPENT'S
CURSE

ILLUSTRATIONS BY BILL PERKINS

 KATHERINE TEGEN BOOKS
An Imprint of HarperCollins Publishers

Katherine Tegen Books is an imprint of HarperCollins Publishers.

The Copernicus Legacy: The Serpent's Curse
Text copyright © 2014 by HarperCollins Publishers
Illustrations copyright © 2014 by Bill Perkins
www.harpercollinschildrens.com

Library of Congress Control Number: 2014937634
ISBN 978-0-06-219446-6 (trade bdg.)
ISBN 978-0-06-235159-3 (int.)

Typography by Michelle Gengaro-Kokmen
14 15 16 17 18   CG/RRDH   10 9 8 7 6 5 4 3 2 1
❖
First Edition

To Guardians everywhere

CHAPTER ONE

New York City
March 17
8:56 p.m.

Twelve hidden relics.
One ancient time machine.
A mother, lost.

Seven minutes before the nasty, pumped-up SUV appeared, Wade Kaplan slumped against his seat in the limousine and scowled silently.

None of his weary co-passengers had spoken a word since the airport. They needed to. They needed to talk, and then they needed to act, together, all of them—his father, astrophysicist Dr. Roald Kaplan; his whip-sharp cousin Lily; her seriously awesome friend Becca Moore; and his stepbrother—no, his brother—Darrell.

"Ten minutes, we'll be in Manhattan," the driver said, his eyes constantly scanning the road, the mirrors, the side windows. "There are sandwiches in the side compartments. You must be hungry, no?"

Wade felt someone should respond to the older gentleman who'd met them at the airport, but no one did. They looked at the floor, at their hands, at their reflections in the windows, anywhere but eye to eye. After what seemed like an eternity, when even Wade couldn't make himself answer, the question faded in the air and died.

For the last three days, he and his family had come to grips with a terrifying truth. His stepmother, Sara, had been kidnapped by the vicious agents of the Teutonic Order of Ancient Prussia.

"You can see the skyline coming up," the driver said, as if it were perfectly all right that no one was speaking.

Ever since Wade's uncle Henry had sent a coded message to his father and was then found murdered, Wade and the others had been swept into a hunt for twelve priceless artifacts hidden around the world by the friends of the sixteenth-century astronomer Nicolaus

Copernicus—the Guardians.

The relics were originally part of a *machina tempore*—an ancient time machine that Copernicus had discovered, rebuilt, journeyed in, and then disassembled when he realized the evil Teutonic Order was after it.

What did an old time machine have to do with Sara Kaplan?

The mysterious young leader of the present-day Teutonic Knights, Galina Krause, *burned* to possess the twelve Copernicus relics and rebuild his machine. No sooner had the children outwitted the Order and discovered Vela—the blue stone now safely tucked into the breast pocket of Wade's father's tweed jacket—than the news came to them.

Sara had vanished.

Galina's cryptic words in Guam suddenly made sense. Because the Copernicus legend hinted that Vela would lead to the next relic, Sara would be brought to wherever the second relic was likely to be—to serve as the ultimate ransom.

Wade glanced at the dark buildings flashing past. Their windows stared back like sinister eyes. The hope that had sustained his family on their recent layover in San Francisco—that Sara would soon be freed—had proved utterly false.

They were crushed.

Yet if they were crushed, they were also learning that what didn't kill them might make them stronger—and smarter. Since their quest began, Wade had grown certain that nothing in the world was coincidental. Events and people were connected across time and place in a way he'd never understood before. He also knew that Galina's minions were everywhere. Right now, sitting in that car, he and his family were more determined than ever to discover the next relic, overcome the ruthless Order, and bring Sara home safe.

But they couldn't sulk anymore, they couldn't brood; they had to talk.

Anxious to break the silence, Wade cleared his throat.

Then Lily spoke. "Someone's following us. It looks like a tank."

His father, suddenly alert, twisted in his seat. "A Hummer. Dark gray."

"I see it," the driver said, instantly speeding up. "I'm calling Mr. Ackroyd."

The oversize armored box thundering behind them did indeed look like a military vehicle, weaving swiftly between the cars and gaining ground.

"The stinking Order," Lily said, more than a flutter of fear in her voice.

"Galina knew our plans from San Francisco," Wade said. "She knows every single thing about us."

"Not how much we hate her," said Darrell, his first words in two hours.

That was the other thing. If their global search for the Copernicus relics—Texas to Berlin to Italy to Guam to San Francisco—had made them stronger, it had made them darker, too. For one thing, they were armed. Two dueling daggers, one owned by Copernicus, the other by the explorer Ferdinand Magellan, had come into their hands. Wade was pretty sure they'd never actually use them, but having weapons and being a little more ruthless might be the only way to get Sara back.

"Galina Krause will kill to get Vela," Becca said, gripping Lily's hand as the limo bounced faster up the street. "She doesn't care about hurting people. She wants Vela and the next relic, and the next, until she has them all."

"That's precisely what I'm here to avoid," the driver said, tearing past signs for the Midtown Tunnel. He appeared to accelerate straight for the tunnel, but veered abruptly off the exit. "Sorry about that. We're in escape mode."

Roald sat forward. "But the tunnel's the fastest way, isn't it?"

"No options in tunnels," the driver said. "Can't turn or pass. Never enter a dark room if there's another way."

He powered to the end of the exit ramp, then took a sharp left under the expressway and accelerated onto Van Dam Street. The back tires let loose for a second, and they drifted through the turn, which, luckily, wasn't crowded. Less than a minute later, they were racing down Greenpoint Boulevard, took a sharp left onto Henry, a zig onto Norman, a zag onto Monitor, then shot past a park onto a street called Driggs.

Why Wade even noticed the street names in the middle of a chase, he didn't know, but observing details had also become a habit over the last days. Clues, he realized, were everywhere, not merely to what was going on now, but to the past and the future as well.

Becca searched out the tinted back window. "Did we lose them?"

"Three cars behind," the driver said. "Hold tight. This will be a little tricky—"

Wade's father braced himself in front of the two girls. *Dad!* Wade wanted to say, but the driver wrenched the wheel sharply to the right, the girls lurched forward, and he himself slid off his seat. The driver might have been hoping that last little maneuver would lose the Hummer. It didn't. The driver sped through the intersection on Union Avenue and swerved left at the final second, sending two slow-moving cars nearly into each other. That also didn't work. The Hummer was on their tail like a stock car slipstreaming the tail of the one before it.

Lily went white with fear. "Why don't they just—"

"Williamsburg Bridge," the driver announced into a receiver that buzzed on the dashboard, as if he were driving a taxi. "Gray Hummer, obscured license. Will try to lose it in lower Manhat—"

They were on the bridge before he finished his sentence. So was the Hummer, closing in fast. Then it flicked out its lights.

Becca cried, "Get down!"

There were two flashes from its front passenger window and two simultaneous explosions, one on either side of the car. The limo's rear tires blew out. The driver punched the brakes, but the car slid sideways across two lanes at high speed, struck the barrier on the water side, and threw the kids hard against one another. Shots thudded into the side panels.

"Omigod!" Lily shrieked. "They're murdering us—"

As the limo careened toward the inner lane, the

Hummer roared past and clipped the limo hard, ramming it into the inside wall. The limo spun back across the road, then flew up the concrete road partition. Its undercarriage shrieked as it slid onto the railing and then stopped sharply, pivoting across the barrier and the outside railing like a seesaw.

The driver slammed forward into the exploding air bag. Lily, Becca, Wade, and Roald were thrown to the floor. Darrell bounced to the ceiling and was back down on the seat, clutching his head with both hands.

Then there was silence. A different kind of silence from before. The quiet you hear before the world goes dark.

Looking out the front, Wade saw a field of black water and glittering lights beyond.

The limo was dangling on the bridge railing, inches from plunging into the East River.

CHAPTER TWO

"Is everyone . . . ," somebody was saying when Wade lifted his throbbing head. The Hummer had spun around fifty yards up the bridge, pulled into the outside lane, and was now aimed at the damaged limo, revving its engine.

Wade yanked up on the door handle. "Get out of the car!" The door wouldn't open. He kicked it. Pain spiked his leg. "Darrell—"

A thin stream of blood trickling down his cheek, Darrell kicked too. The door squealed open a crack. Lily and Becca threw themselves at it. The hinges groaned and the door fell to the roadway. The sudden loss of weight in the back sent the limo teetering forward. There was a moan from behind the wheel.

"The driver!" Wade's father said. He shattered the divider to the front compartment, then grabbed the man's shoulder and squirmed carefully over the seat to him. First puncturing the air bag, he jerked open the passenger door to his right and dragged the driver through it onto the pavement, just as the Hummer pulled up. Four black doors flew open and four oak-sized men emerged.

One of the men walked out into the road and gestured for the oncoming cars to go past. Was he smiling?

Yes, he was.

Wade's frantic thoughts drew to a point: stay close, physically close, to Darrell and the girls. He huddled them together, himself in front. His father staggered over with the driver leaning on his shoulder.

One thick-necked thug, somewhere between seven and ten feet tall, glared down at them with eyes the color of iron. His face was dented and garbage-can ugly.

"Make no movements," he said in a voice like a truck shifting gears. Then he must have thought better of his words, because he added, "One movement.

Give us relic and daggers."

Seriously? Wade thought. *He's clarifying his threat? Who does that?*

But there was nothing funny in the guy's features. There were lumps all over his face as if *he'd* been the one in the accident, but they were neither recent nor red. He'd grown up a monstrosity, Wade guessed, so what choice did he have but to become a thug?

No, that wasn't right. Everyone had a choice.

"Now," the man grunted, drawing an automatic weapon from inside his tight-fitting jacket. He stood with his big boots planted flat on the pavement like one of the bridge girders.

Sirens sounded from the streets they had just come from.

"Or we could wait for the cops," Wade said, stepping forward as if his new toughness meant being aggressive and blurting stuff at bad guys. His father, still holding up the driver, yanked him back.

In a move Wade didn't quite understand, one of the thugs splayed his thick fingers and grabbed Lily by the arm. Then he lifted her off the ground like a rag doll— probably because she was the smallest—and strode with her to the railing. "She goes over."

Before Wade could react, before he could *think* of moving, his father slid the driver onto him and jumped at the thug, wrenching his arm to let Lily go, which the man didn't—until there was a sudden flash of silver, and the goon screamed.

Shouting incomprehensibly, Becca had thrust Magellan's priceless dagger into the man's arm. Its ivory hilt cracked off in her hand, while the blade stayed in him. She pulled Lily from him and staggered back, stunned at what she had done.

Wade whipped out his own dagger, ready to fight, when a sleek white town car raced up the bridge from the Manhattan side, a blue light flashing from its dashboard.

The other goons dragged their wounded comrade into the Hummer, Becca's hiltless blade still in his arm.

"Ve get you all, dead and dead—" one goon was muttering idiotically.

Not this time, Wade thought, staring at Becca. *Because of you . . .*

The town car shrieked to a stop, and the passenger door flew open. "I'm Terence Ackroyd," the driver said. "Everybody in!" Then he helped Wade's father slide the limo driver inside. As the Hummer tore back to

Brooklyn, the others piled into the town car, and they roared away, shaken but alive and mostly unhurt.

Wade couldn't breathe, couldn't speak. *Becca was amazing,* he thought. *She saved us. She . . .* He quaked like an old man, his hands trembling uncontrollably as they sped across the bridge into the winding streets of lower Manhattan.

CHAPTER THREE

Madrid, Spain
March 18
2:06 a.m.

Thin, pale, and slightly bent, the brilliant physicist Ebner von Braun stepped wearily inside a nondescript building buried in a warren of backstreets off the Plaza Conde de Barajas in old Madrid.

Madrid may well be one of the most beautiful cities in the world, Ebner thought, but that entry hall was disgusting. It was dismal and dark, its floor was uneven, and its grotesquely peeling walls were sodden with the odor of rancid olive oil, scorched garlic, and, surprisingly, turpentine.

Breathing through a handkerchief, he pressed a button on the wall. The elevator doors jerked noisily aside. He stepped in, and the racket of the ancient cables began. A long minute and several subbasements later, he found himself strolling the length of a bank of large, high-definition computer monitors.

Here, the smell was of nothing at all, the pristine, climate-controlled cleanliness of modern science. Ebner gazed over the backs of three hundred men and women, their fingers clacking endlessly on multiple keyboards, text scrolling up and down, screen images shifting and alive with video, and he smiled.

Such busy little bees they are!

Except they are not little bees, are they? he thought. *They are devils. Demons—Orcs!—all recruited, mostly by me, for the vast army of Galina Krause and the Knights of the Teutonic Order.*

The round chamber, one hundred forty feet side to side, with multiple tiers of bookcases rising to a star-painted ceiling, reminded him of the main reading room in the British Museum.

Except ours is better.

In addition to the NSA-level computing resources collected here, the bookshelves and glass-fronted cases alone were laden with over seven million reference books in every conceivable language, hundreds of thousands of manuscripts, many more thousands of early printed works, geographical and topographical maps, marine charts, celestial diagrams, paintings, drawings, engravings, ledgers, letters, tracts, notebooks, and assorted rare or secret documents, all collected from the last five and a half centuries of human history for one purpose: to document every single event in the life of Nicolaus Copernicus.

Behold, the Copernicus Room.

After four years, the massive servers had at last come online, and this army of frowning scientists, burrowing historians, scurrying archivists, and bleary-eyed programmers was now assembled to collect, collate, and cross-reference every conceivable atom of available knowledge to track Copernicus's slightest movement from the day of his birth, on 19 February 1473, to his fateful journey from Frombork, Poland, in 1514, with his assistant, Hans Novak, to his discovery of the time-traveling, relic-bejeweled astrolabe in a location still unknown, and every moment else, all the way to his death in Frombork Castle, on 24 May 1543.

All to determine the identity of the twelve first Guardians.

Now that the modern-day Guardians had invoked the

infamous Frombork Protocol, which decreed that the relics be gathered from their hiding places around the world to be destroyed, Ebner found himself wondering for the millionth time: Who were these original protectors, the good men and women whom Copernicus asked to guard his precious relics? One was Magellan, yes. They knew how his relic was secreted in a cave on the island of Guam. Another was the Portuguese trader Tomé Pires, who brought the poisonous Scorpio relic to China, a relic nearly recovered in San Francisco two days ago. But who were the other ten? And what of the mysterious twelfth relic?

If it was possible to know, the Copernicus Room would tell them.

And yet, Ebner mused as he strolled among the Orcs, *at such a cost.*

The rush of the Order's recent renaissance, their rebirth at light speed over the last four years under Galina's leadership, had not been without blunders. The unprecedented and impatient Kronos program, the Order's secret mission to create its own time machine, had resulted in catastrophically botched incidents:

The ridiculous Florida experiment, an ultimately insignificant test that was still trailing its rags publicly. The spontaneous crumbling of a building in the

17

bustling heart of Rio de Janeiro. And, perhaps worst of all, the strange, half-promising, half-calamitous episode at the Somosierra Tunnel, a mere hour's drive from where he stood right now.

Somosierra was particularly troublesome.

Ebner drew the newspaper clipping from his jacket.

The incident remains under investigation by local and federal crime units.

Of course it does! A school bus vanishes in a tunnel and reappears days later, bearing evidence of an attack by Napoleonic soldiers from 1808? To say nothing of the disappearance of two of its passengers or the subsequent deadly illness of the survivors?

To Ebner, these mistakes meant one thing: only Copernicus's original device—his Eternity Machine, as a recently discovered document referred to it—could ever travel through time successfully.

Every effort otherwise seemed doomed to failure. That was why he had issued a moratorium. No more experiments until further data was amassed and analyzed.

Meanwhile, the workers worked, the researchers researched, and the Copernicus Room, Ebner's beloved brainchild, hummed on.

For example . . . him . . . there . . . Helmut Bern.

The young Swiss hipster sat hunched over his station as if over a platter of hot cheese and sausages. With an improbably constant three days' stubble, an artfully shaved head, and a gold ear stud, Bern had just been relocated from Berlin. The man was now dedicated to uncovering the errors in the Kronos program, and especially Kronos III, the time gun used in the Somosierra mess.

Ebner was strolling over to question him on his progress when the thousands of fingers stopped clacking at once. There was a sudden hush in the room, and Ebner swung around, his heart thudding wildly.

It was she, entering.

Galina Krause—the not-yet-twenty-year-old Grand Mistress of the Knights of the Teutonic Order—slid liquidly between the elevator doors and strode into the Copernicus Room.

As always, she was dressed in black as severe as raven feathers. A silver-studded belt was nearly the only color. But then, who needed color when the different hues of her irises—one silver, one diamond blue, a phenomenon known as heterochromia iridis—took all one's breath away, made her so forbidding, so strangely and mysteriously hypnotic? The very definition, Ebner mused, of dangerous beauty. *Femme fatale.*

Draped around her neck was a half-dollar-sized ruby carved into the shape of a kraken, a jewel once owned by the sixteenth-century Grand Master Albrecht von Hohenzollern. Galina's personal archaeologist, Markus Wolff, had found that particular item, though he, Ebner, had been the one to present it to her last week.

Ebner bowed instinctively. Anyone standing did the same.

Observing the attention, Galina waved it off with her hand. "Vela will inform the Kaplans where the next relic is," she said, her voice slithering toward him as she approached. "If they are intelligent enough to decipher its message. Where are they at this moment?"

"Newly arrived in New York City," Ebner said. "Alas, after Markus Wolff left them in California, they are once again safe and sound. Our New York agents got nothing from them but the blade of Magellan's dagger. We have dispatched a more seasoned squad from Marseille."

"The Kaplan brood is learning to defend itself," Galina said. "Continue to have them watched closely and every movement entered into these databases. Assign one unit specifically to monitor them, but do not stall them. We may need their lead, if all of this"—she flicked her fingers almost dismissively around the vast chamber—"does not offer up the names of the original Guardians."

"It shall," Ebner said proudly. "No expense has been spared. One hundred interconnected databases are now online."

"Alert our agents in Texas to watch their families, too, and ensure that they know they are being watched."

"Ah, an added element of fear, good," said Ebner. "On another matter, we have traced a courier working with the present-day Guardians."

"Where?" she asked.

"Prague. He recently returned there from somewhere in Italy. We do not have his Italian contact yet, but the courier's identity is known to us."

"Curious," she said softly. "I have business in Prague. I will . . ." Galina suddenly looked past Ebner at a tall, broad-shouldered man with a deep tan stepping off the elevator. He wore wraparound dark glasses.

Who the devil is this, thought Ebner, *a film star?*

The man approached. Ebner raised his hand. "You are?"

"Bartolo Cassa," he said. "Miss Krause, the cargo from Rio is now on Spanish soil."

Galina studied him. "The cargo from South America. Yes. Sara Kaplan. Have it transferred to my hangar at the airport."

"Yes, Miss Krause." He bowed, turned, and left the room the way he had come.

Good. The fewer minutes this "Bartolo Cassa" is around, the better. Something about him is simply not quite right. Not . . . normal. And those sunglasses? Is he blind?

Galina gazed across the sea of workers. Her voice was low. "Despite all this data gathering, Ebner, there are holes in the Magister's biography. We require someone on the ground."

"On the ground? But where?" he asked, gesturing to the tiny lights glowing on one of two giant wall maps. "From Tokyo to Helsinki, to London, Cape Town, Vancouver, and everywhere in between, our agents span the entire globe—"

"Not here. Not now," Galina said. "Then. There. We need someone in Copernicus's time to follow him. One hundred databases, and yet there are far too many gaps in our knowledge of the Magister. We must send someone back."

"Back?" Ebner felt his spine shudder. "You do not mean another experiment?"

"One that will succeed," she said, her eyes piercing his.

"With a human subject?" he said. "A subject who can report to us? From the sixteenth century?" Ebner found himself shaking his head, then stopped. It was unwise to deny one so powerful. "Kronos Three is by far the most successful temporal device we have constructed, yet you see the untidy result at Somosierra. Two souls were left behind in 1808! These experiments are far too risky for a person. The possibility of simply *losing* a traveler is too great. You must realize, Galina, that only the"—he barely whispered the next words—"only Copernicus's original Eternity Machine has been proved to navigate time and place accurately. The Kronos experiments are far from foolproof—"

A desk chair squeaked, and Helmut Bern hustled over, breathing oddly. "Miss Krause!"

Helmut Bern! Always Johnny-on-the-spot, lobbying for Galina's blessing.

"What is it?" Ebner snapped.

"Two things. Forgive me, I heard you discussing the Kronos program. I believe I have just pinpointed the central error of the devices. A rather long and twisted string of programming. A difficult fix, but I can manage it. Three days, perhaps four."

"And the second thing?" Galina asked.

"A bit we've just picked up," Bern said, grinning like an idiot. "Copernicus sent a letter from Cádiz in May of 1517. It mentions a journey by sea. Much of it is coded, but we have begun to decrypt it."

"Cádiz," Galina said, studying the other large map in the room, one illustrating the sixteenth-century world of the astronomer. "Fascinating. The Magister sails the Mediterranean. Good work, Bern. Continue with all due haste."

"Yes, Miss Krause!" Bern returned gleefully to his terminal.

"There. You see, Galina," Ebner said. "There is no need for another Kronos experiment. This information will help us track—"

"Send her."

His eyes widened. "Send . . ."

"You told me our recent experiments were too risky," Galina responded. "A trial, then. A minor experiment. With someone expendable. Send Sara Kaplan."

"No experiment in the physics of time is minor!" he blurted, then caught himself. "Forgive me, Galina, but that woman was to have been our insurance that the Kaplans would give us the relics."

"All the family needs to know is that we have her," she said. "Fear will do the rest. What actually happens to the woman is of little consequence."

"But, but . . ." Ebner was sputtering now. "Galina, even assuming we manage to get the woman to *report* to us, *how* would she do it? By what mechanism? To say nothing of the havoc she might create five centuries ago. Any tiny misstep of hers could shudder down through the years to the present. Her mere presence could cause a greater rupture—"

"Ready Kronos Three for her journey. In the meantime, I go to Prague to persuade this courier to reveal his Italian contact. A message was delivered. I want to know to whom." Galina turned her face away. It was a face, Ebner knew, from which all expression had just died. She was done listening. She had issued her command.

So.

Sara Kaplan would go on a journey.

A journey likely to result in her death.

Or worse.

CHAPTER FOUR

New York

"That didn't just happen," Becca heard someone saying.

She turned. It was Darrell.

"Oh, it happened," someone else said. That was Wade, who was looking at her when he said it. There was a hand on her arm, urging her gently out of the town car and onto the street. Even at night, New York City was noisy. And cold, bitter cold for the middle of March. But she hardly registered those things. Her head buzzed. Her eyes could barely focus enough to keep her from smashing into stuff.

She had just attacked a man.

Stabbed a man.

No matter that he was a thickheaded creepy goon, or that he had mauled poor Lily and threatened to toss her off a bridge, or that three days ago his boss, Galina, had shot Becca herself with a gas-powered crossbow, giving her a wound that still hadn't healed. Forget all that. Becca was a girl who read books, a girl with a loving family, a girl who was just a girl. The Hummer goon was maybe a goon, but he was also a human being, and she had *stabbed* him. With a *dagger*.

She glanced at her hands. One was shaking like a leaf in a storm, but at least there was no blood on it. She would have freaked if there'd been blood on it. The other hand? Lily was holding it. Tightly. Comfortingly.

"It's okay, Bec," Lily said, pulling her along the sidewalk by her unhurt arm. "You saved my life. You were awesome. Really. *Thank you* doesn't begin to cover it. I was so scared and . . . well . . . I guess you knew that and that's why you . . ."

Becca's cell phone vibrated suddenly, and she didn't hear the rest. She pulled it out and glanced at the screen. She saw who was calling her. She let it vibrate.

Before they had departed the San Francisco airport that morning, Uncle Roald had picked up new phones for each of them. Despite the danger of their phones being tracked, he said it was unrealistic to think that the five of them would always be in the same place at the same time. They needed to be able to communicate with one another at a moment's notice. Though Lily had immediately cross-programmed the phones with all their numbers as well as family numbers, they all kept their batteries out most of the time. The first thing Becca herself had done was to call her mother to say she was safe. Her mother hadn't answered. No one had answered. So she'd left a voice mail. She realized now that she must have forgotten to remove the battery, because someone was calling back.

The dark screen was lit with four large white letters. *Home.*

But how could she answer it? She had just . . . she had just . . .

The phone stopped vibrating, and Becca watched the number 1 appear next to the voice mail icon. She slipped it back into her pocket. Lily was still talking.

". . . are definitely my hero, and I *so* owe you one, or probably way more than one, but we'll round it off to one big one . . ."

"Uh-huh," Becca said. "Uh-huh."

What would Maggie say if she knew what I just did? Becca's younger sister was the reason for so many things in her life. After nearly dying two years ago, Maggie was always on her mind, and when that creep grabbed Lily on the bridge, Becca saw Maggie in the thug's powerful grip. How could she not jump at him? And if her hand went to Magellan's dagger first, well, she couldn't stop herself. But no way could she talk to anyone at home. Not yet.

The doors of the Gramercy Park Hotel whisked open, and warm air engulfed them. After raising his hand to the man and woman behind the check-in desk, who smiled warmly, Terence Ackroyd led the Kaplans into the elevator, pressing the button for the seventh floor.

It was Mr. Ackroyd who'd originally told them that Sara had disappeared. Sara was supposed to fly from Bolivia to New York to meet him, but her luggage arrived without her. His rescuing them in the car, not an instant too soon, was their first actual meeting with the famous writer, though Becca had started reading one of his books, *The Prometheus Riddle*. The spy thriller she'd picked up in Honolulu was like their lives now. Full of death and near death. She wondered where the novelist got his ideas. He didn't look like a spy as much as a rich man. He was tall, casually dressed, with longish dark hair, graying at the temples. He moved easily among all the glitter and obvious wealth in the lobby, as if he owned the place.

Maybe he did.

She was coming back to herself now. Observing things. Beginning to remember stuff and hear things in real time. Happily, their limo driver was all right, just shaken up, and had already retired to his own room on a lower floor. Darrell's forehead was gashed slightly from the limo's ceiling light and had been bandaged using the first aid kit in Mr. Ackroyd's car. There was talk about getting a doctor to look at her arrow wound, which she hardly felt at the moment.

They entered the elevator. It was warm. Her breathing was slowing down, her breaths becoming deeper. She took her place between Lily and Wade at the back of the glass-and-wood-paneled car and clamped her elbow tightly on her shoulder bag. The bag held not only the cracked hilt of the Magellan dagger, but something even more priceless. The secret diary of Nicolaus Copernicus.

Written by the astronomer and his young assistant, Hans Novak, from 1514 to about a decade later, the diary was the main source of what they knew about the time-traveling astrolabe. The book was composed in several languages and was heavily coded. Thanks to her maternal grandparents, Becca had a gift for foreign languages, and with the help of Wade's science and math smarts she had already translated pretty good-size chunks of the diary into her red notebook. In fact, it was on the jet here from San Francisco that they'd discovered what Copernicus had come to call his time-traveling device.

Die Ewigkeitsmaschine.

The Eternity Machine.

It seemed the perfect name for something so mysterious, and so deadly.

"Here we are," Terence Ackroyd said as the elevator opened directly into his suite.

Whoa. The suite was huge, a multiroom apartment with broad windows looking out over lower Manhattan. It was furnished like a billionaire's home, with a combination of antique chairs painted gold and white and modern leather sofas, two of which shared a lacquered Japanese coffee table that Mr. Ackroyd went straight to. He motioned for them to sit. "Please, rest, while we brew some fresh tea."

We?

"I have it, Dad."

A boy entered the room, carrying a tray with a steaming teapot and several cups on it. He seemed a couple of years older than the kids, and had long, sandy-colored hair and very blue eyes. He set the tray on the table between the couches.

"I'm Julian," he said.

Terence smiled. "My son. Excuse me for a moment." Then he slipped off into a room with double doors, leaving them open. It was a study, from which a keyboard suite by Handel was playing softly from hidden speakers.

Is that where he writes his thrillers?

"I have to apologize for your welcome to New York," Julian said with as pleasant a smile as his father's, which he kept while they introduced themselves. "The Knights of the Teutonic Order have been violent since their first appearance in Jerusalem in 1198. Lawless in Poland and other northern European cities after the Crusades. Copernicus himself fought them several times. They were finally abolished by Napoleon in 1809, but a sect related to Albrecht von Hohenzollern has continued underground since then, hanging on through bloodlines, mostly, and has grown suddenly very wealthy."

His way of speaking was a bit PBS, Becca thought, but he went straight to business, which was what they needed right now.

"But Mr. Kaplan, I'm sorry," he said, suddenly bouncing to his feet. "Of course you want to know about Mrs.

Kaplan. Let me bring her luggage."

"Thank you. And call me Roald, please."

Julian trotted down a hall as his father returned from his workroom. "Becca, the hotel doctor is on his way up to take a look at your arm," Terence said. "In the meantime, Dennis, our driver, sends his heartfelt regards." He breathed out. "Now . . . you've been through—are *going* through—a terrible shock, and I'm very sorry."

"We appreciate anything you can tell us about Sara," Wade said, with a look at Darrell. "About Mom."

Terence nodded and sat among them. "First, let me say this. I have sources on the ground all over the world. For my writing, you understand. This apartment is one of a few research stations I have that's fully equipped: a workroom, communications study, and so on. I'm trying to say that my research team and I are fully at your disposal."

"And why are you helping us exactly?" Darrell broke in. "I mean, sorry, but you don't really know us, and we've learned we can't trust new people."

"Whoa, Darrell," Lily said. "That's rude."

"No, no. Fair question," Terence said. "It's simple. The moment I received Sara's things, I knew something was off, you see. Something was dreadfully wrong. Since I'm a mystery writer, my antennae shot up. More

33

than that, I've just started, well, a foundation for causes that are actively fighting injustice here and around the globe. The Teutonic Order is far more powerful than you. More powerful, actually, than any international organization I've come across. And they've become that mainly in the last four years. I've asked myself, what exactly is going on here?"

"War," said Darrell gloomily. "That's what's going on. Galina Krause and the Teutonic Order have declared war on us."

"I completely agree," Terence said. "And on the world, too, which is why my foundation and I want to help you however we can . . . but there will be time later for that. Here's Sara's suitcase."

The moment Julian entered the room with Sara's main bag and set it down on the coffee table, Becca watched Uncle Roald and Darrell. Roald practically leaped on the suitcase. But his fingers shook, and she saw the blood drain visibly from his cheeks. Darrell hovered over the suitcase next to his stepfather, his fingers poised but apparently unable to touch anything. Becca wanted to help, but stupidly couldn't think of how. It took Roald a full minute to open the clasp and unzip the case, and by the time he lifted the top, he had to wipe away tears.

Sara's clothes, toiletries, books, shoes—everything was stowed neatly in its place, just as Sara must have packed it for the return flight from South America, the flight she never made. A lump forced its way into Becca's throat, and she teared up, too. On the table in front of them was the clearest evidence so far that Sara was lost, and that no one knew where.

Darrell put both hands over his eyes. "Oh, Mom . . . Mom . . ."

Becca looked at the floor. Her heart thundered as loudly as it had when she'd thought of Lily and Maggie on the bridge.

CHAPTER FIVE

" I hasten to say that I have every reason to believe that right now your mother is safe," Terence said earnestly to Darrell. "Step by step, here's what we think. . . ."

The voice blurred in Darrell's ears, then faded away.

Something had cracked inside him when his mother's suitcase was opened, and it was still cracking. Seeing her clothes like that was like looking at stuff belonging to somebody who was dead. His throat tightened. He threw himself back on the sofa to be able to breathe, but just as quickly bent over the suitcase again. His ears were hot, like something was screaming into them. His stepfather was on his feet now, looking away.

When Lily patted him awkwardly on the arm,

Darrell realized that the room was quiet and everyone was waiting for him. To do what? He glanced up to see them all staring at him; then he brushed his hand over his face. *Oh, right. To stop crying.* He wiped his cheeks. "Sorry. Go on, Mr. Ackroyd."

"No need to be sorry," the man said, glancing searchingly at Julian.

Uh-huh, and what was that look?

"To continue, when I realized that Sara's luggage had arrived here without her, I immediately examined it, without actually *moving* too much. All of her belongings, including her phone and wallet, everything seemed to be here and intact."

"As my dad told you on the phone in Guam, we didn't contact the police because of what else we found," Julian said. He was now sitting in a chair across the room, alternately looking down from behind the curtain, as if he was surveilling the street, and tapping the keys on a laptop.

"Exactly," said Terence. "We've discovered two things. The first is what I take to be a warning, hidden cleverly in the inner lining." Terence carefully peeled back a portion of the patterned lining. It had been pried open and reclosed with a safety pin. Tucked into the space behind the lining was a charm bracelet.

Roald lifted it out. "I know this bracelet. Sara's had it for a long time, but . . ."

One of its charms was wrapped inside a self-adhesive Forever postage stamp depicting the American flag.

"May I?" Carefully unpeeling the stamp, Terence revealed the charm inside. It was a silver skull.

"I don't like the way this looks," Darrell said. "Dad, a skull? Mom's not a skull kind of person. And I don't remember this charm. When did she get it?"

Terence was about to speak when Roald said, "I think she got it last year at a conference in Mexico. It's a standard icon there. 'Day of the Dead' and all that."

"But wrapped inside a picture of the American flag," said Lily. "Is that like something against our country?"

"No, no." Terence shook his head vigorously. "Not at all. I attended that same conference. It was, in fact, where I met Sara for the first time and decided to donate my manuscripts to her archive in Austin. I believe this part of the clue was actually meant for me. It is a direct reference to a silly thing I wrote about in my first novel—"

"*The Zanzibar Cryptex,*" Julian said from across the room. "Not one of your best, Dad. The ending on the ocean liner?"

Terence smirked. "Everyone's a critic. But seriously,

in that book there was a similar clue, an item wrapped in a stamp. And it meant something very specific, which Sara well knew. You see, the skull represents, well, death, or at the very least danger. The flag quite simply means the authorities. The message in the novel—and here—is plain: contacting the authorities will put Sara in more danger. At least she thought so. She must have been threatened or somehow understood that bringing the police in—"

"Or the CIA or FBI," Julian added.

"—would not help," Terence said. "For the moment, then, finding her should remain a private matter. But not without resources."

"Sara's in danger but she's sending us codes and clues?" Lily said. "What a mom."

"You better believe it," Wade whispered.

The elevator chime rang behind them, and Terence hopped up. "Ah, Becca. Your doctor." A middle-aged woman entered, smiling, and Becca went with her to the dining-room table, where they chatted softly, so Becca could also listen.

Roald stood anxiously. "All right, so Sara is telling us to be cautious. Terence, you said you found two things."

"That's my cue," Julian said, leaving his chair by the window after one last look at the street and setting his laptop on the coffee table. "Three hours ago we received a heavily encrypted video from our investigators in Brazil. I've just been decoding it and cleaning up some of the images." He adjusted the screen, and hit the Play button.

A fuzzy nighttime video image appeared, showing an old station wagon creeping slowly along what appeared to be a utility road behind a large building. There were words on the side of the building: *Reparação Hangar 4.*

"Hmm. An airline-repair hangar," Terence whispered, shooting a glance at his son. "In Rio de Janeiro."

In the video the car stopped abruptly. Behind it, a set of double doors slid aside on the hangar, and two shapes emerged from it. The driver and a passenger climbed from the car, opened the back of the station wagon, and began to tug something out, while the two men from the hangar assisted. It was a coffin. The four men carried it like pallbearers into the hangar. A few minutes later, the two from the station wagon reappeared, closed the rear door, and drove off. The video ended.

Darrell stared at his stepfather, not wanting to believe what he saw, but his lips formed the words. "Mom is dead?"

"No, no," said Terence, rising and putting his hand on Darrell's shoulder. "What we have just witnessed means precisely the opposite. The shipment of coffins is a well-known but poorly policed method of moving people from country to country without documents. The time stamp tells us that this occurred at two twenty-seven a.m. last night, Rio time. Precisely thirty-six minutes later, two small private jets took off, both heading east on different routes, possibly to Europe or Africa. By tomorrow, we will know where each landed. If your mother is indeed in that coffin, it means that the Order is flying her somewhere, *smuggling* her to another country. Excuse me for being blunt, but if Sara were . . . dead, the Order would not go to such lengths. This video not only means that she is alive, but that precautions are being taken to ensure her safety."

It didn't sound right to Darrell, but Terence's face—and Julian's—betrayed no sense of hiding the truth. "She's alive? You're sure?"

"I quite believe so," Terence said, nodding heartily. "It is a matter now of tracking down both jets to see where they may be moving her."

"We had heard something about Madrid," said Becca from the dining room. "In San Francisco, we discovered that the Order has some servers, big computers, there, and Galina might have been there, too."

"Good. I'll alert my people. This may be a solid lead."

"We've been tricked before," said Lily.

"I understand your disappointment in San Francisco," Terence said. "But my network is largest in Europe. I've taken the liberty of arranging a meeting between Dr. Kaplan and myself and Paul Ferrere, the head of my Paris bureau, tomorrow morning, here in the city. Ferrere is ex–Foreign Legion and has a team of detectives spread across the length and breadth of Europe. We have hopes of finding Sara Kaplan before very long."

"Hopes?" Darrell grunted.

Roald patted him on the arm. "Not false hopes. Never again. But we can inch ahead. Keep moving forward."

Darrell wanted to believe him. "Okay . . ."

His stepfather took one more look at the paused video on Julian's laptop and began to pace the living room. "Here's the way I see it. Galina Krause may be waiting for us to lead her somewhere, and we'll be in danger the moment we make a move. I get that, but while we're waiting for a solid lead about Sara, we have to continue our search for the second relic, the one Vela is supposed to lead us to. Wade, you have my notebook; Becca, you have the diary. Lily, you're the electronic brains. Darrell, you cracked some riddles in San Francisco that baffled the rest of us. Together, we *will* find the second relic, and we *will* find Sara."

Darrell got it. He understood. It made sense, and having Terence and his detectives on the case gave them a way forward. His lungs were gasping for a deep breath, and his heart pounded like pistons in his chest, but being scattered or afraid wouldn't help them or his mother. He wiped his cheeks. "Okay. Good."

The doctor left, with a silent smile and thumbs-up to the family, and Becca rejoined them, a clean bandage on her arm.

"All set," she said. "It feels great. Thank you, Mr. Ackroyd . . . Terence."

"Not at all," he said.

"And now . . . Vela," said Roald.

Still worrying about his mother, Darrell watched his stepfather move his hand inside the breast pocket of his jacket. When he drew it out, he was holding the brilliant blue stone.

CHAPTER SIX

"I'm Sara Kaplan," she told herself for the thousandth time. "I'm an American. I've been kidnapped. I don't know by whom, and I don't know why. I had no time— almost no time—to alert anyone. It happened too fast."

She had rehearsed these words over and over so she could tell the first person she saw in as short a time as possible. But she hadn't seen anyone at all since . . . since when? Since the hotel on the morning of her flight from La Paz, Bolivia, to meet Terence Ackroyd in New York City. She'd rehearsed *that* scene over and over, too.

A bright tap on the hotel room door.

"Just a minute!" she'd said.

Thinking it a hotel employee come for her luggage, she opened the door.

The man—broad shouldered, mean faced, in sunglasses—was on her in a flash. Hand over mouth, pushing her back into the room, kicking the door shut behind him. "Resist and your family will be killed. If they notify the authorities, you will be killed. Silence. Silence—"

She twisted away from him, threw herself at the bathroom door, and locked herself in. "Do not panic!" she'd told herself. Look around, look around. *Her suitcase was in there. She'd been packing to return home. Her phone, her pocketbook, everything was there. No time to make a call. Futile to scrawl a message on the mirror—he would smear any message to illegibility.*

Then, inspiration. The silliest thing in the world, but it made sense. Her charm bracelet. She slid it off, wrapped the skull in a stamp. It seemed idiotic, but Terence would recognize it. From his novel. The Madagascar Codex. *No,* The Zambian Crypt? The Zimbabwe—

The door split open on its hinges as she stuffed the bracelet into the lining of her suitcase and pinned it closed. The face above her was flat and brutal. The eyes . . . the eyes were invisible behind those black-lensed sunglasses. She was screaming now at the top of her lungs, and couldn't imagine how she could not be rescued, when there came another thought: she was not screaming at all, but falling silently to the floor of the bathroom. There was a stabbing pain in her neck, and her cries, if they ever came out at all, were choked to silence. She stared up at the ceiling as she slipped to the floor, wondering if she would crack her head on the tiles.

Seconds passed. Minutes? Then there was the sound of a zipper coming from somewhere at her feet, and then flaps of black plastic were being folded over her face, and all the light was gone.

Darrell's face came to her then, in a swift sequence of his ages from birth up to when she saw him that last morning in Austin. And Wade. And Roald. What would they . . . what would . . .

Then all her thoughts faded, and she fell away to a place of no dreams.

Nothing for hours and days until today. She was unable to move. There was a freshness to the air in the . . . what *was* she in, anyway? A bag? A box? There were tubes in her arm. She couldn't raise herself or move her hands to find out. *I'm in restraints.* But there was air in there, so he wanted her alive, whoever he was. The man in the sunglasses . . . Zanzibar! That was it!

The Zanzibar Cryptex.

She wanted to scream that she was alive and being

taken somewhere, but . . . The waves that had been falling over her became more rhythmic, and sleep took her,
or what she thought might be sleep, but she wasn't very
sure of that.

CHAPTER SEVEN

New York

Even under the Ackroyd living room's subtle lamp-light, Vela shone as if it were its own star. Like a heavenly body not of this earth. *Which it might actually be,* thought Lily. What did any of them really know about the shadowy origins of the relics? Copernicus had supposedly found an old astrolabe built by the Greek astronomer Ptolemy. But that was all pretty hazy.

"Let's bring it into the study," said Julian.

Julian seemed to be really bright. His father was kind of brilliant, too. How many books had he written? Ten? A hundred? She and the others were surrounded by smart people, so you had to think they really would get Sara back *and* find the relics.

The study off the living room was large and lined with thousands of books—not all of them written by Terence Ackroyd, thank goodness. It was traditional in a way, sleepy almost, but also equipped with a really high level of computer gear.

There was a long worktable with a wide-lens magnifying device perched on it. Several shelves of cameras, printers, and scanners were next to the worktable along with stacks of servers. On the wall behind them was a range of twenty-four clocks showing the current time in each of the world's major time zones. Except for a gnarly old typewriter on a stand by itself like a museum piece from another century, the room was like she imagined a secret CIA lair would be.

The only other thing I'd need would be . . . nothing.

"First things first," Julian said, opening a small tablet computer that lay on the worktable next to five sparkling new cell phones. "These are for you. We've loaded this tablet with tons of texts and image databases that can help with the relic hunt."

"Wow, thanks," Lily said, practically snatching it from his hands. "I'm kind of the digital person here."

Julian laughed. "Ooh, the tech master of the group. The intelligence officer. Very cool. I've modified each phone's GPS function with a software app I invented. The tablet likewise. Except to one another, and mine and Dad's, these units will emit random location coordinates, making them essentially blind to most conventional GPS locators." He passed a phone to each of them, and turned to Roald. "Now . . . the relic . . ."

Roald set Vela gently on the worktable. When he did, Lily realized they'd been so completely focused on hiding and protecting Vela over the last few days that this was only the second time since Wade and Becca discovered it that they'd been able to bring it safely out into the open.

Wade and Becca, she thought.

Wade had been giving Becca goo-goo eyes ever since Mission Dolores in San Francisco, where they'd discovered that the Scorpio relic was a fake. Maybe it was because of the stare the Order's assassin, Markus Wolff, had given Becca in the Mission. Or maybe Wade realized something about the twelfth relic that Wolff had been all cryptic about. Either way, something was up, those weird looks meant something, and Lily would find out. She could read Darrell. He was hot or cold. Not so much in between. And by hot or cold she meant either hilarious or ready to explode. Wade was a different story. Becca, too, for that matter, and . . . *Wait, where was I? Oh. Right. Vela.*

Triangular in shape, about four inches from base to upper point, with one short side and two of roughly equal length, Vela was something Roald called "technically an isosceles triangle." Except that one of its long sides curved in slightly toward the center like a sail in the wind. Which made sense, since Vela was supposed to represent the sail in the constellation Argo Navis. It also had a slew of curved lines etched into it.

When they examined the stone closely they saw that even though it was about the same thickness from the front side to the back—about a quarter of an inch—Vela was undoubtedly heavier in the middle than in any of the corners, a fact that she was the first to voice. "Look." She placed it flat across her finger and it balanced. "Something's in there."

"Maybe an inner mechanism," Roald said. "Something hidden inside its heart."

"Yes, yes," Terence said, taking it now from Lily. "I can see the faint design on both sides of the stone and a series of very tiny, even infinitesimal, separations that could mean that the stone somehow opens up. It is far too heavy to be a normal stone."

Passing it around, they gently tried to coax the stone to reveal its secret, but short of prying it open and maybe busting it, they couldn't find a way. Vela told them nothing.

"Have you considered that it's fairly dangerous to be lugging this around with you?" Julian said. "There are vaults in the city that are pretty near uncrackable, even by the Order."

Roald nodded. "A good idea, I agree. But the legend says 'the first will circle to the last,' meaning that something about Vela is a clue to the next relic or maybe its Guardian. We need to discover something soon or we won't know where to look."

"There's also this." Becca slid her hand into her shoulder bag and tugged out the cracked hilt of the Magellan dagger. "The handle cracked when I . . . you know. I'm sorry . . ."

"I'm so glad you did," Lily said, shuddering to see the hilt again. "It was, well . . ." She was going to say that what Becca had done—stabbing the goon on the bridge and saving her life—was something so *beyond* amazing, but she felt suddenly on the verge of tears, which she never was, so instead she just closed her mouth, which was also pretty rare, and smiled like a dope at whoever, which turned out to be Wade, who, as usual, was staring at Becca with his googly eyes.

"That's quite something," Julian said, drawing in a quiet breath when Becca set the hilt on the table. "Italian, by any chance?"

"Bolognese," said Wade, finally tearing his eyes from Becca.

"Yes, yes." Julian picked it up gently, but it suddenly separated into two pieces of carved ivory and fell back on the table. "Ack! I'm sorry!"

"Hold on . . ." Lily used her slender fingers to tug something out from inside the hilt. It was a long, narrow ribbon. "What is this?"

Terence stood. "Oh, ho!" He pinched one end of the ribbon and held it up. It dangled about three feet.

"Microscope!" said Julian. He snatched the ribbon from his father, then jerked away from the table to the far end of the room, where he sat at a small table. Not ten seconds later, he said, "Dad, we've seen this kind of thing before."

They all rushed over to Julian in a flash, but Lily pushed her way through the crowd to be the first one leaning over the lens. "Letters," she said. "I see letters. They're pretty faded, but they're there, written one under the other the whole length of the ribbon."

Darrell moved in next. "*T-O-E-G-S-K*, and a bunch

more. We've done word scrambles and substitution codes. Is this one of those? They look random."

Terence took his own look and smiled. "Not random at all, actually. These letters are one half of a cipher called a *scytale*." He pronounced the word as if it rhymed with *Italy*.

"Invented by the ancient Spartans, the cipher consists of two parts: a ribbon made of cloth or leather with letters on it, and a wooden staff," he continued. "The staff has a number of flat sides on it, rather like a pencil. You wrap the ribbon around the staff like a candy cane stripe, and if the staff is the right size, the letters line up in words."

Julian grinned. "The trick is that you always have to keep the ribbon separate from the staff until it's time to decode the message." He paused and looked at his father. "Dad, are you thinking what I'm thinking? Two birds?"

"Two birds?" said Wade. "Is that code for something?"

Julian laughed. "It's a saying. Kill two birds with one stone. The Morgan Library up the street has an awesome vault for Vela. It also happens to have probably the best—and least known—collection of scytale staffs on the East Coast. I'll bet we can find one that works with this ribbon."

"I suggest we hit the Morgan Library at eight tomorrow morning," Terence said.

"Don't museums usually open later than that?" said Becca.

"Yes, but for Dad and me, the Morgan is never closed," said Julian with a smile that seemed to Lily like the sun breaking out after a long darkness.

Chapter Eight

Prague, Czech Republic
March 18
9:13 a.m.

Galina Krause kept her hand inside her coat, where a compact Beretta Storm lay holstered against her ribs. Its barrel, specially filed to obscure its ballistics, was still warm. She would be gone long before the police discovered the body of the Guardian's courier, Jaroslav Hájek, or the single untraceable bullet in his head.

She disliked killing old men, but the courier had refused to reveal his Italian contact, although his flat did contain a collection of antique hand clocks, which was likely a clue to how the message had been transferred.

In any case, a dead courier working with the Guardians was never a bad thing, and one obstacle less in her overall journey.

As Galina walked the winding, snow-dusted streets of Prague's Old Town, she passed through deserted alleys and passages barely wider than a sidewalk. Finally, she entered into the somber "antiquarian district." This section of Prague deserved its designation. A neighborhood forlorn, yet rich in history and the smell of a past carelessly abandoned by modernity. For that reason alone, she adored it.

She halted three doors down from a tiny low-awninged shopfront on Bělehradská Street. Antikvariát Gerrenhausen appeared as it must have generations ago: crumbling, forever in shadow, hauntingly like those sad, cluttered storefronts in old photographs of a forgotten, bygone era.

A man entered the street from the far end. He was tall. His close-cropped white hair cut a severe contrast with the stark black of his knee-length leather coat.

Markus Wolff had recently returned from the United States.

She moved toward him, though their eyes would not meet until the standard subterfuge was completed. Wolff approached her, passed by, and then, after scanning the street and its neighboring windows for prying eyes, doubled back to her.

"Miss Krause." He greeted her in a deep baritone, a voice that was, if possible, icier than her own. He unslung a black leather satchel from his shoulder and set it on the sidewalk at her feet. "The remains of the shattered jade scorpion from Mission Dolores. The Madrid servers can perhaps make sense of them."

"Excellent," she replied. "Do you have the video I asked you to take in San Francisco?"

"I do." He pressed the screen of his phone.

A moment later, a file appeared on hers. She opened it. A boy, seven and three-quarters years of age, ran awkwardly across a field of green grass, kicking a soccer ball. The camera zoomed in on his face. The tender smile, the pink cheeks, the lazy blond curls flying in the wind. She paused it. The boy was oblivious to his own mortality.

"Splendid," she said sullenly. "Wolff, take note of this street. This shop."

"I have."

"You may be asked to return here in the weeks to come," she said. "For now, I want you to look into the Somosierra incident. Ease my mind."

"The stranded bus driver and student," he said. "I

will search for physical evidence."

She felt suddenly nauseated and wanted the conversation to end. "In six days' time I will be in Istanbul. We will meet there."

Markus Wolff nodded once and left.

Man of few words, Galina thought. *How refreshing.* Shouldering the leather satchel and drawing a cold breath, she entered the shop. A cadaverous gentleman, the seventh generation of Gerrenhausens, stood hunched and motionless behind a counter cluttered with books and rolled maps, yellowed file folders, and an assortment of wooden boxes. He listened as a gramophone on the shelf behind him emitted a scratchy yet plaintive string quartet movement. She recognized it as Haydn. The D-minor andante.

"You have the item I requested?" she asked. The sound of her voice was nearly swallowed by the yearning violins and the thick, paper-muffled air in the old shop.

The slender hands of the emaciated proprietor twitched, while his lips formed a smile as thin as a razor blade. "It has just arrived, miss." He reached under the counter and withdrew a small oak box, burnished nearly black with age. He opened the lid.

Nestled deeply in maroon velvet was a delicate

miniature portrait of a kind common in the sixteenth century.

The framed circular painting, two inches in diameter, was a product of Hans Holbein the Younger. "Incorrectly dated 1541, it was created actually between 1533 and 1535, during the painter's years in England at the court of King Henry the Eighth, as you know," the proprietor said.

The portrait featured the face and shoulders of its sitter, a brilliant bloom of flesh in a setting of velvety black and midnight blue. It was a three-quarter view, in which the sitter, aged somewhere between seventeen and nineteen, gazed off, a sorrowful expression on the face, eyes dark, lips pursed, almost trembling. It was not a peaceful portrait, and Galina found herself shuddering at the sight of it. She closed the box.

"The fee is one hundred seventy-five thousand euros," the proprietor said softly, as if only slightly embarrassed by the number. "Its former home, a boutique museum in Edinburgh, will not soon realize it is displaying a forgery. Such workmanship is costly."

To Galina the miniature was worth ten times as much, a hundred times. It was not the money that mattered in this instance. She had become aware over the last years that she required the strictest loyalty and silence from an antiquarian such as Herr Gerrenhausen and knew how pitifully easy it was to gain such loyalty and silence when a loved one was threatened. Smiling at the old proprietor, she swiped her phone open to the frozen video. "Do you recognize this young boy?"

The man squinted at the phone and beamed. "Why, yes! That is my grandson, Adrian. He lives with my youngest daughter and her husband in California. But why . . . how . . . why do you have a video of Adrian . . . ?" He trailed off. His face turned the color of white wax.

Galina slid a list of several items across the counter to him. "This is what I need. You will acquire the items for me. There will be no end to our relationship until I say there is. Currently the boy is safe. But he is within our grasp at any moment. You do understand me."

Rapid nodding preceded a long string of garbled words, which the man punctuated finally with "I understand."

She felt her expression ease. "I am wiring the purchase fee for the miniature to your Munich account. The first item on the list is to be auctioned at the Carlton Hotel in Cannes in June. You will acquire it anonymously."

"Of course! I will. Yes, everything."

The Haydn andante ended morosely behind him.

Galina swiped the image of the boy from her phone, then inserted the blackened oak box into her leather satchel and left the shop, short of breath and shivering, but not from the cold.

CHAPTER NINE

New York

The morning after the discovery of the ribbon in the dagger's hilt, Darrell woke early from somber dreams about his mother to hear his stepfather and Terence Ackroyd working out an elaborate plan for that morning, a ruse intended to throw off any agents of the Teutonic Order who might be watching the hotel.

"The first of many new plans," Roald had told him.

"I hope they work," Darrell grumbled to himself.

The plan involved three cars, the family of the Gramercy Park Hotel's assistant manager, two retired New York City policemen, a traffic officer, and a crew of window cleaners—all creating multiple distractions while the kids zigzagged uptown with Julian, and Roald and Terence headed on foot to the West Side to meet the detective Paul Ferrere.

A half hour later, Darrell and the others were streaming up Madison Avenue, shielded by crowds of commuters and early shoppers. Since he had no sense whatsoever of anyone watching them, Darrell accepted that their plan had actually succeeded.

Despite the latest storm having dumped nine heavy inches of snow that was now aging into black and crusty walls, narrowing the streets and the sidewalks to half their width, their walk uptown was brisk but still not fast enough for him.

As soon as Darrell pictured his mother tied to a chair or pounding on a door or lying bound up in a locked closet, his mind went red, and blood rushed like waves inside his head until he couldn't see straight.

But he had to hope, right? He had to put his mother's situation in a pocket and get on with what he knew he had to get on with. *We're doing everything possible. We have detectives. We have Terence's assistance. Sooner or later, Mom will be where the next relic is, because that's where Galina will take her.*

So fine. Get your head in the game.

He managed to refocus himself in time to hear Julian

saying to Wade, who was five steps behind him, "I was born in Mandalay, actually. Myanmar. What they used to call Burma. It's where my mom died. I was four. I never had much time with her."

So. That was why Terence had given his son that look last night. Julian had lost his mother, too. How do you even deal with not growing up with your mom, having so little time to be with her? And Myanmar? Myanmar was right next to Thailand, where Darrell's father had grown up.

They came to the southwest corner of the intersection of Madison Avenue and Thirty-Sixth Street and waited for the light. Lily nudged him and nodded at two low-roofed Renaissance-style mansions—one of brown stone blocks, the other white—with a modern glass-and-steel atrium joining them.

"We are going to get so much help here," she said. "I have a feeling."

Becca nodded. "Like Wade said in San Francisco, the more relics we find, the more leverage we have."

"I know," Darrel said, mustering up a smile. "I get it."

The truth was that he *wanted* to go after the next relic. Not as much as he *needed* to find his mother, of course, but a real close second. This was important.

The Copernicus Legacy was life-alteringly amazing. It was cosmic. Time travel blew his mind, and if Galina wanted to reassemble the astrolabe, that was enough to make him vow she never would. He needed to be a part of what they were doing, no matter how dangerous or scary.

We have to stop Galina. At all costs.

Lily was very impressed. And, seriously, not a lot of stuff impressed her. But exactly as Julian had promised the night before, even though the Morgan Library and Museum was still closed to the public, its doors whisked open for them and sealed solidly after they entered.

Wow.

"You'll be rather astounded at their collection," Julian told them when they filed into the tall, glass-walled atrium. "And their security." He nodded at a pair of hefty guards by the doors who looked more than a match for the oak-headed thugs from last night.

"I should also tell you that your new tablet contains a slew of one-of-a-kind documents from the Morgan's private holdings," he added. "Sixteenth-century biographies. Maps. Astronomical treatises. Code books. It'll take you months to go through it all."

"I could do it in a few days," Lily said, shrugging.

"I'm sure you could," he said with a smile.

Lily had felt special last night when the Ackroyds, both father and son, had recognized that she was, in Julian's words, "the tech master of the group. The intelligence officer."

I so like that! Intelligence officer. That's exactly what I am.

"Good morning." A slender man in a dark blue suit with soft-heeled shoes, who Julian whispered was one of the two chief curators, met them in the atrium. The kids took turns explaining why they were there.

"Scytales and the vault," the curator said, tapping his fingers on his chin. "Got it. Vault first. Please follow me." He spun around and led them through several still-darkened galleries to a bank of elevators. They took one down into the library's underground level. "Perhaps Julian has told you, but the lowest level runs beneath the entire length of both the library and Pierpont Morgan's original residence."

"This is where my dad is suggesting you keep . . . the object," Julian said. "For the time being at least. We have extensive vault privileges here."

After leading them through several passages, the curator paused at a large steel door. "When Mr. Morgan had the house built, he constantly rotated his collection between what he displayed upstairs and what was stored in the vault. In the century since then, security has been updated countless times. The vault is now virtually invulnerable. Even in the case of nuclear attack, which, surprisingly, is a factor . . . no matter how slight."

For instance, what if the Order . . . never mind.

He opened the door with a pass code and a fingerprint scan. Inside stood a narrow entry hall leading to a second door. "Built into the side walls is a kind of electronic gauntlet," the curator said. "You have to pass through it to reach the vault."

"You'll like this," Julian said to them as they entered. "Gates trip and floor tiles sink if you take the wrong route to the inner chamber. Any intruder would be trapped between the walls long before any theft or damage could occur."

The curator nodded. "For example, several infrared sensors are scanning us as we're passing through right now—"

Beeep!

The curator turned to Wade. "Er . . . you appear to have something on you . . ."

Even in its unique protective holster, one that had fooled various airport security scanners, Wade's antique dagger now set off the Morgan's sensors. "It's the first time that's happened," he said. "You have the best security I've seen."

"About the dagger," Julian said. "Your dad wanted it in the vault, too, didn't he?"

Wade nodded reluctantly. "He told me this morning. He's right, I guess." He slipped off the holster with Copernicus's dagger housed invisibly inside and handed it to the curator.

Lily hated weapons of any kind, but Wade giving up the dagger? Wouldn't they need it? He'd carried it since Berlin last week, and the Magellan dagger had saved her life just yesterday. They were, after all, at war with the Teutonic Knights. On the other hand, Copernicus's own private weapon was far too precious—and, she supposed, too dangerous—to carry around. *So, yeah. Good idea.*

The large steel door opened on a staggeringly wide, deep, and high-ceilinged room.

Becca started to wheeze.

"Indeed," said the curator, grinning for the first time since they'd met him.

One side of the room was lined with numerous three-tiered display compartments and multishelf bookcases. On the far end was a honeycomb of hundreds of narrow slots built up to the ceiling. Paintings were shelved upright in these spaces. Classical sculptures of people and animals—some realistic, some fantastical—were clustered here and there the entire length of the vault.

The curator set the dagger and its holster reverently on a worktable, then stepped over to a portion of the wall containing built-in safe-deposit-type boxes.

"What is your birth date, Wade?" he asked.

"Me?"

Lily remembered how the deciphering of Uncle Henry's original coded message had involved a reference to Wade's birthday. That was what had started their quest.

"October sixth."

"So . . ." The curator selected and removed one of the boxes, which he said was "made of a titanium alloy," and brought it to the table. He placed the holster and dagger inside the box, sealed it, tapped in a key-code combination, and returned the box to its slot in the wall. He then withdrew the box directly below it. "The, ah, object you wish to store here?"

Darrell drew Vela from an inside pocket.

Raising his eyebrows very high, the curator took the heavy blue stone—the relic with something buried in its interior—and swaddled it carefully in new velvet.

"It's priceless," Lily said.

"I believe it," the curator responded. He set the velvet-wrapped stone in a wooden box. Then he placed that box inside a second titanium container, which he inserted below the one with the dagger inside. When he pushed it all the way in, there was a low whump followed by the clicking and rolling of tumblers that stopped with a hush.

"Now you'll want to see our head of antiquities," the curator said, leading them all briskly out of the vault and security corridor. "I'll ask her to meet you upstairs in the atrium. If anyone can help you decode your message, she's the one."

Taking one last look at the sealed vault door, Lily breathed easily. Vela, the first of the Copernicus relics, was now hidden safely underneath New York City.

CHAPTER TEN

The curator led them back up to the atrium.

As Wade watched the man disappear, Darrell's hip pocket began to ring. "It's Dad," he said, and stepped away, listening, Lily along with him. Becca turned to follow them when Wade stopped her.

"How's your arm?" he asked.

She smiled. "Okay. Better all the time."

"Good." He was still deciding if he should tell Becca about *the dream*. The one he'd had leaving Guam in which Becca had seemed to be, well, dead. He'd so far been unable to say it out loud. It was too upsetting, even for him. Naturally, he worried that his dream had something to do with Markus Wolff's intense look at her in the Mission in San Francisco, although that was clearly impossible, since his dream had been earlier.

"What about the Mission?" Becca asked.

"What?"

"You said *Mission*, just now."

His face went hot. "I did? Well . . . it's just . . . I wonder what Markus Wolff meant about the twelfth relic. That we should ask ourselves what it was."

"Me, too. Strange, huh?"

"Yeah."

That went nowhere.

Darrell was off the phone now. "Good news. Investigators are spreading across Europe."

"He said we have to be prepared that they won't find your mom today or probably tomorrow," Lily added. "That it'll take some time, but everybody feels good about it."

"Excellent," said Julian. "It may not be long now before we know what the ribbon says and where it points."

"Find the relic, find Sara," Becca said.

"That's the idea," said Wade.

There was a slow click of heels on tile, and a tiny,

very old woman hobbled into the open atrium as if wandering in from the long past. She wore a dark beige pantsuit with a bright pink scarf flowing up out of her vest like a fountain. Her eyes flickered like a pair of tiny flashlights low on battery, and she bleated, "I'm . . . ancient . . ."

Wade glanced at the others, then back to the woman. "Oh, not so much—"

". . . curator here at the . . . Morgan," she said, scowling at him. She huffed several more breaths as if each could be her last. "Dr. Rosemary Billing . . ."

"Pleased to meet you, Dr. Billing," Becca said.

"Ham," the woman said.

"Excuse me?" said Lily.

"Ham," the woman repeated. "Billing*ham*. My name is Bill . . . ingham. Why won't you let me . . ." Three, four breaths. ". . . finish? Now . . . who are . . . you all . . . and how . . . may I help you?"

One by one they told her their names. She frowned severely at each one until Julian's. "Julian?" she gasped, adjusting her glasses. "There you are! Well, if you're . . . here then it's quite all right. Fol . . . low me."

Stopping and starting several times, like a car backing up in a tight space, Dr. Billingham turned around and toddled down the hallway she had just come from, wheezing the whole time. What seemed a day and a half later, they arrived at a small, windowless room. Rosemary flicked on the lights and, after much finger motion, unlocked a glass-topped display case.

"Despite these . . . scytale staffs being, in many cases, also used as . . . weapons, they're old, and . . . we must consider them extremely fragile. Rather . . . like me . . ."

Wade didn't know whether to laugh or not, but he knew to wait.

Five breaths later, she added, ". . . dieval manuscripts."

Then Rosemary waved her hand over the contents of the case like a game-show hostess. She was right to do so. As Julian had promised, the library's collection of scytale staffs was special. They were obviously ancient, and all were roughly between five and ten inches long. Two were carved in thick ebony, one appeared to be cast in bronze, and the others were shaped of ivory or wood. Each was nestled in its own formfitting compartment and labeled by date. The earliest was from the sixth century BCE—"Before the Common . . . Era," Rosemary explained—the most recent from Germany in the eleventh century. The smallest staff was little bigger around than a pencil, while the largest bore a circumference similar to the handle on a tennis racket.

"Now show me your rib . . . ," Rosemary asked Becca alarmingly, then finished with ". . . bon."

Becca removed the ribbon carefully from her pocket, unrolled it, and laid it flat on the table.

The curator frowned through her spectacles as she examined the ribbon. "About a . . . hundred letters?"

"Ninety," Becca said, glancing at Julian, who nodded.

"Ah, just . . . like . . . me . . ."

Wade waited six, seven breaths, but that turned out to be the end of her sentence.

Rosemary tugged either end of the ribbon lightly. "The fabric is silk. Without . . . running tests, I would guess it was woven sometime in the fifteenth or sixteenth century."

"That fits our date," Darrell said.

The curator raised a finger as if to shush him. "Also, it doesn't . . . stretch very much. This is good. It means we'll have better luck finding an exact fit. Let's start small . . . and go up from there." Then, chuckling to herself, she added, "The narrower the staff, the larger the mess . . ."

Two breaths.

". . . age."

Rosemary took up the narrowest of the staffs, more of a dowel than anything else, with five equal sides. Pinching the top end of the ribbon against one of the sides, she gently spiraled it around the dowel like the stripe of a candy cane, making sure that the letters sat next to one another. The first line of the message read:

TGOSNOTSTPHID

Which, because of the peculiar wiring of his brain, Darrell said aloud before anyone could stop him. "'To go snot stupid.' No, wait. 'Togo's not stupid.' Is that the dog from *The Wizard of Oz*? Who's Togo?"

"You are," said Wade, glaring at his stepbrother. "And we're not sure what language it's in, remember that. Copernicus knew several. Either way, that's obviously not the right staff. Can we try a bigger one, to spread out the letters—"

"Keep your pant . . . s on, young man," Rosemary growled at Wade, who she suddenly seemed to like less than she liked Darrell. "I shall choo . . . se what we do next. And I choose . . . a bigger one, to spread out the letters more." She returned the first dowel to the case, then selected a thicker one and carefully wrapped the ribbon around it. It produced the following sequence of letters:

TOSMNHTTHLDE

"That's not a word," said Lily. "Another one?"

The curator's wobbly cheeks turned red, and Wade wondered if she would explode and what that might look like. He stepped back. Rose . . . mary waved a hand in front of her face as if to cool off, then pulled out a staff with ten sides and a diameter of about one and a half inches. Wrapping the ribbon around it produced the following first three lines in English:

TOTHELAND
OFENDLESS
SNOWTOBEG

"To the land of endless snow . . ." Becca gasped. "That's it! Yay, we found it!"

Rosemary's face was purple when she whirled it around to Becca's. "*Who* found it, dear? Did *we* . . . find it? Because I rather th . . . ink *I* found it."

"You did, Rosemary," said Julian. "As usual, you

are being tremendously awesome. My friends here, as grateful as they are, are simply super anxious to know what the rest of the message says. Forgive them, please."

"Dear . . . boy!" Rosemary said, pausing to pinch Julian's cheeks a few times. "Here then . . . is the whole th . . . ing."

> *TOTHELAND*
> *OFENDLESS*
> *SNOWTOBEG*
> *THEATHOSG*
> *REEKCONCE*
> *ALTHEUNBO*
> *UNDDOUBLE*
> *EYEDBEAST*
> *FROMDEMON*
> *MASTERAVH*

Wade drew out the notebook containing the major clues they'd discovered so far and, after much scribbling, broke down the text into individual words.

> *TO THE LAND OF ENDLESS SNOW TO BEG THE ATHOS GREEK CONCEAL THE UNBOUND DOUBLE EYED BEAST FROM DEMON MASTER AVH*

And there it was, a riddle to the location of the second Guardian and the second relic.

"We're all thinking it, right?" said Becca. "'Demon Master AVH'?"

"Albrecht von Hohenzollern, Grand Master of the Teutonic Order in the fifteen hundreds," said Darrell. "I like that Copernicus finally called him what he was."

Wade set his father's college notebook on the table, closed his eyes, and tried to think. *Land of endless snow, Athos Greek, conceal the unbound . . . double-eyed beast . . . double-eyed . . .*

"If I close my eyes . . . for that long . . . people think I'm dead!" Rosemary cackled.

"No, no," Wade said, opening his eyes. "It's just that . . . *double-eyed beast* describes the object we're looking for, and it's based on a constellation." From his backpack, he took out and unfolded the celestial map his uncle Henry had given him.

"Oh, there are several star charts in our collection," Rosemary said, "but that's a very nice one."

"Thanks." Carefully running his fingers over the constellations, Wade searched the chart's colorful illustrations, hoping something would pop out at him. His mind flashed with the idea of the twelfth relic, but he waved it away. Right now there were at least a dozen candidates for *double-eyed beast*—constellations named for dogs, wolves, dragons, monsters—but not one of them suggested that it and it alone was the one Copernicus referred to on the ribbon. "If I study this long enough, I bet I can figure it out."

"Then my work here is done," Dr. Billingham said. She slid the ribbon from the staff, pressed it into Becca's palm, replaced the staff in the display case, snapped the case shut, and locked it away. "For the further meaning of your message, I suggest you all trot off to Hell . . ."

CHAPTER ELEVEN

" ...**E**nistic archives," Rosemary finished. "The phrase *the Athos Greek* undoubtedly points to Hellenistic culture. You should start with section five in the reading room. Good-bye."

The curator brusquely shooed them from the room by flicking her fingers toward the door, and they headed back to the atrium.

"That took a week," Lily said, blinking her eyes as if coming out of a cave.

"But we have the message," said Becca. "Now we just need to know what it means." The truth was, the instant Becca had heard the words *reading room*, her pulse had sped up. As always, she had the Copernicus diary in her bag and knew it was as precious as just about any rare book anywhere. But the Morgan's collection was world famous for a reason. Gutenberg Bibles, Dickens manuscripts, diaries, biographies, histories, artwork, political documents. The Morgan had them all.

"The Athos Greek," she said. "Land of endless snow. Those are awesomely definite clues to who the Guardian might be. Greece is in the south of Europe, but endless snow sounds like the north. I'm sure the diary will tell us even more."

"And I can't stop thinking about the double-eyed beast," Wade added, looking back at her as he had *so* many times since San Francisco. What *that* was all about, Becca didn't know. "If I keep studying the star map, I might be able to narrow it down." Then he started chewing his lip, that little thing he did when he was thinking.

Before entering the Morgan's upstairs reading room, they were asked to stow their belongings—except for notebooks and computers—in special lockers outside the room and, interestingly, to wash their hands.

"Because of the oils," Darrell said, wiggling his fingers. "The oils in our skin can damage original materials. Mom knows stuff like that."

"And now so do you," said Lily.

After they explained the basic reason for their visit—"Greek monasteries and monks of the early sixteenth century"—the young man who'd let them in gave them a brief tour of the holdings, and they each decided to take on a different aspect of the research. Wade unfolded his celestial map and sat his notebook by its side. Julian pulled down from the shelves a large photographic book on Mediterranean monasteries as well as several maps of the world and Greece for the exact location of Athos. Lily gave herself the task of scanning the five Copernicus biographies loaded on the new tablet, while Darrell hunted down a handful of books on sixteenth-century Greek history.

As they got to work, Becca stood staring at the filled bookshelves and glass bookcases, at the dozens of reference stacks, and at the lone, lucky, lucky librarian behind the counter, and she wondered how in the world she could ever get his job.

Imagine being the master of this room! I would totally live here.

"Becca, are you with us?" asked Lily. "Or lost in your own head?"

"Yes, yes," she said. "I mean, no. I'm fine."

She set down on the table in front of her a book disguised in a wrinkled copy of the London *Times*, knowing that the librarian would envy *her* if he only knew that, ten feet away, was the five-hundred-year-old diary of Copernicus.

Before running for their lives in San Francisco, Becca had discovered in the diary's final pages a sequence of heavily coded passages along with a *tabula recta*, a square block of letters. When she'd discovered the right key word, the square had allowed her to decode a particularly difficult passage. That passage, among other things, had confirmed that the original Guardian of the Scorpio relic was a Portuguese trader named Tomé Pires. The clue had eventually led to them locating not the original relic, but a centuries-old decoy.

Then, just this morning, when the pain in her arm had woken her, she'd distracted herself by studying the other coded pages. As in San Francisco, where she'd come across a tiny sketch of a scorpion in the margin of a page, Becca had discovered a date written in tiny letters—*xiii February 1517*—and another drawing. It was so faint as to be nearly invisible.

At first, she'd thought

the image—almost certainly sketched by Copernicus himself—was meant to be two diamonds touching end to end. But now the "double-eyed beast" of the scytale message suggested that the drawing was really of two eyes, and that the passage next to the drawing might tell the story of the Guardian whose name they were searching for. Either way, the first line of the double-eyed passage was impenetrable.

Ourn ao froa lfa atsiu vlali am sa tlrlau dsa . . .

Without the right key word, it might prove fruitless to try to decode it, but maybe she had to try anyway. Still, where to start? *Ourn ao froa . . . ?*

"Becca, can you read Greek?" asked Darrell, holding an old volume bound in red leather. "This one's about the lives of monks in the time period we want."

"Sorry," she grumbled. "I feel like I'm doing it now."

"I can help," the librarian whispered at the counter. He then showed Darrell to a scanner whose output was linked to a translation program. "I suggest you scan the book's table of contents first, find the pages you think you want, then scan *them*. The translation will appear on this computer."

"Perfect," said Darrell.

After some minutes of quiet work, in which they all searched for anything that might connect to the scytale message, Julian sat back from the table. "First of all, there are over twenty monasteries in Athos. Some are like fortresses built on cliffs over the ocean. You have to climb these endless narrow stairs cut into the rocks. But it makes me wonder if Copernicus ever visited Greece. I mean, how did he meet the Athos Greek?"

Lily did quick word searches through the several biographies on the tablet. "Copernicus traveled, but it doesn't look like he ever visited Greece. At least I can't find any journey recorded in these books. So we're back to square zero."

"I think you mean square one," said Wade. "But they're pretty close together."

"Um, yeah, until me," said Darrell inexplicably. "It scrambles my brain, but I think I found something. It's from a Greek book called something like *Holy Monks of Athos*. The translation is rough, but listen to this."

He cleared his throat and read the words on the computer. "'One big monks Athos be Maximus, living 1475 until 1556 when he became no longer.'"

Wade stared at him. "Which I think means . . . the same time as Copernicus."

"I think so, too," Darrell said. "Now . . . 'unlike monk

brothers of his, Maximus studied far Italy, Padua, when 1502 came round.'" He grinned. "Nice style, huh?"

"Padua," said Becca. "We know Copernicus was in Bologna . . . Lily?"

Lily scanned the indexes again. "Yep. He was a student at the University of Padua from 1501 to 1502."

Becca looked up from the diary and grinned. "Darrell, it proves what you said."

"Probably. What are we talking about?"

"That everybody knew everybody back then. The world had lots fewer people, and they all gathered in the same places."

Darrell nodded. "I did say that. So, yes, I am right. Plus, Italy, right? Everybody went there because of the weather."

"Well, that's just it, isn't it?" said Julian. "*The land of snow and endless night* doesn't sound like either Italy or Greece. Something more northern, maybe . . ."

Darrell squinted at the screen. "'Maximus can be known as Greek Maxim or Maxim Grek or Maximus Grekus or Grekus Maximus.'"

"Huh," said Lily. "Greek Maxim. I get it."

"You do?" asked Wade.

"Sure, I mean, I ask myself why they would call him Greek Maxim, right?" They shook their heads. "Well, think about it. Would you call a Greek a Greek when he's in Greece? No, you wouldn't, because they're *all* Greek in Greece. So . . . anyone—"

"Ooh!" Becca said. "They called him 'the Greek' when he lived in another country!"

"A country with snow?" asked Julian. "Darrell, what does the book say?"

Darrell squinted at the screen. "Um, yeah. Lots of snow. The endless kind . . ."

"Norway!" said Wade. "No! Iceland!"

"Russia, my friends," Darrell said, pleased with himself. "At least I think that's what this says. Listen. 'Come later Maxim was by Russia Duke Vasily the Three invited Moscow to. There he Russian make of Greek into Russian word pages.'"

"That makes sense," said Becca. "They wanted Maxim to translate Greek stuff into Russian because the Greeks probably had all kinds of books they didn't have in Russia."

Darrell grumbled. "Which is exactly what I said."

"When did Maxim go to Russia?" asked Wade.

"*If* you'll let me continue—"

"It's hard to listen to," said Wade.

"So are you." Darrell cleared his throat and started up. "It says . . . 1515. Exactly when we need him to be in the land of endless snow. I totally bet Maxim Grek is the second Guardian."

Becca stood. "Darrell, this is huge. I think maybe you did it—"

"Russia is huge, too." Lily pushed a map to the middle of the table. "Look at it. Where do we even begin?"

"Wait. There's more." Darrell scanned another page of the book. "'His life problems came big in Russia. Duke Vasily make him prison for Maxim when Maxim say Duke no marry.' Which means that after going to Russia things turned pretty rough for Maxim. Vasily threw him in jail because Maxim didn't like him marrying some lady."

"As opposed to who?" asked Becca.

Darrell scanned the text. "His wife."

"Oh."

Julian stood and paced the length of the table. "Did Maxim die in Russia? If he did, the relic may still be there. Besides that, sometimes people do important things on their deathbeds. Like the Frombork Protocol, right? Maybe before he died, Maxim left a clue about where he hid the relic."

Darrell stood away from the computer. "I anymore read cannot. Eyes of me blur big. Anyone . . . ?"

"I'll do it," said Lily. She slid over to the computer

and read the screen for a few seconds. "Oh, and double oh. It says . . . 'Duke Vasily many had of alliances. One of with' . . . ack! Guess who?"

"The pope," said Darrell. "Napoleon. Dracula! Final answer!"

She shook her head. "The Demon Master, AVH himself!"

"Seriously?" said Wade. "Duke Vasily's ally was Albrecht von Hohenzollern?"

"'Albrecht of Hohenzollern Prussia,'" Lily read. "The one and only Grand Master of the creepy Knights of the Teutonic Order, and the creepy nemesis of Copernicus!"

The reading room went quiet.

Becca closed the diary, unable to read anymore. "So . . . Copernicus meets Maxim Grek in Padua when they're students. Later, when he has to hide the relics, he remembers his college friend, who is now in Russia, where Maxim quickly becomes the enemy of Vasily *and* Albrecht at the same time. Maxim Grek is very possibly our Guardian!"

Lily smiled. "And because the first will circle to the last, Copernicus leaves the clue in Magellan's dagger, which we only found when Becca cracked it—saving *my* life. In other words, you're welcome."

Darrell eased back to the computer. "It goes on . . .

'War plenty. Maxim prison was after and after for his life. Last years in Saint Sergius monastery inside out of Muscovy. Only after Maxim die is he buried. This can be 1556!'" Darrell blinked. "To translate the translation, Maxim was jailed in one monastery after another and finally spent his last years in a place called Saint Sergius, a monastery 'inside out of Muscovy.' He never made it back to Greece. They buried him in the monastery after he died."

"Here's Saint Sergius." Julian turned a large photographic book around. Spread across two pages was a picture of the massive Saint Sergius monastery. It was an enormous and opulent fortress. Towering over its high white stone walls were dozens of plump domes painted brilliant gold or deep blue and flecked all over with silver stars.

"Can you imagine how many places you could hide a relic there?" asked Lily. "Seriously, it makes sense to start at the end of his life and work backward. It's how we zeroed in on Magellan."

Which Becca realized for the first time was true, as it had been for Uncle Henry, too. It was at the end of *his* life that he had passed the secret on to them.

"Man, I wish I was going with you," said Julian.

"Going with us?" Wade asked. "To Russia? Are we

seriously thinking the relic is in Russia?"

"Go to where he died. That's where I would begin," Darrell said. "Russia. The monastery at Saint Sergius. For which, by the way, *you're* welcome."

"All right, then," said Wade. "It would be totally amazing if we think we've already figured out who the Guardian might be. But I'm getting nowhere on what the double-eyed relic is—"

Julian's cell phone buzzed. He swiped it on and answered it. He nodded once, ended the call, and stood up. "We have to go right now."

"Did the Order find us?" said Darrell. "Are they here? Why do we have to leave?"

"For brunch," Julian said. "Our dads are meeting us in half an hour!"

CHAPTER TWELVE

As a precaution, Lily, Julian, and a guard left the Morgan from the old entrance on Thirty-Sixth Street, while Wade, Becca, Darrell, and another guard exited the brownstone through a pair of glass doors at 24 East Thirty-Seventh Street. They met one another a block east of the museum, on Park Avenue, where a brown four-door Honda sedan was idling at the curb. Dennis, the Ackroyds' driver, sat behind the wheel. He smiled and unlocked the doors, the kids climbed in, and the two guards trotted back to the museum.

"Dennis, how are you feeling this morning?" Julian asked.

"Fine today," he said. "Where to?"

"The Water Club."

"I hope they have food, too," said Darrell.

Wade laughed. Darrell was feeling good. They all were. In a couple of short hours, they had gained a solid idea of who the second Guardian was. That was real progress.

Ten minutes later, after zigzagging from block to block across streets and down avenues, they arrived at a broad, low restaurant overlooking the river. Julian thanked Dennis, who drove off to park nearby.

"Your father will arrive in . . . seventeen minutes," said a man at the desk, checking his watch. "Your table is ready for you now."

The dining room smelled deliciously of hot coffee, fried eggs, bacon, and pastries, and Wade's stomach wanted all of them. They crossed the floor to a large round table by a wide bank of windows. Snowflakes, heavier now, were falling gently and dissolving into the river outside.

Becca took a seat next to him. "What's this river?"

"The East River," said Julian. "You can just make out the Williamsburg Bridge."

"Oh." She shivered. "Better to look at it than be on it."

As soon as they were all seated, Wade drew the star

chart from his backpack and unfolded it. "The constellation is here, somewhere," he murmured. "The double-eyed beast has got to be one of Ptolemy's original forty-eight constellations. But which one?"

"There are a dozen or so 'beasts,'" Lily said, making air quotes around the last word. "And I'm including dogs, birds, Hydras, dragons, and bears."

Wade nodded. "But some are profiles. Not all of them have both eyes visible." As he looked at his antique sky map, Wade imagined Uncle Henry's kind, old face, and he felt something shut off in his brain. The table, the windows, the snow vanishing into the river, even Becca and the others around him, seemed to fade into the background. His talent for blocking out noises and distractions—so tested lately—came forward.

He mentally ticked off the constellations that couldn't for an instant be considered "double-eyed." That still left a number of water creatures, centaurs, a lion, bears, a dragon, a horse, and more. Studying the golden and silver constellations, he remembered what his father had taught him about stars, and a small thought entered his mind.

Could *double-eyed* refer to the astronomical phenomenon known as a double star? "Huh . . ."

"Huh, what?" asked Lily.

"Well, maybe Copernicus meant that there's a double star in the constellation's head."

"What's a double star?" Darrell asked. "And don't say two stars."

Wade laughed. "Well, they kind of *are* two stars—"

"I asked you not to—"

"Which is why I did. A double star is really where two stars are so close together that they sometimes appear like one really bright star. It's only when you observe them for a long time that you discover that there are two of them. Lily, can you cross-check double stars against Ptolemy's forty-eight constellations?"

"Smart," she said, her fingers already moving over the tablet's screen, "for a non–intelligence officer, that is. I'm searching, searching, and . . . oh."

"You found something already?" asked Julian.

"Actually, no. There are a ton of double stars in the constellations and a bunch where the eyes could be."

Darrell leaned over Wade's notebook. "Well, then, what about this 'unbound' beast? What does that even mean? A wild beast? A beast out of control?"

"Right," said Julian. "Or maybe it's loose somehow? Not together—"

"You mean like Wade?" said Darrell.

"Good one," said Julian. "I mean like in a bunch of

different parts? Is there a constellation, *one* constellation, in more than one part? That *also* has a double star in its head?"

Wade studied the star chart carefully before ruling out one constellation after another. Then he stopped, shaking his head. He ran through the constellations a second time. He felt a smile coming on that he couldn't hide. "You got it, Julian. There *is* one constellation that has two stars in its head, and it *is* in two separate parts," he said. "Just one . . ."

They waited.

"Wade. Seriously," said Becca.

"And they call the name of that constellation . . ."

Lily narrowed her eyes at him. "Tell. Us."

"Serpens," he said, tapping the chart directly on the constellation appearing in the northern sky. "Serpens. Which stands for—"

"The Serpent, yeah," Darrell said. "We figured it out. Let's go find it."

"Except . . . look at it," said Wade. "The Serpens constellation really *is* in two parts. In the west is the serpent head and in the east is the body. In between is the figure of the guy who's wrestling it—Ophiuchus—and he's got his own other constellation. Serpens is actually divided into two parts. It's odd that way."

"You're odd that way," Darrell said, squinting over the chart.

"I get it from you," Wade said. "I'm just hoping the relic isn't in two pieces, each one hidden in a different place."

"We'll still find it," Darrell said. "Both of it."

Wade was wondering what it might really mean if the relic was split and hidden in two places when his father and Terence Ackroyd entered the restaurant. They both wore cautious smiles.

"Paul Ferrere is already on his way back to Paris, certain that Sara is in Europe, probably southern Europe," said Terence. "All other destinations for the two jets have been ruled out, and the detectives are paying particular attention to Madrid's several municipal and private airfields."

"Which is very good," Wade's father added. "Their extensive team of investigators is fanning out across the continent."

"Really good!" said Darrell. "This is soooo good!"

"From this moment on, I will be the go-between for the detectives and you," Terence said. "Now, what did you learn at the Morgan?"

"Maxim Grek."

"Serpens."

"Russia."

That's what Wade and the others told his father and Terence. Both men countered their arguments here and there, and the kids countered back. This went on during their three-course brunch, until both men agreed that, given the evidence, they were very likely on the right track.

"Russia," Roald said finally. "As soon as Galina finds out, and she *will* find out, she'll bring Sara to Russia, too. If we have no other leads, then Russia is a start. Don't travel visas take several days to get?"

Julian glanced at his father. "Are you thinking what I'm thinking? Comrade Boris?"

Terence seemed strangely reluctant, then nodded. "I think so, yes. There is a man. A Russian fellow. His name is Boris Volkov. He's lived in London for the past few years. I think you should fly there first and see him. He can likely be of help to you."

"Likely?" said Becca.

"Volkov is a scholar of languages and a historian of Russia's medieval period," Terence said. "I met him when I was writing a book about the treasure the Crusaders brought back from the Middle East. He knows a lot about the Order, perhaps the Guardians, too. Whether he is an agent of one or the other, I can't say.

He's quite cagey about what he reveals. But he may be able to help you get into Russia quickly and aid you while you're there. Boris Volkov seems to have . . . connections."

"Well, we can't afford—" Wade's father began.

Terence waved his hand to stop him. "Think no more about that. I told you, my resources are yours. Since you don't have the authorities on your side, the Ackroyd Foundation will bankroll your continued travels. I'll do everything in my power to help you get Sara back safely and find the relic."

"Awesome," said Lily, smiling at both Ackroyds. "Thank you, again."

Wade's father took a breath, then raised his eyes to the two girls. "There's . . . something else," he said. "Becca, I called your mother this morning, and Lily, your dad, about you going home or going on. You both need to call your parents, not at home, but on their cell phones."

Becca's face fell. "What is it? Oh, I should have answered when I got the call last night. I didn't want to. What's happening—"

Roald held up his hands. "Everyone is fine, they're fine, and in fact Paul Ferrere has already alerted his people in Austin. But there was an incident at Maggie's school the other day, and Lily, your father was followed home from work. Nothing happened, nothing at all, but as of this morning, both of your families have been relocated temporarily."

Lily held one hand over her mouth as she dug furiously for her phone.

Becca did the same. "Maggie, Maggie, I should have answered!"

For the next few minutes, both girls were sitting at different tables, glued to their cell phones, deep in conversation with their parents, while Terence filled in the details.

"The stinking Order," Darrell grumbled.

"Dad—" Wade started.

"I already talked to your mother," his father said, assuring him. "She's fine and traveling in Mexico. She doesn't appear to be on their radar at all."

A weight had been lifted, but Wade realized it had been days since he had spoken with her. "I'll call her right after this."

"Basically," Terence said, "it's best for none of you to return to Austin until we're sure of what we are dealing with. The Order could simply be flexing its muscles. I have no doubt that whatever they are doing comes from Galina herself, but my feeling is that she won't want to spread herself too thin with actions as intimidating as doing anything to the girls' families. Her empire is huge. She will need to focus it."

Wade shared a look with Darrell, who muttered something about Galina that Wade knew he probably shouldn't repeat. That was when his father produced a narrow silver tube from his pocket. It was the size of a fat ballpoint.

"It's a stun gun," he said. "A miniature Taser. Totally legal. The investigators gave one to me."

"Do we each get one?" asked Darrell.

"Absolutely not. And it's for defense only."

"A little something," said Terence. "It can be handy in tight quarters, without being a dangerous weapon."

Minutes later, Lily returned, wiping her cheeks. "They're all right. Way upset, with, like, a million questions, but they don't think I should be there right now." She started crying again behind her hands. "I'm sorry." Darrell put his arm around her shoulders, and she leaned into him.

Becca came back to the table looking like a zombie, blinking tears away from her eyes, unable to sit down. "Maggie's okay, worried like crazy. My parents, too, but they said I should stay with you. I never even thought of going home, and now I really want to, but I guess I should stay. I don't know."

Lily pulled away from Darrell and put her hand on Becca's wrist, and Becca sat. It was like that for a long while, everyone quiet, eyes down, not knowing what to say.

Wade once more remembered his dream of the cave: Becca lying lifeless on the floor. Then the way Markus Wolff had stared at her in San Francisco. He suddenly feared that Becca might be in some particular kind of danger, but he still didn't know how to express it. He just gazed at her, then at Lily, then at Becca again.

Finally, dishes were removed and dessert came, and that seemed to reset things.

"Is Boris Volkov a friend of yours?" Roald asked over a final coffee.

"No, not a friend," Terence said, waving a waiter over and asking for the check. "But he's useful. Listen to what he has to say. He knows many people in Russia who may be able to help you. However, I wouldn't entirely trust him. Boris doesn't do anything for nothing."

Wade felt uneasy to hear those words. But he hoped that the mysterious Russian would shed light on the relic's whereabouts. At the very least, the family was, as his father had hoped, moving forward.

To Russia. To the second relic . . . and Sara.

"In the meantime," Julian said, "Dad and I will focus on finding out what we can from our side. The instant we discover anything, we'll call you."

"Night or day," Roald said, looking around at the children.

With a final firm pledge of assistance, Terence made a call. Seven minutes later, Dennis pulled up outside the Water Club in yet another limo. Their luggage packed and safely in the trunk, the kids and Roald began their roundabout journey to JFK, to await their evening flight to London.

CHAPTER THIRTEEN

Madrid; London
March 19

Ebner von Braun woke to the tinny ascending scale of a digital marimba that suddenly sounded like a skeleton drumming a piano with its own bones. It was a ringtone he was determined to change at his first opportunity.

He blinked his eyes onto a black room.

Where am I?

More marimba.

Right.

Madrid.

He slid open the phone. *"¿Hola?"*

It was an Orc from the Copernicus Room. He listened. *"¿Londres?"* he said. *"¿Cuándo?"* The voice replied. Ebner pulled the phone away from his face. *"¿Quién es el jefe del Grupo de los Seis?"*

"Señor Doyle."

"Then send Señor Doyle."

Click.

The aroma of grilled tomatoes greeted Archie Doyle when he woke up. He gazed through sleepy eyes at the bedroom of his three-room flat at 36B Foulden Road in the Borough of Hackney in London. He yawned.

It was 5:51 a.m., and his wife, Sheila, and his son, Paulie, were already awake.

Ah, family.

He flapped his lips and blew out the stale breath of sleep. "Bbbbbbbbbb!" This habit, and other exercises of the face and vocal cords, were ones he had learned in his unsuccessful years as an actor, which, alas, were all of them. As an actor, a mimic, a stand-up comedian, and the sad clown Tristophanes, in whose guise he appeared at birthday parties and bar mitzvahs, Archie Doyle had struggled.

He was far better at his other calling.

He liked to kill people.

And he'd be getting to do more of it soon. A recent and bizarre auto accident involving no less than three operatives had left Archie next in line to head Group 6 of the East London section of the Teutonic Order, a post he held while Berlin made up its corporate mind about more permanent arrangements.

Archie was determined to make a good impression.

"The rrrrrain in Spppppain stays mmmmmainly on the pppplain!"

"That you, dear?" came the call from the kitchen. "Breakfast in five minutes."

"Coming, luv," Archie responded happily. Sitting up, he slid his laptop from the end table onto the bed and opened it. He then typed in seven distinct passwords, and the screen he wanted came up. On it was a photograph of five rather downcast people, a man and four young teenagers, at a departure gate in what his trained eye told him was JFK airport in New York. Did they know they were being tracked? Their expressions suggested they might. It was next to impossible to avoid detection in such places when the Order was after you. On the other hand, a father and four children? Where was Mum?

Mine not to reason why.

Beneath the photograph were the names of the five persons, and these words:

Guardian alert: 19 March. NY flight Virgin Atlantic 004.
Arrival 7:25 a.m. Heathrow Terminal 3.

"Oh, brilliant!" he whispered with a smile. There was a standing order to terminate all Guardians when identified as such. Five kills in one day. This would be a rather lovely way to convince his superiors that Archie was the man for the top job.

When he scrolled down a little farther, however, his smile crinkled to disappointment. Beneath the names and destination of the people in the photograph was a series of items with little boxes to be checkmarked as to Archie's course of action.

☐ *Terminate immediately*
☐ *Terminate off site*
☐ *Kidnap and report*
☑ *Follow only and report*

"Blast it all!" he breathed softly. "I am a termination machine!"

Still, a job was a job, and pleasing the Order was far preferable to displeasing them. And by *them* he meant *her*, and by *her* he meant Galina Krause. He'd seen her angry once. He hoped never to see it again.

Pulling up the train schedule, Archie calculated that the journey from his local railway station of Rectory Road to Heathrow would take a total of ninety-four minutes. Just before 6:30, he would snag a seat on the excruciatingly slow one-hour service west to central London, disembark at Paddington Station, dash over to Platform 6 for the 7:30 Heathrow Express to Terminal 3, and arrive twenty minutes later. Given another twenty or so minutes spent deplaning, collecting bags, if any, passport control, bathroom time, etc., the gloomy family couldn't be expected to be out of the arrivals hall until eight a.m. at the earliest, anyway. He checked the time again. Six o'clock.

I do have to get a move on.

Archie Doyle was of normal height and build with features that were, in the best tradition of foreign agents, nondescript. He leaped from bed, cleaned himself up, dressed in a smart wool suit of dark blue and a white shirt with muted tie, and topped it all off with a crisp bowler hat. He then slipped his briefcase onto his dresser and flipped up the lid.

Inside were the tools of his trade: several thicknesses and shades of adhesive mustaches and matching eyebrows, a range of eyeglasses, a tube of rub-on tanner, two false noses, three slender vials of poison, a small pistol and silencer, a stiletto, and assorted untraceable cell phones. It amazed him how many of these items he also used for his party activities. He placed his computer inside and clamped the briefcase shut. Then he slid his brolly—umbrella—from the closet, opened and closed it once, then tapped one of two small buttons inside its handle. With barely a breath, a hollow two-inch needle emerged from the umbrella's tip. Such a weapon could inflict a range of wounds, from a simple annoying scratch to a deadly puncture, if the needle was infused with poison. That was what the second button was for.

Archie wondered for an instant: Who *were* the Kaplans, anyway? Why "follow only and report"? Why not terminate? With no answers coming, he carefully retracted the umbrella's needle, gave his bowler a slap, and was in the kitchen—all in less than ten minutes from the time he woke.

His lovely wife, Sheila, turned to him, her smile like sunshine on the lawn of Hyde Park. In the tiny room with her, and taking up much of the floor space, was a portable crib. Fingers in mouth, sippy cup wedged between his plump legs, sat Paulie Doyle, fourteen months of pudge and drool and grins.

"I'm nearly plating the tomatoes, dear," Sheila said. "Kippers this morning?"

Archie Doyle sighed. "Sorry, dear. Must leap to the office immediately. I'll grab an egg and bacon on the way to the train. Save the tomatoes, though. Should be home for lunch."

"All right, dear," she said. "You have a wunnyful day."

"Thanks, luv," Archie said, kissing her ample cheek. "And bye-bye, Little Prince Paulie." He ruffled the wispy hair on the head of his son on his way to the door.

Archie was out, down the stairs, and on the sidewalk in a flash. Brisk day. Gray but pleasant. A perfect day for a termination—or five—he thought, but good enough to follow only and report.

"We shall see," he murmured, fingering the second button on his umbrella, "what we shall see."

CHAPTER FOURTEEN

London

Knowing there was little escape from airport cameras, Becca emerged head down from the Jetway in the arrivals terminal at London's Heathrow Airport. She trailed Lily, who as usual was acting as a sort of guide through the crowded world of crowds. It was the morning after the flight, and early, only a few minutes after eight a.m. But already the gates and concourses were busy, and Becca couldn't look up without feeling nauseous.

A really annoying personality trait.

It was like shouting, *Hey, everybody, look at me! I'm not looking at you!*

"You'll have to learn to do this one day, you know," Lily said over her shoulder.

"Not if you're always here."

"I just might be!"

Before the flight had left New York the previous evening, both girls had received a second and third round of phone calls from their parents, and Becca had had a very long talk with Maggie, which had managed to settle them both so that by the end they'd been laughing through their tears and whispering promises to each other to be good and safe. Becca felt that for her and Lily, hearing from their families was like Roald, Darrell, and Wade hearing from the investigators: all of them were now more or less assured that things were as okay as they could be for the moment and moving in the right direction. Without that, Becca didn't know how they could possibly focus on the relic and Russia and whatever else was to come. But here they were, on their first leg of the Serpens quest, and they were doing it.

"Oh, brother, now it begins," Lily grumbled as an airport official waved them and a hundred thousand other international passengers into the same skinny line.

There was no hiding here, Becca thought. No possibility of evasive action. Everyone had to go through passport control. And they were undoubtedly being filmed. In San Francisco they'd learned about the Order's awesome "Copernicus servers," with a computer power most first-world countries would envy. The family had probably been spotted at Kennedy airport, back in New York, so the Order *had* to know they were already in London. Eyes were on them. Of course they were.

Nearly an hour of blurring movement and bouncing from one line into another and opening bags and zipping them up and showing documents and squeezing into another line finally ended, and they were out of the terminal, and it was great, but not that great.

London might have been the home of Oliver Twist and Sherlock Holmes, but Becca's first experience outside the terminal was a stabbing downpour of cold, heavy, exhaust-filled, vertical rain.

"Absolutely fabulous, it's not," Lily grumbled. "Who knew it rained in England?"

"Uck, okay. Stay together," Roald urged, and they did, sticking close as he moved them quickly across the lanes of bus and shuttle traffic to the taxi stand, where they piled into a bulbous black cab that looked very much like the old one they'd seen in San Francisco last week. The sight of it started a superfast stream of memories in Becca's mind, culminating with a gun at her head at Mission Dolores, which, thankfully, hadn't gone off. Best not to live those days again. These days were bound to be scary enough.

"We'll be stopping at various places," Roald told the driver from the backseat. "First destination, Covent Garden."

"Certainly."

The taxi, piloted by a very quiet driver who wore a Sikh turban, was soon grinding its way from the airport and up onto a broad highway known as the M4. One of the things both Terence Ackroyd and the investigator had advised, to confuse would-be followers, was to take a roundabout route wherever they went. Terence Ackroyd's private apartment—or "safe flat," as he called it—was near the British Museum, but it would likely be a couple of hours before they actually reached it.

"Evasive maneuvers," Roald called them.

In the same spirit, Darrell and Wade had worked out a set of secret finger gestures on the plane. "To use if something bad is happening but you can't tell anyone," Darrell had said.

Lily gave them a blank look. "Um . . . what?"

"The complete range of bad things can be said with only five fingers," Wade insisted. "You raise them to your face in a casual way, and the rest of us know what to do."

"What?" she said again.

They explained it this way:

One finger: The Order is near—run.

Two fingers: Meet me at (location to be determined).

Three fingers: Create a diversion.

Four fingers: Help.

Five fingers: Just get away from me.

The last one was added by Darrell specifically, he said, for use between the brothers. Becca and Lily spent a long time rolling their eyes, then shrugged and practiced the gestures. Roald woke from a brief nap as the plane was descending and learned them as well, but he thought he might be able to come up with a better set of commands.

"I dare you, Dad," Darrell quipped.

Becca watched out the cab window as they motored swiftly past brick and brownstone neighborhoods with names that exuded Englishness: Cranford and Osterley, Brentford and Shepherd's Bush. She could practically see the sheep grazing in pastures, though that was a scene from old novels and, by now, there weren't many pastures that hadn't been developed and built on.

Still, the slower the taxi went, the more clogged the streets were, and the more Becca began to feel the aura of "London, England" breathing from the sights around her. It came powerfully. All those English novels by English writers! They were written here, about here, and they were everywhere, as if those books had spilled their pages out into the living city. Even the presence of the Sikh driver spoke of the once-great colonial empire that was Great Britain, and how London gathered in its vast geography everyone from everywhere it had ever ruled.

"My first time to London in ten years," said Roald, his neck craning around here and there to catch every moment, just as she was doing. "There was a conference at the University of London. I presented a paper on Europa, one of Jupiter's moons. It was my first international paper."

"So cool," Becca breathed, aware that there was little volume in what she said.

"Only if you don't read the paper," he said with a laugh. "Pretty dull stuff."

"Still," she said. "London."

Trying not to annoy or alarm the driver, Roald gave him several addresses to drive to—as if they were sightseeing—before the final one. After Covent Garden, a bustling market in the heart of the city, they drove through the madly snarled traffic of Piccadilly Circus, around to Selfridges department store, across a bridge to Southwark, and back over another bridge to Saint Paul's Cathedral. When, finally, they motored toward their final stop, Darrell suggested they call the telephone number Terence had given them, "to get things started." Roald tapped a number on the cell phone installed with Julian's homemade alert software.

"Galina probably knows we're in London," Wade whispered; then he frowned. "There's no probably about it. She knows. We have to be supersmart."

Becca shared a grim look with the others. Despite their hopped-up phones, if for some reason Galina Krause *didn't* already know their exact location, she would soon.

"I've never been not smart," said Lily. "An intelligence officer can't afford to be. That witch is out there. Her and her thugs. I'm sure of it."

The Sikh driver half turned. "*Thugs*, miss. This is a word coming from the Hindi term *thuggees*, the name given to some fanatic followers of Kali. The goddess of destruction."

"Thank you," Lily said, her eyes widening. "How weirdly . . . accurate. . . ."

Becca's blood tingled in her veins. The quest was on, and she believed, as they all did, that if Maxim *was* the Guardian, and Serpens *was* the second relic, then Russia was the place, and she hoped Boris Volkov would help confirm it.

"Hallo? Who is?" The voice crackled loudly from Roald's phone.

"Hello. Is this Boris Volkov?"

"Ya. Hallo. Who is?"

"Excuse me," Roald said as they eased deeper into the streets. "This is a friend of Terence Ackroyd's. He told us—"

"Ah, yes, Terry! Dear friend, Terry. Yes, yes. Family Keplen. Come see me. Is Boris. Boris Volkov." There was the sound of ice clinking into a glass on the other end. "You come Promenade. Ten thirty this morning. Dorchester Hotel."

"Uh . . . we would prefer somewhere more private," Roald said.

"No. Public is safe. Witnesses be there. Public only. Bring item with you, yes?"

"Item?" said Roald. "I'm not sure I know exactly—"

"Park Lane. You find? Yes? Good. You come."

Click.

"Dad, what does he want?" Wade asked. "We don't have any *item* for him."

Roald tapped the phone and returned it to his jacket pocket. "I think we'll find out soon enough. Hotel Cavendish, Gower Street," he told the driver.

"Certainly."

CHAPTER FIFTEEN

The Hotel Cavendish was a small boutique hotel near the corner of Gower Street and Torrington Place in the neighborhood surrounding the British Museum. Wade wondered what their rooms were like. He would continue to wonder. When their taxi wove through a series of narrow streets and passages and finally stopped outside, his father paid their driver handsomely. They entered the hotel, where they booked two rooms, made sure the taxi was gone, then turned and walked right back outside, to the bewilderment of the desk clerk, who was dangling two sets of room keys for no one.

"That looked kind of comfy," said Lily. "And expensive."

"Paul Ferrere always books a room he never stays in," Wade's father said. "This is the kind of life we're living right now. Our flat is a few short blocks away."

He then led the kids up Gower Street, took a left onto Torrington Place, and hung a right into the narrow Chenies Mews, an L-shaped passage whose long side ran parallel to Gower. They walked along the Mews to the corner of the L, where Roald paused in front of a nondescript and, Wade thought, seedy-looking brick building. But the narrow street was quiet and the building more warehouse-like than domestic, both precautions Wade appreciated as Terence's way of keeping them under the radar.

"Just for a day or two," said Roald. "And just so we're all clear: this is our 'location to be determined.' Memorize where we are in relation to the neighborhood."

"Got it," said Becca.

Wade and Darrell quickly left their bags in their ample rooms inside. It was 10:03 a.m. On their return to the Hotel Cavendish by a different route, Wade kept scanning the neighborhood. He noticed no slowing cars or anyone loitering suspiciously. He saw only a young couple in running gear heading to breakfast and a businessman in a blue suit and bowler hat, shaking out his umbrella under a bus stop shelter. But then, according to Darrell, he wouldn't see an agent of the Order until it was too late.

They assembled on the sidewalk in front of the Cavendish while the desk clerk gawked from the lobby. Roald hailed a black cab. The roundabout twenty-minute drive took them past the massive and imposing British Museum, which drew an extended gasp from Becca.

"Next time," she said. "Next time, all the sights."

"Maybe the Ackroyds have special privileges there, too," said Darrell.

Becca's jaw dropped playfully. "Don't kid me."

The cold rain continued to fall on the street, on the cars, on the gray buildings. Wade thought it made the city look sadder than it probably was, but they likely wouldn't get to see much of London anyway. Not if Boris Volkov told them what Wade hoped he would. By this afternoon, they'd be flying to Russia, to find both the relic and Sara.

"We should buy winter coats in London before we leave," Lily said out of nowhere. "*If* we leave. For Russia,

I mean. We should go back to Selfridges. For parkas and scarves and gloves. And Uggs."

For what seemed like a day and a half, they drove past the famous and huge expanse of lawn known as Hyde Park before coiling into an area congested by expensive cars, where the cab left them off. A five-minute evasive walk brought them finally to the graceful Dorchester Hotel. Under its broad awning a top-hatted doorman directed them through the revolving doors into the marble lobby. With a quick look around them, they wove their way into the bustling Promenade room.

CHAPTER SIXTEEN

A tuxedoed man stood behind a tall desk at the entrance to the restaurant.

He nodded politely when they told him who they were there to meet. "Yes, yes. Mr. Volkov has been waiting. One moment." He stepped out and cast a glance over the restaurant.

The Promenade was a deep, busy room lined with elegant tables and chairs on either side, with a central bank of velvet-cushioned sofas. Short potted palm trees were placed every few feet, and gold-topped columns rose to a tiered ceiling. There was also a lot of gold in the other fixtures and hangings, and a jungle of enormous flower arrangements on tables.

The place boomed with the sound of clinking cutlery and tinkling glass and the bubbling murmurs of dozens of breakfast conversations. It was also filled with the smell of toast and coffee, which was fine, but Wade wondered if they'd ever heard of the basic bacon, egg, and cheese on a hard roll.

The maître d' adjusted his glasses and pointed. "Mr. Volkov is right over . . ."

He didn't have to go on. A very big man wearing a very big suit waved both arms from the end of the room as if he were trying to stop traffic.

"You must be Keplens!" he bellowed.

"Great," Darrell whispered. "Three seconds in a public place and already we've been outed."

By a really enormous guy.

Wade's antennae went up instantly. "Dad, I don't get it. Why did he want to meet here?" he whispered. "The whole world sees us."

"Unless it's a trap," Darrell said.

"Maybe," Wade's father said. "He *is* right that being in public might protect us from outright attack. Remember, the Order doesn't want to get caught, either. Maybe he knows something about being careful that we don't."

Boris Volkov was completely huge, and seemed to grow more huge the closer they came. He appeared to

Wade every bit as cagey and suspicious as Terence Ackroyd had suggested. Weaving around the tables toward him, Wade kept a lookout for anyone paying special attention to them, but after turning to see who the "Keplens!" were, the other patrons seemed to have gone back to their private conversations. *Good,* he thought. *I'd rather eat than run.*

The large Russian bounced up awkwardly when they came over, nearly taking the tablecloth with him, and wrapped his arms around them in a weird group hug.

Wade wanted to trust him, but he didn't care for the heavy, fumy smell that blossomed from him. Alcohol in the morning? What sort of person had Terence hooked them up with? Everyone, he told himself, every single person was under suspicion until proved otherwise. That was a lesson they'd learned in San Francisco, with the killer Feng Yi, who had betrayed the kids *and* the Teutonic Order.

His father introduced them all, and Volkov forced them into a very precise arrangement at the table. He asked Becca and Lily, who he called by each other's name—*Lee-lee* and *Bake-ahh*—to squeeze in alongside him, while he gestured Wade, his father, and Darrell to take seats on the other side. Settling in, Wade tugged out his notebook and turned to the first clean page, ready for whatever the strange man told them.

In the few moments that followed, during which they ordered, Wade eyed Boris Volkov as best he could without staring. First off, everything on the guy was sweating. His jowly cheeks, his forehead, the ridge above his chin, his levels of neck. The front of his shirt was soaked through. There was a drop of sweat dangling from the tip of his nose, which he didn't wipe away, but which never appeared to fall, either.

It was when the man's eyes turned on Wade that he noticed Boris Volkov's real distinguishing feature. It was neither his plump lobster face nor his short chubby fingers, but the two large dark eyes that were severely misaligned. The left one slanted to the left, while the right one stared straight ahead.

Which one do you look at?

And did it mean anything that this guy *and* Galina Krause both had eye things going on? Hers, two colors; his, wandering around?

"So, so," the man said, turning his head completely to Wade's father, which didn't help answer the question of which eye to address. "Promenade safe place. Over there, deputy head of MI6, British Secret Intelligence Service. At table alone, British foreign secretary. Safest place in all of London, right here!"

"Thank you for meeting us," Wade's father said. "And yes, I agree, a good location."

The Russian arched up in his seat. "You want to know who is Boris Volkov, yes? Why is Russian in the country of Wimbledon and Big Ben?" He shrugged and breathed out a flammable gust. Wade was glad there were no candles on the breakfast table.

"I graduate Moscow State University," he said. "Scholar for many years. Dead languages. Boris love dead languages. Russia is land of the dead, no? But, I say wrong things at wrong time. Government not like so much. I spend time in famous Lubyanka prison, yes? Not serious. Just questions, you see? I notice there the wood floor. Oak. Very nice. Like this, yes?" He paused, flattening his big hands and angling them, one to the other.

"Parquet," Darrell said.

"Yes!" Boris boomed, patting Darrell's hand on the table. "You very smart American boy. How you know parquet?"

"My mom's office in the archives at the University of Texas has parquet floors," he said.

"Ah, yes. Mother. She in this, too. Terry tell me. Sad, sad."

Wade didn't know what Boris knew, but wondered

once again what exactly Terence had told him.

"So, future of Boris is not in Russia. Zoom-boom! I come London, yes?" He slapped his chubby palms on the table. "I perch now in small flat owned by friend. Is beautiful little birdcage. Tiny. Top floor. Five stairway. No elevator. Is hard for old legs, but this is way I live now. Boris walk everywhere. He never take car. Car take you to Lubyanka, yes?"

I don't know, does it?

Boris paused a moment to move the sugar bowl from one side of his place setting to the other. "But enough. You call me Uncle Boris now, yes?"

No, thought Wade, *we don't. You're not our uncle. I had an uncle, Uncle Henry, and he was murdered by the Teutonic Order, and so was nice Mr. Chen on the plane to San Francisco, and we don't know if you're with the Order or not.*

It wasn't that Wade wanted his mind to go there, accusing everyone, suspicious of everyone, but how could he do anything else? Heinrich Vogel's death had been sudden and brutal—an old man murdered in his home. It was fresh, barely a week and half in the past, and, like Sara's kidnapping, Wade realized it was hovering like a shroud over everything they thought and did. It was Uncle Henry's murder that had sent them on the relic hunt in the first place, the quest that had quickly become their urgent mission. The quest that was changing them in ways he didn't fully understand.

After a few pleasant remarks with Roald about the weather and hotels and so on, Boris Volkov tapped his meaty fingers on the tabletop. His smile dropped away.

"You see, it is this. History of Russia is history of pain. Invasions? Countless invasions. Poland. Napoleon. Hitler. Then invasions from inside—Lenin, Stalin, demon masters buried now with honors in Red Square. Horrible history. Still Russia survives."

"We know that the Teutonic Order was friends with the Duke of Moscow," Becca said. "Vasily the Third had an alliance with Albrecht."

"Teutonic Order of Ancient Prussia." Boris's face reddened. "This is the way of the Order. They seep everywhere, like poison." He lowered his voice. "In Russia, you see, the Order is known as Red Brotherhood. Keplens, you do not know this, but Teutonic Order kill Boris's brother. Galina Krause murder him while she in Russia. Yes, is true! Dental records prove it. I see his teeth. I *have* his teeth." And he raised a finger behind his open collar and tugged out a chain on which hung a blackened molar. "It belonged to Aleksandr in his mouth. Alek was doctor, very fine doctor. His tooth is all I carry. No money. No wallet. No key. See, I have

132

nothing." Boris tugged at his pants pockets to show they were empty. "Of course, Alek's name not really Volkov. Nor he, nor me."

Meaning what, exactly?

"I'm so sorry to hear that," Roald said. "We didn't know. Terence did tell us about your knowledge of the Order in Russia. It's part of the reason we've come here today. We need to do research there. In Russia. Terence said you might be able to help us."

"Yes, yes." Boris tucked the tooth back behind his collar. Then he slid his hand inside his voluminous jacket and produced a narrow manila envelope. He set it on the table and pressed a stubby finger on it. "Documents necessary to get into Russia this very day. Terry phone me with names, so these ready to use. Russian tourist visas. Completely genuine. Notarized by Russian embassy. Smuggled, of course, but what is little smuggling among friends, yes? After you are settled there, I must take side trip, but is not for some days. All us go tonight, yes? You pay? I tell you I have no money."

They went quiet.

"All of us?" said Wade finally. "I didn't think we *all* had to go."

"Perhaps Mr. Ackroyd didn't explain our journey to you," his father added. "It's, well, rather a private family project. We actually don't need—"

"You must have me," Volkov said. His face darkened and his misaligned eyes flashed with anger. "You need Boris. Boris has urgent journey. Boris have friends you require. I did not suffer Lubyanka prison for nothing. I go. I help. For price."

Here it is, Wade thought. *He doesn't do anything for nothing.*

Volkov leaned over the teacups toward them, fixing his eyes on both Darrell and Wade at the same time. "I am collector of unique objects. I want Copernicus dagger."

Wade's blood froze.

How does Boris Volkov—or whatever his real name is— know about the dagger? Is he a Teutonic Knight? Is this a trap?

"I . . . don't know exactly what you mean," Roald said, lying. "A dagger?"

Boris Volkov snorted angrily. "Then go back to Texas, USA. No tea. Good-bye. You are liars, try to trick Boris. Like all the rest. You have nothing!" He slumped back into his chair with such force the table shook. Again, the room hushed.

Texas? How much does he know about us?

"No. Wait," his father said. "We don't actually have . . . what you want."

"But you can get it? As sign of good faith?"

"Let me call Terence." Roald rose and pulled away from the table. "I'll get in touch with him right now."

"More like it," Volkov said, mopping his brow with his napkin, then bouncing right back with a big grin. "Take moments, Dr. Roald Keplen. Time, she does not matter, does she?"

At the word *she*, Darrell fidgeted in his chair, and his face darkened even more than the Russian's had a moment before. "Oh, yeah?" he said. "Yeah?"

"Darrell," Becca whispered. "Not here."

Surprisingly, he calmed down, but Wade could feel his legs pumping under the table.

Right. The real point of meeting this guy is to get Sara back. Time, she does not matter? Time matters more than anything.

His father disappeared into the lobby with his phone at his ear. Volkov stood to massage his right leg as if he weren't in public. It was hard to look at. "Old body hurts, yes?" He thundered back into his chair and pressed his giant bulk across the cups and plates, gesturing the four of them closer. Given how he took up so much table space, there was hardly any room to *be* closer.

"You," Boris said, apparently looking at Wade. "You are Vade, yes? Vade Keplen?"

"Yes."

"Good. You are scientist, yes? I hear it from Terry in New York. And Darrell, you are brother of Vade. I tell you story about scientist and his brother." He set his wandering eyes on the kids, one after the other. "I amuse American children with little story."

The words were sinister enough, but they were nothing compared to the way his wild eyes beckoned them. When he began to speak, slowly and almost in a whisper, the sounds of clacking cutlery and plates, the tinkle of glassware, the murmuring of voices around them—all seemed to fade away.

Even with his seriously broken English, Boris Volkov became suddenly—and inexplicably—a master of words, losing the trappings of the blustery, moody exile. Right there in the middle of a bustling London restaurant, amid the whirl of modern life, he conjured up another time, a forgotten world.

"Listen. Listen to words. Listen to Boris. . . ."

CHAPTER SEVENTEEN

Perhaps you know this already, but long ago there was a man and his brother. Nicolaus and Andreas Copernicus. A scientist and his brother. Andreas was, alas, dying. Illness took people young in those days.

Wade and the others had learned the story of Andreas Copernicus in San Francisco. In fact, it was precisely *because* Andreas had become ill from handling the deadly Scorpio relic that Copernicus had asked his friend Tomé Pires to hide it inside a jade figurine. Wade and later his father believed Andreas might have died from radium poisoning.

"We know a bit about that," said Lily, shooting Wade

and Darrell a glance.

Ah, yes, the bond of brothers is strong. My own brother, Alek, was very skilled doctor. We grew up together in coal mine. A strange place to grow up, is it not?

You see, after Russia's Great Patriotic War, in 1945, our father was sent to labor camp to dig coal day and night in a mine in the gulag. Forced labor, for what they said was his defiance of the government. Camp is far away in Siberia, north of Arctic Circle. You do not know cold like this. Pray you never do.

Two years later, we are born. Twins. Mother dies in childbirth, so Father names us. Alek born first, so he A, for Aleksandr. Me. I am B, for Boris. Is humor. You get?

His eyes bounced back between Wade and Darrell. Did this old Russian see something in them, a kinship that proved they were all Guardians in this together? Or was he weaving a story like a spider weaves a web, drawing them in and snaring them before they realized it was too late? Words mattered, Wade knew. Words had power.

As boys we send message to each other, even in . . .

Boris said something then that Wade wrote in his notebook as *log punked.*

World-famous code is solved when we are boys. Is joke to

us, yes? A and B? He send code to me, me send to he. Even when we grow up and go our ways, we send messages. Oh, the vastness of Russia. Me to Moscow, then here, never to return to dark circle of Mother Russia. He to Saint Petersburg, jewel on the Gulf of Finland.

Then the real horror begins.

Four years ago, Galina Krause appears out of the night. Alek works for her. What he does for the Order no one knows; he is doctor! But there is fire. Alek vanishes, is never heard from. Messages stop. I ask friends in Russia, what happen to my brother? They say the girl, Galina. His teeth are sent to me to prove he is dead. Me? I feel something break inside my heart. I cry—"Alek is dead! Galina has killed him!"

The restaurant hushed momentarily, then resumed its noise.

Galina Krause has murdered my brother, Aleksandr. In my heart, all is gone. Father, mother, Alek, even log punked is gone. But from London, I can do nothing. Until now today with you Keplens. We shield each other, yes? I have traced Red Brotherhood. I arrange gift for Galina. We go together in group, me to avenge my poor brother, Andreas . . . I mean Aleksandr . . .

The large Russian paused to wipe his eyes and his cheeks, then slumped back into his chair, making the table quake. "Me, I am nothing. I am like brother with disease. Leper. I am like dead languages that I study. My brother, he is the real one. He had pain. Much, much pain. He was the great one of these two brothers. Then Galina kill him."

CHAPTER EIGHTEEN

In the silence that followed, even through her own misty vision Lily couldn't help staring across the table into the Russian's jiggling left pupil. Not that she wanted to.

Look away! she told herself. *You really have to be more accepting of other people's different little things.*

Boris vacuumed in a long breath. "Russia is a grave, you see? Not only of fathers, not only of brothers. But of the past. But perhaps *you* tell Boris now what *you* know?"

Um, sure, Lily said in her head. *We found out from the coded ribbon in the Magellan dagger that Copernicus wanted to give Serpens to a monk named Maxim Grek, who was invited to Russia, then thrown in jail. Serpens is maybe a two-part serpent-shaped relic representing the northern constellation of the same name. It fits into the big wheel of Copernicus's astrolabe.*

Lily didn't say any of those words. Boris Volkov—which he said was not even his real name!—could simply be trying to trick them into telling what they knew.

I'll try to be okay with the eye, but I'm not going to spill the beans to any old person. Or young person. Or anybody.

"We'll let Uncle Roald tell you what we know," Becca finally said.

"Ah? Yes, of course. Caution. This is wise."

Lily surprised herself that she'd become as wary of others as Wade and Darrell had. Generally, she liked people, even if she made fun of some of them, like Darrell and Wade, but that was so easy to do, and anyway it was friendly, and sometimes they didn't even get it until she explained it to them. This was new to her, meeting these kinds of people she'd never met before except in a movie or a book, but those were fake and this was real. Except maybe for one of his eyes.

"Well, thanks for the story," she said, and Becca nodded with her.

"Is but story. A tale of long time past. Four years ago,

sixty years ago, five hundred years ago, all same. The clock ticks many hours. The journey to the end of the sea is long, yes? Copernicus himself wrote these words. But what do *we* know? Who can say what is true, yes?"

You're right about that, Lily thought. There were so many names and dates in his story that she wished she'd recorded it. *The journey to the end of the sea is long?* It sure is. *Wade's jotting things down, but somebody should be taping the whole thing. Wearing a wire. Like a real spy.*

Roald finally wove his way back through the tables, off the phone now. "The dagger is secure, out of the country, but I think we can make some sort of deal, once we get into—and safely out of—Russia."

Lily tried to read her uncle's face. He was fibbing, right? She hoped he was. They should *never* give up the Copernicus dagger. *Ever.*

"Yes!" Volkov lifted his teacup as if it were a beer mug, chugged it down, then "cheered" the cup into the air. "To our journey, then. I shall close up my flat, then to Russia we go—"

He sucked in an enormous groan and lurched to his feet, like a sea monster rising from the deep. Silverware clattered to the floor because he had stuffed the table-cloth into his belt. His teacup hung out in the air, his sausage-like fingers dwarfing its tiny size, when it fell from his hand and crashed on the table.

"Kkkk—kkk!" Boris's face twisted and bulged as if he were turning into a werewolf.

"Doctor!" Roald yelled. "Is there a doctor—"

The man's cheeks went deep purple. He pawed his leg mercilessly. Roald struggled to wrap his arms around Boris from behind to give him the Heimlich maneuver while both Darrell and Wade held him up, but the Russian was too big, and now his arms were flapping straight out. Suddenly, his eyes ballooned, and he clutched his neck with both hands, gasping for air that wouldn't come.

Customers at other tables were jumping to their feet, some rushing over to help. A waiter dropped his tray and raced back to the desk for the phone.

Boris spat out breaths, trying to form a word, but nothing would come. Roald held him up. "Boris, do you have any medication with you? Someone you want us to call? Anything I can get you?"

The huge man stared down at Lily. Right at her! *Why?* He suddenly blurted "Bird!" right into her face.

"Excuse me? What?" she said, backing up.

"Cage!" He seemed to want to fall on top of her. She stepped back again, saw a bloodstain on his pant leg where he had been rubbing it. She frantically scanned the chaotic room for someone who might be a doctor. On the far side of the restaurant, a calm-looking middle-aged man in a dark blue suit rose from his table. She beelined between the tables to him. "Are you a doctor?" she said. "Sir, can you help him?"

Boris bellowed, then slammed facedown on the table like a whale free-falling from the top of a building. The whole table went over, everything splattered, and Boris slumped to the floor, clutching at Wade for a moment, then slid away, motionless.

Lily screamed, grabbing the sleeve of the man in the dark suit. "Help him!"

"Alas, child," the man said, gently removing her hand, then patting her arm. "I am not a doctor." Tipping his bowler, he swung his umbrella toward the lobby and wove through the tables to the sound of sirens howling up the street.

CHAPTER NINETEEN

Madrid

Galina Krause watched two men in overalls roll a shiny brown coffin across the floor of her private hangar at the Madrid-Barajas Airport. Her mind ticked with a hundred possible scenarios for what might happen over the next hours and days.

Ebner leaned toward her. "We will be in Berlin in three hours' time," he said. "We can take the coffin to Station Two, if you are still intent on sending the woman, which I would not—"

"Yes, Berlin," Galina said.

But is Berlin the best destination after all? she wondered. She didn't like that the Copernicus Room had come up

with nothing useful so far except, perhaps, the astronomer's supposed 1517 voyage south from Cádiz, a coastal
city less than an hour's flight away. The Kaplans were
in London now, but what if they suddenly jetted off to
Spain or other parts south? Berlin would put her that
much farther away.

"*¿Señorita? ¿A dónde?*" one of the men ferrying the
coffin questioned. He pointed from one to the other of
two small jets in the hangar.

"*En el avión negro, por favor,*" she replied.

They pushed the coffin to her dark, gunmetal-gray
Mystère-Falcon and up a short ramp into its cargo hold.
They collapsed the legs of the coffin stand like one would
with a hospital gurney, secured the coffin in place, and
left the hangar.

Ebner paced annoyingly. "Is *he* to be with us the
entire time?"

Galina turned to see Bartolo Cassa stride into the hangar from the sunny tarmac. "You object? Do you think
he cannot be trusted? He brought the cargo undamaged
from South America. He removed three . . . obstacles to
bring the coffin to us. Can he not be trusted?"

Ebner seemed to be debating his answer to that question when the breast pocket of his coat sounded with
the tinkling scale of a frantic marimba. He reached for

his phone, slid his thumb across the screen, and held it to his ear. "Speak."

Hitching a long, box-shaped canvas bag over his shoulder, Cassa strode easily to the Falcon, walked up its stairs, vanished for a moment, then reappeared in the cockpit.

Galina fixed her eyes on Ebner. "Who is it?"

"Mr. Doyle with his report." Ebner flicked his phone to speaker.

". . . early this morning," Mr. Doyle was saying in a clipped British accent. "The Kaplan family, all of them, met a gentleman, a native Russian known currently as Boris Volkov, for breakfast at the Dorchester Hotel. Papers were passed between them. As directed, I have not interfered with the family, but per protocol, Volkov has been removed. He suffered a leg wound laced with ricin."

"Volkov? You mean the dissident scholar?" asked Ebner.

"Indeed," chirped the Londoner, "although Volkov is not his real name. Up until he was expelled from Russia, he was known as Rubashov. Boris Rubashov."

Galina breathed in suddenly, her eyes flashing. "Rubashov?" Her limbs stiffened for what seemed like an eternity before she said, "They are going to Russia."

"Ah, that explains the papers," said Mr. Doyle from the phone. "They had the look of tourist visas. In a rather curious turn, the smaller girl came up to me, thinking I was a doctor. The bowler, perhaps. I am tracking them, in case he gave them something I didn't see. I am also monitoring the stages of poor Boris's demise. Group Six has an agent in the hospital system."

Ebner seemed to want Galina to speak, but she could not find the words. "Very efficient, Doyle," he said. "This bodes well for your promotion in Group Six. Keep close to the family. Request backup if you need it."

"I shall. Cheerio!"

The fingers of Galina's right hand rose to the three-inch scar on her neck, then fell to her side. "The Kaplans," she said, "have met this Russian for one reason only. Ebner—"

"Galina." Ebner shuddered as if freezing. "Galina, the name Rubashov could simply be a coincidence."

"—the Kaplans are going after the Serpens relic."

Silver, diamonds, and hinges of sparkling wire swam in her vision.

"But surely they know nothing of the full story of Serpens," Ebner said softly. "They could not. The two parts, where they may have ended up—and why. I am certain it is but a stab in the dark, consistent with all of their . . . advances in the quest." He took a breath. "Still, I will inform the Copernicus Room to direct all their research on it now. But any more than that would be premature—"

"Alert the Red Brotherhood to follow the Kaplans wherever they go."

Ebner now appeared to swallow with difficulty. "Galina, the Red Brotherhood are hooligans, gangsters, thugs. They cannot *follow*. They maim; they kill. That's all they know. Let me bring in the Austrians."

"There is no time. Alert the Brotherhood. Naturally, you and I must fly directly . . . there."

"Not the castle—" The word escaped Ebner's lips before he could unsay it.

"Have the Italian brought to the castle, too. And Helmut Bern, as well."

"Tell me you do not mean . . ."

She turned her eyes on him. "I had hoped to wait, but there is no waiting. Ebner, we return to Greywolf immediately."

Greywolf—the Order's Station One—was an estate three hundred kilometers east of Saint Petersburg. It was a huge property: fifty square kilometers of steep, forest-thickened hills, at the summit of which stood a sixteenth-century fortress that the Order had abandoned to a destructive fire four years before.

"Galina, no. I beg you, another place. Kronos One lies in ruins after all this time. Lord knows if the main tower even exists any longer. If you are set on experimenting with Sara Kaplan, I beg you let me send for a newer device."

She laid her hand gently on his and then began to squeeze it under her iron fist. "Greywolf. Kronos One. We go now."

"All because of Rubashov," Ebner muttered, sulking away to the jet.

At the mention of the poisoned Russian's true name, and at the memory of Greywolf, the aircraft hangar around Galina began to vanish, and she soon saw herself laid out, comatose, on a vast slab of undifferentiated white, a wasteland of permafrost and tundra. She had hoped and prayed—bled, even—never to return to the monster country, and certainly not to the fortress. Serpens was in that bleak wilderness somewhere, or half of it, at least. But she was hoping to avoid ever entering that poisoned land to dig for it.

As she climbed the stairs to the Falcon, Galina realized that this flight to Russia was very nearly

superfluous. In her mind, ticking like a geared clockwork, like a sequence of tumblers in a combination
lock, she had never left.

Wherever she was, there would always be Russia.

CHAPTER TWENTY

I am moving.

Again.

Sara knew this as the cushioned walls so tight around her tilted side to side, inclined up, then leveled out, and stopped. Her moment of clarity wouldn't last long. *They'll soon drug me again,* she thought, *and I'll be out another I-don't-know-how-many days.* She tried to think, to process. She'd read Terence's spy novels, his international thrillers. What could a kidnap victim do? What could a victim learn from her surroundings?

One thing was the conditions of the kidnapping. Here, there were elaborate measures taken, not only for her restraint but also for a kind of comfort. Her hands and feet were bound, and there was some kind of thick belt across her forehead, in addition to an impenetrable blindfold. She was gagged. But she also knew a tube was attached to a needle in her right arm. There was oxygen, pure and cool, being pumped into her nostrils. She was cushioned like an artifact in a box.

She was being cared for, if *cared for* could ever be the proper term.

Though the low pulse of an oxygen pump some-where near her feet obscured most sound, her ears were open. *Listen!* She made herself still. Unless it was her own mind, she detected a murmur of voices nearby. Faint, almost like whispering. Then a whirring sound around her. And . . . bolts? One, two, three, four. Then the box jostled. Air—real air—swept over her face, her arms. The lid of her prison was open. Was it her keeper? The man with sunglasses, her handler from Bolivia? *Handle me, and I'll bite your arm—no, scream—no, both!* She couldn't, of course, do either.

"*¿Está viva?*" a voice said.

Yes, I'm viva! Sara snapped. Then she thought: *Span-ish. Spanish, yes, but not the accent of Bolivia or even of New York. Spain? Am I in Spain?*

A sharp poke in the arm. Sara screamed—tried to scream—but the pressure went straight into her brain like a magician's sword through his assistant in the box, and she was falling again. Quick. Remember. *Spain.*

Roald! Darrell! I'm in Spain! RoaldDarrellRoaldDarrell-WadeDarrell . . .

The lid of her prison crashed shut, and the roar of an engine thundered through the cushioned walls so tight around her, and . . . and . . .

CHAPTER TWENTY-ONE

London

Seemingly within moments of Boris Volkov's thundering fall to the floor, the Promenade was invaded by squads of police and scurrying medical technicians.

In the chaos, Becca saw Uncle Roald sweep the envelope of documents from the table and subtly tuck it into his jacket pocket just before he was called away for questioning by several plainclothes policemen. Lily simply stood there, shaking her head, hands poised in the air as if not knowing what to do with them, her mouth gaping open, nothing coming out.

She's terrified to death! Boris spoke to her. Why?

Becca wrapped her fingers around Lily's wrist and pulled her gently to the far side of the room with the others. "Boris was telling us a lot. Too much," she whispered. "Someone wanted him to stop talking, and stop him going with us."

"That was no heart attack," Darrell growled. "No way."

Wade shoved his hands deep into his pockets. "Do you think we should try to find his flat? He practically told us where it was. Five floors, no elevator."

Two police officers were standing in front of Roald now.

"Either Dad's waving to us or he's doing the code," Darrell whispered. "Look. Five fingers. What's five fingers? Create a diversion? Like a food fight?"

"No, that's three fingers. Five fingers means get away from me," said Wade. "Which I thought was just for us."

"Apparently not," said Becca. "He keeps doing it. We should leave." Bowing her head, she urged them with the other guests toward the lobby just as the medical personnel loaded the giant man onto the gurney. It took three technicians plus two policemen, hissing at one another to make sure he didn't fall off it. It was horrifying to see the once-animated Russian hanging limply over the sides of the gurney. Tables and chairs squeaked and knocked as a handful of remaining customers pulled them aside to make way for Boris to be wheeled to the ambulance.

"Where are we going to go?" asked Lily, still shaking. "What are we even doing?"

"Look, Uncle Roald wants us out of here, and Wade's right," said Becca. "Boris told us he only walks. So his flat is walking distance from the Dorchester. Lily, maybe we should check maps. Can you?"

"Maps?" she said, turning to her. "Are you thinking we should find his place? How are you thinking about anything?"

"I don't know, but he said his flat is on the fifth floor," Becca said as they gathered under the hotel awning. "There's no elevator, remember? Plus, he said he never takes a car or a cab. He walked here. Boris was way out of shape, so it can't be far away."

"His last words were *bird* and *cage*," Darrell added.

"To me," Lily said. "He was talking to me."

"Plus, he gave me this," Wade said, digging into his pocket. "I don't think it's a clue, though. I think . . . he just wanted us to have it?" He opened his palm. In it lay the blackened tooth of Boris's brother.

"Seriously?" said Darrell. "He gave you the tooth?

Why did he give you the tooth?"

Wade shrugged nervously, then said, "I don't know, to keep us moving? To remind us of what the Order and Galina are capable of?"

Becca glanced through the doors and saw Roald sitting in the lobby now with one of the policemen, who was writing in a pad. "Your dad always does the dirty work," she said. "Lily, the maps."

"All right, already," Lily said, finally coming back online. She flipped out her tablet and keyed in several words as she spoke them. "London. Five-floor building. Near Dorchester Hotel. Bird. Cage. No elevator." After a few moments, she perked up in surprise. "That was easy, even for me. I guess the reason Boris was saying stuff to me was because I'm the tech brain of the family. A real estate site just gave me a couple of addresses on a street called"—she turned her tablet around for them to see the map—"Birdcage Walk. Twenty-four minutes from here on foot."

Becca nodded. "Boris was telling us to go to his flat to find another clue. We can swing by his place before we head to our safe flat. Wade?"

They peeked in as Roald's face grew exasperated, one more policeman came over, and they all sat at another table. Roald caught the kids watching him and seemed to deliberately raise a single finger. *The Order is near—run.*

"Whoa," Wade said. "We'll text him later. Let's beat it!"

Following Lily's map, they doglegged quickly to Stanhope Gate, South Audley, Curzon Street, then to the quaintly named Half Moon Street and across a large park that practically connected to another park. Twenty minutes later, they arrived at the short, classy street known as Birdcage Walk.

Trying to determine which building might hold Boris's flat, they dismissed those that were offices or complexes that undoubtedly had elevators. That left a brief half block of older buildings. Each had a stately, crisp exterior, and all of them were set deep on bright green lawns closed in by tall wrought-iron fencing. The neighborhood appeared very exclusive. It was hard for Becca to think of rumpled, maybe-dead Boris living there, but then she remembered that he was staying in a flat owned by someone else.

"You know how I know when we're being followed?" Darrell said. "It's a gift, I understand, but someone's after us now. Whoever Dad warned us against must have followed us."

They looked down the street in both directions and across to the park.

"No one," said Lily. "Which to you only proves that someone is there."

"You bet it does," Darrell said. "We should definitely hurry this up and get back to the safe flat."

"Right. So some of the buildings only have four floors," Becca said. "That leaves seven houses old enough not to have elevators, and where the fifth floor is the top floor."

They were the narrow-fronted row houses of the charming sort she had seen on the way from the airport, though now they were shrouded with the aura of a possible death. She didn't want to think about it, but Boris's fall, his great booming crash onto the table, kept playing in her head.

They spread out across the housefronts and knocked on the doors. What could have been a lengthy process of elimination was made unnecessary by a middle-aged woman who came to the door for Wade, the third door they'd tried. He called them over.

"The *Russian* fellow?" the woman said, a tiny dog nestled in her arms. She narrowed her eyes at them. "I don't *know*. I mean, I *know* him, of course. *Borrrris.*

So does Benjy here, don't you, *Benjy*? You remember *Borrrris*."

The dog started yapping and didn't stop for a full minute.

"Can you tell us where he lives?" asked Lily.

"Where he *lives*?" she said, her eyes squinting even more, if that was possible, and stepping back from the door. "Oh, I *could* tell you, dear. Certainly I *could*, but why, my dear, *that's* the question, *why*? He's not there, no, I *seen* him walk out of his flat just this *morning*. Cross the park. But I don't know as I should tell *you* where he lives, no, because, as I say, *why*?"

That stumped them. There was no reason why the woman should volunteer such information to random people who came looking for a neighbor. Until Darrell said the obvious.

"We know he's not here," he said. "We were just with him across the park at the Dorchester Hotel for breakfast. And . . . but . . ."

He started to falter when Wade jumped in. "He left something behind that we need to return to him."

"*Oh?* And what did Boris leave behind?" she asked, edging even farther back into the hallway.

"Show the lady," said Lily, apparently guessing right away and nodding at his pocket.

Wade held up the black tooth. "This."

"Oh, *goodness*!" the woman screamed, and Benjy growled. "That *awful* thing. He shows everyone. He'll be wanting *that* back for certain. Number Five, two doors over," she said. "Top floor. *Mind* you don't trip on Boris's *bottles*!"

Two minutes after thanking her and petting Benjy to calm him down, they stood in front of Number Five Birdcage Walk. The building door was, happily, unlocked. They entered. The lobby was quiet. They ascended the stairs quickly. The top-floor landing was small, half the size of the others. The flat's door was closed. Wade tried the knob. That door was, unhappily, locked.

Wade and Darrell put their ears to the door as if it were a thing brothers normally do.

"We should just break it open before the cops come and seal it up," said Darrell. "Cops always do that when there's a crime. Everywhere becomes a crime scene." He stepped back and lifted his foot.

"So we're sure it's a crime?" said Lily. "Because I'm not a hundred percent sure. It could be a heart attack."

"You should be sure. The restaurant was the scene of the crime," Darrell said. "Now, stand back. . . ."

"Stop!" Becca said. "Boris said he carried no money,

no wallet, no keys, remember? Well, if the door is locked, but he didn't have the door key, how did he get in? He must have left the key somewhere—"

"I can still kick it open," said Darrell.

"Will you wait!" Lily snapped. "Becca's thinking."

Becca scanned the landing. The only other door in sight was narrow, as if to a utility closet. She tried it. It was unlocked. Looking all around, she reached to the top of the closet's door frame and felt along the outside first. Nothing. Then the inside. She stopped. "Yes!" She pulled her hand away. She was holding a key.

Lily grinned. "Well, aren't you the genius."

"I try."

Becca inserted the key in Boris's door and turned it. The door inched open. It was small and cold inside. And dark. A petite table lamp sat on a desk inside the door. Lily tried the switch several times. There was no power.

"Maybe there's a coin box here," Becca said. "I've read about them in novels. If the electricity is coin-operated, you can only use it if you pay for it. Boris was frugal. Or maybe he wasn't planning to stay very long. Anyone have change?"

Wade cast a quick look around and found a dish of coins sitting on the counter in the kitchenette, near the electric box. He pushed some coins into the slot, and several dim lights turned on.

The furniture in the three spare rooms was plain. The bed was unmade. The kitchen, such as it was, was a small nook off the living room. There was next to nothing of any personality about the place, except for one whole wall of Russian books.

"Boris was a scholar, right?" said Darrell. "So maybe one of the books is a clue?"

Becca found herself drawn to the shelves, even though she couldn't read any of the titles. "I don't know any Cyrillic. I should learn. I'll buy a phrase book before we leave." She suddenly hoped they had interpreted Roald's signal correctly. *Was* the Order near? How did he know? Was he in danger? Should they really be helping him? Did he mean to raise four fingers instead of five? She was finally only certain of one thing: that she felt afraid in Boris's dark apartment. Boris, who might already be dead.

"Come on, everybody," said Wade. "It's here, and we're not seeing it. Boris *wanted* us here. I think we're all pretty sure of that. So what did he want us to find?"

"Maybe it's not here," said Lily. "Maybe we should get back to your dad. Or the safe flat. Or somewhere else. This place is kind of sad. If Boris is, you know . . ."

"Dad would call," said Darrell. "And if he doesn't

call, it means he's tied up. If he's tied up, it means *we* have to move forward. His words. He told us to."

"Okay, you're all witnesses," Lily said. "Whatever happens, it's Darrell's fault."

"Fine," he said. "But if there's something here Boris wanted to give us, it'll take us closer to my mom, so yeah, bring it on."

Wade and Lily started opening every drawer they could find, while Darrell looked into and under every piece of furniture in all three rooms. For her part, Becca found herself unable to leave the books. She fingered them one after another, as if they would somehow make sense to her the closer she was to them. Rows and rows of old bindings, some with dust jackets with faded colors, others with dented spines, wrinkled boards, and vanished titles. Then she stopped. She tugged a book bound in black cloth from the shelf. She read its title aloud. *"The Teeth, in Relation to Beauty, Voice, and Health."*

"You *can* read Russian," said Darrell. "That didn't take long."

"No," she said. "It's in English. It's the only book in English out of all of them." She turned. "Wade? It's about teeth. Do you think—"

He moved next to her, and she handed it to him. He opened the cover, only to find that a rectangular area had been cut out of the pages to a depth of about one and a half inches. Inside the hole was a black plastic box.

"A videotape," he said. "Do you think he wanted us to see the tape?"

"How can we play that?" said Lily. "That's like 1970 or something, isn't it?"

Becca whirled around. There was a low cabinet against the opposite wall. She knelt to it. A small television was inside. On top of the television was a tape player. "Oh, man. This is it. This is what Boris wanted us to find."

She turned on the television, popped the tape into the player, and hit Play.

The screen slowly came alive with gray snow, then went black with a flicker of color, and there was Boris, reaching his hand away from the screen and plopping his bulk down on a couch that was not the same as the couch in the room with them.

Boris was as large as he had been in the restaurant, but younger, as if the video had been made some years ago and somewhere else.

"So . . . ," he began. "Is Boris here. If you find this, you know. My little time here is over. Your time has just begun. Your journey? Miles, miles, and more miles.

The clock ticks many hours, and still you may not find what you wish to find. But as last final thing, Boris tell what *he* knows."

He had said some of those words at the restaurant, Becca recalled. It was strange and sad to see his large face staring at them from beyond the television, maybe from beyond the grave. *Was* Boris dead? They might have resuscitated him in the ambulance, or at the hospital. Maybe . . .

"We all want to know secret, yes?" Boris went on. "This is why we are here on this earth. Starting with great astronomer Nicolaus Copernicus, then with Guardians, secret is hidden inside secret!" His face, even on the video, grew dark, and the gleam of perspiration was already on his forehead. "Secret is hidden, and is hidden, and is hidden like layers of onion. In the center . . . is relic."

"This is meant for the Guardians," Darrell said. "He's going to tell us—"

"Once comes powerful man," Boris said urgently. He twisted his body this way and that, apparently unable to settle into his surroundings, until his own story took him, and he looked away from the camera. "He is ruler of men. Of nation. Many nation. His name, Albrecht von Hohenzollern. Grand Master of Teutonic Order. He live in castle far away. Today it is in Mother Russia. Not so then. Not so in 1517 . . ."

And just like at the restaurant, his tortured English dissolved, and, despite themselves, the four of them fell under his heavy spell.

CHAPTER TWENTY-TWO

Moonlight falls over the frosted ramparts of a castle on the banks of a black river.

It is Schloss Königsberg, crowning fortress of the Teutonic Knights.

The year is 1517, the month February, the day the eighteenth.

A figure wrapped in long robes stalks the snowy walls silently. It is he, the Grand Master, Albrecht von Hohenzollern. His face is a mask of sorrow, wet with tears he futilely attempts to wipe away. Bitter howling coils up from the rooms below, a tender voice in agony. Albrecht slaps his hands over his frozen ears, yet louder, louder come the shrieks. Then—clack-clack!

It is the clatter of hobnail boots.

"What is it?" Albrecht growls.

Two knights appear: his nephews, sons of his sister. "Grand Master, we have returned from the wastes of Muscovy with words from Duke Vasily—"

"Words? Only words? What of the astronomer? His machine? I sent thirty knights after one man! Where are the others?"

"Dead," says one nephew. "We two alone have returned."

"The others were slain by the astronomer's sword," says the other. "Their bodies prayed over by a monk. But we managed to steal part of the relic."

"Part of it? Part of it! What part?"

"The head, Grand Master. The double-eyed serpent's head."

Suddenly in Albrecht's palm sits a jeweled device, glittering in the moonlight. The twin diamond eyes of the serpent are surrounded by a complex fixture of filigreed silver and more diamonds.

"Duke Vasily sends a hundred knights in pursuit of the astronomer and the traitor monk," says one nephew.

"To honor his alliance with you," says the other.

Albrecht breathes more calmly, or so his nephews think. "You have accomplished half your mission. Kneel before me."

Without a word, they do.

He draws his sword and swings it once, and the head of one

nephew rolls across the stone to his feet, where he kicks it over the wall into the snow.

To the other, Albrecht says, "I have another task for you. The child below . . . the child must leave here with its nurse. There is a ship departing Königsberg in three days' time—"

A deafening shriek freezes his voice, his blood.

The Grand Master turns away, all too aware that the journey to the end of the sea is long, so very long.

"Child!" he cries. "Child, cease your cries! Your mother is lost . . . lost . . ."

Alone once more, Albrecht stalks the walls over and over, night after night, lamenting, pondering, waiting . . .

And that was all. Boris slumped back into himself and said no more.

"Boris, where is Serpens now?" Becca asked, staring at the face on the screen as if it could answer her, until the screen went black again.

Darrell switched off the player and the television. "So Albrecht had his goons steal the head of Serpens when Copernicus was in Russia, and after that Albrecht had it. But . . . is Boris also saying that Albrecht had a baby, and that his wife died?"

"I think so," Lily said. "At least maybe. But did everyone hear that? He said 'the journey to the end of the sea is long.' He said at the restaurant that it's a quote from Copernicus. What did he mean? What sea? Whose journey? Ours? Albrecht's? And 'the clock ticks many hours.' Boris talks like a fortune-teller."

"One thing is sure," said Wade. "And it's kind of what I suspected. That Serpens was, and may still be, in two parts. The head that Albrecht stole, and the body that Copernicus still had."

As they sat in the cold room, staring at the blank television screen, the fence gate outside squealed on its hinges, the front door down below edged open, and someone stepped inside the building.

CHAPTER TWENTY-THREE

Wade rose to his feet. "Don't anyone move."

"You just did," said Darrell.

"Shhh!"

The buzzer on the wall next to the flat door sounded. Wade shot his finger to his lips. The buzzer sounded again. After a few moments of silence, slow footsteps echoed up the staircase.

"What do we do?" Lily whispered.

Wade listened. The footsteps were closer, louder, but slow, like those of an elderly person. And . . . what was that? . . . The clacking of a cane up the stairs. "Maybe it's . . . let's just be cool." He went to the door and pulled it open casually as if they had not just entered a possibly dead man's apartment and weren't being hunted by international assassins.

A man with a mop of gray hair and a beard made his last slow steps up to the fifth-floor landing. He wore thick spectacles and a bulky buttoned sweater, and he used a slender umbrella as a cane. He wheezed for breath, adjusted his glasses, and gazed blinkingly at the children. "You . . ." His voice was hoarse. "But you are not Boris Rubashov. Where is my dear friend Boris?"

Rubashov, Wade thought. *Is that Boris's real last name?*

"No. We were just looking in his flat. He . . . asked us to come over. But he's not here . . . yet."

"Ah," the man said, scratching his chin and leaning inside. "He asked you to pick up the, er, thing, did he?"

Darrell stepped forward next to Wade. "What thing?"

The old man blinked quizzically through his glasses. "You know, the, er, thing. You know." He cupped his free hand on the side of his mouth and whispered, "The relic!"

Suddenly, Lily pushed her way between the boys. "You're *him,*" she said, pointing to the umbrella. "The man . . ."

"Man? Me? No, no. I'm not him. Him who?"

"The man at the Dorchester Hotel. You wore a suit. You pretended to be a doctor."

"No, I didn't. You *thought* I was a doctor because I am such a good actor!"

"You poisoned Boris!" she screamed. "It *is* murder! You killed him. That umbrella. And this . . . beard . . ." She grabbed it and pulled hard.

"Owww!" the man cried as his beard peeled halfway off his cheeks. "Bloody rude, that was! Now you've changed the game. Ex-ter-min-ate! Ex-ter-min-ate!" He swept his umbrella up like a sword. There was the sound of a spring letting loose, a slender silver point thrust itself from the tip of the umbrella, and he stabbed the air in front of Wade. "You—die—now!"

"Murderer!" Becca shouted, tugging Lily past the boys and back into the room.

Wade felt his hand move instinctively to his left side, but the dagger was in a vault in New York. Instead he grabbed the nearest unattached thing—the small table lamp by the door. He yanked its cord from the wall and knocked the end of the umbrella down. But the guy, with his fake beard still dangling from his chin, swung the weapon around in a neat O and jabbed. Its needle point gleamed in the half-light and pierced the lampshade. The man danced back like a stage actor in a duel.

"She forbade me terminate you, but I have a duty to defend myself!" the man said. "For the Order!" He slashed away madly in the air, while Becca spun around in the flat and grabbed a handful of fat Russian novels from the shelf and threw them at the weird little man.

He batted them away one by one. "I also play cricket!"

Wade's cell phone began to ring. He couldn't answer it, but he managed to pull it out and throw it to Lily, as Becca and now Darrell both heaved things at the man. Wade sliced down and brought the umbrella close enough to grab the shaft of it. Dropping the lamp, he yanked the umbrella hard to get it away from the man, who growled and held on with both hands, pumping it at Wade.

"Your dad is on the phone, screaming to know where we are!" Lily said.

"Tell—him—the—morgue!" the man said, his face a gnarled grimace, until Becca heaved the videotape player, trailing cords and all, at his head. He groaned once and fell backward. The umbrella dropped to the floor, and Wade kicked it off the landing. It clattered between the stairs for five floors before crashing to the lobby below.

"We shall meet again!" the man coughed at them. "Oh, yes, we shall!"

"Can it!" Darrell snapped. He had Wade by the forearm and dragged him from the landing and down the stairs behind Lily and Becca. They all hurried down two flights when Darrell stopped suddenly and spun on his heels. "You know what? Tell Galina," he yelled, his chest heaving, "tell Galina that we're coming for my mother. And then we're coming for her!"

Out on the street, the rain had begun again.

Lily paused for a second. "Wade, your dad wants us at Victoria Station right now. He's already got our stuff from the safe house. We're flying to Moscow on the next flight." She handed him the phone. "Everybody, Boris is . . . Boris died."

CHAPTER TWENTY-FOUR

Northern Europe

Galina Krause's jet droned low over the Baltic Sea, skirting the northern shores of Poland. In her mind, she conjured the burning tower in Frombork. How Nicolaus Copernicus, sword in hand, had rushed down the stairs outside the tower to save Hans Novak from Albrecht's knights. The flames, the snow, the furious attack on the tower were sights and sounds she imagined often.

And now, if she turned just so in her seat, she could see that other momentous location, the spot where Albrecht's castle at Königsberg had stood so long ago.

These two places—the Magister's tower and

Albrecht's castle, barely one hundred fifty kilometers from each other—were deeply and inextricably linked.

And the words came back to her.

Eine Legende besagt . . .

One legend says . . .

Four years ago, Galina first entered the ruins of Schloss Königsberg. She was barely sixteen years old and as near death as a human can be and still breathe, yet even then her mind was filled with tales of that burning Frombork tower.

Buried under the monstrous Cold War architecture known as the House of Soviets in the renamed city of Kaliningrad, the ruined foundations of Albrecht's castle concealed a history as grand as it was bleak. Among the fallen stones and crumbled walls she squirmed her way, snakelike, to the undercrypt. There she had located the legendary Serpens relic she had heard stories about, but which only she had known was there.

"Why did Albrecht not hide *both* parts of the relic in the same place?"

Ebner von Braun, sitting against the windows on the opposite side of the jet, raised his head from a pristine second edition of *Faust*, part one, from 1828. "Excuse me? I didn't catch that."

"The legend," Galina said. "If it was true, as one

legend says, that Albrecht had *both* parts of Serpens, why were they not both at Schloss Königsberg?"

Ebner gazed at the sea below, a finger marking his place in the book. "The legend. Yes. Perhaps it is false. Perhaps Albrecht did hide both parts there. After all these centuries, we do not know. If he did, possibly the other part was stolen before you got there. We know only that you discovered the head before it was lost again."

Galina knew it was still a puzzle to Ebner—and to the entire ruling circle of Teutonic Knights—how a young dying girl could possibly have known what the great Albrecht von Hohenzollern had possessed five centuries before, let alone where to find it so long after the Grand Master's death. The answer was trivially simple, but letting the puzzle fester kept them convinced of her brilliance.

"It must have been the war," she mused. "When the Soviets invaded East Prussia in April 1945, they sought to retrieve Russian treasures looted by the Nazis. One nameless soldier likely discovered the body of Serpens. Bedazzled by it, he took it home with him in his rucksack. He kept it for years on the shelf between his bottle of vodka and his jar of borscht. There is only the legend, Ebner, but I believe both body and head of Serpens remain in Russia to this day. In fact, I am certain of it. As I am certain that we shall find them both."

Ebner returned to his reading, silently turning a page as the jet droned.

She watched the slender wrist of the Baltic Sea widen into the Gulf of Finland. In the farther distance, she could just make out that glittering and audacious jewel dredged from an abysmal swamp, the czarist refuge of incomparable wealth and the source of so much beauty and pain: Saint Petersburg.

Take me to the clinic, she had told Ebner at Schloss Königsberg that stormy night four years ago, nearer death than when she had entered the ruins, but with the head of Serpens clutched in her shivering hands. *Take me now.*

More than three hundred kilometers east of Saint Petersburg lay the dark den of Greywolf. As horrifying as crawling through the ruins of Königsberg had been, as near a nightmare as one could possibly conceive, she would soon be in a worse place.

All because both parts of Serpens might still be on Russian soil, as one legend said.

Eine Legende besagt . . .

CHAPTER TWENTY-FIVE

Moscow
March 21

"**C**ome sroo. Sroo!"

In a species of English, a stout middle-aged woman in a vaguely official outfit shooed Wade and the others through passport control at Moscow's Sheremetyevo airport.

"Thank you," he said, not really knowing why. She didn't acknowledge him anyway.

The cramped, airless arrivals hall smelled of too many people jammed into too small a space, but to Wade it was a kind of progress. They had not, as it turned out, been able to take the next flight to Moscow. They'd been on their way to Victoria Station for the train to Heathrow when the police had stopped them. Their renewed investigation of the sudden collapse and death of Boris Volkov—officially revealed as Boris Rubashov—had taken nearly the full day. After spending the evening at their safe flat in Chenies Mews, the children had finally been interviewed by the police the following morning. They'd replied to questions they had no answers to, then languished back at the flat for several more hours, until the ruling came down—false, they knew—that, awaiting toxicology results, there were no immediate signs of foul play.

While the medical examiners waited for the findings, the authorities had no reason to hold the Kaplans, so Roald had booked seats on the earliest possible flight to Moscow. They were finally off the ground by the very late evening of the day of the interview, but not before Wade's father had blown up—several times—about actually fighting with an agent of the Order, as they'd done at Boris's flat.

"An assassin!" his father called the umbrella man. "You totally went off script! I clearly raised five fingers!"

"Which means get away from me," said Darrell.

"No, it means meet me at the safe house."

184

"No, meet at the safe house is two fingers," said Becca.

"No, two fingers is wait for me!" Roald said.

"Dad, wait for me is not any of the fingers," said Wade, flipping open the notebook. "See?" His father grabbed the notebook, read the finger gestures of the family code, and grunted. "Oh."

"Dad, maybe it looks like we were careless—" Darrell started.

"You *were* careless!"

"Excuse me, Uncle Roald, but not really so much," Lily added boldly, but also sweetly. "I mean, it might seem like we got away with something, but we thought you gave us a message, and we used our instincts. Plus we were smart, never splitting up from one another, and the thing we got away with was . . . a clue. A pretty big clue."

Wade's father stared at them for a full two minutes; then, just as it appeared as if he was going to go on another tirade, he got a call from Paris. "Paul Ferrere, the investigator." Listening for a few moments, his father nodded, then said, *"Merci."* He pushed End Call. "Sara left Madrid, flying northeast. To Russia."

"That settles it," said Darrell, jumping up. "We're going to Russia."

And now they were. Slowly. Even after catching the

plane, a four-hour time difference, plus a Siberian snow front that delayed by nearly three hours a normally four-hour flight, it was now three days since they'd left New York City. But they were on Russian soil at last and were ready to move forward once more.

"Hurry sroo!" the official repeated, waving the line ahead.

Darrell piled into Wade. "Even the lady with the bun thinks this is going way too slow."

"Poor Boris," Lily whispered, zipping and unzipping her bag nervously. "He should be coming sroo with us."

"Wade," said Becca, "I hope you wrote down what he said at the restaurant."

"The key words."

"Well, I made a video of the videotape at his flat, which may be against copyright, but I don't think so," Lily said as Roald ushered them gently along the line, then positioned himself at the head to speak with the passport-control officials.

"Whatever you do, bro, don't look guilty." Darrell nodded toward the officers.

"Of what? I haven't done anything."

"Doesn't matter. Did you know that when your adrenaline spikes, you suddenly need the bathroom?"

"Eww, Darrell, gross!" said Lily. "Get away from me."

"You have to do five fingers if you're going to say that," said Darrell. "But most of all, bro, don't sweat. Fear is all about stuff coming out of your body. They'll know you're lying if you sweat, plus you'll need the bathroom, but you won't get to go because they'll send you straight to Sumeria without a key."

"Siberia," said Becca.

Darrell smirked. "Sure, if you're lucky."

"Bags be open. Computers be in themselves bins. Passports and visas be out."

Wade pushed his stuffed backpack between Becca's and Lily's bags on the conveyor and suddenly wanted to thank Boris for everything he'd given them. The visas were one thing, but there was also the tooth. Why Wade hadn't gotten rid of it, he wasn't sure, except that it was like a voice urging him on to do whatever he had to do. His father had said they should keep it in case it turned out to be another clue, so he'd stowed it in his backpack among his socks.

Oddly, or maybe not so oddly, since Boris had made a point of his possible "side trip," they'd also found a ticket to a theater performance among the documents.

The ticket was for an opera performance in Venice, Italy, the following evening.

"Mozart's *The Magic Flute*," Becca said. "The last line of the ticket says, 'The bearers are allowed entry to Box Three-Seventeen.' *Scatola del teatro* means 'theater box.'"

What was so necessary about Boris attending an opera eluded Wade, and he wondered what would happen if the Russian didn't show up, but he lodged the question in the back of his brain anyway. *Everything is a clue. Everyone is suspicious. Nothing is coincidental.*

"You first. Others stay," a stern-looking immigration official barked at his father, who had been successfully keeping them together as a group. Glancing back, his dad went to the counter and spoke with the official, who looked past him at the kids. Finally the official nodded and let him through.

"Cool. We're in," Lily said. "Saint Sergius monastery,

here we come." She was next with her documents, then Darrell, then Becca, and finally Wade.

As the others had done, Wade handed over his passport and the tourist visa that Boris had filled out in his name. His chest spiked with a sudden fear. Was there any way the officials could tell just by looking at them that the visas were "smuggled," whatever that actually meant? And if not here, how long *would* it be before they were stopped, pulled off into a small room, and interrogated?

Or worse. You could be arrested, right? Jailed like Maxim? What was Boris's prison with the parquet floors? Kremlin? Red Square? No. Lubyanka. A somber word.

The official nodded him forward, and he breathed with relief, when a male guard with one hand on a holstered handgun stopped him abruptly. "No, no," he said, planting his feet in front of Wade. "No, no. Step aside. Here."

For a half second Wade imagined they had discovered the dagger, but he didn't have the dagger. Certainly not the tooth?

"Excuse me," his father said, "this is my son—"

"Stand back, sir," the guard snapped, shooting his father a look. Then, fingering Wade's passport and visa, he nodded at the officers tending the security gate. "Vade Keplen of America, step aside. Others go through."

When they didn't move, the guard repeated, "Go through!"

Wade's heart misfired. The back of his neck froze. He watched blurrily as his father and the others stepped down the narrow hallway toward the terminal, staring back at him. He fought an icy stream of nausea coming up his throat.

Don't sweat, bro.

Yeah, that ship had sailed. His armpits were soggy; his forehead was beading up.

"I really didn't do anything . . ."

A heavyset woman with gray hair waddled through the mass of officers surrounding him. She smelled of boiled food. Her name tag read *I. LYUBOV.* She snatched his documents from the guard and flicked her eyes from them to Wade without raising her head. "You are Vade Keplen from Texes."

If it was a question, it didn't sound like one, but he answered anyway. "Yes, ma'am. Wade Kaplan. From Texas." A moment later he thought to add, "America."

Another long minute of nothing. No movement or sign from the stony face. He wiped the sweat under his eyes, careful to raise his hand slowly in case they thought he was going for a weapon. His insides were turning to water. How had Darrell known? He glanced down the hall. His family was nearly invisible now among the crush of approved passengers. *Becca, is that you?* The woman shifted heavily from foot to foot. Her eyes told him nothing. Steel hatches bolted closed. *She's trying to get me to crack. That's what she's doing. She expects me to blurt out the name of the relic and its original Guardian and the monastery we're going to—*

"Yes. Fine. Go now vis femily. Enjoy stay." The woman handed him back his documents, spun on her low heels more lightly than he'd imagined she would, and slid into a glass booth, where she picked up a telephone.

Startled, he emerged into the hallway and into the arms of his father.

"What did she ask you?" his father asked him.

"Nothing. Nothing at all."

"Russia," Lily said. "Our grandparents have stories."

Wade swallowed hard. "I need to go to the bathroom."

Becca wanted nothing other than to yank Wade away from the plump woman with the bun and the constant scowl. She saw his eyes find hers out of the crowd and tried to lock on to him, but things moved too quickly from that point on and didn't stop until they were out in the stale air of the main terminal, and the noise crashed in on her again.

"What was that all about?" she asked when they piled on an escalator down to ground level.

"I don't know." He was shaking all over. His voice was hoarse. "I don't even know."

"Maybe now we're tagged," Lily whispered. "They tagged us."

"Tagged?" said Darrell.

"Like when you take clothes into a dressing room," she said. "Some stores scan the tags to make sure they know exactly what you went in with. There might have been something about your tourist visa. I saw Bun Lady make a phone call after she let you go. Maybe we're being followed by the Russian police right this minute."

"Or KGB agents," Darrell said. He glanced quickly around them. "They're in disguise, of course. Much better than Lily's umbrella killer. You never see them until they pounce on you; then it's too late. James Bond could tell you."

"The KGB is called the FSB now," Becca said, "and anyway, we should totally expect it. Duke Vasily was a friend of Albrecht's, remember. Maybe they're still working together. The Order and the FSB. As scary as

Berlin was, or London, this is worse. So much worse."

It was a lot of words for Becca, she knew that. But she felt she had to get it out there.

Because when you think about it . . . what just happened with Wade almost certainly means that the Order knows exactly where we are and what we're doing. The Russian safe house, she thought. *How will we get there without the Order's agents tracking us? Even with Julian's untraceable phones, going to an airport tells everyone where you are.*

They walked unhindered through the terminal and outside into the icy, smoke-thick, and diesel-clogged air. It was frigid, a new kind of iron cold that froze your bones.

"Even though we pretty much know that Umbrella Man killed Boris," Lily said as Roald led them to the platform for the shuttle that was supposed to take them to the rental car center, "does it mean we automatically believe everything Boris told us? He did hide his real name from us. Could our trip to Russia be a setup?"

Darrell stomped his feet to keep warm. "Yeah, we have to think of that. Even though his visas got us in here safely. All except Wade, I mean. He's on borrowed time. Lubyanky, here you come."

"Funny," said Wade, splaying five fingers in Darrell's face.

"Calm down, everyone," Roald said. "We'll talk when we get into our car." He waved down the rental car shuttle bus like a soccer dad on the sidelines. The driver seemed to make the stop grudgingly, as if picking up passengers were voluntary. Scowling, he whisked the door open but didn't leave his seat or help them stow their bags.

"Let's keep focused," Roald whispered as they mounted the steps to their seats. "The car ride to Saint Sergius will take us a couple of hours. But we have to remember, it's a holy place and a shrine, where Maxim and thousands of monks lived, all the way up to now. We are polite, we're tourists, we're Texans, but we watch our backs, stay together, and if we find ourselves against a wall, we *don't fight anyone*." His voice grew louder with the last three words, but he lowered it again. "There's always another way to solve things. After Saint Sergius, we'll drive back to Moscow. We'll be here again before it gets dark."

"If you ask me, it's already dark," Darrell grumbled. "Let's go already."

CHAPTER TWENTY-SIX

It was just after two o'clock in the afternoon when Lily and the others emerged from the rental car center under a grim sky swirling with gray clouds. Uncle Roald squeezed behind the wheel of a boxy blue Aleko sedan like a giant on a tricycle. The rest of them squished in wherever they could. The car stank of diesel fuel inside and out, but it drove perkily enough to push Lily back in her seat when Roald hit the accelerator.

"Finally, we're moving," Darrell said with a sigh.

"Agreed," said Wade. "Thank you, Boris."

"And Terence Ackroyd," Roald reminded them. "This car will free up our movements. Public transportation here is too public. There are CCTV cameras everywhere.

After the monastery, we'll hole up in the Moscow safe house, but until then we have no footprint. We spend as little money as we can. We slip in and out of wherever we are like ghosts."

Lily wasn't sure he expected or wanted a response from anyone, but she gave one anyway. "I'm totally into that." She liked their new secrecy and felt safer because of the precautions, even the troublesome finger gestures. *But ghosts? I really like that.*

The roads out of the airport were surprisingly simple. But the weather was turning grayer by the minute, more bitterly cold, and the clouds announced that serious snow was on its way. The Aleko's heating system was loud and ineffective.

"If, as we all pretty much hope, Maxim Grek *does* prove to be the second Guardian," Becca said, turning to the double-eyed figure sketched in the diary's margin, "the monastery where he lived his last years might actually give me something to decode these pages, which I am now calling 'the Guardian Files.'"

Darrell nodded, smiling. "Nice. I think we should name everything. It makes it seem more important that way."

Wade turned. "I name you . . . Darrell."

Darrell grinned. "I already feel important."

For the next hour, Lily searched online encyclopedia entries about Saint Sergius on the tablet, covering as much history as she could. "Sergiev Posad," she told them, "is the first stop on the western side of what is called 'the Golden Ring,' a four-hundred-mile drive through a bunch of ancient monastic towns stretching northeast of Moscow. The monastery of Saint Sergius was founded in 1345 and is still the most important monastery in the country. It's also the center of the Russian Orthodox Church. It's called a *lavra*, which is a monastery including a bunch of cells for hermits. There are over three hundred monks there now."

"An army, if they're all working for the Order," Darrell said.

"Darrell, they're not," his stepfather said.

There was little information about Maxim's stay there, except to say that cells from around the time of his death might still exist. "Which is good," she said. "But the monastery's also under renovation, which could be a problem. The original cells were built inside the walls. We should start there and see where it takes us."

After a good stretch of highway driving, Wade

arched up in his seat. "I think I see it. The monastery."

They were still miles from the city proper, but a cluster of towers rose over the landscape like beacons. The monastery seemed enormous, perched on a hill and surrounded by tall, powerful, whitewashed stone walls set at irregular angles. Some portions of the walls were fitted with scaffolding, while dozens of domed towers loomed over the walls, some dazzlingly blue and spangled with stars like the night sky, others brilliant gold, and every one of them dusted with a ring of fresh snow.

All told, the drive to Sergiev Posad had taken a little over two hours, putting them there at roughly half past four. The large parking area had only a few cars in it, a smattering of work trucks, and one police vehicle, idling at an angle to the front gate. Roald parked at the far end of the lot, and they got out. They walked quietly through the mounting wind toward the entrance gate in the shadow of the walls.

Then Roald paused and checked his watch. "Kids . . ." His voice was low, almost hoarse from not speaking. "This is a different land, one with centuries of history that Western visitors might not understand. Be on your guard, all of you. And I'll say it again. Absolutely *do not* confront anyone. This is serious. More serious than serious."

As if the few birds and the roaring of traffic and even the movement of the air understood his words, the instant they passed through the massive monastery gate, quiet fell over them like a low, gray, heavy, ominous shadow.

CHAPTER TWENTY-SEVEN

Greywolf, Republic of Karelia, Northwest Russia

When her silver Range Rover stopped three hundred kilometers northeast of Saint Petersburg, Galina Krause's stomach twisted like a cloth being wrung out.

In one sense, Greywolf, the secret sixteenth-century fortress of Duke Vasily III, seemed like any private lair built outside any city the size of Saint Petersburg: a summertime resort used by those in favor with the current political regime.

Except that in 1515, there *was* no Saint Petersburg, and Greywolf was hundreds of miles from any shadow of civilized life. It was constructed in a time of blood law, betrayal, and murder, the menacing fortress of a powerful and quite paranoid ruler.

Vasily III had built the blocklike main structure using an army of slave labor—who he'd then had slain because they knew far too much. Greywolf—or *Seriyvolk*—was, in fact, where Vasily and Albrecht had cemented their mysterious and violent alliance. The building was born, existed, and aged nearly two centuries before Saint Petersburg existed. By that time, Greywolf was already buried deep in the wolf-ridden wastelands, far from the prying eyes of any human being, let alone an intrigue-besotted royal court.

To Galina Krause, Greywolf represented the deepest circle of torment she had ever endured in her young life.

"Open the doors," she said.

Ebner tore himself from his heated seat in the Range Rover, slogged past the burned-out husk of the east wing, whose beams had been blackened four years earlier by a violent inferno, and trod up the wide stairs to unlock and unbolt the heavy front doors.

Glancing up at the fortified tower that protruded from the castle's heart like the hilt of a dagger, Galina ascended the steps behind him. He shifted aside. She entered, intent on ignoring the shadow passing over her, although—inauspiciously—the Madrid coffin followed her in.

Two faceless men from the Red Brotherhood rolled the box through room after spacious room and into a windowless chamber in the center of the ground floor. From there they moved into an elevator installed in Stalin's time. A half minute later, they reached the summit of the tower, and the box was wheeled out. The room was a broad, circular, and high-ceilinged laboratory with a gallery running around the upper level. Save for a very large object in wraps, the room was bare.

"Galina," Ebner began, "there is still time to rethink—"

"We have different concepts of time, Ebner. Remove the cover."

He sighed and walked to the center of the room. He tugged at the heavy black cloth. It fell away from a construction of gears and rods and barrels that vaguely resembled an alien weapon.

Kronos I.

Despite the airy promises of the Copernicus Room, or the chance of overtaking the Kaplans in their freakishly successful run for the relics, to Galina it was Kronos I that held out the most hope.

"Miss Krause . . ." Ebner cleared his throat. "This prototype was a failure. Built before I could conduct the necessary and exhaustive tests. Built, Galina, you must recall, in the horrifying days of your recovery four years ago. The poor creatures we sent God-knows-where never had a chance of survival. Kronos One was born of impatience, constructed years before I could assemble the data needed to—"

"You built it."

He paused. "I did. I did build it. I built Kronos to your specifications. And the concept was brilliant. To mimic the Copernicus astrolabe in such a manner, with such inconceivable detail, was a lofty goal. But after four years of improvements, even Kronos Three, our most effective model, is fatally flawed. Our goal of a faultless time journey has proved unattainable. Heaven knows how you ever conceived of something so devilishly . . . magnificent, particularly in your weakened state. But your—our—ideas were frighteningly incomplete."

"Helmut Bern will complete them."

"Galina, please—"

She raised her hand with such suddenness it must have taken his breath away. He coughed and stifled himself.

She approached the ten-foot spoked wheel of platinum. The barrel protruding from its center was winged with a series of angled flanges, large at the body of the gun and narrowing to a point at the tip. There was no helical coil of superconducting fiber, which they had implemented on later models, and little finesse to the targeting mechanism.

On the other hand, no machine, not even Kronos III, had ever attempted to send a living thing back half a millennium. Their only real success, the botched Somosierra test, had been a mere two hundred years. Kronos I, unlike any subsequent version of the machine, contained a seat of sorts, a kind of cage, which held the passenger, though the controls were set wisely out of reach.

"Kronos One was both crude and audacious," Galina said softly, running her fingers along the machine's razor-sharp angles. "And therein lies its beauty, Ebner. Open the coffin."

With an even sadder breath, Ebner undid the four latches around the perimeter of the death box. His face grimacing like a weightlifter's, he lifted the upper half of the lid to reveal the blindfolded, unmoving body of Sara Kaplan.

Her unkempt brown hair had twisted across her face during the flight from Madrid. Her clothes, a summer-weight linen camping suit, were wrinkled, stained, sunken. Her face was pale white but bore a surprising rosy tinge in its cheeks.

Galina turned to the two silent men. "Move her into the cage."

The two men undid the restraints and removed Sara from the coffin. They carried her dead weight to Kronos I and inserted her in the cage's reclining seat. They closed the cage door and chained and bolted it shut.

"Leave us," Galina said to the men. They bowed wordlessly and left.

She untied the woman's blindfold, then removed a small black case from her belt. From it she withdrew a syringe and a bottle of clear liquid. She tapped the syringe's glass barrel. Pressing her thumb on the plunger, she watched the needle release a tiny bubble of air, then a narrow fountain of the liquid.

How often Galina had seen the same thing done by doctors over the last four years. First here in Greywolf, then in Argentina, then in Sydney, Oslo, Myanmar, and most recently Budapest. A seemingly endless series of injections, endured for but one end.

She sank the needle into the woman's arm.

I know exactly how this feels, my dear. The cold pinch. The pressure on the skin. The heat in your arm as the chemical swims into your bloodstream.

The body in the cage jerked violently, ripping its worn camping suit. Her legs stiffened against the iron bars, her head convulsed, the jaws ground each other, her eyes shuddered open, and she screamed, her first words for days.

"You insane crazy *freak*—"

Sara Kaplan screamed and screamed, then coughed and gagged until her lungs gave out and her head fell back.

"Perhaps I am such a thing," Galina said, stroking the scar on her neck. "On the other hand, you are, thus far, unhurt. You will remain alive as long as you help us locate some stolen property."

"In your dreams, witch—"

"You will help us," Galina repeated in a dry, unemotional tone. "Or not only you, but Roald Kaplan and your two sons will die. Then we shall simply close this house and walk away. No one will think to look for you here. No one comes to Greywolf."

"Except maniacs like you," Sara gasped, looking around at the cage and the machine. "Did you invent this nightmare? Is this, like, the inside of your sick head?"

"You, my dear, are ransom," Galina said, suddenly smiling. "And your future is controlled by this nightmare. Think of Darrell and of Wade. Think of your husband. Soon, your family will discover that you can be saved in only one way. By giving me the Copernicus relics."

"I have no idea what you're talking about."

"If they do not give them to me, well . . ."

Sara started yelling at the top of her lungs.

"Shall I?" Ebner asked.

With a nod from her, Ebner roughly gagged Sara with a cloth soaked with sedatives. He strapped the gag to her face with a band stretching around her head and retied her blindfold. He retested the cage's locks and bolts and stepped away.

Helmut Bern entered the chamber, dusting snow from the shoulders of his Prada overcoat and gawking like an idiot. "What *is* this place? It looks like the set of a Frankenstein movie. . . ." He trailed off when he saw the machine. Puzzled, he looked to Ebner, then to Galina, then back at the machine. "There's a woman in that thing."

"Which is no concern of yours," Galina said impassively. "Bern, I want you to reprogram Kronos with what you discovered in Madrid. You will also incorporate at the moment of transport a particle injection into its passenger."

"A *particle* injection?" Bern said. "What sort of particle?"

"A radioisotope," she said. "For tracking purposes."

"But that will poison the passen . . . *her*. It will poison *her*."

"Once more, this does not concern you. Finally, I wish you to decrypt the Magister's Cádiz code and enter its coordinates into the computer. You have until"—she glanced at her phone—"the end of the day on Sunday. Let us say midnight."

"Midnight on Sunday?" Bern said. "That's barely two days!"

Galina leaned over to a clockwork mechanism that was mounted outside the cage near the spoked wheel. She touched a number of minute levers sequentially, and the sound of clicking began. "The timer is set at fifty-six hours, eleven minutes, twenty-two seconds . . . twenty-one . . . twenty. . . . No delay, Bern."

"But, how can I work with such a deadline?" he said, his voice gaining pitch with each word. "Miss Krause, please. I will certainly labor as hard as I can, but by midnight Sunday? What the devil will happen then?"

"Kronos will do what it was meant to do."

"With unfinished programming?" Bern's voice was

at toddler pitch now. "What if I need ten minutes more? Three seconds more?"

"I have an appointment in Istanbul Monday morning that cannot be missed. No delay, Bern. Please do not make me say this a third time." Galina turned away from the incredulous expression on his face, her lips warming into a smile as Bartolo Cassa entered the chamber, pushing in a second coffin.

"Ah, the Italian shipment," she said.

"Leave it against the wall," Ebner said sharply. "Is there anything else?"

"A message from the Copernicus Room," Cassa said. "They have just traced the Prague courier's contact in Italy, the agent who was to pass a message to Boris Rubashov tomorrow night, and where." He handed Galina his phone.

On it was a single image.

She felt a shiver run up her spine to the base of her skull. "Is this all? No other word?"

"None."

Ebner stole a look at the image, then lifted his eyes to her. "I shall join you—"

"We shall both," Cassa said.

"No. See that Bern does not leave the machine. I will

return by Sunday at dawn." She breathed in the frigid air of the tower, then moved to the elevator, managing only in the final seconds to shake off her sense of imminent doom.

"*Der Hölle Rache*," she sang, "*kocht in meinem Herzen!*"

CHAPTER TWENTY-EIGHT

Sergiev Posad

Wade felt his guard go up the instant a tall bearded man in a stiff black hat and long robe strode over the monastery's cobblestone court toward them. The Teutonic Knights began as a religious order. He knew enough of their history, and Boris's story, to be cautious.

"Ah, English," the young man said with very little accent. "I can tell by your clothing. Welcome."

"American," Roald said pleasantly. "But you're right. We just arrived from London, where we bought these winter coats."

"So, I am a detective," the man said with a bright

laugh. "I am Brother Semyon. You wish a tour of Trinity Saint Sergius monastery? The last of today's English-language tours will begin in approximately fifteen minutes. I will deliver it myself." He spoke English easily and well. He handed them a map, which Darrell took.

"Perfect. And are the old fifteenth- and sixteenth-century monks' cells on the tour?" Wade asked, trying to sound as casual as his father.

"We read online that you still have some of the old monks' cells here," Lily added. "We'd love to see them if we could."

The young monk's smile began to fade. He looked them over, studying their faces methodically, lingering on Wade's the longest, as if his brain were doing a quick calculation. "Unfortunately not . . . ," he said.

A man in civilian clothes strode across the cobble-stones toward them. The young monk turned. "One moment, please," he said softly to Roald. He went directly to the approaching man and stopped him with a raised hand. They spoke quietly to each other while the second man glanced over the monk's shoulder at them.

"Uh-oh," Becca whispered as Wade turned his face away. "We've been outed again. Do you think they already know the relic we're after?"

Wade's father put on a false smile. "Let's not panic. Not yet. It may be nothing."

The young monk returned to them. "I am sorry, but foreign visitors must sign waivers first. This is policy, I'm afraid. We are a monastery of meditation and prayer."

"And the gentleman you spoke with?" said Roald, smiling. "He is . . . ?"

"Alas, there exists a complex relationship between the monastery, the government, and their security at public sites," the monk said. "Besides, it is perfectly true that some areas are not on view this time of day. There is no way otherwise, and it would be better to comply than to leave at this point. Please, sir," he said to Roald directly, "I hope you understand and come with me. Children, remain here, won't you? Sir, please do come with me." Gesturing firmly ahead of him, he took hold of Roald's elbow and directed him toward what appeared to be an administration building. The other man followed on their heels, leaving the children by themselves.

"Oh, man," said Darrell. "Now we've done it. Or, more accurately, Wade's done it."

"I have not—"

"Tagged," Lily whispered. "I knew we were."

"Well, something's up," Becca said softly. "Monk or no monk, praying or not, this isn't right. Why is some guy in a suit telling the monks how to run their place?"

"Did you see the way his smile just died when we asked to see the old cells?" said Wade. "He knows exactly why we're here. We can't be this open with people, even religious people. I know that doesn't sound right, but we can't trust anyone."

He saw his father briefly in the doorway of the building, looking out at them. He did not use any finger signals, and Wade couldn't be sure he had memorized the family code correctly anyway. Then a third man, an older monk, drew his father gently back inside.

"Not again," said Lily. "They're taking your dad away?"

No. Not again. Wade's father was out a moment later, his forehead furrowed in a frown. "Sorry, kids, not today," he said loudly.

"Dad—" Wade started.

"Shhh," his father said. "We're to go to the Saint John gate. Brother Semyon will meet us there. Darrell, do you still have the map?"

Darrell flipped it open. "Back the way we came in from the parking lot. The Gateway Church of Saint John the Baptist."

"He's helping us?" Wade asked as they headed back across the cobblestone court.

"As much as he can. The security man is with the government. He doesn't appear to suspect us, but he may have ties to the Red Brotherhood. Brother Semyon will try to get us to the oldest cells. He's really risking a lot."

By the time they had crossed the courtyard, a bank of heavy gray clouds had moved in from the west. It was going to snow. *Soon and hard,* Wade thought. He pulled his cap low.

They were only halfway through a thick arched doorway, which was more like a tunnel, when Brother Semyon appeared from the shadows. "We must hurry," he whispered. "Our government friend is a bit thick-headed, but even he will check up if I do not return soon."

Wade's father nodded. "Thank you for what you are doing."

"How did you know about us?" Becca asked.

Brother Semyon turned to a door inside the tunnel. "The Guardians in Russia are known as the Circle of Athos. Surely you have heard the name Hans Novak?"

"Of course. He was Nicolaus's assistant," said Lily.

"Hans Novak was young, yet he spent his life

protecting the Legacy. You—you four children—because you are young, have been called *Novizhny*, the new followers of Hans Novak." He pronounced the word "no-VIHSH-nee."

"Cool," said Darrell. "*Novizhny*. I told you things need to have names. Wade, write it down."

Brother Semyon smiled. "A friend of the Circle of Athos told me to expect you. I have been waiting for days."

"A friend?" said Wade's father. "Do you mean Boris Volkov, from London?"

"I do not know him. We have little time. This way. Come."

Brother Semyon led them through the door into a high-ceilinged room. Every inch of wall space was fixed with religious icons, frescos, and beaded and jeweled paintings.

"These are the prizes of Russia," he said, moving quickly. "But Saint Sergius chapels and ancient art are not important to you just now." They entered a narrow stone corridor that was lit by fat candles set into niches in the wall at eye level. Because they had to walk in single file, Wade couldn't see what they were approaching. It was a blank wall. The young monk turned to face them.

Wade's sense of alarm went up. "What's going on?"

The monk bowed his head. "The cells the tourists see are reconstructions. Back when there were many more of us in the Circle of Athos, we hid Maxim's true cell behind a false wall."

He turned to the blank wall and pushed firmly at five blocks on it. They seemed five random blocks, until he stepped away and Wade saw that the blocks formed the shape of a large letter.

M

A moment later, the entire wall shifted backward into darkness.

"Silence, please, from here on," Brother Semyon said. Gathering the folds of his robe in one hand, he led them up a set of steep stairs that ran inside the monastery wall.

Wade counted forty steps until they reached a level stone passage. It was narrow, although dim light from the end of the passage gave enough visibility to see that it ran forward twenty or thirty feet. A single wooden door was set into the wall on the left, the outer side of the monastery wall.

"Maxim's cell," the monk said. He led them past a wrought-iron panel set against the passage wall. "It is

nearly bare, as it was in the time when he occupied it."
Brother Semyon paused and stepped closer to them.
"We members of the Circle are now very few in number.
The Order and its Russian allies, the Red Brotherhood,
have diminished our forces to a piteous handful. I have
only become aware of the invocation of the Frombork
Protocol, but my duty is to keep the great legacy of
Copernicus from being reassembled. I leave you here to
discover what you can."

"Don't you know what the relic is or where it is?"
Wade's father asked.

Brother Semyon shook his head firmly. "I am a
Guardian of Guardians. My role here and now is to
keep the *Novizhny*, and their father, safe. You are the
hunters; I am your servant. The only thing I can say is
that other than his bones, nothing belonging to Maxim
exists here anymore, except for seven religious icons he
is said to have painted in his last months."

He then pointed to a switch box on the wall. "Ring
this when you wish to be released. Please do your work
quickly."

"Released?" Wade's father said. "What do you
mean?"

Reaching to his right, Brother Semyon pulled the
iron panel closed and locked it on them. "I am obliged

by the Circle of Athos to protect you. I alone will hear the bell. It rings in my cell. Hurry and do your work." Moments later, he was gone.

Breathing in slowly, Wade turned toward the single cell in the passage.

Lily went up and tried the gate. "Okay, this is way against every rule. This is locked solid. The Circle of Athos is part of the Guardians. Brother Semyon says he is a Guardian. Do we believe him? Do we believe anyone? I'm kind of freaking out now."

"Calm down, Lily," said Darrell, tapping the monastery map. "I'm already planning our way out of here."

Then Wade stepped down the hall and entered Maxim Grek's tiny cell. "Everybody, get in here!"

CHAPTER TWENTY-NINE

L ily stepped into Maxim Grek's square cell, a tiny, cold, stone space that barely held the five of them.

The room was completely featureless except for a high horizontal upper window, from which they could see the storm-clouded sky, and seven small icons, paintings on wood panels hanging on the inside wall.

The images were plain, flat, and almost crudely painted, though the colors were brilliant and rich— red, gold, and green, with strokes of blue as deep as on the domes outside. The five men and two women wore halos—plain gold circles—behind their heads, and were shown in a variety of poses, some at labor and others at prayer.

"Saints," said Becca.

"The backgrounds of all seven pictures seem to be the Saint Sergius monastery," said Roald. "There's the Red (Holy) Gate, the courtyard, and the older towers. The saints are identified in Greek."

"Oh, boy," said Becca. "Lily, can I borrow your tablet?"

While Becca searched the tablet for a Greek dictionary, Lily examined the images for clues. There were either hundreds or none at all. She felt a little helpless. Wade and Darrell were standing around looking bewildered, too.

Becca had better luck, soon identifying one of the women, kneeling in prayer in a kind of chapel, as Saint Matrona. One of the men, who was holding two books with crosses on their covers, was Saint John Chrysostom.

"This one here is Saint Anysia," Becca said. "She's often shown standing on a mountain of gold because she gave away her money. Next to them is Saint Joachim of Ithaca. He's holding a tiny church. Saint Achillius of Larissa and Saint Nikon are praying. The last one is Saint Dominic, who is tending his garden."

"Wade, my notebook," his father said. "I remember Uncle Henry lecturing once and mentioning something about saints."

"Do you think there's a clue in there about who the saints are?" asked Lily.

"Maybe," Roald said, flipping the pages slowly.

"If all the saints are Greek," Wade said, "Maxim was probably remembering his home. He painted them at the end of his life—"

"No," said Roald. "Not all of them. Six are Greek, but Saint Dominic is Italian. That's what I was remembering. Here it is, from Uncle Henry's first lectures about cosmology. He told us that Saint Dominic was the patron saint of . . . guess what?"

"Uncle Roald, that's my line," said Lily.

"Astronomy!" he said. "Uncle Henry told us at the beginning of his survey course. Of all the seven icons, this one might be the real clue."

Lily stood in front of the painting and snapped a picture of it on the tablet. "There aren't any astronomy things in the picture," she said. "Dominic's right hand is pointing to a tall tower, while his left is holding some kind of stalky plant with a white bulb dangling from it."

"That's an onion," Becca said.

"An onion," Wade mumbled, taking the notebook back from his father. "Boris said 'onion' on the videotape . . . 'secret is hidden,' he said, 'like layers of onion.'

Does everyone remember that? Then he said 'In the center . . . is relic.'"

The cell went quiet. Lily suspected it was because they were all remembering Boris Volkov, or Rubashov, as they found out his real name was. Boris was the first victim of the hunt for the second relic. "Maybe Maxim is saying he *planted* the secret," she said. "Or he hid it in the ground somewhere, like an onion."

"The domes in the monastery are called onion domes," said Roald.

Lily recalled that from her reading. Was that a clue, too?

Darrell looked up from the map and tried to listen to the crisscrossing voices, even his stepfather's, but all he could see was the tiny prison cell, and he couldn't *not* think of his mother. Her cell might be like this, clean and white. Or more probably it was filthy and dark and cold and horrible. . . .

Don't go there.

Dad said it isn't healthy and it doesn't help. Be useful. Back to the map. My job is just to plan a way out of here.

He rubbed his face with one hand, then tried to match up the nearly sixty numbers on the map with the list of names on the facing page, to pinpoint their current position in the vast monastery. If they had to escape, how would they do it? Which route would they take, leading to where? *Here's the wall above the Gateway Church of Saint John the Baptist . . .*

There was the sound of an engine stuttering in the parking lot below the window, and Roald instantly looked out. "Two cars just pulled in. And it's snowing harder now."

. . . and there's the Good Friday Tower . . .

"Saint Dominic was also the patron saint of people who have been falsely accused," Becca said, still reading Lily's tablet. "Like you, Wade."

"Thanks for reminding me—"

"Darrell, you look at art all the time," Lily said. "Your mom and everything. What do you see when you look at the painting?"

He lifted his head from the map and stared squarely at the icon. "A saint. He's pointing to a tower with one hand. In the other he's holding . . . he's holding an onion. . . . Holy cow. Could it be that simple?"

"What's simple?" asked Wade.

Darrell flipped the map around. "Look at this right here. Two towers away. This one on the corner is called the Good Friday Tower, right? The next one is called the

Onion Tower. Right here on the south wall of the monastery. In the painting, Dominic is holding an onion and pointing to a tower. He's saying Onion Tower. The relic is in the Onion Tower—"

There came the sudden sound of footsteps from the bottom of the stairway outside.

"Dr. Kaplan! Children!" someone called. "We know you are up there!" The voice was unfamiliar.

Roald peeked out of the cell, then quickly jerked back in. "The government man from before. He must be with the Brotherhood. He's not alone."

The stairway groaned with several sets of feet. "Dr. Kaplan, come out this instant," another voice shouted. "You are all in violation of the laws of Holy Trinity— Saint Sergius Lavra and the Russian Federation!"

CHAPTER THIRTY

Becca held her breath as at least two, maybe three or even four people stomped up the stairs and into the passage outside Maxim's cell, only to find the gate at the far end of the passage padlocked. The urgency of the raised voices and the rattling of the gate told her they didn't have the key with them.

There was a good deal more yelling before the men hurried back down the steps. One of them yelled over and over, *"Poluchit' klyuchi!"* The final word sounded enough like *key* in both French and Italian for Becca to know that the men would soon be back.

"I hope Brother Semyon is okay," said Lily.

"We'll have to hope he can take care of himself."
Roald peeked out again. The hall was empty. "Darrell,
how do we get to the Onion Tower?"

"Without going back down the stairs? Only one way.
Over the roof on the outside wall. But I don't see how
to get up there."

"There's scaffolding along parts of the outside wall,"
said Wade.

Roald shook his head. "Let's see what's at the other
end of the passage."

They scurried out of the cell and down the narrow
hallway to where it ended in a brief L, a dead end that
led nowhere except for a small window set high in the
wall. Becca suspected it might offer the only way to go,
besides back down the stairs and into the hands of men
who were most certainly from the Red Brotherhood.

"The window is our only way out," she said softly.

"Like you know," said Darrell.

"Do you have a better idea, smarty?" asked Lily. "As
the intelligence officer around here, I'm siding with
Becca. Which is like her getting an A and you getting . . ."

"Yes?"

"Not an A," she said. "But can we even get it open?"

Roald reached to the sill and pulled himself up high enough to see out. "There's scaffolding right outside. I guess we'll have to go this way."

More shouting from the hall, then the clank of chains hitting the floor. There was only the bolt now that kept the men from getting to them. Together, Wade and his father pushed out on the window. It groaned. "Careful, Dad. You're pushing too hard—"

More groaning; then the window fell away. Snowflakes flew in on them. Becca expected to hear the glass shatter down the side of the wall to the courtyard below, but it clanked to a stop just under the window.

"Let me test the scaffold," Roald said.

"It's probably slippery. Be careful," said Lily.

Roald clambered up to the sill, reached his arms through, and pulled himself outside. "It's slippery as anything, but strong enough to hold us. Come on, who's next?"

Wade and Darrell both boosted Becca up; she took Roald's hand and slid forward through the window, scraping her wounded arm, though she tried to ignore the sudden pain. When she was out, she found herself standing on a slightly slanted scaffold running along the inside walls, with cold snowflakes whirling in her face.

An iron framework supported the narrow planks all the way to the corner. Lily crawled out next. Wade went after her, then Darrell, who immediately pointed to a green-topped tower midway between the nearest corner and the one next to it. "That's Maxim's Onion Tower."

A rough voice yelled out suddenly from the court-yard below. "Do not go any farther. You have nowhere to run!" It was the rumpled-suited man from before. He was with three other men wearing lousy suits. One of the men held two phones and yelled into both. The men were soon joined by a half-dozen others, who started up the scaffold from the ground. Brother Semyon stood by helplessly.

"Never mind them," Darrell snapped. "To the corner." They made their way quickly along the planks as far as they could. Another stretch of boards ran along the outside walls from the corner to the Onion Tower.

"Dad, we can make it over the roof to the other scaffold," Wade said. He didn't wait for a response from his father, just crawled over the roof. Minutes later, they were all standing on the boards running along the outside walls.

Becca pointed to the parking lot. "Look. Our car.

Uncle Roald, what if you got the car and drove it down the outside wall under the tower? We can get to the tower, find the relic, and get down from there. We won't have to run into the guys climbing up."

Roald looked both ways, down the scaffolding to the ground and back at the men slowly climbing up. He wagged his head. "All right. Five minutes. I'll try to draw the men away. You be down there right below the Onion Tower. I'll meet you. Go!"

As Roald carefully worked his way to the ground outside the monastery, Wade led the others to where the scaffolding intersected with the Onion Tower's top floor, just below a set of high-arched windows. "I'm going to slide down to the gutter to get a foothold and open a window. Break it, if I have to."

Once down there, he found one of the three windows unlocked. He pushed it in easily. Darrell was right behind him. They dropped down onto a wide-planked wooden floor. Lily and Becca slid in next.

They were in the Onion Tower.

It was empty; the walls were simple and bare. It had a wooden floor that looked, at most, a hundred years old—a bad sign, if Maxim hid something in 1556. Walls of plain gray stone led up to a wooden ceiling that was nothing more than the inside of the cupola.

"Not a lot of hiding places," said Darrell.

Wade quietly lowered two planks that barred the doors. They were sealed in. "So now what?" he asked.

"Back to the picture," Lily said, bringing it up on her tablet. "Maxim is pointing—I mean, Saint Dominic is—to the base of the middle window."

"Do you think he was being that exact?" asked Darrell.

Becca looked around the small space. "Each side of the tower has three windows, but he's standing on the ground in front of it, which eliminates the sides where the walls meet the tower. So there are only two walls where it could be—"

"Actually, one," Lily said. "Dominic is obviously standing inside the monastery, because he was a prisoner like Maxim was. So it's got to be on the inside wall."

"It," said Darrell. "I sure hope we're talking about the relic. Either way, Maxim can't have known how long his secret would need to be hidden, so he probably hid it in something made of stone."

Wade peeked out the window. "Dad's in the car. There's a van in the parking lot now. Hurry this up."

As quickly as they could, they went over the entire inside wall, and especially the window area, but saw nothing, until Becca, brushing away stone dust accumulated over the years, ran her fingers over the shelf at the bottom of the middle north window.

At the base of the mullion, the pillar between the windows, two small figures were scratched into the surface of the stone, deeply enough to have endured for a long time.

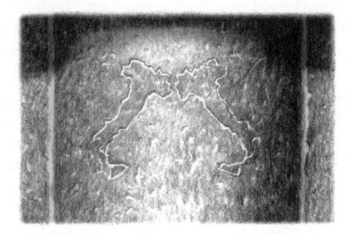

"Boots?" said Darrell. "A pretty gnarly pair of boots, if you ask me."

"Or the gnarly outline of Italy," said Becca. "Which makes perfect sense. Dominic was Italian. Maxim and Copernicus were in Italy at the same time."

"But why *two* Italys, and why is one of them backward?" Darrell asked. "Italy against Italy?"

"Or . . ." Becca dug Copernicus's diary from her bag and quickly leafed to the final pages—the Guardian Files—she had isolated. "Or . . . Italian against Italian?"

"Meaning what?" asked Wade.

"The coded passage," she said. "Maybe it's coded in the same language, only one of them is used backward."

"I am so not understanding you," said Wade. "Plus we need to hurry."

Snow flew in the open window behind Becca. The storm was getting worse. She had to block it out. "What I mean is that two Italys, one facing the other, might mean that there aren't two code languages, only one, and part of the message is backward."

"Up there!" said Lily, searching the wall above the Italy drawing. "The boots are pointing to something. I'm not . . . tall enough to see what it is."

Wade almost smiled. "The oldest cryptogram in the book. You point to the answer." He reached up and slipped his fingers into a small gap between two stones. He carefully drew out a rolled-up strip of parchment. It was nearly black with dense writing. There was a date—xvii January 1556—followed by a brief passage in a language that seemed like gibberish. "Becca, can you read—"

Footsteps scraped the floor heavily in the passage outside the tower. Something slammed roughly against the door. A similar sound fell against the opposite door.

"They're breaking in," Darrell whispered. He moved to the far window. "We need to get down the scaffold to the car."

More footsteps stomped down the halls outside the tower. The doors thundered. A hinge tore off one door frame and clanked to the floor.

"Out the window!" Lily said. "Now!"

CHAPTER THIRTY-ONE

Wade crawled first out the window and onto the ledge along the wall. At that point, the scaffold was a single slippery board. He hated this, hated heights, and the snow didn't make any of what they were doing smart or easy.

"Where's Dad?" Darrell asked, sliding out next to him.

Lily was next. "They got him," she said. "They got him, and they arrested him, and now they're coming for us—"

Then there he was, his tiny car sliding around the corner too quickly for the snow, nearly crashing into the trees that edged the wall, but he managed to right it and skidded to a stop beneath the tower. They climbed down the scaffolding as quickly as they could, jumping the last five feet, where there were no more boards. Then the van appeared, roaring from the parking lot onto the snowy ground, until its driver realized it was too large to fit between the trees and the outer wall. The van slid to a stop. The doors opened, and several men bolted out.

"The Brotherhood!" Roald said from the open window of the car. "Get in!"

As soon as they were safely inside, Roald gunned the engine. The Aleko spun down the narrow strip of ground and around the walls, losing their pursuers as they slid and careened over the property. They finally thudded onto an actual road and bounded up the entrance ramp of the highway. Roald swerved abruptly into traffic and crossed like a crazy man to the fast lane, gaining as much speed as the rattletrap could handle. It was approaching seven o'clock, the traffic was still heavy, but they were on their way back to Moscow.

"Good work, Dad," said Darrell. "You were awesome."

Roald grumbled under his breath. "I feel like a teenager," he said. "And not in a good way. What did you discover in the tower? Not Serpens?"

"No. A small document," said Becca. "And a decryption key. I think it's a decryption key, maybe to the passage in the diary. I hope it is . . ."

"It's a start, anyway," his father said.

Which only reminded Wade of that line Boris had told them twice. *The journey to the end of the sea is long.* Well, their long day was ending, they had all risked their lives, and they had no relic, only a tiny scroll of paper that they *hoped* would be a part of the puzzle, but they weren't even sure of that. Sara was still lost, somewhere in Russia. But Russia was enormous. Maxim Grek was looking like just the beginning of a very long journey. But they wouldn't know for certain until they deciphered the scroll. Even if they did find something, it might be just one clue leading to another and another . . .

Is hidden, and is hidden, and is hidden like layers of onion.

Roald switched lanes suddenly, then switched again, just as abruptly.

"Dad?" Darrell said. "What is it?"

"They found us. The van parked outside the monastery. Hold on—"

He swerved boldly across the highway and took the nearest exit ramp onto a side road. They bounced onto the street at the bottom of the ramp and headed for the highway underpass, where Roald spun the car around. He switched off the headlights.

The large gray van screeched down the exit ramp after them, then paused when it spotted them hiding under the highway. It motored slowly toward them. A moment later, a black car appeared. They could see the man in the rumpled suit from the monastery behind the wheel.

"This is not good," said Lily. "Should we get out and take cover?"

"We can take the little guy," said Darrell.

"No way," said his father, staring in each direction as if memorizing what he saw.

Suddenly the driver of the black car jumped out and approached them, his gun drawn. Wade's father glared at him intently. "Wade, get in the driver's seat, foot on the brake, put it in gear, and don't take your eyes off me."

"Dad, I can't drive!"

"You might have to. The rest of you stay put." His father jumped out of the car, leaving the engine running, and started talking, babbling really, as Wade warily shifted behind the wheel.

"I have what you're looking for!" his father yelled. "We found it at the monastery. The monk tried to stop us, but we found it. You can take it. We don't even know what it is, but you can take it. Just leave us alone. Let us leave in peace, and that's it. We'll go home."

Wade knew his father was bluffing, but what else he was planning he had no idea, until he saw his father reach into his hip pocket and palm the little silver device the detectives had given him in New York. The stun gun.

"You are being smart," said the man in a thick voice. He waved his gun casually, not at anyone.

Keeping the thick-voiced man between himself and the van, Wade's father marched right up to him, still jabbering like a lunatic, waving his arms. All at once, he crouched and jerked the Taser into the guy's chest. The man went spasmodic. He cried out and arched backward, dropping his gun. He fell in a quivering heap onto the snowy pavement. The goons from the van bolted over on foot.

"Wade! Now!"

He couldn't believe his father actually wanted him to drive the car, but his father was obviously trapped. The only way he could escape was if Wade jammed his foot on the accelerator and plowed the car between the charging men and his father.

"Omigod, Wade!" Becca cried. "Do it!"

"I—ahhh!"

The squeal of tires and the groaning of the engine weren't the worst things. Becca and Darrell both shrieked when he nearly ran his father down. At the last second, Wade stomped his foot on the brake. The car skidded ten feet toward the goons. They scattered. Lily reached over the seat and swung the front passenger door open. Wade's father dived into the car.

"Heads down! Gas!" his father yelled. Wade pressed the pedal to the floor.

His father grabbed the wheel, and together they swerved at the men again. The air exploded with shots. The car skidded between the van and the black car, then back up the wrong way onto the exit ramp. Bullets thudded into the side panels and blew out the rear window. With a crazy turn of the wheel, they spun into traffic and righted seconds before they would have smashed into a tractor trailer.

"Good . . . good . . . ," his father said, finally lifting himself over Wade and switching places with him. Under cover of quickly thickening snowfall, they tore back down the highway to Moscow.

CHAPTER THIRTY-TWO

Greywolf

Sara Kaplan woke up to ticking.

It sounded like the teeth of one gear joining with another's. Or the rhythmical oscillations of a giant clockwork. Either way, it wasn't normal.

"Where am I?" she mumbled through gagged lips. No answer. Blindfolded, she listened with every atom she could muster. No sound but the strange, loud ticking behind her head. The man who always seemed to be humming wasn't nearby. She was alone, still caged in that horrifying machine.

It had been hours since the troll and the supermodel had had her removed from the coffin. While her brain was still oozing forward like sludge, making only the most obvious connections, Sara deduced that the coffin had been used to keep prying eyes away as they smuggled her from place to place. She also reasoned that she had taken a series of airplane flights since she was first drugged in La Paz and could be just about anywhere now.

It was cold here. What did that crazy witch call it? Greywolf? What in the world were the Copernicus relics, and what did her family have to do with them? And of all things, a coffin! What sort of people . . .

But Sara guessed what sort of people they were. Not what they were all about, of course, but the kinds of things they did. Evil things. Very expensive evil things.

This wasn't your ordinary kidnapping for ransom.

At the thought of ransom and the image of her family around the living-room table waiting for a call, her eyes welled up. Then her brain sparked again. No. Not the living-room table. Roald had taken the children to Europe. Berlin. She'd received that message on her phone before she landed in Bolivia. A series of messages, even a couple from Darrell a few days later, put them somewhere—Italy?—with Roald's niece and her friend. Seriously? What was going on? What in the world was her family doing, traveling across the globe while she was transferred from a coffin to a horrible ticking engine? At least there didn't seem to be any more flights for her. She was where her kidnappers wanted her.

Greywolf.

Wherever that was . . .

Footsteps approached.

"Please tell me where I am," she gasped, scarcely more clearly. The footsteps came closer. She took in a breath and tried again. "Where—"

"Hush, my dear. Quiet!" A woman's voice, her breath hot and stale.

"Who's there?" All at once, Sara's blindfold was lifted and her gag removed. She blinked in the light, and the face before her clarified. The woman was her age, maybe a few years older. Her dark hair was limp, dangling over her face, her clothes filthy, stained. In one hand she held . . . a kitchen knife? Was there blood on it?

"Don't hurt me, please," Sara said. "I've been kidnapped."

"What? No," said the woman. She placed the knife carefully on the floor at her feet, then set about struggling with the chains that bound Sara into the machine, but her weak, bruised fingers could do nothing. "I must get you out of here," she said. An accent. Italian?

"Who are you?" Sara asked the woman.

"You have . . . I heard them saying . . . two days only."

"Two days? Before what? Who are you?"

The woman seemed half delirious, her thin fingers shaking, her eyes darting back and forth over the clock-work mechanism whose ticking had woken Sara. "Two days before the machine does what it does! The clock-work. Look. It counts down!"

"Who are you?" Sara repeated. "And these people? Where is Greywolf? Please, you have to get a message to my husband. His name is Roald Kaplan. His cell num-ber is—"

The woman's fingers froze. She stared at Sara. "Roald Kaplan . . . you said Roald Kaplan? You are Sara Kaplan! They took you, too! Because of the relics!"

"Wait, how do you know Roald—"

"I will try to find him. I have a friend at Moscow State University."

"Moscow? We're in Russia?"

Something clanked from outside the room. The door to the upper gallery swung open, and the humming man in the lab coat entered in a rush, holding a tray and focused on keeping whatever was on it from spill-ing. The woman quickly replaced Sara's gag and the blindfold. Sara heard her pick up the knife and duck around behind the machine. *Who are you?* she wanted to scream, but she let her head drop to her chest as if she were still drugged. She'd read enough Terence Ackroyd stories to know to do that. When she heard the man in the lab coat humming as he trotted down the stairs to her, and smelled the hot coffee, she realized he hadn't seen the woman. She had escaped.

Whoever she is, she knows Roald! She'll find him. She'll tell him where I am. He'll come for me. Darrell and Wade, too. Soon they'll come for me!

CHAPTER THIRTY-THREE

Moscow

Strangely, to herself at least, Becca didn't freak out after the insanity of the car chase. Even racing to Moscow in a smoking, sputtering, nearly windowless rental car with a bullet-riddled engine didn't faze her. And while everyone else was either breathless (Lily) or crazy anxious (Wade) or jabbering his head off (Darrell) or staring zombielike down the road ahead (Uncle Roald), Becca was calm.

More than calm, she was serene.

Something had clicked, and her mind was blocking everything out and holding a single image. The mirrored outlines of Italy.

She was certain they were the key to decrypting the Maxim passage in Copernicus's diary, the one marked with the date "xiii February 1517."

If they were *also* the key to the tiny scroll from the Onion Tower, she would translate both texts here and now. She would do it in that freezing, smoking, cramped Aleko, and she would conjure the astronomer's words and Maxim's five-hundred-year-old message.

Badgering Wade and Darrell to shield the diary from the wind, Lily focused the tablet in flashlight mode overhead so Becca could work out the double-eyed code.

Like a television chef preparing a delicious dish, she ran her finger along the diary page and narrated everything.

"First, we have the coded passage. Here is the beginning line."

Ourn ao froa lfa atsiu vlali am sa tlrlau dsa . . .

"If I'm right about the two facing Italys, the double-eyed passage is created by sort of *braiding* the words from the beginning *and* the end. To decode it, we have to separate every other letter into the two halves of the message. So the first, third, fifth, and so on give us *this* line." She wrote the letters carefully in her notebook, hoping she could hold on to the slender thread of how she thought the code worked.

o r a f o l a t i v a i m a l l u s

"And the second, fourth, sixth, and so on, give us *this* line."

u n o r a f a s u l l a s t r a d a

She wrote those letters down beneath the first. She recognized a word in that line—*strada*, for "street"—but it could be meaningless if the backward half of the code didn't work too.

"Will there be a quiz on this?" asked Darrell. "Or do you want us to know this because you are planning to leave us?"

"Neither," she said.

"Good," said Lily.

"I just think you should know this stuff," she added.

"We should," said Wade, leaning over her and her notebook.

The snow had let up a bit, and traffic was faster now. She spied the dim lights from skyscrapers in northern Moscow in the distance. Somehow that comforted her.

"So . . . since the backward shape of Italy was on the *left*, or *first*, if we're reading left to right, the code actually starts at the *end* of the message. This means that *o-r-a-f-o-l-a-t-i-v-a-i-m-a-l-l-u-s* is backward. Turned around it becomes *s-u-l-l-a-m-i-a-v-i-t-a-l-o-f-a-r-o*."

She wrote that down as neatly as she could, bouncing along in a wrecked car at eighty miles an hour. She saw a word there, too. "Now, because the passage *starts* with the end of the message, I'm going to guess that the *lengths* of the coded words—*O-u-r-n a-o f-r-o-a l-f-a a-t-s-i-u*—correspond to the length of the words of the final words of the message, starting from the end. In other words, four letters, then two letters, four, three, five, and so on."

Becca doubted whether they could follow this, but she felt she needed to explain it as thoroughly as possible, praying it actually did what she hoped it would.

"So, assuming it means something real, we break up *s-u-l-l-a-m-i-a-v-i-t-a-l-o-f-a-r-o* into words, starting from the end, of four letters, two, four, three, five, et cetera. The letters form the words like this . . ."

sulla mia vita lo faro

Becca had to pause. She read the separated words over and over, stunned to realize that her method actually *had* worked. She had deciphered the code.

"What is it? What does it mean?" asked Lily, still holding the light over the notebook. "Anything?"

Becca could barely bring herself to speak it. "It's the last line of the passage. It means, 'Upon my life I will.'"

"Astounding," Roald said from the front.

"Oh, man." Darrell breathed out a cloud of cold air. "You did it. You totally cracked the cipher."

After that, it was short but brain-heated work to translate the first half of the diary passage, though a bit tougher to discover exactly where the forward and backward messages met. She tugged her woolen hat down low and finally finished. Shivering between Lily and Wade, she read the deciphered passage aloud, even as the Aleko slowed in the approach to Moscow's center.

xiii February 1517.

One hour ago on the frozen road to Muscovy, Maxim Grek and I were ambushed by the knights of East Prussia.

The battle was brief but fierce. Sword in hand, I flew and struck like a Persian dervish. Thirty men came at us. Many will not return to their homes this night, but two escaped with a treasure beyond belief.

"Half of Serpens is in their hands," I tell Maxim. "I need a strong man to guard its other half, to keep it hidden

from men's eyes. From Albrecht's, from Vasily's as well."

"Friend, why me?" he asks.

"Sir," I say, "I have sailed with ancient Caesar. This cut above my brow was gained when I fought side by side with the great Alexander. These bruises on my hands? From crawling through a trench battling iron monsters!"

"Holy cow," Wade interrupted. "Dad? It sounds like World War One."

"What do you speak of?" he asks me.

"The past, the future, all times between. Maxim, three years ago I discovered a device that, used by the wrong men, can be a terrible weapon. This is why I have disassembled it. This is why, my friend, I am asking you to hide a piece of it."

He bows his head. "Tell me, Nicolaus, what would you have me do?"

I loosen the straps of the bag. The relic falls into my palm. Maxim's eyes widen. "It glitters like Vasily's jewels!"

"All told," I say, "this relic is a construct of nine diamonds, one for each star in the Serpens constellation, set in a hinged device of silver. The artifact, when whole, breathes like a living thing. It now lies lifeless

in my hand because its head, three diamonds circling twin eyes of such blue splendor, was stolen this night by Albrecht's men. It is the head that makes the body move. It is the head that gives it life. Many have died because of it."

"Boris's story about Albrecht and the crying baby was on February eighteenth, five days later than this," said Lily. "Sorry. Go on."

"Serpens, indeed, sounds cursed," Maxim says.

"Pain. Loss. Greed," I say. "These are the serpent's curse. I am asking you to take it with you wherever you go. Where would you like to be?"

Maxim smiles. "Italy, without a doubt. My days with you and your brother, Andreas, in Padua were the happiest of my life. I dream of Italy."

"Then bring Serpens with you. And devise a code to speak with future friends. You will need it."

He nods slowly. "I think backward to what I have said to you, and there is my code."

"Good," I say. "Now, Maxim of Athos, will you guard the relic, keep it safe from Albrecht and the eyes of sinful men?"

He blesses me and whispers the words that the first

252

Guardian himself spoke.

"Upon my life I will."

Uncle Roald made a sound through his lips. "This is one of the first times Copernicus has talked about his journeys. He met Caesar? And Alexander the Great? Excellent work, Becca. It's extraordinary." He was forced to slow the car several streets away from the rental agency.

"Does the same decryption key work for the scroll, too?" asked Lily. "We need to hear from Maxim."

Becca studied the first words of the scroll that appeared under the date. *Laonmd brrea sdmeo lrliar moonro . . . .* "I think so. Give me a few minutes."

The traffic eased a bit, and Roald pulled the damaged car into the rental center garage to the astonished stares of the desk agents. While he endured the agents' screaming and arguing, and a mountain of paperwork, Becca kept going. Wade held the diary and Darrell her notebook as she used the same system—two sets of words folded into each other back to front—to translate the scroll Maxim hid in the Onion Tower.

xvii January 1556

Andreas died one brief year after I took the Serpens

body from Nicolaus.

Nicolaus himself has been gone more than a decade.

I never saw Italy again. Saint Sergius has become my tomb. I prepare for death. Then, one day, I have a visitor.

"I am Rheticus," he says. "I was the Magister's friend. Trust me with Serpens now."

I can tell from his eyes that Rheticus is a good man, but the serpent has cursed me. I do not want to give it up. To save my soul, I hand the relic to this good man. "Take it."

To find the body of the serpent now, follow the man named Rheticus.

I have done my duty to Nicolaus.

The shadow of death comes soon.

Uncle Roald led them from the rental car center into the bitter Moscow night, listening while Becca read over the coded scroll. "I remember Rheticus," he said.

"You took good notes at Uncle Henry's lectures," Wade said. "It's all in the notebook. Rheticus came to Copernicus at the end of his life and convinced him to publish his proof that the earth revolves around the sun."

"So we have to follow him now?" asked Darrell. "Does this mean the quest will take us somewhere else?"

Becca frowned. "It might, if all this is just another layer of the onion."

"Possibly," Roald said. "Rheticus was the one who really made the world aware of Copernicus's brilliance. Interestingly, he came into Nicolaus's life at least twenty years *after* the relics were hidden. I guess what Maxim is saying is that Rheticus knew about the time machine, the relics, everything. We can talk this over in the safe house."

CHAPTER THIRTY-FOUR

Terence Ackroyd had booked the Kaplan family into a tiny flat of three rooms. It was located on the fourth floor of a building operated as part student hostel, part long-term hotel, run by an expatriate Austrian couple in their sixties. Just two streets off the broad-laned Teatral'ny Proyezd, the flat was not too far from Red Square and the Kremlin, the centuries-old seat of the Russian government. Wade tried to imagine a warm room, food, and rest, but he couldn't.

In the center is a relic, he thought as he marched through the stinging, almost horizontal snow. *Copernicus to Maxim to Rheticus to who? One clue to another and another, but how far away from the center are we?* It seemed to Wade that the layers of the onion were all they'd seen so far. What he was certain of, as they stomped block after frozen block toward their rooms, was that another day was gone, Sara was still missing, and they had a clue or two, but no relic.

"A few more intersections," his father called over his shoulder. "Stay together."

The flat was still a half-dozen snowbound blocks away when, as they tried to turn onto Teatral'ny, they found several police vans parked end to end across the avenue. A brigade of policemen with automatic rifles was busy cordoning off the street at the corner.

Becca dug into her bag for her phrase book. She sidled up to a group of spectators. "What's going on?" she whispered in halting Russian. The man she'd asked said nothing or something unintelligible, then snapped his fingers at a uniformed policeman, who trotted over.

Wade's first thought: *What if the police are looking for us?*

But the officer took only a brief glance at them and jetted off some harsh-sounding words, one of which Wade recognized: Lubyanka. The Soviet prison Boris said he had spent time in. It was just up the hill from them right now.

"Lubyanka Square is the scene of some kind of

protest against the government," Becca told them. They now heard yelling and raucous singing from up the street. "He said it's none of our concern, and we should go away."

"But our flat," Lily said. "And I'm frozen, and my poor feet. The ground is cold—"

"*Nyet!* No go here!" The policeman scowled, making a show of regripping his rifle for effect. "All you, go away!"

Roald pulled them back, smiling to the officer as he did. "If we can't get there this way, we can't," he said under his breath. "We don't want to get tangled up with the authorities. All they have to do is check with passport control, and who knows what the flak is from our performance at the monastery? Let's backtrack until we find an open street. I'm sure they're not just closing off a big part of the city where people live. I have a street map. Let's try another way."

They slid back among the streams of people moving down Teatral'ny Proyezd from Lubyanka Square. Wade's father studied the map to find a side street that might swing them back around to their flat. The sidewalks were iced over, narrowed by mounds of shoveled snow. When they reached the end of the street, police vans were parked end to end one way across that road, too, while on the far side of the street another crowd was assembling.

"Is this the same demonstration or another one?" Lily asked. "What now?"

Someone barked out loudly on a bullhorn. A banner unfurling awkwardly among the protestors seemed to galvanize the growing crowd into movement. The thump of footsteps, a roar at first, quickly became a kind of rhythmic thunder. A flag appeared suddenly.

"What is this, *Les Miz*?" said Becca. "We shouldn't be here, Uncle Roald."

"Let's make our way around the crowd to the far end of the block," he said firmly. "Don't get separated. Always have one another in eyeshot. Yell out if something happens. Look for signs for Teatral'ny Proyezd. That's the street our flat is off of. Teatral'ny. Ask if you need help. Use your phones if we get separated, but *don't* get separated, but here's cash and change in case," he said, dividing up the currency he had in his pockets. "The demonstration can't last all night. Stay close. Come on."

Wade's father began weaving along the sidewalk, his hand up for them to focus on. But the crowd was large, spilling beyond its original shape and rolling like a wave now.

Darrell nudged Wade's arm. "Look." A group of men in black parkas and wool caps emerged from the crowd. They were moving slowly toward them. "I don't like this."

Following Wade's father, the kids pushed through the stragglers on the fringes, when the police abruptly moved into position behind the vans, like soldiers defending a wall.

Wade expected to hear the crack of gunfire any second. "Dad, maybe we should—"

The men in parkas weren't visible now. Wade's attention was taken by a tall flat-faced man in a long overcoat who snapped orders to the officers crouched behind the cars. He was bald and had a bushy black mustache. The police shifted not only behind their cars but on both sides of the avenue. A second bullhorn squealed angrily. The front of the crowd stopped, but the back kept pushing forward. The shouting was punctuated by screaming now.

"Wade, get over here!" his father yelled, and Wade saw the mustached policeman spin around on his heels as if he'd heard Wade's name—seemingly impossible in all the noise. The man stared in their direction until he fixed on Wade. The men in parkas were there again, too, striding toward Wade. *Oh, no. No.*

Lily threaded her way through the crowd. Wade saw Becca's ponytail swinging. They were together, at least. Where was Darrell? The protestors were moving again in waves. He swam against the tide of bodies, trying to reach the girls, while Darrell was suddenly deep in the crowd, abreast of their father. The demonstration was all around him now and frightening. Strange faces yelled angrily. He felt a punch in his side. Spittle sprayed his cheek. He looked up. The men in parkas were closer. But his father wasn't where he'd last seen him.

Jumping to see over the crowd, he yelled, "Dad!" then heard a sudden loud pop. Becca whirled around toward him, cringing, while Lily slid past a cluster of protesters to Darrell. There was his father again, reaching backward for them but being dragged farther away. Wade muscled through the crowd and snagged Becca's sleeve. "Bec, let's get out of this. There's a subway over there somewhere."

"You want to eat? *Now*?"

"No, a metro!" Wade said. "We can ride it back to the flat—"

They broke free of the jostling bodies and ducked between close-set stone buildings, hurrying to where the subway arrows pointed. He searched the crowd. His father, Darrell, and Lily were already across the street, looking back to find him and Becca. Wade waved his arms, but they didn't see him. There was another pop, then a shout. He couldn't see the men in parkas. Groups of demonstrators were spilling around quickly as if they would start running. Then Wade spied the stairs. Together he and Becca entered the heated subway. He held her by the hand, afraid without his father and the others, but responsible for himself and Becca. When they reached the bottom of the stairs, heat washed over them, and being underground had never felt so good.

"This is like Boston a little," Becca said nervously. "They call their subway the T."

"Good. Then you lead."

She cracked a smile. "I think we follow the noise down the stairs."

After paying for tickets with pocket change, and snatching a color-coded map of the subway system, they jumped down the nearest steps to the platform. They huddled behind a vending machine for minutes before boarding the first train that came screeching to a stop. It was immaculate and filled with passengers.

"If this station is called Okhotny Ryad, we'd better get off at the next station, wherever that is," said Becca, reading the map on the subway wall. "It's pretty far anyway. We'll either walk back or take a cab to the flat.

Maybe the demonstration will have moved on by then."

"That was crazy, huh?" Wade said. "Those guys were chasing us, weren't they?"

"I didn't see them, but Darrell seemed to. There were so many people."

They were crammed together face-to-face in the standing-room-only car. It was a sea of thick coats, knit caps, shopping bags, and teetering bodies as the train lurched forward. Wade wasn't sure exactly why, but he suddenly wanted to say something comforting to Becca. All he came up with was "How's your arm?"

She cradled an area between the elbow and shoulder of her left arm. "It itches, so that's a good sign, right? Like it's beginning to heal?"

"Good," he said, trying to smile. The truth was that her bandages, when he'd glimpsed them under her coat, were dark, as if she had bled some. "We need to find another clinic to have it looked at. The Austrian couple who run the hostel will know where to go."

She shook her head. "I don't want to slow us down—"

"Becca. You won't. We need to protect you." Was that comforting? He didn't know. He tried to follow up with something more promising than what he was thinking when the tunnel outside the windows brightened, and the train began to slow.

"We'd better get off," she said, rummaging through her bag. "The next stop is way beyond Red Square, and too far to walk back. And I actually don't think we can hail a cab. I must have lost my phrase book in the crowd, and I didn't get to the taxicab page. We don't want to end up even farther away."

Wade snorted a laugh. "Agreed."

He eased through the passengers to be ready to jump off when the train stopped. Before it did, the door from the next compartment opened with a breath of air, and Wade's heart thumped. The tall policeman with the bushy mustache pushed in. His gray overcoat flapped open to reveal a thick leather strap across his chest. He gripped something like a phone in his hand, reading it and then staring into the crowd.

"Becca . . ."

"I see him. Did he follow us down here? He's either with the police . . . or he's part of the Red Brotherhood."

"Or both. Watch out for guys in black parkas."

The train screeched to a stop. The doors groaned aside. Wade instinctively took her arm, but it was the wrong one. She winced, and he let go. He jumped onto the platform and turned for her, but a block of people pushed past him into the car, and Becca was forced away from the doors.

"Becca—" He tried to push his way back onto the car, but she was crowded even farther from the doors. He couldn't get on. She couldn't get off. The whistle sounded. The doors began to close. "Becca!" Then the mustached man jumped from the rear door of the car onto the platform. With a single look at Becca, Wade charged away into a warren of tunnels as the subway roared off into the dark.

CHAPTER THIRTY-FIVE

Snow was falling heavily when Wade stumbled up the metro stairs to the street. The flakes were large and wet and flying in his face and down his neck. He pulled his woolen cap low and ran up the sidewalk to the nearest corner. His shirt was soaked through. Everything was soaked, though his chest was a block of ice. He looked back. No one else came out of the subway. He searched the intersection.

"Wait!" someone yelled in English. Or was it "Wade"? He didn't look back. Panicking, he hurried down the sidewalk, slipping, nearly falling. He reached the next intersection. Footsteps thudded behind him. Several sets. Running this time.

At the first break in traffic, he tore across the wide avenue to a park on the other side. He ducked behind a shuttered kiosk. The mustached man paced the far corner, his overcoat flapping and flapping, scanning the intersection. Was *he* the one who had called to him? Why would anyone "wait" for someone pursuing him?

Trying to keep the kiosk directly between him and the tall man, he made himself small and ran as quietly as he could in the opposite direction. He soon found himself in a maze of grim gray buildings that resembled a movie set for the apocalypse.

He ducked into the first side alley he saw. Narrow, barren. Cold.

He'd lost his breath and couldn't get it back. Not from running so much, but deep inside. As if his lungs were failing him.

"Wait!" the voice called.

He stormed deeper into a cement quadrangle and glanced back, and something told him to turn at the first corner. He slipped on the ice, smashing his knee on the pavement. The pain speared up his side. On his feet again, turn, and down the passage, then turn again. His legs were lead. The snow was heavier, wetter. He started to remember the warmth of Rome, that night outside the Museo Copernicano, when they'd slept under the stars. Of being together with Darrell and Becca and Lily. But there wasn't enough of his brain to do anything but run.

He was running on bone. He stumbled to the end of the alley, hoping for an outlet. There was none. It ended in gray stone, a coffin of concrete. Heavy footsteps crashed behind him. Many more than before. Twenty paces behind him. Ten. Five. Three.

Wade rested his head on the cold cement wall, then spun around with a cry—"Help me!"—as a group of men in hooded coats closed over him.

CHAPTER THIRTY-SIX

Becca raced through the slushy streets. The demonstration had broken up as quickly as it had formed. She found the safe house, but Wade hadn't returned.

Roald was on the phone to the police, getting nowhere.

"They have him," she gasped. "The police or the FSB or the Brotherhood. They took him!" She told them everything, and Darrell started doing his caged-animal thing. He eyed the tiny window of their room as if he was going to jump out of it. Then he shot her a look as if it was somehow *her* fault that Wade wasn't there. As if *she* should be lost, instead.

She understood. Brothers. She was nearly as close to

Lily as she was to her own sister, Maggie. If anything happened to her . . .

"I couldn't get off the train," she said. "The crowd was pushy, and I—"

"We know, Bec," Lily said, patting her hand. "It's not that—"

"Of course it's not that!" Darrell practically shouted, then breathed out sharply. "It's this dumb freezing place. Wade could be anywhere—"

The door swung in. Becca jumped for it, but it was a man in a parka and black combat fatigues and boots. Behind him were several other men dressed the same. "Put down the phone," the first one said to Roald. "Gather things. Come with us. No time."

"But—" Roald began, the phone halfway to its cradle.

Darrell shook his head crazily. "No! I'm not leaving! I'm not going anywhere without Wade!"

The lead man pulled his pistol out of its holster. "No words. Put down phone. Chief Inspector Yazinsky has ordered us to bring you to station." Becca then watched as the man did an odd thing. He put a finger to his lips, and whispered, "Red Brotherhood are entering lobby downstairs. They are coming. We do not want firefight in building. Please. Hurry."

And that was it. She went electric and so did everyone

else. They threw their things together. The men—were they even real police?—shut off all the lights but one and hovered at the windows and doors, guns drawn.

The man made a hissing noise. There was a shout from outside their room. The men at the door crouched. A shot exploded through the door frame and crashed back out the window. The men at the door returned fire.

"Stair escape through bathroom," the lead man said. He pushed them efficiently through the room and into the bathroom, where he slammed the bottom sash up as far as it would go. Eight inches. Not enough. He raised a jackboot and kicked it out entirely. Glass splattered onto an iron landing. "Mister first," he said, "then others."

Roald slipped through the opening into the whirling snow and waited on the landing for Becca and Lily. They took the iron steps down to the next landing and the next, while Darrell followed with the officer. An unmarked car was waiting at the bottom. The gunfight above had stopped and been replaced with yelling and the sound of multiple sirens approaching through the snowy streets.

"Who are you?" Roald said as they were hustled into the back of the cruiser. There was no answer. The driver started up, the electronic door locks engaged, and the car slid away, leaving the officer who had helped them on the street, trotting into the hotel, his weapon raised. The cruiser was nearly around the corner when Becca felt the air shudder. Glass and wood and fire blew like a rocket's ignition out of their room, showering the street with flaming debris.

Darrell screamed, "They bombed our room! Those freaks bombed our room!"

A second blast blew fire out everywhere. The cruiser picked up speed and they were on another street and another. More sirens. The driver tore through several blocks north from the safe house, down the hill from Lubyanka Square, whizzing past the ragged remains of the demonstration, slowing only as they entered a wide plaza. In the center of the plaza was a big box of a building. There was a range of brightly lit double-arched windows across the front and a heavy square tower sprouting from the roof. The area in front of it was filled with taxicabs.

"This is . . . I thought we were going to the police station," Roald said.

Becca read the sign: ЛЕНИНГРАДСКИЙ ВОКЗАЛ. "What is this place?"

"Leningradskiy train station," the man said in English. "You leave on next train."

"Dad, what is this?" Darrell cried.

"No talking now," the officer said. He pulled the cruiser to the front of the building and, without looking at them, electronically unlocked the doors. "Inside. Officer will find you. Go. Now!"

They stumbled out into a tumult of circling cars and still heavier snow.

CHAPTER THIRTY-SEVEN

The bag over his head had been the worst. Wade could barely stomach the smell of someone else's face and hair and breath so close to his own.

Even now he spat out a greasy thread. "Gross . . ."

The room was tiny, a small box, four feet by nine feet—he'd paced it out—with only a padded bench in it. It was a cell smaller than Maxim's. They'd thrust him inside and slammed the door behind him. He'd torn off the bag immediately and thrown it on the floor. That was—what—two hours ago? Longer? Was it the middle of the night?

The stained bag sat on the floorboards, a lump of gray canvas. Floorboards. Not a concrete floor. In the dim light of the hanging bulb he studied the narrow oak boards set in an angled pattern, one next to another, like the weave of a fancy overcoat.

His breath left him.

Parquet.

"I'm in Lubyanka prison."

His heart sank, then squeezed tight, and something wrenched up his throat. He wanted to cry. He pounded on the door with his fists. "Let me out. I'm an American! You hear me? You can't do this! I'm an American citizen!"

No answer. But the mustached man knew who Wade was anyway. Of course he did. He and a handful of large, hard men had cornered him, bagged him, and pulled him into a car. Boris's words came back to him. *Car take you to Lubyanka.*

He remembered Lily telling them how Saint Dominic was the patron saint of those who were falsely accused. Like Sara? Yes, like Sara. Thinking that actually gave him hope. He was locked up, but alive. And Sara was, too. She had to be.

Wiping his face, Wade paced the cell front to back, door to bench, three and a half steps, turn, then three and a half steps back. He tried to find a place of calm inside him. If there was silence, if he was alone, he could make use of it.

So far, they had nothing. They didn't have a relic yet. They had nothing but words. But it wasn't just a mess of unrelated words. It wasn't random. It was a kind of history, where things from here and there were connected and made a picture.

It was like . . . what?

A constellation, his astronomical brain told him.

Isolate the things I see. Put them in order. Make the connections. Bring all the stories down to points of light.

He stooped to the floor and ran his fingers along the floorboards where they met the wall, looking for a nail or something sharp. Nothing. Then he remembered. The tooth. He slipped his hand into his pocket and pulled it out. Black, chipped, dead. The tooth of a martyred Guardian, perhaps. A victim of Galina Krause. It was the perfect thing to use against her.

With the tooth pinched between his fingers, Wade scratched a letter into the wall.

C

That was for Copernicus. In 1517 he gave the body of Serpens to Maxim—*M*—who at his death, in 1556, gave it to Rheticus—*R*—who died in 1574. But the other thing that happened in 1517 was that the nephews of Albrecht—*A*—stole the head of Serpens. Albrecht himself died in 1568, a generation after Copernicus's own death in 1543.

So what did that look like? It looked like this:

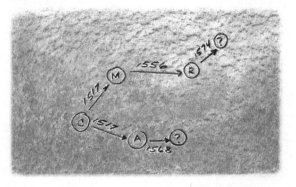

Strangely, reducing the confusion of his thoughts to a clear drawing calmed him. It really did look like a constellation, the shorthand for a long story. A story reduced to glowing points of light, which then became the story again.

His breath slowed. His panic ebbed. Moving from there to there to there was progress. It gave him a direction.

"So now we have two questions," Wade said to himself, pocketing the tooth. "Where did the head go after Albrecht, and where did the body go after Rheticus?"

Keys jangled outside the door. It burst wide, nearly smacking him in the face. Before he could see anyone, he was spun around and his wrists were shackled behind his back. The canvas bag, wet now and smelling of mice, was dropped over his head again.

CHAPTER THIRTY-EIGHT

Darrell was stone. He refused to move or set foot in the Leningradskiy train station. "We're not leaving without Wade. First Mom, now Wade? We're not leaving."

"We're not going anywhere," his stepfather said. "I'm calling the embassy right now. I don't know who Chief Inspector Yazinsky is, but authorities or no, we need help here."

Before Roald could locate the number, a short older man in a gray overcoat hanging loose over a suit and tie—obviously a policeman or secret service officer—pushed out the station doors into the parking lot. "Please close the phone, sir. The inspector wishes no calls. Not from your phone. We cannot take chances. Please . . ."

Roald looked shocked but didn't resist. The man pulled the cell from his hand, swiped it off, removed its battery, and pocketed it. "Follow me, please." His grip on Roald's arm was apparently strong, as he tugged him forcefully to the door.

"Uncle Roald—" Lily started.

"Do as he says."

Cursing to himself, Darrell reluctantly followed him into the station.

It was an enormous open room with a lighted arcade running down each of the long sides. Hundreds of people wove across the floor from end to end, even at that time of night. The air was filled with the din of voices and footsteps, the rumbling of wheeled suitcases, and overlapping announcements in Russian, English, and French. The incessant clink and clatter from late-night restaurants and snack bars added its own kind of roar in his ears. Beneath it all rolled the thunder of the rails running from the station out into the countryside beyond Moscow.

"Wait here one minute," the officer commanded, and strode several feet away.

Becca huddled together with Lily and Darrell. All of

them were mumbling, afraid, trying to be logical, but everything they said came down to some crazy version of "What in the world is going on?"

Then Lily's cell phone rang. "Who's calling me?" she answered. "May I help you?"

The voice on the other end was slow and faraway. "I'm calling from the morgue."

"Ahhhh!" Lily screamed, and dropped the phone.

"What!" Becca cried.

"It's the morgue! Someone's dead!" Lily scrambled for the cell phone, but Darrell tore it from her fingers and punched the speaker button.

"Hello? Hello? Are you there? Is it Wade? Is it my brother? Is he . . . dead?"

"Dea . . . I . . . not . . ." The voice was faint, crackly.

"Can you please speak up," Roald said into the phone. "Is this the morgue? Are you calling from the morgue?"

". . . an Library," said the suddenly familiar voice. "The Morg . . . an Library. In New York City. Is this the Kaplan family?"

Darrell buried his head in his hands, practically sobbing. "Good God."

Roald said, "Hello, you are Dr. Billingham, I presume? This is Roald Kaplan. We're just . . . never mind.

Do you have some news for us?"

"I am a mess . . . ," Rosemary said, " . . . enger for Julian Ackroyd. He says his fa . . . ther has business in London, but will arrive in Mos . . . cow on Sun . . . day morning. There is news, he says. Are you under . . . standing me?"

"Thank you," said Roald. "Thank you so much!"

"That's not . . . all," Rosemary said. "Last night there was a robbery . . ."

"Oh, my gosh, Vela!" Lily said.

". . . attempt at the library. Of course, nothing was taken. The police are hunting for a Germ . . ." There was a long few seconds before ". . . an man and three French ass . . . ociates. That's . . . all. Good day."

The short officer returned and drew them swiftly down the perimeter of the room toward the far inside corner. He scanned the crowd like a hawk, but gave no answer to Darrell's—or anyone else's—urgent questions.

At the same time an unmarked automobile motored swiftly from one snowbound street to the next. The car made constant turns, approaching a yellow-towered public building three times before turning away to begin another series of zigzags and cutbacks.

Chief Inspector Simon Yazinsky sat in the rear seat. He tugged one end of his bushy mustache and turned to the passenger sitting next to him.

"Truly, Wade," he said in lightly accented English, "my sincerest apologies for the filthy bag. A bit dramatic, I know. Lubyanka, as well. All of it. It was for your own safety that you remained anonymous. You see, in Russia the Teutonic Order and its allies here, the Red Brotherhood, are everywhere and powerful. Your visit to Saint Sergius alerted the Brotherhood. They planned to use the demonstration as a cover to kidnap you. I had to intervene. For your own safety, you must leave the city."

Wade nodded slowly, desperately trying to take it all in with the fraction of a brain he had left. "So you arrested me because the Brotherhood was after us? The men in black parkas at the demonstration?"

He nodded. "Although I have a distinguished rank in the FSB, even after I scooped you up, I wanted no one to see you. I can trust my friend here behind the wheel, but few others on my staff. I must also inform you that there has just been an attempt on the safety of your family. An attack and explosion in your rooms."

"Oh, my gosh, are they—"

"They are fine, and waiting nearby."

The car drove smoothly from street to street.

"You were following us, tracking me from the beginning," Wade said, feeling more and more brain coming back to him. "How did you know to do that?"

Chief Inspector Yazinsky cleared his throat. "The Circle of Athos has been aware of you since your arrival at Sheremetyevo airport."

Wade thought back. "The guard who stopped me at the passport control? What was her name . . . I. Lyubov?"

"Cousin Irina," he said, smiling under his mustache. "Carlo Nuovenuto—you know him—sent encrypted pictures to the Guardians in Europe and elsewhere. The clearest image from the fencing school in Bologna was of you. We have eluded our pursuers, and here we are."

The building with the tower reappeared once again, and this time Wade saw its blazing letters.

ЛЕНИНГРАДСКИЙ ВОКЗАЛ

The driver pulled up to it. "The train to Saint Petersburg," Inspector Yazinsky said. "The station is quaintly still named Leningradskiy." He leaned across the seat to Wade, and his voice went low. "The Circle of Athos comprises a handful only, while the Order is a kraken of great size, a monster. Even with our precautions, we must be careful when we enter." The inspector reached across Wade and opened his door. It swung out into the cold. Wade stumbled out, then followed the man into the station.

CHAPTER THIRTY-NINE

W ade was bewildered by the massive, brilliantly lit hall. It was elegant and insufferably loud. His father was not visible; neither were Becca, Darrell, and Lily. He didn't like it. The roar of noise and movement could drown out any number of dangers.

"Be careful," the inspector repeated. "This way."

His senses on high alert, Wade followed the inspector, hugging close to the side of the huge open room. They went under one of the two large arches to an office door. "Railroad security," the inspector whispered.

"Are they Guardians, too?" he asked.

"Guardians? No. But they are friends, even if they do not know exactly why we're here." The inspector knocked three times, paused a moment, and then knocked twice more. The door opened, Wade entered, and his shoulder thudded with a series of blows from behind. He went into an immediate crouch, but hands were suddenly all over him, spinning him around.

"Wade, Wade, Wade!"

Darrell, Becca, and Lily wouldn't let go of him, as if he'd been missing for a year. He coughed out, "I'm okay, I'm okay," a hundred times, but they barely let him breathe.

When he finally pulled away, his father wrapped him in his arms. "Wade, we were worried sick about you!"

"Really, I'm okay," he said. "I heard there was a bomb."

They told him about their last-second rescue from the safe house, then that Terence was on a jet flying to them right now. It was several minutes before Wade could properly introduce them to Chief Inspector Yazinsky.

"I apologize for all the secrecy," the inspector said to them, nodding at a short, smiling security officer. "The reason you are here is twofold. As I told young Wade on the way over, the Red Brotherhood has closed in, and you must leave Moscow. But this is what you might wish to do anyway. Dmitri?"

The short officer stepped forward. "One hour ago, we arrested someone at the station, coming in on the train from Saint Petersburg. No identification, no story. A vagrant, we thought. Or worse. She was armed—"

"She?" said Darrell. "A woman?"

"Not your mother," said Inspector Yazinsky. "We are certain. Continue, Dmitri."

"She was armed," the officer continued. "And she bears bruises on her face and hands. She is dehydrated, weak. She is being treated right now for shock, exposure to extreme cold, exhaustion, cuts, bruises, frostbite—"

"Oh, my gosh," said Becca.

"Who is she?" Roald asked.

Dmitri lowered his head. "The woman will not speak to us. She will say nothing."

Roald looked at the inspector, then back at the short officer. "Then, I'm sorry, but what does this have to do with us?"

"She will say nothing, sir," the officer continued, "but your name. Roald Kaplan."

"Dad!" said Wade. "Who is it?"

"Allow me to bring you to her," the officer said. "The station clinic is this way."

The inspector motioned them through the door, and

they hurried down a very narrow corridor toward a white circular sign beaming with a flickering neon red cross. The short officer turned the knob, then bowed at the doorway.

"I take my leave of you here. She has been sedated, but is awake."

The clinic inside was clean and spacious for a railway station. It smelled of chemicals and food. In a cubicle surrounded by thin curtains sat a low hospital cot. A woman lay on it, her arms connected to tubes, her hands and feet and cheeks bandaged. No, it was not Sara. It was, in fact, no one Wade recognized, but his father let out a gasp.

"Isabella! Isabella Mercanti!" He knelt to the cot and gently took her hand. Her eyes flicked open, then closed again. "Isabella," he said, "it's Roald. . . ."

The children watched as the woman slowly turned her face to him. "Roald? Roald!" She reached for him, but the tubes held her back. She started to cry.

Isabella Mercanti was the Italian professor Wade's father had told the children to meet in Bologna last week. She was the widow of Silvio Mercanti, a member of his father's old college circle, Asterias. When she had gone missing, and even her university hadn't heard from her, they had all presumed the worst.

Wade felt his knees give way. He plopped into a chair next to a rolling cart. On the cart were instruments, bloodied gauze bandages, and, strangely, a kitchen knife. Why was Isabella Mercanti in Russia, of all places? And on a train originating in Saint Petersburg, four hundred miles from here?

Was this anything but another weird layer of the onion?

"Some water, please," his father said, and the inspector stepped into the next room. "Isabella, tell me what happened to you? Why are you in Moscow?"

"I saw her," she whispered. "I saw Sara . . ."

Darrell knelt to the cot. "My mother? Where is she? Is she okay?"

"She did not escape, not like me," she said, taking a sip of water. "But yes. Alive. In a horrifying castle many kilometers outside Saint Petersburg."

"When did you see her?" Becca asked.

"It is after midnight now? Then yesterday," she said. "Yes, yesterday. She was captive. In a tower. I could not get her out of the thing. I wounded a soldier. No, not a soldier. A brute, an animal. Maybe he died. I do not know. I stab him and escape."

Wade glanced back at the knife on the cart, then at Becca. She was staring at it, too, wiping her cheeks.

"I run barefoot to a small city. Far, many hours away. People pity me, get me to train in Saint Petersburg, pay for me. I come here. I have friend in Moscow. Sara"— she paused, looked at Darrell—"your mother is in a . . . device. Horrible. Big device."

Darrell stood and pounded the nearest wall. "What kind of device? Tell us!"

"Let her speak," Roald said softly, cradling Isabella by her shoulders.

She sat up, her eyes wild. "I only caught a glimpse of the machine. Then a man comes in. I have to run. Sara is a prisoner of clockwork. Something happens at midnight some days from now. No, not some days. Sooner. It is Saturday in the early morning, yes? Then tomorrow. Sunday at midnight. That is what I heard them say."

"Mom is being tortured?" Darrell slammed his fist once more on the wall.

"No, not tortured. It is clockwork. Gears and wheels."

"What does the machine do?" asked Lily.

"I don't know!" Isabella answered.

"Do you know where the place is exactly?" Roald asked.

Isabella shook her head. "I hear some things. A German woman. Young."

"Galina Krause," muttered Wade.

She nodded. "I hear her voice. She say, *'Der Hölle Rache'*? It is German, but what is this?"

No one knew. Becca asked for Lily's computer.

"And I hear one word. The name of the horrible place where we are held. A fortress. It is called . . . Greywolf."

"Greywolf." Roald rose to his feet and began to pace around the cot. "Inspector?"

"I do not know of it," he murmured, dragging his phone from his pocket. "I will find out."

"Dad, we're going to get Mom right now," Darrell said slowly and in a whisper. "It's nearly three a.m. Saturday morning. Only forty-something hours to Sunday midnight. We have to go get Mom before that machine does anything to her."

"We will," Roald said firmly, looking deeply into Darrell's eyes. "We will. We'll find out where this Greywolf is, and we'll go for her. I'll phone Terence to change his flight plans and meet us in Saint Petersburg."

Isabella was breathing more easily now. "I cannot go back there and I do not know the way. Roald, I am sorry. But I must return to Italy as soon as possible. My husband discovered a secret before he was murdered. That is why the Order took me. The clue is in our apartment in Bologna. I must go there as soon as possible to protect it."

"Oh, man . . ." Becca stood, Lily's computer tablet quivering in her hands. "Boris's ticket . . ."

Wade turned to her. "Ticket? You mean to the opera in Italy? What about it?"

"*Der Hölle Rache kocht in meinem Herzen,*" she said. "What Galina said. It means 'Hell's vengeance boils in my heart.' It's a line from *The Magic Flute*. The opera in Venice that Boris had a ticket to see. He was going there Saturday night. Tonight! Galina is going there, too! That's what she meant when she said those words. She must have heard that Boris was going to meet someone, and now she's going! We have to go to Venice!"

Wade felt the tooth in his pocket. Aleksandr. Boris. Andreas. Nicolaus. The connection between brothers. "A message for Boris. It was about the relic. A message about Serpens, maybe. We need to know what someone wanted to tell Boris—"

Darrell shook his head vehemently. "No we don't. We're going to Greywolf. Dad, I don't care where Galina's going. Mom is tied up in some death machine, and we're going to save her. We're not leaving Russia!"

"Darrell, calm down," his stepfather said. "We're not going anywhere. We're not."

"Dr. Kaplan." The inspector cleared his throat. "May I make a suggestion? I feel responsible and will make the trip to Italy to escort Dr. Mercanti home. If you approve, I will also escort anyone who wishes to go to Venice for the rendezvous. I will protect them as if they are my own. Clearly the Circle of Athos cannot keep you safe against the Order here. I suggest you continue to Saint Petersburg. I will personally provide all assistance to ensure Dr. Mercanti's safety. Perhaps Wade and another of the children should accompany us, to follow through on the meeting at the opera house. We will then return together. I leave it to you."

Wade knew the gears were moving in his father's head. His dad would never want to split the family apart. But now that there was a deadline in one place and a clue in another, they might have to. "Dad," he said, "the inspector might be right."

His father looked at him, then at the others, and finally at Isabella. "What do we think?" he asked softly. "Isabella, I know it's a lot to ask, but what do you think about stopping in Venice before you go home to Bologna? With some of us. I think we need to know what will happen in Venice tonight. Can you—"

"Yes," Isabella said quietly. She sat up more firmly, her bandaged feet resting on the floor. She teetered a little, but took a deep breath and steadied herself. "Yes, Roald, of course. Thank you, Inspector. I will help as much as I can. It is my place to do so. My husband was a Guardian. This makes me one, too."

"Wade, girls?" his father asked.

"Venice," said Lily.

Becca nodded. "Venice."

Darrell looked at Wade. "Dude, go. We'll have Terence. Plus, you're kind of klutzy and will probably slow us down."

Wade knew it was Darrell's attempt—a weak one—at humor. But it allowed him to say what he felt he should say. "All right, then. Venice."

Becca passed the tablet back to Lily. "Airlines . . ."

"Oh, I know," she said, smiling over the screen. "Five tickets to Venice. Trust me. We'll be there in plenty of time for the opera."

"Darrell and I will go to Saint Petersburg," Roald said. "We'll find out where Greywolf is. And we'll find Sara. We will."

CHAPTER FORTY

Saint Petersburg; Venice

Later that morning, following the appearance of Isabella Mercanti, Darrell and his stepfather sleeplessly took the train to Saint Petersburg.

After Chief Inspector Yazinsky had seen to it that Roald's cell phone was returned to him, the first call he made was to Terence Ackroyd, who said he would meet them in Saint Petersburg. The investigator Paul Ferrere and a colleague from Paris were on their way there, too.

For his part, Chief Inspector Yazinsky searched but could discover nothing about Greywolf from official sources. Neither could he promise much Guardian help in the northern city, beyond the offer of the name of a low-level aide at the seldom-visited Railway Museum, "because of their extensive maps of the Russian frontier. Pray you find Greywolf listed on one of them."

Because of Isabella's condition, it was several hours before she felt well enough to fly. Once she gave the go-ahead, Lily booked them all—the inspector, Isabella, Becca, Wade, and herself—on the earliest nonstop to Venice. It would leave at two p.m. Given the time difference, Venice being three hours earlier than Moscow, the three-and-a-half-hour flight was scheduled to arrive midafternoon. That would leave them five solid hours before the opera performance on Saturday evening.

"Venice is quite different from Rome or Bologna," Isabella said as they took their seats on the flight. "But I have always loved it there. So will you."

Lily felt they could trust Isabella. One of the marks of Guardians seemed to be that they didn't press, they didn't force, they didn't make you feel as if you had to *do* or *feel* or *tell them* something. That was plain in Copernicus's conversation with Maxim. He asked; he didn't force. Maxim agreed anyway.

Upon my life I will.

"The relic we're searching for in Russia is called

Serpens," she told Isabella. Remembering that Isabella's husband, Silvio, was a friend of Uncle Roald's, she added, "I'm so sorry your husband passed away."

Isabella shook her head. "Silvio's murder was disguised as a skiing mishap. He was murdered by an agent named Markus Wolff. I know you know him. It was Silvio's obsession with what he called 'number twelve' that got him killed. There is a mystery about the twelfth—the final—relic. It is somehow odd and unlike the others."

"Wolff hinted at the same thing in San Francisco," Lily said. "He said that what the twelfth relic is, is the answer to everything. What did Mr. Mercanti find out?"

Isabella frowned. "I know little, but he was close to discovering something. The Order thinks I know what it is. The answer lies hidden in our apartment in Bologna. I will find it. For Silvio, I will find it."

"We know how terrible the Order is," said Wade. "The death of my uncle Henry—Heinrich Vogel—pulled us into the relic hunt in the first place."

"Heinrich was a good man," she said. "I was calling him when I was kidnapped."

"Thanks to him, we have one relic so far," said Becca. "But Serpens is in two parts, and we have neither, which isn't good."

"But neither does Galina, yes?" said the inspector.

"Right," said Lily. "And that *is* good. Really good."

"Maybe having lots of layers to the onion are all right, after all," Becca said.

It was warm and sunny when they arrived at Marco Polo Airport, a small and clean affair built out over the water six and a half miles north of the city. Lily shed her coat at the earliest opportunity. Though brisk in late March, Italy was already showing signs of spring, and after so much cold Lily began to feel, as they all did, thawed out, rejuvenated, alive. "No more hunching against the cold," she said. "I can stand straight up for the first time in days. No more windburn, either. Or frozen fingers."

Maybe best of all, they weren't being followed yet. Galina might already be there, but likely didn't know that they were.

Becca seemed to be beaming. The attention to her wound by an intern at the railway clinic where they first saw Isabella, and a set of fresh bandages, had obviously made her feel better. And hopeful. They all felt that, too.

"The south," Becca said. "The sun feels so amazing."

Isabella was feeling better, too. She had eaten two large meals since they'd found her in the clinic, had called her friends in Bologna, had slept like a stone, and was anxious to return home as soon as possible. Chief Inspector Yazinsky tried to persuade her to take a police escort back to Bologna, but two friends from her university met her at the airport. After a long round of good-byes and tears and hugs, Wade said, "Thank you for everything you are doing. You are the most amazing person. . . ."

"So are you," Isabella said. "So are you all. I will call your father, Wade, when I reach Bologna. You will all see me again."

They left Isabella with her friends to await a connecting flight.

Then, at a little after three o'clock, after using Terence's Ackroyd's credit card to withdraw euros from an airport ATM, the kids and Inspector Yazinsky climbed aboard a launch called a vaporetto for the hour-long water ride into Venice. They settled into seats by the windows facing east and were soon motoring past long strips of land that Lily's maps told them surrounded and formed the giant Venice lagoon.

"This is great," Becca said. "We can almost pretend we're tourists."

"Almost," said Wade. "We should blend in, but be alert to everything."

Lily knew this was true. They were seriously the furthest thing from being tourists. None of what they saw, heard, or thought about was what a tourist saw or heard or thought about. Everything meant something on their quest for the relic. After all, would this strange place, so far from everything they were learning in Russia, give them the vital information they sought?

She hoped so.

The vaporetto slowed and sidled into the dock. They emerged by a series of walkways and ramps into the Piazza San Marco—Saint Mark's Square.

Now that it was midafternoon on a warm day, the area was thronged with tourists. It was almost too much for Lily not to run over and talk to fellow Americans, but it was out of the question, as the inspector kept telling them.

"We are undercover," he said, "as much as a Russian inspector and three American teenagers can be undercover."

The immense domed Basilica di San Marco loomed over the square on one end. Adjacent to it was the Doge's Palace, a colonnaded structure with rose-shaped cutouts and a long gallery of pointed arches. Everywhere else were outdoor cafés and stalls selling postcards and scarves and every kind of souvenir. Pigeons constantly fluttered up and settled here and there across the stones. And then there were the canals: wide avenues of water between blocks of buildings, and narrower inlets down the side streets, alleys, and passages.

"So beautiful and warm," said Wade, making notes about the sites in his notebook. "Strange sensation. My fingers don't actually ache."

"Going back will be hard," said Lily. "Mostly on my toes."

When they entered the plaza between the twin pillars of San Marco and San Teodoro, Becca stopped dead. Against one side of the piazza stood a tower whose main feature was a giant twenty-four-hour astronomical clock. The face of the clock was brilliant blue, the numbers around its face—Roman numerals, of course—were gold, and at the center stood an unmoving, dull-colored globe representing the earth.

"It is pre-Copernican, is it not?" asked the inspector.

"It is," said Becca. "The earth is in the center of the clock, as if the sun were revolving around it."

"Kind of my line," said Wade, nudging her. "But exactly right."

"The tower is called the Torre dell'Orologio. Saint Mark's Clock Tower," Lily said. "Built in 1497."

The fiery, smiling face of the sun was mounted on the

hour hand. The face was divided into several concentric discs, which, they guessed, turned at different speeds to reflect the movement of the sun and the moon around the earth. The moon was an orb sunk halfway into its circling disc, and turned on its own axis. Half the orb was blue, the other half gold, and when it revolved, the golden half illustrated the phases, from new moon to full and back again.

"It's so beautiful," Becca said. "It makes you think that astronomy—and Copernicus—are everywhere."

"They are everywhere," the inspector whispered as he scanned the piazza. "But Galina is here as well. Let us lay low until the opera."

That brought Lily and the rest of them back to reality. They weren't tourists. They had never been tourists.

After finding reasonably priced clothing shops, where they bought a few scarves and a necktie each for Wade and Inspector Yazinsky, they hid out the rest of the day.

At twenty minutes before nine, under stars glittering like jewels against the blue Venetian sky, they arrived at the old opera house, hoping to peel away yet another layer of the onion.

CHAPTER FORTY-ONE

Saint Petersburg

Near the intersection of Rimskogo-Korsakova and Sadovaya Streets stood Saint Petersburg's Central Railway Museum.

To Darrell it was a world of dust. A bright young man who looked like he did everything from cataloging ancient maps to mopping the floors ushered them into a large, frigid room known as the Cherepanov Archives. The collection included virtually untouched and unexamined historical and topographical maps from the last one hundred sixty years of railway exploration.

Narrowing their search was Isabella Mercanti's vague but vital clue—"Greywolf"—along with a surprise lead the detective Paul Ferrere had brought from Paris: an unidentified private jet had been tracked into the wastelands north and east of the city.

One hour earlier, Paul had met them at the train station and introduced his colleague. "My right-hand operative, Marceline Dufort," he said.

"Dufort?" said Roald as they headed for a taxicab. "Are you related at all to—"

"I am Bernard's sister," she said.

Like Isabella's husband, Bernard Dufort was another original member of Asterias, and a Guardian. His murder in Paris had led directly to the death of Heinrich Vogel—Uncle Henry—which had then led the Kaplans to become involved in the relic hunt.

"Wow, we're pleased to have you with us," said Darrell. "Thanks for helping."

At the museum, Marceline located a large map from 1852 and spread it out on one of the many worktables in the main map room. "Let us begin with this."

Paul traced his finger across it, north from Madrid. "The jet that Galina Krause flies is a Mystère-Falcon," he said. "On a full tank, the Falcon has a flying range of two thousand kilometers. If she flew from Madrid to here, she would have to refuel, most likely in Berlin, where we know she has a private airstrip. Assuming that she did not refuel again, a straight flight from Berlin to the Saint Petersburg area would have landed her no farther than this area."

He circled a two-hundred-mile region of forests and hills to the northeast of the city. "Because we believe the fortress was a former headquarters of the KGB, and thus within heavily monitored airspace, no present-day satellite map we could find shows its exact location. That is why our search of old maps may provide our only real evidence of Greywolf's existence."

Darrell felt upbeat for the first time in days. "We're getting closer, Dad."

"I think so, too."

They each took a different group of maps and scoured the region, with, at first, little luck. Then Darrell found something. He *thought* he found something. While searching a crusty French map from 1848 of the forests of the Republic of Karelia—in the center of Galina's flight zone—Darrell found himself squinting at the tiniest inked writing he had ever seen. Inside a series of concentric circles meant to designate a hill were six almost invisible letters.

Chât. L.G.

"What does *chat* mean in French?" he asked.

Marceline smiled. "It means 'cat.' Where do you see this?"

He pressed his finger on the map. Marceline saw what he was pointing at, and her smile dropped. "No, no. *Chat* means 'cat,' but *chât* with a period and an accent like this means it is an abbreviation. It could mean *château*. 'Castle.'"

Roald was by his side now, bending over the map. "What could the initials *LG* mean?"

"Ah!" said Paul, sharing a look with his colleague. "Your son has found something. *LG* are not the initials for a person. *LG* very probably means *loup gris*."

"Dad?" said Darrell.

Roald instantly put his arms around him. "*Loup gris* is 'grey wolf.' You found your mother, Darrell. You found her!"

CHAPTER FORTY-TWO

Venice

The Gran Teatro opera house was a simple stone box with four columns separating large, dark-paneled entry portals.

Now that they were hiding behind the base of a large statue of a man in armor, knowing that Galina would soon be there, Wade was a mess of nerves. His senses were raw. Everything meant something. Nothing meant nothing, and he needed to take in every detail.

"Let us wait and watch," the inspector whispered. "Once everyone enters, we will lose ourselves in the crowd."

"I feel so out of place," Becca said.

"No way," said Lily. "We're as important as anybody. More important, I'd say. Just think about what we're doing. Who else in this crowd is after an ancient relic *and* a murderer *and* is a Guardian *and* is going to see a famous opera? Nobody but us. Not that anyone will ever know, because real heroes don't seek the spotlight, but we'll know."

"You're starting to talk like Darrell now," Wade said.

"He must have infected me," she said.

At ten minutes before nine, four boys in feathered costumes descended the stairs, ringing hand bells. This was the signal that it was time to enter the opera house.

"That is our invitation," the inspector said. "Let's find our box. Be alert."

Weaving into the crowd, the four ascended the stairs and were greeted by two smiling attendants in muted uniforms. Presenting their ticket, which was apparently good for up to eight people, they entered the lobby. A wide and tall flight of carpeted stairs stood ahead of them. It led to the upper seats.

"Box Three-Seventeen is on the third tier, halfway up," Becca said, holding Boris's ticket. "I feel like we're approaching the scene of a crime now that Boris is . . . you know."

Wade nodded. "Me, too. Everybody, keep your eyes open."

"And ears," said Lily. "This is an opera, after all."

"Well said," added the inspector.

They were finally shown to *scatola del teatro* 317 by a woman in a maroon suit. She unlocked the door and let them into a narrow room opening up to the inside of the theater. A heavy velvet curtain hung from the ceiling of the box, separating the hallway door from the seats.

When Wade gently pulled the curtain aside, he gasped. "Are you kidding me?"

From the square outside, the plain facade of Gran Teatro La Fenice gave little hint of the opulent and enormous theater inside. The walls were painted gold. Sconces of spherical lights outside each box shone like fairy bulbs on the orchestra-level seats below. Dozens of boxes on five levels were filling up, while hundreds of people moved about in the aisles below. The orchestra pit was peopled by black-suited musicians, tuning, playing scales and melodies, chatting, or calmly waiting for everyone to sit.

Their box opened onto the hall like its own stage, while the box itself was luxury Wade had never experienced before. Beside the velvet-covered railing were eight tufted armchairs aimed at a precise angle to the stage. The chairs were gold and white and reminded him of the furniture in Terence's apartment in New York. As if the theater weren't showy enough, a heavy crystal chandelier hung from the center of the ceiling, bathing the hall in brilliant, warm light. It blinked once, twice, and they sat down in the shadows of the box and waited.

Wade knew Mozart, of course, though Bach, being so mathematical, was his favorite composer. Still, he was eager to hear *The Magic Flute* and wished Darrell were there with him to appreciate it. On the other hand, he wanted to be discovering the location of Greywolf with Darrell and his father in Saint Petersburg, too. He decided to phone his father. It went to voice mail. He tried Darrell and that too went to voice mail.

Five minutes passed. No one entered the box from the hall. The lights dimmed. The last remaining guests took their seats; everyone quieted.

"I hope they find where Greywolf is," Wade whispered.

"They will," said Becca.

"I believe so, too," said the inspector. "Let me tell you, I will be happy to get you back together with them as soon as I can. I am far out of my comfort here. But hush now. It begins. Eyes open."

The conductor waved his baton several times, and the audience's quiet turned to utter silence. It was an amazing moment, but nothing like the one that followed, when the conductor flicked his baton up.

Coming from such profound silence, the initial chord of the overture was thunderous and deep, a call to attention and an invitation to the mystery to follow, as if to say, *Wake up! Listen, and you'll hear a fantastic story . . . !*

From that instant on, Wade was hooked.

Whenever Becca heard a piece of music that touched her somehow—and *The Magic Flute*'s overture was exhilarating and deeply moving—she wanted to share it right away with her sister. Maggie was far more musical than she was. As soon as she made it back to Austin, and everyone was safe again, Becca would share this, too.

The overture ended with booming chords, kettle drums, and bright strings, and the audience applauded wildly. This lasted several seconds, until the conductor raised his baton high once more, and the hall quieted again.

With intimations of danger, the stage curtain lifted on a scene of stylized rocks in a wilderness of mountains.

A man named Tamino came in singing urgently. The insistent strains of violins rose and fell behind him. Still singing, he pulled an arrow out of a quiver and shot it offstage.

The arrow reminded Becca that they were looking for Galina. She scanned the rows of spectators below. But would the leader of the Teutonic Order be sitting among them? No, she'd be moving around like a cat, in the halls, maybe in the high seats, searching.

The children in the audience shrieked with delight. A green, scaly, outrageously horned, and slightly comical serpent appeared. A serpent, of all things!

With human feet obviously visible below the scaly hide, the serpent opened its mechanical jaws. It belched out a cloud of red smoke, as if it were breathing fire. It lunged awkwardly at the man, who shot more arrows. Then the serpent wounded the man. He fell. At the same time, three cloaked figures emerged from behind one of the strange rock formations. They carried spears, and—singing, of course—they stabbed the serpent, who fell over in a heap, which set the children cheering once more.

Despite the opera's comedic elements, Becca saw another story unfolding. The evil serpent was Albrecht. Copernicus was the archer, and the three mysterious helpers who slayed the serpent were none other than the Guardians.

Becca glanced over at Lily and Wade. Their mouths were open, their eyes fixed on the stage. She tapped Lily's hand.

Lily turned to her. Her cheeks were wet. "It's so . . ."

"It is!" Becca whispered.

The opera was performed in German, but the supertitles were in Italian. Either way, only Becca and, from the look of it, Inspector Yazinsky understood the story, though it was easy enough to grasp the action. After the serpent-slaying scene, there appeared a comical friend of the archer. This was the bird catcher Papageno, a scruffy-looking guy laden with birdcages. *Birdcages!* She thought of Boris again and grew sad. Though parts of the story were funny, it was hard not to see it as deadly serious. The story centered on a flute with magical powers, but its true meaning was in the trials of the young archer and a young woman who was the captive of a bunch of evil people. That, too, was like their life right now.

Sara was the captive.

After what seemed like a short while but was nearly an hour, Wade leaned over to her and Lily. He was frowning. "If no one's going to show, maybe the message for Boris is hidden in the box somewhere. Or maybe we've been fooled—"

The hall door whooshed open behind them and the velvet curtain twisted aside. An older woman in a gown stood there, clutching the curtain, her face as pale as ice. Inspector Yazinsky rose instantly. "Madam, you are hurt?"

"Where is Boris?" she gasped. "Galina Krause . . ."

"Boris is dead," Wade said, rising from his chair. "Galina killed him. Is she *here*—?"

The woman stumbled forward, tearing the curtain from its rings. She fell awkwardly toward the inspector, then slid to the floor among the chairs. The black handle of a knife protruded from her side.

"She . . . took . . . it . . . ," the woman gasped.

"It? Boris's message?" asked Wade.

The inspector bolted out the door into the hall. "I'll follow Galina."

"I'll get a doctor!" said Wade, and he ran out of the box with the inspector.

"Help is coming," Lily said to the woman as she and Becca knelt next to her.

"I never knew what the message meant," the woman mumbled. "Only Boris . . . the clock . . ." Her voice faded as the music continued.

"What clock?" asked Lily. "Did you have a clock for Boris?"

"Midnight . . ." The woman's eyes glazed, and breath rushed out of her mouth.

"Oh no. Oh no." Becca leaned over the railing. "Doctor!" she cried. "We need a doctor!" People in the neighboring boxes tried at first to shush her. *"Medico!"* she shouted. *"Abbiamo bisogno di un medico!"*

The music stopped raggedly. Faces stared up from the orchestra and the stage. The rear door of the box opened. Wade rushed in with a handful of medical personnel.

"Galina stole the message, a clock," Lily said. "Where's the inspector?"

"Following her. Come on!" Wade took Becca and Lily by the wrists and pulled them after him. "She's escaping, but we can catch her." They pushed against the crushing flow of people running to box 317.

CHAPTER FORTY-THREE

Wade was out quickly enough to see Inspector Yazinsky racing after Galina down a set of stone steps leading to the water. Galina flew like a shadow around a corner and vanished. Wade panicked. She reappeared on the stone landing.

"Is she alone?" asked Becca "I don't see—"

"Not likely," said Lily. "Not if there's a relic at stake."

But is the relic here? Wade wondered as they tore down the steps to the inspector. Or was Galina in Venice only to intercept the message meant for Boris? And a message about what? From whom? Galina wouldn't take this side trip from Russia by herself. Then where were the others?

The Italian faction of the Order they hadn't seen yet?

They reached the water just as Galina hopped into a waiting motorboat. The man at the helm didn't look like an agent of the Order, but he gunned the engine loudly, and the boat roared away. The inspector waved to the boats, calling in Russian. They didn't move.

Becca pushed down the steps in front of him. *"Un motoscafo! Presto!"*

One started up his motor and whirred quietly toward the landing. *"Sì? Per dove?"*

Becca pointed down the canal. *"Seguire quella barca!"*

The pilot wagged his head from side to side when the inspector drew out his badge. Then Lily waved a ten-euro note at him. *"Sì! Sì!"* he said. They jumped in. He threw the boat into gear.

What Wade hoped would be a high-speed chase was anything but. The canal outside the theater, Rio delle Veste, was narrow and clogged with scores of black gondolas moored along the sides. Slicing past them, Galina's boat nearly tore one of them in half.

"Faster!" said Wade.

"Is electric motor," the pilot said. "For eco, yes?"

"That woman stole something from us!" Becca snapped. "Chase her!"

"*Sì,* but, *la polizia,*" said the pilot.

"I *am* the *polizia!*" boomed the inspector, slapping his badge again.

"Not here you not," the driver said.

Lily pushed two more bills into his hand. "Go!"

The pilot shrugged and hit the accelerator. They made up some of the distance, but Galina's gas-powered boat was pulling away. Then, seconds before it vanished around the corner, she turned back, her hair flying around her face. There was a silent flash of light from the vicinity of her hip, a splash, and the sound of a thud striking their motorboat below the waterline.

The inspector tugged out a small pistol. "Keep your heads down!"

"*Che cosa?*" the driver cried out. "*No, no—*"

When Galina's own driver realized she was firing a gun, he cut the engine and began shouting at her. So, he wasn't one of her agents. She whipped her gun at him, and he splashed noisily into the canal. She took the wheel herself.

"Please!" Becca urged. "It's life and death!"

"Death of motor license!" the pilot said, even as he jammed down the accelerator.

They trailed Galina left onto the curving Rio dei Barcaroli. Pedestrians on the bridges overhead shouted in punctuated phrases—curses, Wade was certain— but their boat sped underneath, barely squeezing past gondolas that looked suddenly like bobbing coffins. Galina yelled out something in Italian, and dark figures swarmed out of the shadows on the sides of the canal and darted across the bridges, taking aim with pistols.

Shots slapped dully into the water in front of their boat. The pilot swerved once, twice, eluding them, and made it past the bridge. Galina's boat thundered north onto the Rio di San Luca. Wade saw an approaching marker leaning over the canal like a dented street sign. Rio Fuseri. "She's heading for the Grand Canal. We can cut her off if we go right."

"Please," the driver said. "Too much traffic. Too much police launches. Is forbidden."

"I'll deal with them," said Yazinsky. "Do as Wade says!"

Another ten euros from Lily and the driver roared into the Rio Fuseri, picking up speed as they lost sight of her.

"This better be the right move," Lily growled. "We could lose her altogether."

"We won't," Wade said, hoping he was right. Galina had stolen what they needed desperately—without leverage, his stepmother was in more danger. He wasn't going to leave Venice without it. The canal was blocked at the next intersection with a mangle of gondolas. The driver sped right, then turned left behind the great piazza. They could see the domes of the basilica lit up like giant festive balloons.

They zigzagged right, then left and left again, away from the piazza, and burst suddenly out onto the Grand Canal in a wide sweep of spray. The famous Rialto Bridge arched over the water straight ahead. And there was Galina, headlights glaring, speeding toward them from the opposite direction. Her face was pale, angry, startled.

She cut her engine suddenly. Wade studied her face, her strange, hypnotic eyes glinting in the canal lights, the hanging lamps, the lacquered hulls of the gondolas, the lights from the houses looming over the water. Time seemed to pause for a second. He saw in her eyes that she would do anything to avoid being caught.

Shoot them all dead, if she had to.

Then it was over. She gunned the engine and aimed toward them.

Inspector Yazinsky aimed his pistol. "Full speed ahead!"

"*Sul serio?*" their driver spat. He matched Galina's speed, his motor whirring like a top, then tried to steer away when he realized she wasn't going to stop. Too late. The boats scraped each other horribly, and Wade found himself a bare two feet away from Galina. His legs took over, and he leaped from their boat right onto the deck of hers.

An instantaneously stupid move. He crashed to his knees, then staggered to his feet, pain knifing up his legs. Galina whipped him across the face with the side of her hand. Her hand!

It was ice-cold and strong as steel. It flattened him. He tried to climb to his feet, but she had the engine at full throttle. He thudded awkwardly onto the deck, half on and half off the boat, water spitting into his face. He arched up again. "You! Always you!" she cried, kicking his legs out from under him.

He slammed back to the deck but managed to swing his arm around, clamping onto her leg. He pulled with all his strength. She fell to the planks. The engine idled while the wheel was locked in an ever-widening turn.

"Wade!" Becca yelled from somewhere. "You—"

"Stop at once!" the inspector bellowed at Galina.

Wade couldn't hear the rest. He grasped at Galina's hand, trying to force the gun away from her, when he saw a shiny disc on the deck. The clock! She had dropped it! Releasing Galina, risking that she would turn the gun back on him, he dived for the clock with both hands, when she swung her gun at his head. It was like being struck by a baseball bat. He was up and over the side, half falling, half jumping, and fell headfirst into the canal.

CHAPTER FORTY-FOUR

"Wade! Omigod, Wade!"

Becca was half out of their boat as it drew alongside, grasping at the water with the inspector. Wade flailed and splashed like a drowning man. Together they lifted him out.

"I have it," he gasped, spitting out a mouthful of canal water. "I . . ."

"Here come the police launches," said Yazinsky.

"Galina took off," Lily added. "She's gone. We can't get stuck here. Come on."

Becca draped her jacket over Wade's shivering shoulders, and she and Lily squashed him between them. Their awesome driver, to whom Lily gave another twenty euros, motored them quickly to the nearest landing. Hurried away by the inspector, the kids disappeared into the crowded streets just as the Venice traffic police arrived with sirens blaring.

At the first corner, Wade stopped hobbling along. "Wait," he said. "Look."

When he showed them what he had stolen from Galina, Becca recognized it instantly. "That's a souvenir of the Saint Mark's clock. The astronomical clock in Piazza San Marco. The messenger said it was a clue for Boris that only he would understand."

"She also said 'midnight,'" Lily added.

"It's nearly midnight now," Yazinsky said. "Do you think that Boris was to go to the clock in the piazza?"

Wade shivered in Becca's jacket. "I don't know. But there's probably something with the clock that we need to see. There are bells, right? Chimes? Maybe something will happen when they ring at midnight, something that Boris was supposed to see."

"Quickly, then," the inspector urged.

They zigzagged through the streets, the inspector leading them along the fringes of any piazzas they had to cross, joining bunches of tourists as a shield. They saw neither Galina nor any agents she might have in Venice. Four minutes before midnight, they emerged from the Salita San Moise, through the colonnade, and into Piazza San Marco. Even at that late hour, the crowds were heavy and noisy. Soon the bell atop the tower began to chime, struck by two monumental bronze figures with hammers. Twenty-four slow, momentous peals that seemed to roll beneath the stones under their feet and out into the lagoon.

At the fading of the last of the echoes, everyone resumed their strolling and talking. Becca, Wade, Lily, and Inspector Yazinsky just stared at the clock. A minute passed, another minute, five minutes.

"Nothing's happening," said Lily. "What did the messenger mean? 'Midnight'? Are we supposed to go up there and find something behind the clock or in the mechanism or something? What's the message? Don't tell me we have to climb up there. . . ."

"I can get us in, if it comes to that," Yazinsky said.

On a whim, Becca hurried over to a vendor's stall just closing up. She quickly found souvenir clocks similar to the one meant for Boris. But they were not identical. She called them over. "These souvenirs are trinkets, not nearly as detailed as ours is. Ours is metal, not plastic, with movable faces and all. It's much more like the real one."

Wade took Boris's clock from her. Even before being

aware of it, his fingers started working the miniature like a Rubik's Cube, twisting and turning its various faces and dials, trying to match its faces to the one on the tower, setting the time to midnight.

A shrill whistle sounded from the motor launch landing along the water's edge. It would soon make its final run to the airport.

"We should go," said Lily.

"Hold on," he said, still working the miniature clock, shifting its movable parts to show the exact moment of midnight. Nothing happened. It was a dead metal toy in his hands, until he twisted the tiny moon's face a fraction backward, so less gold peered out of its face. Then—*click*—the back of the clock sprang open in his palm.

CHAPTER FORTY-FIVE

Under the warm blue-black sky, her heart thumping at this new discovery, Becca studied the device in Wade's palm. Inside its open cover were four unusual characters—not inscribed, but scratched, roughly, as if in haste.

"They are not Cyrillic," Yazinsky said. "I have never seen such marks."

Wade moved the clock closer to the nearest lamp-light and turned to Becca.

"Don't ask me," she said. "I was going to ask if they're math symbols or something from physics maybe."

He shook his head. "I don't know all the symbols in trigonometry—my dad does—but these aren't any astronomical or mathematical symbols I've ever seen. Hieroglyphics, maybe?"

Becca didn't think so.

"If Darrell were here," Lily said, "he'd go, 'Aaatheee.' Because if you squint, the letters almost look like they could be *A-T-H-E*—"

Becca breathed in sharply. "Boris was a scholar of dead languages. This message was meant for him. A dead language from some old civilization. Oh, what did Boris say at the restaurant about it . . . ? Wade, your notebook."

His cell phone buzzed. "Here." He gave her the note-book. "It's Darrell. It's three in the morning there!" He switched the phone on speaker. "Darrell, what's going on—"

"Greywolf is a creepy old castle," Darrell inter-rupted, his voice hoarse, faraway, gloomy. "We checked it a dozen different ways on lots of crumbly old maps, and we're sure. It's two hundred miles from anywhere.

Plus it's, well, never mind. You have to meet us in Saint Petersburg. Pulkovo Airport it's called. We'll fly from here. What's happening down there?"

"We got a little wet," Becca said. "Mostly Wade. Galina stole the message meant for Boris, but Wade fought her and stole it back. We don't know what it says yet."

"Don't tell Dad about me fighting her," Wade said. He took a breath. "Boris's contact in Venice was attacked by Galina. We had to leave her. I don't know . . ."

"The Order is taking out the Guardians, one by one," the inspector said, leaning in to the phone.

"Is there any word about Mom?" asked Wade.

"Just get here as soon as you can, that's all."

The call ended with that grim statement. The launch blasted its horn once more for passengers.

"Come, come," Yazinsky said. "There's no reason anymore to remain in Venice. We must return to Russia."

An hour later, the four of them were in their seats on a small jet ascending from the Marco Polo Airport. After a brief layover in Moscow, they would arrive in Saint Petersburg at dawn on Sunday. The day of the midnight deadline.

At which time a weird machine would do something horrible to Sara.

"Listen to this," Becca said, studying Wade's notebook. "Boris said that a world-famous code was solved when he and his brother were young and living in Siberia. That must have been in the 1950s. He said that *A* and *B* was a kind of joke to them. And they sent coded messages 'even when we grow up.' What do you think that means? That *A* and *B* was a joke?"

Lily nodded. "I'm typing it all in—Boris, Aleksandr, *A*, *B*, dead languages, Siberia, the whole business."

Wade stared out the window down at the receding lights of Venice. Only from up there could he truly see the serpentine shape of the Grand Canal that he had fallen into, winding away through the narrow streets of the city. "Aleksandr is dead, so someone else sent Boris this message in their old code."

Lily let out a long slow breath, her fingers poised over the tablet's screen. "Well . . . there was something called Linear A and Linear B, ancient languages discovered in the early twentieth century. No one has cracked A, but Linear B was decrypted in the 1950s."

"When Boris and Aleksandr were boys," said Becca.

"It is a wonder to watch you work," the inspector said. "You are rather amazing."

"Thanks," said Lily. "We're learning." She hit another link, then another, started scrolling and scrolling, then stopped. "Yes, oh, yes! This is it. The message inside the clock is written in Linear B. Look."

She flipped the tablet around for everyone to see.

"The note for Boris uses the symbols of Linear B," she said. "Each symbol translates to the sound shown

underneath each character."

The four characters of the message . . . translated to . . . *wo ro ku ta*.

"What's *worokuta*?" Becca asked. "Lil, again, please?"

She typed that in. "There's 'Wirikuta.' It's a site sacred to the Wixárika Nation, Indians in Mexico. It's supposed to be the place the world was created—"

"No," Becca said.

"It's *not* where the world was created?" asked Wade.

"No, *worokuta* is not *Wirikuta*," she said, "because there are actual Linear B symbols for 'wi' and 'ri,' but the message uses the ones for 'wo' and 'ro,' which means that whoever sent it was saying something else to Boris."

They looked to the inspector. "I am sorry. I wish I could tell you what *worokuta* means, but I studied criminal justice, not dead languages. It means nothing to me."

They all went quiet. Their most recent rest had been on the flight to Venice, many long hours before. Since then, the attack on the Guardian messenger at the opera, the canal chase, the enigma of the clock's strange code, and Darrell's gloomy message had left them drained and exhausted.

They really needed to rest.

But Wade knew they never would.

CHAPTER FORTY-SIX

Saint Petersburg
March 24

D arrell stared from the windows of the arrivals hall at Saint Petersburg's Pulkovo Airport as he had without pause for nearly three hours, hoping every incoming flight would be his brother's jet from Venice by way of Moscow.

His stepfather was pacing as usual, but Darrell found himself frozen to the spot, unable to do anything but scan the sky for incoming aircraft. He feared that the moment he left his post, or moved a single atom of air, the last three hours of fruitless waiting would reset and begin again.

Greywolf was a centuries-old fortress buried in ever-green forests and rocky terrain more than two hundred miles from where he was standing. His mother was a prisoner there, trapped inside a device that was ticking down to midnight that night, a mere fifteen hours away.

But if Galina Krause had kidnapped his mother as ransom to force them to give her Vela—and Serpens, if they had it—why, Darrell asked himself, why was his mother in a machine ticking down to something horrible?

Why kill my mother?

What does the machine do?

A flurry of people broke into the baggage area. Looking exhausted, dragging luggage, they swarmed across the floor. Then he saw three people weaving through the crowd, running when they could, followed by a tall mustached man. There was Lily's worried face. Then Wade's. Finally Becca's. There was no reunion, no time for one.

"Terence will be here soon," Darrell said, hurrying to meet them. "Flying one of those NetJet thingies, a private plane from London. He's a pilot. A good one, they say. Anyway, Greywolf is an old castle, two hundred miles outside the city. An hour's flight. Once we get started."

"Darrell found the fortress," Roald told them. "We confirmed and double confirmed it, but he found it first."

"It's that brain." Wade gave Darrell a soft punch in the arm. "Every once in a while, he blows out the cobwebs, and it works. It even surprises him. Not us, though."

Darrell wanted to laugh, but he couldn't make himself. All he saw was his mother's face and *it*—a giant clockwork machine . . . gears and wheels . . . "Greywolf is a horrible place. But we have help." He nodded toward the two investigators, who were busily checking their computers. "They're coming with us."

Terence landed at noon, two hours later than expected. He'd had to switch jets at the last moment, for one with a greater flight range.

"So sorry," he said. "But the delay gave me time to consult with the archivist at the Ministry of Defence in London. She discovered a rare aerial snapshot of the area taken in 1941. It's apparently the last clear photo of the place before the Soviets completed camouflaging the grounds. The image indicates a private landing strip on the Greywolf property." He enlarged it on his phone. "Pray that the strip is still functional."

As soon as his jet had refueled, the Kaplans, Paul, and Marceline took their seats in the cabin and Terence in the cockpit. The jet was a sleek winged missile with a single large cabin, and a half-dozen swivel chairs and low tables. According to Terence, it was quite fast and nimble.

"There's an arctic blast roaring down from Finland," he said from the cockpit. "We've no time to lose if we're to stay ahead of it."

Within minutes, the jet was speeding down the tarmac. It lifted off into a bleak gray sky, even as the first wave of snow moved in from the west. Darrell checked his watch. It was 1:07 p.m. Ten hours and fifty-three minutes to midnight.

CHAPTER FORTY-SEVEN

Republic of Karelia, Northwest Russia

Now that they were on their way to Greywolf—all
eight of them—Lily wondered if they would bust
into Galina's creepy lair with guns blazing and bombs
booming. Well, guns, anyway. The two private investigators were huddled together, checking and rechecking
their weapons.

"The Red Brotherhood will be in force," Paul Ferrere
said. "We must expect a battle."

"We will shield you to do your work," said Marceline.

Our work, Lily thought. *We know that Sara's there, caged
up in a machine with gears and wheels and junk—whatever*

that is. But is the relic there, too? And what about worokuta?

Becca and Wade were furiously consulting their notebooks to put that latest clue into place. Lily knew that soon her digital fiddling wouldn't cut it anymore. The relic hunt, the *Sara* hunt, would soon become physical. Analog. Trekking through the trees and rocks and snow. Not Lily's area of intelligence officering.

But right now she was ready for the next digital problem they might throw at her.

"Anything?" she asked.

Wade tapped a page in his notebook. "There are words I must have gotten wrong when Boris was talking. He said 'log punked.' Remember that?"

"I do," said Darrell. "He and Alek sent messages to each other 'even in log punked.'"

"Well, I know I got it wrong," said Wade, "but does anyone remember it better?"

Lily had forgotten *log punked*. Probably because she'd been too busy deciding which of Boris's eyes to respond to.

But Uncle Roald tilted his head as if searching the air between their seats. "You told me Boris said he grew up in a labor camp, because that's where his father was sent after the Second World War, right? Well, the Soviet system of labor camps was called the gulag. It's an anagram of some kind, but the 'ag' in Russian is a common thing. Maybe Boris was saying *l-a-g* something, not *l-o-g* something. Whatever that might mean."

"Is that enough to start?" Becca asked Lily.

"Since you asked so nicely . . ." But no sooner had Lily keyed in the letters *l-a-g-p-u* than the search window filled in the remaining letters.

l-a-g-p-u-n-k-t

Holding her fingers up to get everyone's attention, she hit Enter.

The plane bucked once, and her screen froze. The connection was severed.

Terence came on the address system. "Sorry about that. The storm is moving down really fast—" Another slight loss of altitude shook the cabin. "I'm trying to fly south of it. It'll increase our flying time, but maybe we can gain time later. Hold on."

A few rough minutes passed before they were cruising more steadily. Lily tried again. The connection was restored. She rekeyed the search on *lagpunkt* and hit Enter for the second time. The screen refreshed.

"'A *lagpunkt* is a subsection of a forced labor camp,'" she read. "Which is helpful but not too specific." She hit a second link, which featured an excerpt from a book about the history of Siberian labor camps. She silently scanned a paragraph about the day the inmates received the news of Josef Stalin's death in 1953—Stalin being the guy who'd exiled many of them to the labor camps in the first place. It said that Stalin would be buried with honors in Red Square. Boris had told them that, too. Lily quickly read the rest of the piece, then nearly jumped out of her seat.

In a very slow voice, she said, "There is a reference here to . . . to . . . Hey, are you all listening? There is a reference here to a . . . 'Vorkuta *lagpunkt.*'"

Becca gasped. "Vorkuta! *Worokuta!* Lily, you—are—brilliant!"

"I know, right?" Lily said. "There's got to be more." Which there was. Again, thanks to the nifty feature that filled in the letters of a possible search even before you keyed it all in, she typed *v-o-r-k* and, boom, the term was identified.

"Vorkuta is a Russian industrial city in Siberia, about eleven hundred miles from Saint Petersburg. We're actually flying in the same direction right now. It was a big coal mining area from the nineteen thirties. There was a prison camp there until the nineteen seventies. Now it's a giant city with a shrinking population and not much coal. . . ."

"So what are we saying?" asked Darrell. "That's where the relic is? Or part of it?"

"Maybe," said Roald. "But if there were any records, we *might* find that Vorkuta is where Boris and his brother grew up, and where they sent coded messages to each other."

"Whoa." Becca's eyes widened. "Someone sent a coded message to Boris that said 'Vorkuta'?"

"But Aleksandr is dead," said Wade. "I have proof right here in my pocket. So who would send the message, and what would it mean to Boris?"

"Those are the questions," Roald said. "After the witnesses, the dental records, all of Boris's research, he would never have believed Alek was sending him a message. He knew Alek was dead. But maybe Alek hid something in Vorkuta, and a Guardian found it and sent a message to Boris. The Guardian used the old code, knowing that Boris would have to come. He just never got the message."

The nose of the jet dropped suddenly. Water bottles, mugs, whatever was loose flew off the tables. Becca nearly dropped the diary. Overhead lights flickered.

"Whoa!" Darrell said. "What's going on—"

The jet dipped again, this time at a steeper angle,

and the engines shrieked in protest.

"The storm," said Wade. "Maybe the wings are icing over—"

"Stay put!" Roald staggered to the cockpit, throwing the door open. "What's the trouble?"

"Wind shear!" Terence said, working hard to lift the jet back up and keep control. "Unfortunately, we have to head right back into the track of the storm."

"We're close to Greywolf, are we not?" Marceline asked as she studied the chart.

"Very close, I think," Terence said.

"Can you keep going?" Darrell asked, clutching the door frame next to his father. Wade was out of his seat now too, and staggering down the aisle to the front.

"The wings have iced up and are starting to drag us down," Terence murmured. "I don't know how long I can—"

The words were lost under the sound of the crying engines. Lily stared at Becca. They were both clutching their seat handles so tightly neither could move. "Becca, we better not be going to cra—"

"Don't say it! Don't you dare!"

One of the engines began to whine strangely. The jet tilted suddenly. Wade spun down the aisle and landed on the floor in front of Becca. She screamed.

"I have to land!" Terence said. "Brace yourselves; it's going to be rough!"

The next thing Lily knew, everything was bouncing around the cabin. Roald and Darrell slid back into the aisle sideways, then pitched forward again. Paul crawled over to help them. There was a deep groan of metal. The landing gear dropped. The underside of the jet beneath their feet was battered from below. The jet was slicing into the trees.

"I see a clearing—hold tight!"

"We're going down!" Lily yelled.

Branches slapped the wings; then there was a thunderous squeal of metal as the landing gear and the hull of the jet went skidding along the frozen ground. As hard as Lily tried, she couldn't keep herself together. She started screaming.

CHAPTER FORTY-EIGHT

Greywolf

In the large, lead-lined tower of Greywolf, Ebner von Braun observed the miserable form of Sara Kaplan, folded inside the cage at the center of Kronos, shivering like a waif in a storm. It crossed his mind that even if she did not know precisely what awaited her, she must have had an inkling, a premonition, and it was taking its toll on her health. *Expendable.* That was the word Galina had used.

Helmut Bern clacked furiously on his computer, attempting to finish the patch of programming necessary to resuscitate the crude prototype.

Screening out for a moment the machine's pathetic

inmate, Ebner gazed over his own workmanship. If Kronos I was crude, he had to admit that it was also very beautiful. It had survived the terrible fire and suffered four years of disuse, but Helmut, good soldier that he was, had burnished the machine to a brilliant sheen and restored its moving parts to pristine running order.

In a rage since her empty-handed return from Venice, Galina scowled suddenly. "We should send her now! Send her!"

Bern nearly turned himself inside out with shock. "What? No! Please not yet! She'll be destroyed in transit." Then, his breath blooming icily in front of him, he whined, "Miss Krause . . . I beg you . . ."

Galina sneered and looked away. A reprieve for poor Helmut.

"You are an obedient servant, Helmut Bern," Ebner said with, he hoped, a hint of irony.

Kronos was mostly Ebner's own handiwork—based on Galina's fevered vision—and he loved it like a first, awkward child. He was elated to see it humming once more, and horrified to realize that every experiment involving it had claimed at least one life.

The door to the laboratory resounded with a knock. Galina turned. "Enter."

It was Bartolo Cassa, the sunglasses-wearing

muscleman who managed to be everywhere at the same time, like a tabloid celebrity. "Miss Krause," he said, "the injured guard has died of his wounds. Since then, the escaped prisoner must have made contact with the Kaplans. The family has left Saint Petersburg, heading east by jet. They have also had high-level assistance from a Guardian in the FSB."

"Alert the Brotherhood to increase security over every acre of the property," Ebner said. "The family will enter a trap. Is there anything else?"

Cassa nodded. "A report from the Copernicus Room. The messenger Miss Krause eliminated in Venice . . ."

"Yes?" she said.

"The clock she possessed was owned by the courier you neutralized in Prague. The message it likely contained originated elsewhere. It has been traced backward to its source."

Galina merely tilted her head. It was the signal for Cassa to speak.

He did.

One word.

"Vorkuta."

Vorkuta? It was as if Ebner were being punished for thinking he was as cold as he could be. The godforsaken Siberian city of Vorkuta was an iceberg in a land of ice.

"Bring the transport around," she said frostily to Cassa. "We go to the airfield immediately." She turned away from him as if he were no longer there, and in a moment he was not. "Helmut Bern, you will be successful."

The programmer's stubbled head turned to her, his features dappled with sweat, his hands trembling with fear. "Miss Krause, I am working as quickly—"

A frown. "Did I ask you?"

Bern shot a glance at Ebner but must have realized he was floating alone on a frozen sea. "Yes. Of course, Miss Krause," he managed. "That is to say, no, you did not ask, and yes . . . we are on schedule. We will be successful."

Galina smiled icily. "Ebner, we own the best people."

He attempted to match her smile. "We *are* the Teutonic Order."

Galina whipped around and exited the chamber with him, bolting and locking the laboratory from the outside. On the landing, she said, "Greywolf will live up to its name, Ebner. Let the wolves loose in the castle. If the Brotherhood should fail on the grounds, the wolves will protect Kronos until our return."

When they were out the front door, Ebner told the stony-faced local leader of the Red Brotherhood to empty the building except for Bern and the woman and to release the wolves into the fortress. For dramatic effect, he added, "Release the kraken!"

When the guard tilted his head in puzzlement, Ebner pointed wearily to the stables. "Release the wolves into the house!"

"Sir," the guard said, his expression stony once more.

The military transport started up, with the ever-present Bartolo Cassa at its wheel.

"We will be in Vorkuta in three hours, Ebner," Galina said.

Vorkuta, he mused. *Where "warm" is twenty degrees below zero.*

CHAPTER FORTY-NINE

The last thing Wade remembered before he didn't remember anything else was Becca's face, staring into his and screaming. He was on the floor under her seat, and she was screaming at him. Then nothing for a while; then he woke, still under Becca's seat, but she wasn't in it. Pain shot up his legs and into his sides when he tried to stand.

"So . . . we made it . . . ," he said.

"No. We didn't," Darrell grunted from somewhere. "We all died."

Terence Ackroyd had piloted the jet like a bird among the trees, so incredibly precisely that everyone was only banged up, which was still like having been tumbled in a dryer for thirty minutes, but was better than being dead, which he was pretty sure he wasn't, despite Darrell's claim.

But that could change, he told himself.

Marceline Dufort jerked open the cabin door, and the snowstorm flew inside. Bracing themselves, they climbed out into the blinding snow and found themselves in a narrow clearing about fifty feet from a mainly straight road that might have made a better landing strip but had been hidden from above by the trees. Wade and Darrell staggered to their father and the others.

"I'm going to get the radio going," Terence was saying. "I think I can fly us out of here, but NetJet will send a rescue chopper anyway—after the storm passes."

"Wait, no," said Marceline, consulting the aerial photograph. "Look here." The top of the image showed the vague shape of the structure that was Greywolf, but the detective drew her finger to a road winding through the woods at the very lowest edge of the image. "I think this is where we are."

Wade's father stretched, his face grimacing with pain, as he scanned the trees around them. "How far do you think we are from the castle?"

"At the edge of the property, but not too far,"

Marceline said. "Perhaps ten kilometers. And see here. Only one kilometer from Greywolf's landing strip."

"I agree," said her partner, checking a compass and then pointing up into the deeper woods. "The land rises steeply from here on, the forest is thick, and there are ledges and chasms all over the property, many of them man-made to deter intruders."

"What are you saying?" asked Wade.

Paul grunted. "That it will be a hard climb, but I agree that we not wait for a chopper. We lost nearly an hour because of the storm. It is already almost three in the afternoon. If we climb to Greywolf steadily, we can make it by nightfall, with time to spare before the deadline. *If* we don't run into the Brotherhood, a big *if*."

"Are kilometers more or less than miles?" Lily asked.

"Shorter," said Becca.

"Doesn't matter," said Darrell. "We're going on."

"All right then," said Terence. He pulled a handgun from inside the plane and shoved it into his coat pocket.

Wade's father nodded. "Get your gear, everyone. We have a deadline. But first, listen." He brushed snow from his hair and pulled up his hood. "Darrell, you and the investigators know this, but the others don't. During World War Two, Stalin visited Greywolf many times. All the roads on the property were monitored then.

Sometime in the sixties electronic surveillance was installed and probably updated a few times since then. We're entering the enemy camp here. We've never done anything like this before."

"Let's hope we're far enough away that our landing didn't alert the Order," said Terence. "But I guess we have to assume our jet won't be a secret too long."

"Indeed," Marceline added, checking her automatic. "For now we have the element of surprise, as long as we stay smart and keep off the roads. We don't want a firefight, but we must be ready for one."

Darrell swiped on his cell. "Less than nine hours to midnight."

And that was it. They began marching upward in single file, Roald and the children in a group, Terence and the investigators in the lead, armed and fanning out to cover more territory.

Darrell kept his head low. The wind and the blinding snow and ice that had forced the jet down were mercifully less on the ground. The heavy snow seemed to collect in the dense branches above them more than fall on them, but the upward trek was slow and tiring. A half hour—that seemed twice that, Darrell thought—passed without any sense of progress.

Other than the rough track weaving through the trees, the first sign of Greywolf being a "property" and not just wilderness was a head-high stone wall that snaked through a portion of the forest. It looked old. Maybe sixteenth century. Terence and the two detectives studied both directions.

"I'll climb over," Paul volunteered. It was relatively easy for him, an ex-soldier, to clamber up and straddle it, but the moment he reached the crest, he fell hard. The topmost stones were rigged to collapse under pressure. Not only that, but the level of the ground on the far side of the wall was at least three feet deeper than the close side. The earth was chewed up, craggy, and rock-strewn for a swath of fifty feet along the inside of the wall. It had been dug up purposely and the ground left open and treacherous. Using the gap Paul had made, they mounted the wall one by one, dropped down with his help, and kept on climbing. Another grueling half hour of stinging snow and wind came and went. Then a narrow light burst through the swirling gray air. It swept across the snowdrifts ahead of them.

"Patrol! Back off into the trees," Paul barked like a squad commander. He and Roald hustled them all over the rocky ground into a dense cluster of firs. Terence and Marceline looked through their binoculars.

An engine downshifted, and a transport truck camouflaged in white and pale green passed slowly along the road about a mile above them. It had a covered back. Sensors fixed high on the trees on either side of the road blinked in rapid succession as the vehicle crept slowly down the incline. It made a turn and vanished.

"Stay here; we're going forward," Terence said. He darted ahead with Marceline to another copse of trees, then another. A minute later, they returned.

"Galina's in the transport," Marceline hissed breathlessly. "I spied her—"

"Galina? Where is she going?" said Wade.

"Maybe to the airstrip," Paul said. "She'll pass the road not far from us."

After three long minutes, they heard the vehicle again, grinding through the gears. From the sound of the engine, Darrell knew it would weave around to that point in the road in less than two minutes. He borrowed the binoculars from Terence.

And there she was.

Galina Krause, the model-beautiful woman from the Berlin cemetery and the cave in Guam and everywhere they happened to be. Her face was as white as snow, her hair as black as night, a ghostly apparition in an army truck.

"The pale guy with the sunken chest is there, too," Darrell said. "They're jammed in the cab with a guy wearing sunglasses." The transport vanished again among the trees. "Another couple of minutes and we'll see it again."

Suddenly, his stepfather was moving. "Paul, Terence, we need to stop that truck. If Galina has Sara in there, we have to—"

"Rocks, branches, anything, throw them all into the truck's path," said Marceline.

"The bigger the better," said Wade. "Make it look like a landslide or something."

The eight of them heaved rocks and branches down into the road. Before long, headlights flashed at the final turn, and the engine growled into a low gear.

"Pull back; flatten," Marceline said, rolling one last rock down. The truck motored toward the curve. The driver noticed the obstacle and jammed on the brakes. The truck slid to a stop, its rear left tire off the road. He leaped out of the cab, went around the front, and swore loud and long in Spanish. Then he pulled out a pistol and observed both sides of the pass.

Ebner stuck his head out of the passenger window. "Why didn't the rockslide set off the sensors?" he barked, but didn't get out of the cab to help.

"I don't know," Sunglasses replied sharply. "I don't see anyone."

"Clear the road," Galina said. "We must go!"

"Yes, Miss Krause." Holstering his pistol, Sunglasses began heaving the rocks and branches to the roadside.

Darrell rose up to his hands and knees. "If Mom is in the back of the truck, I can check without them seeing me."

His father turned in the snow and held him back with an iron grip. "Darrell, no way."

Before anyone could stop him, Wade slid down the ledge in the truck's blind spot. He lifted up the heavy flap that covered the back opening. Instead of just looking in, he hoisted himself up and crawled inside.

Idiot! thought Darrell. *I should be doing that!*

Then Wade poked his head out and shook it, as if to say, *Sara's not here.*

"Then get out of there!" Becca hissed. "Unless Galina's going for the relic . . ."

Terence grunted under his breath. "Becca may be right. I'll go with Wade. Stay with the investigators. We'll be back."

Lily started moving now. "Galina can't be allowed to steal the relic! I'm going."

"You are not!" Becca said, reaching out for her, but

Lily slid to the end of the ledge and crept down with Terence.

Becca nearly choked on her own breath. Neither Darrell nor his father could move or raise their voices. Paul and Marceline had their pistols out, aimed at the driver with the sunglasses. Then it was too late. Lily and Terence climbed into the back of the truck. Sunglasses hopped into the cabin again and started the engine. He shifted it into gear.

Becca and Roald squirmed away from the rim of the ledge and into the trees with Paul and Marceline, while Darrell gaped, wide-eyed, at the receding truck.

His stepfather urged him back and back and back into the trees, but all Darrell could do was watch the headlights fade and then vanish around the next turn.

CHAPTER FIFTY

Wade hoped his brain wasn't completely wrecked, that it was *merely* the brutal cold, his tumbling in the jet landing, several smacks to the head, his near drowning in the Venice canal, and the specter of a horrifying deadline that had combined to make him think sneaking into Galina's truck was even a thing.

When Lily crawled into the truck hissing, "Are you insane?" he kind of had to admit he was. But then so was she, so he had company.

"Did you think this would help?" she whispered.

"I guess I did."

Then Terence appeared, and Wade didn't know what to believe.

"Your father and stepbrother are rather freaking out back there," Terence said. "I don't know who was holding who back."

"What about Becca? What did she think?"

Lily's mouth fell open. "Are you serious?" She was going to swat him, when the truck bounced suddenly into and out of a pothole, nearly throwing Wade on top of her. He managed to roll off next to a long, narrow case that must have been filled with rocks, because it was as heavy as stone.

"That is a weapon," Terence whispered. "A big one." He unzipped the case. Inside was what looked like a rifle with a huge barrel and canisters alongside. "Ooh, a flamethrower. I burned down a ski lodge with one of these."

Lily choked. "You what?"

"Oh yes. That was chapter seventeen of *The Mozart Inferno*. Hold on, I think I might be able to tweak the fuel line a little bit. . . ." He leaned over the flamethrower and began to pick at the controls with his fingers.

Meanwhile, the truck driver—Sunglasses—seemed to aim for every single bump in the road as if it were his job and he wanted a promotion.

Finally Lily said, "Shh," although neither Wade nor Terence had said anything. "We're slowing down. Listen, I hear engines. Do you hear engines? Shh."

The truck dipped into a half dozen more potholes, then slid to a stop on flat, snowy pavement. The engine turned over for a half minute before giving up in a last cloud of purple smoke, which blossomed into the rear compartment.

Footsteps crunched noisily over the snow away from the truck. No one came around back. Drawing his handgun, Terence peeked out the flap; flakes flew in. "Airfield."

It was a long, straight strip of flat land cleared out of the forest and paved. The engine noise Lily had heard came from two snowplows finishing their work a mile down at the far end. The snowfall and wind had lessened, and they could see a small jet, gray and steely and looking as powerful as it was sleek. It was idling about a hundred feet away, its nose pointing down the strip. Two rough-looking men with hoses sprayed deicing fluid on its wings, while its cargo door hung open, touching the tarmac.

Lily glanced at the black case. "Let's get out of here

before anyone comes for the flamethrower."

"Good idea," whispered Terence, zipping up the case again. "Keep your heads down." He glanced out the back and eased his way to the ground. Lily went next. Wade last. They hurried to the nearest cover, a supply hut at the edge of the airstrip. They crouched behind it.

Galina was busy bullying somebody on her phone as she and Ebner climbed a short ladder into the jet. Sure enough, after checking out the cargo bay, Sunglasses returned to the truck. He removed the long case from the rear compartment, then hitched it onto his shoulder as if it were a violin case. He carried it to the jet and slid it into the cargo hold. Then he stomped over to the hut they were hiding behind. There must have been a phone inside, because Wade heard a chime. Sunglasses spoke a series of quick words. Something, something, Vorkuta. He hung up.

Lily shared a look with Wade and Terence. *Vorkuta,* she mouthed. *The relic!*

The moment Sunglasses ascended to the jet's cabin and the cargo door began lifting, Lily stood up. "We need to get on that jet."

"No," said Terence gently, holding her back. "My jet. We know where she's going, and I'm sure I can get it off the ground. If we can make it back to their truck and drive it to where we landed, we'll only be a few minutes behind her. We have to be careful, though. Those guys with the snowplows are still out there. Come on."

It sounded good. *If* they could get Terence's jet off the ground.

Seventeen minutes after slipping cleanly away from the airstrip, Lily was staring through the cockpit window of Terence's NetJet into a world of white as he tried to get the engines going. The snow was heavy once more. The flakes fell large and wet.

"Won't we just crash again?" she asked.

"Oh, we'll make it," Terence said casually, starting the engines. "It'll be a tad bumpy, of course, bouncing over the ground to the road. And there's a bit of a curve in the road, but if we can get up enough speed on the straight, we'll be okay."

"If?" said Wade.

"Better buckle up," Terence added. "Just in case."

The bounce up to the road was more than a tad bumpy. Twice it felt as if the jet would simply topple over, but Terence finally got it into the rutted tracks. "Here goes!"

The engines' whine changed, thrumming through the fuselage. Lily clung fiercely to her armrests. The jet sped forward, faster and faster, bounding and tilting over the ruts, when a truck appeared on the road ahead of them.

"Uh-oh," said Wade.

"I see it." Terence pulled the steering column back, and the jet tore up from the road just as the truck drove underneath. The fuselage thudded, and they heard two loud pops that reminded Lily of the tires exploding on the Williamsburg Bridge.

"They shot out our landing gear!" she screamed.

"We won't need that for another couple of hours," said Terence. "We'll think of something by then."

"You're pretty calm," said Wade, gripping his seat handles.

"I'm always calm when I'm in the middle of writing a novel."

"You're writing a novel?" said Lily. "*Now?*"

"I'm thinking of calling it *The Greywolf Conundrum*. Hold on while I set the course." Tapping the name *Vor-kuta* into one of the dashboard instruments gave him a sequence of numbers—67°29'18"N, 63°59'35"E—the coordinates for the Vorkuta airport. Though Vorkuta was inside the Arctic Circle, the city was in the same time zone as Moscow and Saint Petersburg, and in Terence's jet, he promised, it would take under three hours.

Two hours and forty-five minutes later, they were descending toward a vast dark city, a blotch of gray concrete on the frozen tundra.

"The airport's still good," Terence said, "but Galina didn't land there. Look." The gray Falcon sat on a vast paved area about a half mile from the airstrip. It appeared to be a parking lot next to a coal mine. "Now this will be rough. Hold tight."

The landing gear grumbled beneath them. Lily knew the tires were in shreds. Her stomach bounced up and up with each hundred-foot descent. She locked eyes with Wade. "I don't like tiny planes."

"Actually," he said, "they almost never . . ." He didn't finish.

The bare rims of the wheels shrieked when they hit the tarmac. Lily shut her eyes as they ground into the surface of the airstrip. She nearly tore the arms from her seat. The landing was rough and long and not very straight. Terence did everything he could to keep the jet from veering off the strip. He was successful until the very last moments, when one of the wheels ripped off the gear, and the plane spun around like a car skidding on ice. It finally came to rest with a jerk, its nose tilted forward and touching the ground. Lily opened her eyes. Terence smiled. Wade was holding a barf bag but hadn't used it.

They had landed, but the jet wouldn't be going anywhere soon. That might have been its last landing. The engines softened, then died altogether.

"Get ready to move," Wade whispered.

"No, really? I was thinking of staying."

"Funny," he said with a fake smile. "Too bad I can't even laugh."

"Oh, you better laugh—"

Terence popped open the cabin door. Frigid air slammed inside. Mustering her strength, Lily crawled down the ladder to the ground. Wade's legs were rubber. He slid and landed like a fish next to her. Terence last. Cold hit them like a wall. It wasn't snowing. It was too cold to snow.

"'You do not know cold like this,'" Lily grumbled. "Boris warned us."

There was a shallow trench running along one side of the airstrip. They took off toward it, hoping no one saw them. No one seemed to. The land around them was more or less flat, an immense plain of rough frozen ground. Wade said stuff like *tundra* and *permafrost*.

"No lessons," she hissed.

In the distance, great concrete buildings clustered like ghosts lost somewhere between life and death. They were gray and massive, but also insubstantial, like shadows in the thick frozen air. Scattered here and there on either side of the airstrip were the remains of tall wire fences—barbed wire, she guessed—some standing, most dented, split open, falling over. Towers made of crisscrossed wooden beams stood like observation towers at national parks. There were the ruins of long, low buildings that Wade couldn't stop himself from saying were "barracks, for the prisoners."

"*Lagpunkt,*" she said.

"The coal mine," said Terence. "That's where Galina is." He pointed to a series of towers and the chutes angling down from them. There were giant many-spoked wheels, barely standing under their own weight, lonely and abandoned. "This is where prisoners were forced to labor, spending their years below the frozen earth."

"And probably where Boris was born," said Wade.

Now that the Soviet Union had collapsed, the mines themselves were in ruins, a mass of cracked smokestacks, frozen cones of black coal, and those things that her tablet had told her must be slag heaps.

When Vorkuta was a labor camp, from the 1930s to the 1970s, tens of thousands of men and women had died there under unspeakable conditions. They had been arrested out of their old lives, sent to Lubyanka, then exiled to Siberia to work and then to die. Like Boris's father.

Galina and Ebner were already across a broad white field, the man with sunglasses following at a distance, the black case hanging from his shoulder like before. They were met by a large troop of armed men—Brotherhood, no doubt—who positioned themselves at several entrances to one of the ruined mines.

Terence blinked ice tears from his eyes. "I don't know mines, but is there an entrance they're not watching?"

"There," said Lily, pointing. "I think we have to run before they see it."

A pack of uniformed men was marching quickly across the airstrip from the jet toward them. "Airport officials," Terence hissed. "Or maybe more Brotherhood. You run. I'll cover for you. Wait for me outside the mine. Do not go inside."

"Yes, Dad," said Lily.

She climbed to her knees, looked around one last time, and scrambled across the airstrip with Wade. The area between the trench and the entrance to the mine was long, wide, and open, but no one was looking at them. Or at what appeared to be a half-collapsed doorway near the rear of the mine.

"Sorry, Terence," she said. "We need to get inside. Wade, come on."

Keeping low, they hurried across the field to the opening. They slipped slowly into the mine entrance. It was as dark as night inside, but warmer. The ceiling beams were in place, and although debris of crushed rock and abandoned tools covered the floor, the tunnel looked passable.

"Use your flashlight app," Wade said, and they both flicked them on. The darkness was so thick, even two lights barely penetrated. Fifteen or twenty paces in, they stopped.

"I hear them," Lily whispered, turning off her light.

Not the Brotherhood, but Galina. Her voice.

Wade pocketed his phone, cupped his ear, and listened. "I think she's on another level. A lower level than where we are. We should search for stairs or—"

"Watch out!" Lily threw her arm in front of him and wrenched him back. Wade's feet were perched inches from the edge of a pit. Moving her light over the pit revealed a sort of cage of metal around a large, perfectly square hole set fifteen feet into the ground.

"An elevator," Wade said. "Stuck between floors."

Lily reasoned that the elevator car had fallen past the level below and lodged there, leaving at its top a gap to the floor beneath them.

"We can crawl through to the lower level," she said.

"What about never entering a dark room if there's another way?"

She shone the light in his face. There was a smile on it. "That was fine in New York. We're in Siberia now." She slid down to one of the iron struts on the perimeter of the shaft. Then to another, and then finally they both lowered themselves onto the elevator roof. It creaked suddenly under their weight. They shared an anxious moment, until they heard the voices murmuring again.

Relying on her years of gymnastics, Lily slipped through the shaft, which opened out into a lower passage of the mine. It wasn't a big drop, but she braced herself firmly to keep from falling, cleared a space for Wade, and helped him down. Glimmers of light and the echo of voices told her they were now on the same level as Galina.

"You know this is absolutely crazy, right?" she said.

"Oh, believe me, I know," Wade said.

"Okay, then. Just so we're on the same page."

"And the same level of a coal mine in Siberia."

Before they were ten feet down the next passage, a thing jerked out of the darkness behind Wade. It clamped itself over his mouth and pulled him roughly back into the shadows. A voice hissed, *"Silence!"*

CHAPTER FIFTY-ONE

The thing over Wade's mouth was cold, powerful, reptilian.

Gollum?

The dry flesh smelled of stone dust and coal and motor oil and something sharp, medicinal. Trying to turn, he imagined he saw a face—but it couldn't have been a face, because not all its features were there. Lily said nothing, her hands over her mouth, her eyes aghast at what was dragging him backward into a long room lit by a single candle.

Around them was a tortured mangle of metal furniture and the broken remains of the equipment of coal mining—drills, saws, picks, and axes—reminding him of a nineteenth-century machine factory.

"Silence!" the voice hissed wetly in his ears. "I release you. Silence, yes?"

Wade nodded. So did Lily, her eyes welling up now. The scaly fingers lifted off his mouth. Wiping his lips on his sleeve, Wade turned slowly.

By the wavering flame he saw a shriveled wire of a man whose nose was mostly gone. It had rotted or burned away. An open hole gaped between his cheeks, giving him the look of a skeleton. The flesh on his forehead was mottled—red, black—and crosshatched with deep scars. His lower lip had been burned almost completely away. The gums that remained were gray. He had no teeth. His lidless, protruding, red-veined eyes appeared to be on fire.

"Every time someone comes," he slurred in a whisper that suggested he couldn't speak any louder, "by plane, by truck, by any way, I come see who. I watch."

"Who are you?" Lily asked tentatively.

"Four long years I watch and wait, knowing it is only matter of time before she come. Four years, I wait for Galina Krause. Finally, she has tracked me to my lair. The circle of horror is completed."

"You know Galina Krause? You know she's here?" Wade asked. "Who are you?"

"Me? I am no one. You are Enklish? Enklish are good people."

"American," Lily said, looking at Wade for an answer he didn't know the question to.

The man turned his face away. "Ah, I thought Enklish. My brother he live London. Maybe you know. Boris his name. Big man. Scholar. They love him in London. But how could you know Boris? You are children; he is famous man. I wished Boris, not Galina. Brother Boris. I sent message for him to come. He has not come."

Lily's knees gave out, and she fell into Wade to keep from collapsing on the filthy floor. After all that had happened since the Promenade room in London, after the countless miles they'd crossed to get here, they *knew* this burned wreck of a man?

Russia felt suddenly as small as the inside of a box.

"You are Aleksandr?" she said softly.

Not that it was even remotely possible for his flesh to move or the muscles that had been destroyed by fire to alter his features, but something softened in his expression.

"You . . . you . . . know Boris Rubashov? My brother, Boris?"

"We met him in London," Wade said, still holding her up. "He helped us to come to Russia. But he . . . he thought *you* were dead. He was convinced that Galina . . ." His hand moved to his pocket, then stopped.

"He thought Galina had killed you," Lily said.

The man, whose brother had called him *A*, stared silently at them with bloodred eyes, eager for every syllable. "Tell me more," he said. "More!" So they related the sad facts of his brother's poisoning. How he had "told" them by video about the Teutonic Order's theft of Serpens from Copernicus. How they had followed his opera ticket to Venice to retrieve what had turned out to be Aleksandr's very own message to his brother.

"*Workuta*," Wade said finally. "That was from you."

"I sent it to a colleague in Prague," the man said. "I hoped it would get to Boris. So that I could see him one more time. To pass on to him my knowledge of Serpens."

"Without Boris we wouldn't be here," Lily said softly. "I didn't realize until now how much he helped us. He hated the Order. He was coming back before they got to him. He loved you. He would have come here, if he had seen your message."

Aleksandr shuddered for minutes without cease. Lily

guessed that his eyes were dry only because his tear ducts had been destroyed by fire. He was sobbing without tears.

"Oh, Boris," he said finally. "Boris—" He stiffened suddenly. He pushed a curled finger to his lips, then picked his way through the ruined machinery. He leaned against the door they had come through. He dragged a dented cabinet against it. "Galina Krause does not know the way to my little home," he whispered, "but she will find it. She circles and circles the passages, looking for me."

"The mine entrances are guarded except the one we came through," said Wade.

"Galina must find me," Aleksandr said, selecting something from the junk on the floor. It was a scalpel. "I will not leave before she does."

"You treated Galina four years ago?" Lily said. "She wouldn't have been much older than we are now. What was wrong with her?"

Aleksandr shook his head. "You have heard of Greywolf? Greywolf harbored a secret experimental clinic for KGB. I was forced. Then, after KGB, the Order. Hideous place. The machine—"

Wade shot Lily a look. "The machine? You know

about it? My stepmother is trapped at Greywolf, *inside* the machine. What is it?"

"Kronos is the Order's experimental time-traveling device!" he said. "They were building it even as I performed the surgery. I know little of physics, but Galina Krause is mad! Time travel simply cannot be done without the relics of Copernicus. Ptolemy knew what he was doing. He lacked only the final brilliance of the Magister. This is the greatness of Copernicus. His wondrous astrolabe!"

Lily tugged Wade to her. "That's what the midnight deadline is. Galina's going to use Kronos on Sara. But my Lord, to do what—"

There were noises echoing into the room from the passages outside.

"Galina's getting closer," Wade said. "We should get out of here."

"She believes I will tell her where the relic is!" he said.

Lily shivered. "Then it's true. You're a Guardian like Boris."

His eyes fixed on her, then on Wade, then on her again. "As our father was before us. As all good people must be. All people who fight the Order . . ."

With that, Aleksandr went into a kind of trance,

speaking much as his brother had in the London break-fast room, drawing them far from the mine and down the long passages of history.

"Behold," he said, "behold the snowbound streets of Kraków, Poland, on the night of February thirteen, in the year 1568 . . ."

CHAPTER FIFTY-TWO

Wade remembered 1568. He had scratched the number on the wall of his Lubyanka cell. It was the year Albrecht von Hohenzollern died.

By this sad time, Copernicus is dead. Albrecht von Hohenzollern is an old man, and yet we see him, struggling through the storm to a small abode on Gołębia Street, in the shadow of the great university, the university that Copernicus himself attended.

Albrecht's spies have told him that a man, one Georg Joachim Rheticus, lives in an upper room. Also in that room is one half of a jeweled serpent, given to Rheticus by Maxim Grek. It is the fragment Albrecht has sought for fifty long years.

It is now within his grasp.

"Wait," Lily interrupted. "Albrecht had the head, and Rheticus had the body. Are you saying . . . they met?"

"Met, knew each other, and on this night saw each other for the very last time. . . ."

Albrecht is accompanied by a handful of men.

One of them is his sole surviving nephew. It is from him we have this story. The men break down the door, mount the stairs. All this happens in moments!

In pain, near death, Albrecht coveted the relic. It is the curse of Serpens, the bloodlust of the relic, which makes all who know of it covet it beyond all things!

Rheticus rises from his lamp-lit desk. He is a younger man by years, but his burdens have reduced his health. The door swings wide. Albrecht enters. Rheticus takes up his rusted sword. They fight. One a Guardian, the other the Grand Master of the Teutonic Order!

Such a battle would be monumental, but they are two old men! They hack away at each other with swords far too heavy for their weak arms. The knights with Albrecht do not intervene. His one surviving nephew watches, catalogs, remembers.

And then the blow. Albrecht's blade across Rheticus's face. The Guardian is blinded, falls. Albrecht grovels on his knees, tears the room apart until he finds the Serpens relic.

He seizes upon it.

He takes it.

Wade couldn't help himself. "So Albrecht had it all."

"Yes!" Alek said. "The Demon Master brings it back to Königsberg. There he connects the two pieces, head and body. The relic moves . . ."

It breathes! Tick . . . tick . . . tick . . . It is said that Serpens stings him. Perhaps, perhaps not. Either way, within a few short months, Albrecht himself is dead.

"What happens to Serpens?" asked Lily. "Is it still at Königsberg?"

"Ah, no. Because, you see, fortune turns. The history of the relic is as twisted and cursed as the serpent itself. The journey to the finding of it is long, as long as . . . But now we must travel forward in time . . . to April 1945. . . ."

My father, Sergei Rubashov, is a private in the Soviet army. He is a weary foot soldier, harnessed to the great engine of Mother Russia.

By April 1945, you see, the Great Patriotic War against Germany is nearly over. My father is sent with his company to take the castle at Königsberg. To search for Russian art treasures the Germans have stolen since the war began.

Bullets and flames fly on the battlefield, but my father makes it to the castle. What Private Rubashov discovers, however, is no mere Russian treasure. It is a discovery beyond belief. Half of a jeweled serpent, a winged body crafted of silver and diamonds beyond worth. It is the Serpens relic. Incomplete. The body only, headless, unnatural. He does not find the head. But this fragment alone is priceless beyond comprehension.

My father is overtaken by its beauty and power.

He cannot control the greed of his eyes, his heart, his hands. He hides the relic in his rucksack. He says nothing to anyone. He brings it home with him, after the war ends.

Father learns soon that the serpent is cursed. He uncovers its terrifying history. Not only its origin with Copernicus, but how it imprisoned Maxim. How it blinded Rheticus. How it killed Albrecht himself.

To save his soul, my father becomes a Guardian.

The Teutonic Order, high in the Soviet government after the war, learns of his theft. They try to force him to reveal where the serpent is. But he is now a Guardian and will not speak.

He never reveals its hiding place. He is sent to Lubyanka prison, then to Vorkuta. Two years later, he marries an inmate, has two sons. Aleksandr and Boris. Mother dies. Father labors for decades in the mines. He never reveals his secret. For more than fifty years, he never gives it up. Boris becomes a Guardian. I become a Guardian. Still, Father never gives it up. Until his deathbed . . .

He took a breath, listened at the door, and went on.

On his deathbed, father gives me the body of Serpens.

He says, "Keep it safe."

I say, "Upon my life I will."

Yet with Father's last breath, already I cannot control my heart and my hands. Even as a fragment, Serpens is magnificent beyond belief. I take it. I hide it. Boris leaves Russia, goes to the West. He is a dissident and must leave to be free. Me, I am already under the yoke of the government. My clinic at Greywolf is my prison. I am forced to stay in the east wing, the surgery. I develop serums, medicines. They work. They cure.

Then, four years ago, a bent little man comes to Greywolf. With him is a girl, young, frail, dying. The man brandishes a pistol. "I am from the Teutonic Order. We have friends in Russia. Many friends. You will cure this girl," he says to me.

"Ebner von Braun," said Wade.

Lily shot a look at Wade. "Galina was dying? Of what?"

"Cancer," Alek said, rubbing his fingertips as if to clean something invisible from them. "But a very rare and almost unknown modality of cancer. I had never seen its like, not until my microscope identified it without question."

Here I am, a Guardian face-to-face with the Order. I am fearful. Yet I cannot refuse to do the operation. I do not want to reject a child of the Order.

The operation is a success. I beg to leave Greywolf, to join my brother in London. The German man refuses, keeps me under lock and key. "Ensure her recovery. We need this girl!" *Then, one night the girl rants in her delirium. Tortured words about a jeweled object in her possession. An object she foraged from Königsberg.*

This is both honey and poison to me!

In this way, I become aware that this young girl possesses the legendary head of the very same serpent! Its double eyes are said to be as large as human eyes, blue diamonds of exquisite cut and quality.

"How did Galina get the head?" Lily asked.

Aleksandr paused again to listen at the door. "How does Galina Krause do many things?"

"But you knew what it was?" Wade said.

"Of course I knew!" Aleksandr said sharply. "The serpent my father brought home from Königsberg had already devoured me with its beauty!"

"Why didn't your father find it when he was there in 1945?" Wade asked.

Aleksandr brushed his burned fingers across his forehead. "One legend says that Albrecht hid the two parts separately. The real reason is lost in the past. But do you understand the gift given to me at that moment? If I let my hands do the bidding of my soul, I could possess the entire Serpens relic, as no one has since Copernicus himself!

"I begin to think, with one relic I can find another. And another. I knew how Serpens was said to move in the palm of your hand as if it were alive. *Tick . . . tick . . .* And how it points its head to the south, and its blue eyes begin to glow, and it moves across your palm as if to join with another. Already it is seeking the next relic!"

Aleksandr paused, falling inside himself for an instant before he went on. "I stole the head of Serpens from her. Even from her recovery bed, the girl ordered that they force me to tell where I put it. They set fire to the clinic. . . . Did you know there existed a morgue at Greywolf? Below the surgery, a small room where the bodies of those who perished were taken. My colleagues and I made errors, you know. Experimental surgery . . ."

Wade tried to follow this new idea. "Yes, I understand. But did you escape with Serpens?" He knew how blunt the question was, but he had no time, and the man was beginning to ramble.

"I escaped! Yes, I did. But the head of Serpens? After so many victims over so many years, Serpens is bathed in the blood of the dead," he said.

"What? Where?" Lily looked ready to jump out of her skin. "Where, Alek?"

"Still this is but half of the story," Alek said. "Fleeing

Greywolf, I stole across Russia to Vorkuta, where my father died. I returned to his mine, where I had hidden the beast. I retrieved the body of Serpens. Realizing that I had sinned with greed, I entrusted the Serpens body to a Guardian far nobler than myself. I bid him hide it away. Since then I live in this mine, the mine that killed my father, and I wait. I knew one day she would find me. She has. Now . . . I will kill her." He raised the scalpel in his hand.

"Alek, no," said Lily. "Let's just escape, get out of here."

"Never!" he said.

"Alek, the Protocol has begun," said Wade. "The relics need to return to Frombork. We have one already. Vela. It pointed to Serpens, as Serpens will point to the next one. Aleksandr, can you help us find both halves?"

"I am the *only* one who can, but . . ." Aleksandr's breath was like the sound of a car wheezing its last. His lungs were damaged, that was plain. "I am at the end now. I will not come with you. But I will tell you. . . . Did you know that below the surgery was a morgue?"

It was maddening, and Wade turned away. "You told us already, Aleksandr. Where are the two parts of the relic? You had them both. We've traveled half the world to find them. Can you just tell us where they are?"

The man drifted off for a moment, as if falling once more into a trance. Then, stirring, he studied their faces closely and said, "Bathed in blood—"

Three shots exploded suddenly in the passage outside. The door bolts flew across the room like shrapnel. The cabinet toppled away. The iron door to Aleksandr Rubashov's lair crashed open.

CHAPTER FIFTY-THREE

Minutes earlier, Galina stalked through the dusty tunnels like a panther on the hunt. Her scar stung as if it were a raw incision. Her memories cut just as raw. She recalled every moment of the operation Aleksandr Rubashov had performed on her at Greywolf. A hundred thousand precise moments of agony.

"We must be near," Ebner whispered.

"We are," she said. "I sense him."

Now, after four years of her thinking him dead, could the good doctor actually be hiding here? In this . . . tomb?

The servers in the Copernicus Room had cross-referenced thousands of fragments of data about the

Rubashov brothers, reducing them to a list of thirty-eight possible origins for the encrypted message meant for Boris. The moment one of those fragments—the name Vorkuta—had been identified as the mine where the Rubashovs' father had died, Galina had been certain. No doubt her failed episode in Venice had given the same information to the Kaplans, if they knew enough to decipher whatever code Aleksandr had used.

"How ironic life and death are," Ebner mused. "A man *we* believed to be dead sends a message to a man *he* believes to be alive. Curiously, we were both wrong."

She slowed and turned to him. "Ironic, Dr. von Braun? We have been wrong far too many times for it to be ironic. We are in Russia, where I nearly perished four years ago. Is *that* ironic?"

"No, no, of course not," he said. He resumed his stumbling, four steps behind her. Cassa strode three paces after him, the heavy weapon slung over his shoulder, so primed she could smell the petrol.

"Once we locate what I have come for, nothing remains," she said. "Cassa, you will use the torch to end it all. Then we leave."

"Indeed," said Ebner. "And not a moment too soon. We must return to Greywolf. Midnight is barely five hours away."

The lengths Galina had to travel to find doctors to supply her the drugs she needed to kill the pain, to repel the black shadow of death into remission. A trail of agony that spanned the world and brought her right back where it began.

She stopped. Her hand shot up. The door to some machine room or other. There were voices behind it. *Voices!* She turned to Bartolo Cassa and nodded. He fired three rounds from his automatic. The door bolts exploded.

And suddenly there was the doctor's face, more dead than alive.

"Rubashov!" she gasped despite herself. "So it's true! You *did* survive." Then she saw the children, and she felt a small part of her brain burst. "Here. Always here. This must end. *You* must end. Cassa, restrain them!" He forced the children against the rear wall of the machine room.

Turning her attention back to the doctor, she shuddered to see his face so destroyed, as if it were burning still. "We thought you dead, Rubashov."

He fixed his ruined eyes on her. "Your scar . . . it is enflamed. You are not well, Galina Krause."

She raised a finger to her neck, slowly dropped it to her side. "More so than you, doctor."

"True. I *am* dead," he replied simply.

"Then it will not pain you to return to the grave. *After* you return what you stole four years ago at Greywolf. Give me the head of Serpens."

"It died in the fire, too—"

She pushed the barrel of her pistol just below his breastbone. "Liar! Relics of the Eternity Machine cannot die! Relics can never die!"

The boy looked surprised. The Kaplans must not have known that the relics were indestructible.

Aleksandr gazed lidlessly at her. "Perhaps the serpent's magic rubbed off on me, allowing me to live just long enough . . . to kill you!" He suddenly shrieked like a madman and fell on her, his scalpel thrust like a sword.

Galina's gun went off before the blade touched her. The surgeon stopped moving as if he'd hit a wall. His mouth formed a horrible, toothless smile. "Now no one will ever know. . . ." He doubled over, hands clutching his torso, then fell to the floor like a limp towel, motionless.

She staggered back a step, lowering the bloody gun. "Why did you do that, Doctor? You made me kill you, again. You, who saved me!"

Shouting something, the Kaplan boy wrenched

himself away from Bartolo and jumped at her. With a single blow of the pistol to his shoulder, she leveled him. The girl screamed when he fell like a deadweight. Galina kicked the still form of Aleksandr Rubashov with her leather boot. Nothing. She turned to the girl. Lily. "Where is Serpens? The head and the body. The doctor told you. Where are they?"

"I don't know!" the girl said. "He didn't tell us. He was about to tell us, but you killed him, you witch. Serpens is lost, the whole thing!"

Galina stepped up to her, shoving her pistol roughly under her chin. It was cold and wet with Aleksandr's blood, and the girl looked as if she wanted to cry but the tears weren't there. She was likely too angry to cry. Galina knew such fury.

"Get that—thing—away from me!" The girl swatted the gun down.

Galina stepped back, wiping the blood from the gun and her fingers on Rubashov's threadbare overcoat. "Ebner, Cassa, search for the relic. If it is here, find it!"

Cassa began turning over the trashed ruins of the room. Ebner did the same, holding a handkerchief over his face like a sissy. In a few seconds, the room that had served as Rubashov's home for four years was more a shambles than it had been when she entered.

"It could be anywhere in the mine!" Ebner shrieked. "Galina—"

There came the high-pitched shriek of sirens, and the thud-thud of machine-gun fire, echoing down through the passages into the mine.

"Miss Krause," Cassa said, "if that is the FSB, we must go. There is a back way. Let me finish the children; then we go. The deadline."

Galina pulled back from the boy and the girl, who stared icily at her. "Finish them? Yes. I am sick of their faces. These two do not matter. Ebner . . . come. We'll return after the fire and locate the relic at our leisure. It cannot be destroyed. Cassa, do the deed."

Galina stepped backward over the rubble scattered across the floor. Cassa threw the girl roughly into the boy, who was groaning in a heap. Backing toward the door, Cassa flicked a lever on the gun. The barrel flared with tongues of white flame. Training the weapon at a metal cabinet on the nearest wall, he let loose a quick spray. The cabinet burst. The wall exploded in a blaze of fire. The girl screamed. He aimed at the opposite wall.

"Wade, get up," the girl said over and over.

Flames bubbled up one wall and licked the ceiling, spreading to a second wall. Soon the room would be an inferno. He sprayed the third wall—tried to spray it.

"Someone has tampered with the gun," Cassa growled.

Galina drew her pistol again. She aimed it at the girl, then at the boy. She lowered it. "Leave them," she said. "Fire will do the rest."

Cassa flipped a lever. The flame on the tip of the barrel vanished in a wisp. He moved back and back until he was in the passage outside with Galina and Ebner. The machine room was ablaze. The girl screamed again. Galina pushed her way through the tunnels to the surface.

CHAPTER FIFTY-FOUR

Greywolf

It was a battle of black and white. The night was heavy and dark even as the snow increased its fury.

Becca marched as close to Darrell, Uncle Roald, and the detectives as she could. They'd kept on like that, plunging for hours through drifts and over frozen streams, slipping, cracking their knees, wrenching their wrists, slowing only for moments to catch their breath, no matter how cold or wet they got or how much it hurt.

They *were* gaining ground, she was sure of it.

The steep, then steeper incline told her Greywolf was up there. Another sound was there, too. Howling echoed down through the trees. She didn't want to believe it was actually wolves. The wolves of Greywolf. But what else could it be—

Something zipped from left to right across the falling snow.

A chunk of tree bark flew off to Darrell's right.

"Everyone down!" Paul hissed, flattening with Marceline, both raising their pistols.

Becca dropped hard into the snow behind the stump of a cracked tree, hurting her wounded arm even more. She stifled a cry. Darrell joined his father behind a rock outcropping. She bit her lip to keep from making noise. The wound ached, throbbed. *Be still!* A spray of gunfire burst among the tree trunks. Paul and Marceline aimed at its source and waited.

"That was a warning!" a voice shouted. "Keplens, surrender. We have you surrounded."

Paul raised himself to his elbows. "No they don't," he whispered. "At the first opportunity, go back down the ridge and around."

"We'll cover you," Marceline added.

Becca watched both detectives settle into the snow and take coordinated aim into the trees. They nodded silently to her and the others as two bursts of gunfire blasted through the tree cover at them. The detectives returned fire, crisscrossing their shots.

"Go!" Marceline whispered.

Darrell crawled on his elbows to Becca. Roald did the same. "Down the ledge," he whispered, nodding behind her. She turned, her arm wet inside her parka. Her wound was bleeding again. *Just move,* she told herself. *No noise, just move.* The gunfire popped and thundered: semiautomatic fire, machine-gun fire, she didn't know what else.

She could die. They could all die. But she kept on, elbowing down the ledge and away from the firefight, from Paul and Marceline.

"Behind the ridge," she said over her shoulder, seeing a path forward. She went first, on her hands and knees initially, then on her feet, running. Darrell was right behind her, Roald last. They were out, away, and heading up again. Seconds stretched to minutes. Longer. The fire was sporadic now.

Then a noise. A whining engine. A snowmobile was heading to the gun battle.

Darrell whispered, "Let's pretend to give up, then steal the snowmobile."

"You're nuts," Becca hissed.

"Actually . . . we need speed," Roald said.

"What? No!"

"Only four hours left," Darrell snapped.

The snowmobile zipped past a knot of trees, fully visible. Suddenly, Roald stood bolt upright in the snow, his hands raised high. The driver was startled; then he recovered and aimed his pistol, slowing his vehicle.

"Stand still," he barked in English. "Both of you!" Darrell reluctantly did as he was told.

Oh, perfect.

The driver reached for his radio transmitter. Becca knew it was up to her. *Something* was up to her. The radio crackled. That was the moment. She jumped to her feet, making sure she registered on the periphery of his vision. She dived down again. It was enough of a distraction. The driver swiveled his head, not his gun, and Darrell and his stepfather flew like ghosts and pushed him off the snowmobile. He hit the ground hard, his gun sinking into the snow. Roald pressed his Taser on the man's neck. It was a low charge. The man continued to grapple with Roald. Darrell pounded his fists on the man's arm. The man jerked his hands loose of them.

The snowmobile rolled, then stopped, still idling. Becca went to it immediately and searched the compartment under the saddle—for what, she wasn't sure. Roald and Darrell wrestled the half-aware driver facedown in the snow and pinned his arms behind him.

"We need to tie him up or something—" Darrell started.

"Wire!" Becca said. "I found wire."

"Take off his coat first," Roald said. "I'll wear it."

"Why?" asked Darrell.

"If we're spotted, they'll think I'm him. It'll buy us time, at least."

"Good idea," said Becca. She knelt next to Darrell and removed the driver's parka, while Roald undid the man's ammunition belt, bound his hands with the wire, jerked him to his feet. He twisted the wire once around a tree before securing it. Darrell stuffed the man's mouth with his own scarf and tied the excess around his head.

The gunfire behind them continued unevenly. Becca knew they had to make the most of the distraction Paul and Marceline were risking their lives to create. After slipping the driver's parka on himself, Roald dug into the snow for the dropped pistol, holstered it in the ammo belt, and tied the belt around his waist.

"Dad . . . ," Darrell said. "Really?"

"Just in case."

Becca watched Roald gaze through the trees up the hill. The fortress still wasn't visible. But now they had the snowmobile. He pulled the parka hood low. "Let's move it."

The firefight was moving too, down the hill and away. Paul and Marceline were in retreat, drawing the Brotherhood away from them. Roald got on the snowmobile, with Darrell behind him and Becca on the back. They had to squeeze, but it felt so good to be sitting on something softer than stone.

"You safe back there?" Darrell asked over his shoulder.

"Maybe."

She clutched the sides of the seat, and Roald twisted the grips on the handlebars. The gunfire started up again, furiously this time but still farther away. Without a pause, the snowmobile lurched forward up the treacherous rise to Greywolf.

CHAPTER FIFTY-FIVE

Vorkuta

When Wade struck the floor, he was sure he cracked his skull. His forehead thundered. His temples burned. His eyeballs ached and saw double when he tried to blink them into focus. Galina was nowhere. The freezing air had turned viciously hot. The room was on fire.

"Lily? Lily!" he cried.

"Help Alek," she coughed.

The doctor moaned and rolled over. "Friends . . ."

Flames had blackened two walls and were scorching the third. Wade scrambled over on his hands and knees. If Galina had shot Aleksandr in the arm or leg, there might have been a way to stop the bleeding. But the wound was just under his sternum, in the stomach, and his ratty clothes were soaked. Aleksandr would bleed to death all too soon.

"How do we get out of here?" Lily asked, searching everywhere.

"There is a passage behind the gas canisters," Aleksandr groaned, his face strangely peaceful. "Do not worry; the canisters are empty." He pointed to the back corner.

"We'll make it out." Wade coughed.

"You, perhaps—"

"All of us."

Together, Lily and Wade rolled the canisters aside and crawled through a low passage into another room, dragging Alek between them.

"There." Alek nodded at a padlocked exit door. "Try to open that. I must tell you about the relic. There may be no time, later."

Wade wrenched the leg off a metal chair. He battered the lock. "What did Galina mean that the relics can't die?"

Aleksandr coughed for a full half minute. "Simply that Copernicus himself tried to destroy them but could not."

"Then where is Serpens now?" he asked for the third time.

"Have I told you that there is a morgue at Greywolf?"

"Yes, Alek, you did," said Wade. Was the man losing his mind? Losing his blood *and* his mind? Then it struck him with the power of Galina's punch. "Are you saying you *hid* the Serpens head in the morgue at Greywolf? That it never left?"

Aleksandr gasped. "I did! It never left! It lies bathed in the blood of the dead. The body, however . . ." With difficulty, he lifted up his right pant leg. The leg itself was burned and scarred as badly as his face and neck, but there was something else, too. A section of several square inches of scarred skin covered his calf. It was sewn on one side with haphazard stiches like those on the Frankenstein monster.

"It looks as if you operated on your—" Lily started.

Aleksandr nodded once. "There was no place closer to me than myself."

Using a shard of glass, Aleksandr laboriously slashed away at the stitched skin. It bled little because of the thick scarring. Slowly he pried the wound open. From it, he withdrew a small white capsule, two or so inches long. He wiped it clean and pulled it apart, then tilted the open capsule into his palm.

"Knowing I could no longer protect the relic my father found in the ruins of Königsberg, I sent it to a friend of mine. An Egyptologist in Moscow. He perished last year. Even so, Serpens remains safe. Once, I dared to ask where he hid it. He did not respond until on his deathbed. Then he sent me this. Along with the Magister's own words. You will be happy to hear that the twisted path of the Serpens body ends with this clue. Now I give it to you." He pulled a rolled strip of paper from the capsule and passed it to Wade, breathing out a long, ragged breath.

On the paper was a square box drawn in ink as red as blood. Filling the inside of the box was a large upside-down *V* with a sequence of numbers running up the left side to the top and three question marks running down the right side.

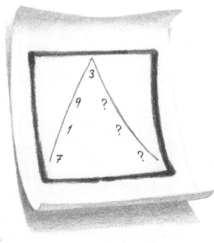

"What does it mean?" Wade asked. "You said he was your friend in Moscow?"

"I never knew the significance. My friend told me just this: no matter how many codes are devised, this will override them all. What that means, I do not know. But if you wish to locate the body of Serpens, this is nearly all the help I can give."

"What were Copernicus's words that your friend told you?" Lily asked.

"'*Puteshestvye do kontsa morya dlinoy,*'" he whispered. "Which means 'the journey to the end of the sea is long.'"

"Boris told us that!" said Lily. "What does it mean?"

Aleksandr seemed relieved, as if released of a great burden. "It is a quotation we Guardians have always known. As Nicolaus's journey was long in the hiding of the relics, the Guardians' journey is just as long. You will find Serpens soon, but your journey will continue!" Then he began coughing, and his breathing grew rapid, shallow, and labored.

Wade hacked once more at the lock. It broke off. He whipped the door open to find a clear passage, but opening the door sucked the fire into the room.

"Up! Out!" Aleksandr choked. "You cannot die like this!" When he lifted himself up from the floor, he bled freely. Yet he managed to push Wade and Lily ahead of him through the door, into room after room, then hung between them, huffing, "This way . . . no, there! That tunnel! Up. Up! You *must* find the relic before Galina. You must!"

Wade's legs felt like lead. The fire burst into the passages behind them faster than they could run. Aleksandr grew suddenly heavy. Was he dead? "Lily . . ."

Tears cut through the grime on her cheeks. "I feel cold air. That way. That way!"

Together, they pulled Alek up a narrow side passage. There *was* cold air, streaming in on them. A ceiling beam crashed down across the passage. Then two more. They were trapped. A voice shouted from the other side of the fallen beams. No, it was the roar of the fire. No, a voice. A call from so far away that Wade wasn't sure he even heard it. Lily's fingers tightened on his wrist. She stopped her breath to listen.

There was a crash, and the voice yelled, "Stand away. Get back!"

Lily pulled Wade flat with Aleksandr behind the fallen beams as the wall burst in at them. Voices came clearer now, even above the screams of the fire. Terence stumbled in with a stream of Russian police behind him. Wade could tell from their uniforms and the expression on Terence's face that they were real police, not Brotherhood. They threw fire cloaks on the children and Aleksandr.

"Out of here!" Terence cried. "Hurry up!"

And they were running, Terence and the police carrying the limp form of Aleksandr from the burning mine. They tore up a last set of broken metal steps and fell onto the frozen ground as the mine threw up a howling gust of flame.

The entrance collapsed; the rumbling and thundering was now underground. They were out of the mine. Bitter cold rushed over them. They laid the burned man on the ground. He was limp, completely still. His mouth gaped. His eyes stared upward. Terence and two policemen worked over him. Sirens wailed in the distance, coming closer. Ambulances, fire engines. Wade turned to see a plume of black smoke pouring out from the mine in three columns. "Lily, Terence, we have to—"

"Maybe they'll come in time to save him," she said.

"Sure," he said.

The quest for Serpens. We're closer than ever to the center, but we're not done.

Terence helped Lily and Wade to their feet. They left Aleksandr Rubashov on the icy ground surrounded by policemen and medical technicians rushing from their trucks, and ran back across the tundra toward the paved strip.

"To the airport," said Terence. "We'll find a plane. We can be at Greywolf in under three hours."

"No," said Lily. "Alek gave us one last clue. We have to go to Moscow!"

* * *

On the airstrip, an old woman with a mop of white hair bent under the nose of Terence's jet. She supervised a mechanic changing the last of the three blown tires.

"What's going on?" Lily asked. "Who's that?"

"I think she believes she's the new owner of our jet," Terence said, trotting quickly over the tarmac. "While I was with the police, she commandeered it."

The woman was dressed in what looked like ten layers of clothing, and she had a rifle over her shoulder. At the sound of their footsteps, she pulled a hidden revolver from inside her coat. "*Stoy!*" she snarled, a word that obviously meant "Stop!"

"Let me handle this," Terence whispered. "Hello— this—is—our—jet!"

The woman narrowed her eyes at both of them but did not lower the pistol. She shook her head and said a long string of Russian, ending in, "*Nyet*. Is my zhet." Then, without taking her tiny eyes off them, she tapped the gun barrel on the fuselage. The door of the plane squeaked open from the inside, and a young woman poked her head out. "I am Ekaterina," she said. "I speak English."

"This is really our jet, and we need to fly to Moscow right now," Wade said.

The younger woman shook her head. "It *was* your

jet. We are taking it."

"I have an idea," whispered Terence. He offered the Ogienko family, as they called themselves, ten thousand rubles to fly them to Moscow in the jet. They hesitated. When Lily searched the net and discovered that ten thousand rubles was about three hundred dollars, Terence quintupled it, which made the old woman and her family ecstatic.

"But I fly zhet," the old woman insisted. "Is my zhet."

"Fine," said Terence. "Just let's go!"

As soon as they muscled their way into the tiny cockpit, the pilot gunned the engines. A little girl, the English-speaking woman's daughter and the pilot's granddaughter, immediately began to kick Wade in the shins, then laugh as if it were the funniest thing in Russia. Maybe it was.

"We have to tell your dad about the morgue," said Lily.

Wade pulled out his phone. "No service. Excuse me, do you have a radio on board?"

"Yes," said the pilot's daughter. "But you cannot call a cell phone."

"How about FSB headquarters in Moscow?" asked Lily.

The woman's eyes widened. "Do not turn us in."

Terence assured them they would not, and Wade radioed Inspector Yazinsky. He was rerouted and put on hold several times before finally reaching the inspector's answering machine. "This is Wade. Tell my father that the head of Serpens is in the morgue at Greywolf. Aleksandr said it's in the east wing of the fortress. Serpens is 'bathed in the blood of the dead.' Sara is trapped in a time machine. We'll go to the airport with Terence when it's all over, but right now we're flying to Moscow—"

The connection crackled and died.

"The relic is in Red Square," Lily said. "We're going to Red Square."

"What?" said Wade.

"Red Square?" said Terence.

"Pfft!" muttered the old woman.

"Look at it," Lily said, holding up the sketch Alek had given them. "It's a red box. A red square. The body of Serpens is hidden in Red Square!"

"Seat belts. We fly now," said Ekaterina.

Terence offered to copilot the jet, but the old woman refused his help. Without much experience at the controls, the pilot moved the wheel first too much, then too little. The plane lifted, then sank toward the blank gray face of a giant high-rise. She tugged the wheel back again, and they rose but barely gained altitude.

The tires bounced across the icy roof of a second building; the jet dropped off the far side, nearly crashing into a third building until the pilot veered left and the nose lifted at the last second. They cleared the next roof and the next.

At last, the city below them, an unruly mass of streetlights and lighted buildings, surrounded by the vast darkness of the Siberian landscape, began to shrink and fade away.

They were airborne.

CHAPTER FIFTY-SIX

As her Mystère-Falcon shot over the tundra back to Greywolf, Galina studied the satellite image she'd just received on her cell phone. Three figures were running away from the burning Vorkuta mine toward a jet standing on the airfield. There was a force of police and a man lying in the snow. Emergency vehicles surrounded the mine.

"They are charmed, these children," she said softly.

"Rather than charred," Ebner offered.

Bartolo Cassa sat stonily in the pilot's seat. "They would never have escaped without help," he said quietly. "The flamethrower was sabotaged."

"I should have shot them myself," Galina said.

Then why didn't I? Seeing them there, children only a few years younger than herself, she'd found herself unable to take the shot. Did she *want* the children alive? Why would that be? They had followed her, sometimes even led her, to something that was so deeply a part of herself. How could she tolerate such an intrusion?

Was it that . . . one of the children *might* turn out to be . . . the one who . . .

She could not think it.

Calmly, she tapped in a text and waited as the jet climbed. *Triangulate their course.* The cockpit was silent for two minutes until her cell lit up with a single word.

"Moscow," she read. "They are en route to Moscow."

"Shall I change course?" Cassa asked her.

"No. Ebner will return to Greywolf. You will pilot me to Moscow. Ebner, have a troop of the Crows meet me at Sheremetyevo in Moscow, with a transport. The Russian surgeon has obviously given the children a clue. I will follow them. Midnight comes soon. You shall oversee the completion of Bern's programming and the successful transportation of Sara Kaplan to Cádiz in 1517. Complete this mission. We need a body there . . . and then."

The physicist nodded. "It shall be done, Miss Krause."

Galina withdrew a pair of earbuds from a zipped

pocket on her coat and inserted them. She tapped an icon on her cell phone and heard the plaintive andante from Haydn's string quartet opus 33, number 6. It was the same piece that had been playing in the antiquarian's shop five days prior. As the cello's insistent funeral march rolled on and the yearning violins begged fruitlessly for comfort, Galina cradled the miniature portrait from Prague. She stared at the face that breathed as if it were alive even now, five centuries later. Inwardly, if not visibly, tears melted down the inside of her breast. Why she loved old artifacts like this was simple . . . and complicated.

A living portrait, yes, she thought, *but how many years did you actually live?*

The portrait's eyes gazed back as if to ask her the same question.

CHAPTER FIFTY-SEVEN

Greywolf

The gunfire at Greywolf grew increasingly sporadic until it died under the roar of the wind through the trees. Midnight was only an hour and a handful of minutes away.

The final push to the summit was excruciatingly slow, despite the speed of the snowmobile, and far longer than Becca expected. They had to take a meandering route to avoid the main road, and twice had to shut off the engine as motorized patrols fanned out over the property in response to the gunfire.

They'd heard Galina's jet return, just before it took off once more. It was over an hour since Chief Inspector

Yazinsky had called Roald's cell to relay Wade's message.

"Galina must be following Wade and Lily to Moscow," Roald reported.

"Then why stop here at all?" asked Darrell. "To let someone off . . ."

The jet taking flight again was followed later by a transport returning from the airfield to the fortress, proving Darrell right. The way the transport had shifted its gears on the road above them had told Becca that the summit was near.

Then the air shuddered. A blast rolled up the hill from below.

"That sounded like a bomb," said Roald. "Or a grenade. Keep moving."

Minutes later, the hulking stone fortress loomed into view. It was larger and more menacing than Becca had imagined. A haunted, gloomy pile of stones dotted with black windows and pierced by a frightening tower that flickered with light like a mad scientist's lair. Roald stopped the snowmobile inside the tree line, cut its engine, and scoured every compartment for more ammo, which he took.

The howling began suddenly, and Roald stiffened in fear. "Wolves. In the house."

"Why are they *inside* the house?" Darrell wondered. "That's just sick."

The howling was horrific. The wolves were in some kind of pain. Or maybe they smelled food approaching. Becca imagined their snarling faces, snouts, jaws, fangs.

Roald unholstered the pistol. "The wolves are there to make sure no one gets in before the deadline."

Becca pushed the idea of guns and wolves out of her mind. "Wade said there was a morgue below the operating room. Let's get moving."

Her legs were freezing, barely with feeling, but they moved her forward.

Together, the three hurried across the clearing. They came to rest behind what were likely the original stables, now the garages. The air was unbearably frigid. Becca couldn't move the muscles of her face. Roald's beard was frozen. They kept in motion, shifting their feet, wrapping their arms around themselves for warmth. The chorus of ghostly wails from inside the fortress rose and fell, crisscrossed, subsided, rose again.

"If Galina is after Wade and Lily, then who's still here?" whispered Becca.

"Ebner, maybe," said Darrell. "Or the goon with the sunglasses."

Then the sound of a snowmobile sputtered behind

the stables. They whirled around, Roald crouching, gun aimed. It was Marceline in the saddle. Marceline alone, an automatic in one hand, a machine gun hitched over her shoulder.

"Paul was shot twice," she whispered. "He is below, out of danger of the Brotherhood. He will survive."

Becca felt her heart sink, her neck go numb, as if she might pass out. She stomped her feet to regain feeling. "Will the Brotherhood come back up here?"

"They will. Though they, too, lost troops. And their transport was destroyed. Still, we must do this quickly."

Roald filled her in on Wade's message while he checked and rechecked his pistol. "Isabella escaped from the back of the castle. That could be the weakest entry point."

"I will go there," Marceline said. "You search for the morgue. Ten minutes exactly is all you have while I create a diversion at the back. Ten minutes. If you have not found Serpens by then, leave it. Once you hear me shooting, you enter the front. I'll do what I can to stop the wolves, then join you in the tower to get Sara out."

That was the end of the talking.

Becca pulled Darrell and his stepfather away from Marceline and hurried to the side of the building. Her heart was pounding. The wolves went crazy against the windowpanes on the ground floor, sensing their presence. Their faces, their teeth, their horrible eyes glimmered in the snow light. Roald skirted the edge of the stables, then loped across the clearing to the back of the house.

"Ten minutes is nine minutes now," said Darrell.

The east wing was a hulk of three freestanding walls, doorless, roofless, and windowless. It hung off the body of the fortress like a ghost limb. But it was free of wolves. Roald pushed into the ruins.

The charred machinery of medicine lay twisted and mangled, a horrifying mess across the floor. The debris was covered by a thick blanket of snow. Rusted poles, girders, ceiling beams, overturned cabinets, and wrecked carts protruded from the white.

"The morgue," Darrell grunted, nodding his head at a portion of the floor that had collapsed, through which they could glimpse a chamber down below. "What did Wade say—bathed in the blood of the dead? The whole morgue is bathed in the—"

He didn't go on—couldn't make himself go on, Becca figured. She found the stairs and climbed tentatively down to the floor below. Four minutes had elapsed since they'd left Marceline.

The morgue was a black pit, a hole, a concrete-lined

grave. It was a crypt for the victims of the Order through the years, the KGB before them. Becca shone her light on the ruined equipment, drills and saws and undertaker tools, mangled with the beds and carts and monitors that had crashed through from the floor above.

"How in the world are we supposed to find anything in this junk?" she asked.

Roald trained his light. "Bathed in blood? It's a riddle. But what does it mean?"

There was a shot, then two more. Roald jerked back. "Marceline? It's too soon."

"Dad, go," said Darrell. "No one's going to find us here. We'll scrounge through the junk, then meet you in the castle. Go!"

"Take this." Roald gave Darrell the Taser. "Be careful when you—" But he was off in the direction of the shots before he finished his sentence.

Becca pushed carefully through the equipment, while Darrell kicked at it angrily. He shoved aside burned-out cabinets and overturned stretchers and the remains of octopus machines with charred hoses dangling from them. He muttered about time and midnight and his mother. Becca tried to find something, anything that could be a hiding place for a handful of jewels, but the morgue was a heap of junk covered in snow and ice.

"Darrell, it could be anywhere."

"We have to find it! We both have to! The Legacy! We have to stop that witch from . . . from . . ." His fingers froze unmoving above the floor. "Becca . . . Serpens is bathed with the blood of the dead."

"I know that! What does that mean?"

"Where does the blood of the dead go in a morgue? The drain. Becca, they wash away the blood down a drain!"

She watched him push across the floor until he came to the very center of the room. He kicked at the snow covering the floor. Then his body jerked in several directions at once. He was frantic, tearing around in the debris until he found something, a tool—a two-foot length of pipe. He slammed it on the floor. The air rang with the sound of metal on metal. He did it again and again, swinging at the floor as if he were chopping down a tree. She heard the chink of metal, and then suddenly the drain—a crosshatched ring of metal—flew up sharply and nearly struck him in the face.

He dropped the pipe, fell to his knees, and drove his hand into the floor, into the drain hole. There must have been so much blood washing down there over the years, but Darrell obviously didn't think of that; he just pushed his fingers into the hole. When he brought them back up, they were twitching and twisting and . . . glistening.

She shone a light on his hand. He held an object, a device. It looked more mechanical than a piece of jewelry. Maybe it was both. It was a delicate construction of silver. Twin blue diamonds gleamed prism-like in the rays of her flashlight.

"It's . . . Darrell, oh my gosh. You found it! The head of Serpens—we have it!"

He rose to his feet and came toward her, the object seeming to draw the light into it while at the same time shooting it back out in a series of flashes or pulses that set the dark room glowing. Darrell's face shone. He blinked at the intensity of the light.

So did Becca. "Is it magic?" she asked. "Is it?"

"No," he said. "Something else. It's heavy. Becca, it's like ten pounds. It's hot and it's heavy and it's humming or something—"

A series of shots cracked the air like multiple explosions. Another and another, followed by the spray of machine-gun fire. There was a thunderous howl, then more shots. Roald and Marceline were at the rear of the house, shooting the wolves, and the wolves were out, charging from the fortress and onto the property.

"Hide the relic. Give me the pipe. Come on!" said Becca firmly.

Darrell wrapped it in his scarf and shoved it into the pocket of his parka. They ran back up the stairs, out of the operating room, and around to the front of the castle. The timbered doors, studded with iron bolts, looked impregnable.

She jumped first up the steps and twisted the pipe into the iron door handles. She pulled it down. The handles squealed. She did it again. They squealed more.

"Together," Darrell said. They both gripped the pipe and pushed up first, wedging it tight; then Darrell kicked it down. The handles groaned awfully and fell. They shouldered into the doors together. They swung in. The wolves were still pouring out the rear of the house. Here in the front rooms, there were none.

"The stairs," Darrell said. "Isabella said Mom is in the tower. Hurry up!"

CHAPTER FIFTY-EIGHT

Moscow

R ed Square. The heart of the city. The dead of night. It had all come down to this.

Thirty minutes before, they had landed safely at Sheremetyevo airport. Then, disaster. Terence and the Ogienkos were held in a cramped room for violating Russian airspace without proper clearance—or something—a trumped-up charge they immediately credited to the Red Brotherhood. Irina Lyubov was not on duty. This left Wade and Lily alone and free, which they realized was simply because the Brotherhood planned to tail them directly to the relic.

"Take a roundabout route to Red Square," Terence

told them privately before he was led away. "Switch cabs, zigzag, do what you can to lose any pursuers. I trust you'll get there eventually. When you do, stay put. Do nothing. I will meet you. Seriously, do nothing until I get there, understood?"

"Yes," Wade said, then thought, *It's just us again.*

Out on the street, Wade and Lily hailed a cab, awkwardly made their first destination known to the driver, and quickly crossed the city. Two cars were obviously following them. "Stopsky heresky please," Lily blurted out at a busy intersection, which the driver surprisingly understood and forgave, even as she apologized. She overpaid him in euros, then they jumped out and raced down one street, cut through to another, and snagged another taxi before their pursuers could spot them. They left that taxi three dark blocks from the enormous Red Square. Strong winds blew snow in tiny cyclones up and down the empty street. The cab drove away. They waited in the shadows of a deep doorway.

Satisfied that the Brotherhood had not followed them, Wade pulled out the paper Aleksandr had given them, huddled against the wind, and tried to study the drawing. But all he saw in his mind were Sara and Darrell and Becca and his father, and he could only imagine the terror of what was happening at Greywolf. "I hope they're okay. The others, I mean—"

"I know who you mean," Lily said, crouching up against him in the doorway. "I'm thinking about them, too. But we have work here. Come on."

He tried to reset his thoughts and focus on the paper again. "Okay, if you're right, the first clue is Red Square, but what do we do when we get there?"

"Hey, I deciphered the first clue," she said. "Now it's your turn."

"Thanks so much."

"While you think, let's keep moving," she said. "And I mean it. You think."

They marched out of the doorway into the wind, crossed two streets, doubled back, and moved forward until the tunneled arches of the famed Resurrection Gate loomed ahead of them. They waited where they had agreed to meet Terence, but he didn't come and didn't come.

Lily shook her head. "We need to go on. Terence may be hours. We don't have hours. The journey to the end of the sea is long, and we're nearly there. What does the triangle inside the square mean?"

Wade had asked himself the same question. "It's technically an upside down *V*; the bottom isn't closed, as in a triangle."

Lily gave him a face. "Helpful, Einstein. Alek said his Guardian friend was an Egyptologist. They're all about pharaohs and pyramids and deserts and mummies—" She stopped, whipped out her tablet, and powered it on. "I'm searching 'Red Square' and 'Egypt' to see if there's any kind of clue here. What about the numbers? Come on. Figure out the numbers while we walk."

They crept through under the gate's deep archway and came out alongside the bulky, ornate, redbrick State Historical Museum. Its gold awnings were heavy with new snow. They paused at the corner and looked south across the vast, deserted square. It was already covered by a thickening blanket of white; snow was blowing around in more twisters.

"The numbers, I don't get," he said, slowing under the first streetlight. "Forgetting for a second the upside-down V, I've been trying to find a pattern in the numbers, but I don't see one. Seven, one, nine, three, blank, blank, blank. If there was a pattern, I might be able to figure out the last three. They might be a combination or an entry code. But I can't find the sequence. Maybe I can use the calculator on the tablet—"

"Oh."

"What?"

She pointed across the square through the squalling

snow. Against the high red wall of the Kremlin fortress stood a stumpy pyramid of red and black stone. "There."

"What about it?" he asked.

"Well, (*a*) it's a pyramid. And (*b*) it's the Lenin mausoleum. Not John Lennon, but Vladimir Ilyich Lenin, one of the leaders of the Russian Revolution. And (*c*) maybe your eyes aren't as good as mine because of all the reading you do, but if you look at the lettering on the front of the tomb, the red lettering against the black, you'll see what I see. It says *Lenin*. Of course, it's in Russian, so the *L* in *Lenin* is not a regular *L*, as in Lily, but an upside-down *V*. Look at it."

He did. Through the whirling flakes he read the letters.

ЛЕНИН

He made a sound. "Whoa . . . is that it?"

"I don't know," she said, tugging Alek's scroll from him, "but if the outside box *does* mean Red Square, then the upside-down *V* could mean a building *in* Red Square. That would make me think that maybe the numbers tell us something *about* the upside-down-*V* building. Maybe that's the way the clue goes. From outside to inside."

From outside to inside? Lily was being pretty brilliant.

Wade studied the tomb. It sat snugly against the Kremlin wall, a squat, five-level pyramid of granite and marble, forty feet tall. It vaguely reminded him of a stepped Aztec temple. In one way it was small, like the foundation of a much taller structure that was never built. In another way, the building was grimly impressive, its multiple levels catching the light of the square in odd and ominous ways.

Because it was the resting place of a maybe-controversial Russian leader, it was heavily guarded. From that distance, it appeared to have eight, maybe ten fully armed soldiers stationed around it.

"Okay, but why there?" he asked.

"Because Lenin is *embalmed*," she said, wagging her tablet. "It says here that every year and a half they redo the embalming to keep him looking fresh and natural. I'm guessing that Alek's Guardian friend was an Egyptologist who knew about embalming, and that he worked on Lenin and hid Serpens in there while he was doing embalming stuff."

"Your face turns green whenever you say *embalming*, you know," Wade said.

"I feel it doing that."

On either side of the tomb and following the Kremlin wall was a loose row of blue spruce trees. They were impeccably trimmed, of nearly identical size, and now ornamented and sagging with heavy late-season snow.

"So . . . the Copernicus relic is in Lenin's tomb?" Wade said.

"One plus one equals Lenin's tomb," she said.

"Speaking of numbers, what *about* the numbers?" he asked.

"That's so your department, math head," she said. "Come on."

They paused close to the facade of the Historical Museum, then darted over the cobblestones to where the Kremlin wall jutted out. They peeked around the abutment to scout out the mausoleum guards.

"Two guards on this side of the tomb and six spread across the front," Lily said. "I don't see any at all covering the back. There are probably two or more on the far side. You know, maybe the numbers are a Russian phone number."

He gave her a look. "I think modern Russian phone numbers have more than seven digits."

"Digits, huh?" She counted the guards again. "Maybe it's an old number."

"Right. Maybe it's Lenin's home phone number from 1924, but nobody knows the last three digits because how do you phone a dead guy?"

She looked at him. "You could try a little harder, you know. We're out of time. We need to do this. Then we need to get out of Russia forever."

At the word *Russia*, Wade's brain twitched. In their time there, he'd never come to terms with the country. His "map" of Russia was false, based on the insane things they'd done over the last few days, the danger they'd been in, the number of times they'd nearly died, the terror about Sara's fate. The dread of what was happening at Greywolf weighed on him like lead. He'd seen Lubyanka and Vorkuta, but he'd never really gotten to know *Russia*. Now, like Lily, all he wanted to do was leave it.

"Our best bet is to make our way behind the trees," Lily said. She slid past him, weaving through a stretch of temporary fencing. They flattened together against the Kremlin wall. Wade figured they were a couple hundred yards from the tomb. His chest ached. This was ridiculous. A movie. What if they were actually spotted? Caught? Fired on?

And yet, the moment the tomb guards looked off toward the cathedral, he trotted down the narrow space between the trees and the Kremlin wall, toward the back corner of the tomb, with Lily right after him.

Ridiculous or not, they were doing it and getting closer to the center of the onion.

Then Lily went to stone. "Look."

There was a narrow set of steps at the back of the structure, leading down several feet from ground level to a steel door at the bottom of the steps.

"A basement."

"Do tombs have basements?" he whispered.

"Maybe. This is Russia. What do we know?" She leaned out as far as she could and stared at the tomb. "Besides, there's something on the wall next to the door. I think it's a keypad. There are your *digits* for you, math boy."

The soldiers shifted slightly, then froze like columns, unmoving, except for their eyes, which were staring forward. The kids waited for some kind of noise distraction, and after a few breathless minutes, it came. A siren blared several blocks away from the square. An ambulance or fire engine, wheeling through the streets, honking and wailing. Then a second one, following the first. Wade and Lily left the cover of the trees and darted the twenty feet to the back corner of the mausoleum and down the narrow steps before the sirens died. The keypad was set at eye level next to the door frame.

"This is where you shine, number boy," she said. "Or get us killed. Your choice."

His chest tightened. His heart didn't stop booming. Keypads. Lily was right. A single wrong entry and they were done for. A squad of Russian soldiers were only yards away, and they probably had orders to shoot to kill, no questions asked.

"Have you figured out the pattern yet?" she asked.

He shook his head. "There are a thousand combinations. Just let me think." And he tried to. He nearly did. But the thought of all the possible combinations froze him. *Key in the wrong numbers and we're dead.* With one unknown number, he might have had a chance to determine the pattern, but *three* unknowns? He stared blankly at the keypad as if it would somehow tell him the answer. It didn't. He looked at the strip of paper for the numbers. He didn't have to. He had memorized the sequence.

7, 1, 9, 3, ? ? ?

He tugged off his glove, then ran his shaking index finger over the keypad, not touching it, but tracing out the first four numbers. Seven. One. Nine. Three. He did it again. A third time. A fourth. Something unfroze in his brain. Something thawed and shifted.

"Your fingers aren't touching the pad, you know," Lily said.

"I know," he said. "But look at this." He repeated the sequence twice for her. "See?"

"Your finger not touching the pad? I do see that."

"No, look again. There's a shape. What shape does it make when you key in seven, one, nine, and three?" He moved his index finger once again over the keys.

"Um . . . *N*," she said. "So seven, one, nine, three is *N*, as in . . . Wait, you're not saying *N* for *Nicolaus*? Are you saying the next three numbers form a *C* for *Copernicus*?"

He found himself grinning at her. "Why not? It's what Brother Semyon did at the monastery, moving the stones in the shape of an *M*, for *Maxim*. It's an old trick, a simple one, but unless you know where and when to do it, you wouldn't guess it. If this *is* it, making the shape of a letter with numbers, the three numbers for *C* would be two, four, and eight. The whole sequence, for *N* and *C* is seven, one, nine, three, two, four, eight. I'm going to do it." He glared at her. "Unless you stop me."

She crossed her arms.

"Okay, then." He raised his trembling finger and tapped in the numbers.

Seven . . .

One . . .

Nine . . .

Three . . .

Two . . .

Four . . .

"Wait!" Lily whispered, clutching his hand suddenly. "It's not eight. It's zero. The last three numbers aren't two, four, eight; they're two, four, zero."

"What? Why?"

"Because of the other clue. The Copernicus quote, remember? 'The journey to the end of the sea is long'? Everybody's been telling us this line, but what if sometimes it isn't *sea*—as in splash-splash—but *C* as in *Copernicus*? The journey to the end of the *C* is long. And the Egyptologist meant it that way, as a trick or a pun. Guardians have to be tricky. So the leg of the *C* doesn't end at eight. It goes as long as it can. All the way down to zero. Do it, do zero now!"

"Did you say 'splash-splash'?"

"Just. Do. It."

Wade lifted his right index finger, held it steady with his left hand, and keyed in the final number.

Zero.

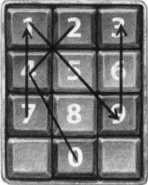

7, 1, 9, 3, 2, 4, 0. For *NC.* Nicolaus Copernicus.

Nothing happened for a full five seconds. Then there came a soft click. It was followed by a slow sequence of sliding bolts and levers behind the door, ending in a dull thud. Wade stared at Lily. She stared at him.

Breathing deeply, they pushed on the door together. It opened soundlessly. And side by side, they slipped into the tomb of Vladimir Ilyich Lenin.

CHAPTER FIFTY-NINE

Greywolf

Wolves howled and guns blasted as Darrell and Becca pushed from hall to room to passage to the center of the fortress. It stank of animals.

"Becca, trade you, the jewels for the pipe. I'll break them."

"Not likely, but yeah." She inserted the relic into the inner pocket of her parka, where Darrell knew she kept the diary. Both relic and diary, he suddenly realized, had belonged to Copernicus.

The man who'd started this quest.

The man who, in a roundabout way, had led them here to Darrell's mother.

"Darrell!" Becca cried. He turned to hear the frantic scampering of paws. Three wolves broke into the room. They were emaciated and gray. They slid across the floorboards, momentarily startled to see the kids. Their growling was like the grinding of gears.

"The door at the top of the stairs," Darrell whispered. "Go!" The wolves leaped up after them, but Roald and Marceline were suddenly there, startling the wolves with gunfire. Two of the creatures bared their fangs and growled, but ran out of the room. The third stood its ground for a second, arched up its hind legs, then ran out, too.

"Go with the children," Marceline said to Roald. "I'll stay here. Go on!"

"Hurry!" Roald snagged their sleeves as he rushed up with them. "She's got ammo, and she's a great shot."

From the top of the stairs, they turned to a mirrored hallway. Darrell ran down the hall and found a final set of stairs. Now that they had the Serpens head, it was all about finding his mother. They climbed to the landing. Roald shot at the locked door, a double-wide set of doors, and pushed into a large circular room. It was the inside room of the tower.

"Sara!" Roald cried out.

Darrell nearly vomited.

His mother hung, limp and drugged, inside a cage of metal bands at the center of a horrifying engine of gears and wheels and pistons. A haggard young man jerked out from behind the machine. He had an enormous handgun trained on them.

"You were never supposed to make it this far," the man said. "You were supposed to die at the hands of the Red Brotherhood. Or at least the wolves!"

"What have you done to her?" Darrell screamed. "Get my mother out of that thing!"

The man barely registered the words, but shot wildly. The bullet ricocheted powerfully off the wall behind them. "Stop or die. I must finish Kronos. I must . . ." His eyes widened, then narrowed, as if his brain was completely fried. Keeping his pistol leveled at the three of them, the man moved his free hand. It scrambled with lightning speed over a keyboard attached by a cable to the machine. The machine resembled a kind of gun, its barrel hinged inward at his mother.

"We're taking her out of there," Roald said, moving toward the machine. The man raised his gun and shot him.

In the forearm. Becca screamed. Roald reeled back, dropping his pistol, but stayed on his feet. It was a graze, not serious. "I'm fine," he said.

Darrell pulled out the Taser. "We're going to get her—"

"Please stop, or I will kill you all!" the man screamed, firing his pistol at the floor in front of Darrell, exploding the flagstones at his feet. "Twelve minutes! Twelve min— No! Eleven! Look! See!" He pointed the gun barrel at a clock mechanism mounted next to Sara. "If you move, I will kill her. And then I will kill you. I must do this."

Darrell heard footsteps coming toward them in the hallway. Marceline? The shooting had stopped. Had she neutralized the wolves?

Marceline Dufort leaped up the stairs and burst into the laboratory, her machine gun raised. The man at the device was startled to see her, and her gun. He thrust his pistol at Sara's head. "Drop your gun. Kick it here. Or she dies right now." Marceline placed her gun on the floor and followed his order.

"You see I *must* do this," the man said, his pistol still trained on Darrell's mother. He moved his free hand back to the keyboard and tapped three times in rapid succession.

The machine made an urgent sound.

One very large wheel began to turn.

CHAPTER SIXTY

Moscow

Lily quickly pulled the tomb's utility door closed behind them and held her breath. No alarm. The *NC* code had worked. With, naturally, her own brilliant correction.

She and Wade wound through a sequence of basement hallways until they found a cement staircase with a door at the top. They climbed up. The door was locked, but there was another keypad. Assured by Aleksandr that the Guardian code could override any other, they used it again, and the door lock clicked. They opened it and entered the mausoleum.

"Oh, man," Wade breathed.

She totally agreed.

The inside of the tomb resembled a modern hotel lobby more than a crypt, except, of course, for the giant coffin.

There were lights embedded in the ceiling, bare stone walls, marble floors. It wasn't as frigid as outside by any means, but it wasn't room temp, either. *Tomb temp*, Lily thought, then dismissed it. This was a place of reverence, whatever you thought of the man lying there.

Wade was dumbstruck, barely moving. "Where would you hide a relic here?"

"The shorter list is where *couldn't* you hide one," she said. "Serpens could be anywhere." Though not, she hoped, inside the coffin.

Or *sarcophagus*, as the websites had called it. It stood on a raised platform in the center of the large square room. The base was framed in marble. Above it was a bronze sculpture of cloth spilling tastefully out from the open casket. Several feet above the casket itself stood a construction of four tiers of marble and wood. In between were walls of thick glass, angled slightly outward from the base to the larger top. Inside the glass, lying in the casket as still as stone, was the embalmed body of Vladimir Lenin.

She swallowed hard and took a step toward it.

The dead leader's head and shoulders were—nice touch—tilted upward on a dark ruby pillow. To make for better viewing by the daily crowds, she guessed. Lenin's eyes were closed, but the embalming was so good that they looked as if they had just recently shut themselves. His hands were poised individually, not crossing each other at the waist, but separated. They had, if Lily could bring her mind to say it, a kind of personality. The right hand was folded on itself as if holding something. She really hoped it wasn't a diamond serpent. The left hand rested lightly on the upper left thigh.

"Okay, let's get to work," Wade said.

She shook her head to focus her thoughts. "Take two walls. Go over every inch of them. But remember that people are here all the time to pay their respects. So maybe the best hiding place will be a place where people don't go very much."

"Good point," Wade said softly. "I guess we have to be as clever as the Guardian who hid the relic. We have no real information on who he was, but we know the *NC* trick with the keypad. Maybe there's something like that going on inside, too."

"I just hope it's as far away as possible from *him*," she said. "You know, the third person in the room." She thought she heard Wade chuckling.

She hoped it was Wade chuckling.

For his part, Wade wanted to think logically about their search, but Guardian code makers were among the most sophisticated in the world, so it could be devilishly clever. Or devilishly simple. Or intuitive. Or impossible.

The four walls were clean, just flat or stepped marble blocks up to the ceiling, with minimal ornaments and light fixtures, none of which looked like it held a relic, and all of which was far too public anyway. So they moved toward the center of the tomb, or rather Lily did, because Wade found he had stopped moving.

"What's the matter? Outside the obvious one of breaking into a tomb?"

"I don't know." Wade slipped the strip of paper that Alek had given them from his pocket and stared at the simple cleverness of the solution to the entry code. Then he scanned the four corners of the room and the public entrance on the front wall, an entrance that jutted out into Red Square. That entrance was just like the zero on a keypad. He looked down at the floor, then up at the ceiling.

"What are you thinking?" she asked. "Because I hope you're thinking."

"I think I am thinking," he said. "And I'm thinking that the *NC* thing *could* be more than just the entry code. I mean, it's what Aleksandr told us. No matter how many times codes are changed, this will still work. Well, maybe that's the beauty of it. The simplicity. Because look at the layout of the floor. It juts forward, like the zero on the keypad. What if we trace the same two letters in the room, as if they form the same shape as the letters?"

Lily visually took in the four corners, the middle of the back wall, the right wall (from Lenin's perspective), and the entrance. "I don't know what we'll see that way that we didn't see before."

"Maybe it isn't what we see," he said. "Or what *we* see."

"Fine, be cryptical. I don't have a better idea."

Together, they stood under the ceiling light in the lower left corner. It suddenly flickered out. They walked slowly to the upper left corner, making the first "stroke" of the *N*. There was another ceiling light there. It too went out when they stood under it. They made their way around the sarcophagus to the lower right, then finally to the upper right, completing the *N*. There were ceiling lights in both corners, and both went out.

"That was the *N*. Now the *C*," he said. Starting at the

middle of the back wall, where there was also a ceiling light, they went to the middle of the side wall, then down to the entrance—the long journey to the end of the *C*—where there was a final ceiling light. Those three blinked and died, too.

"The lights are sensors!" she said.

All seven lights came on again, and from the center of the room came the sound of something sliding. To Wade, it seemed more mechanical than electronic. The sound continued for another few seconds, then stopped with a click.

"The sarcophagus," he whispered. His arms and legs tingled as he walked slowly to the large glass coffin, but Lily focused on the source of the noise first. She scurried over to the foot of the coffin. The marble molding around the base was unbroken except in one spot, where a short length of black marble was protruding two or three inches. As the ceiling light haloed her face and hair, she knelt and pried at the close-fitting molding.

It slid out another three inches and stopped.

Wade watched as she pushed her fingers behind the molding, and felt around and around, until her whole body quivered.

"Lily?"

From inside she drew a small rectangular item and held it up to the light.

It was a burnished wooden box, two inches deep and as long and wide as two decks of playing cards set end to end.

She gasped. "The box is so heavy. Wade? Could this be it? Omigod, what if Darrell and Becca find the head? We'll have both parts."

"We don't have anything yet," he said. "Open the box."

She let out all her breath. "Okay . . . okay . . ." Holding the bottom of the box in her hand, she undid the simple clasp and tilted the lid.

Silver light bloomed out of the inside of the box. She glanced away, blinked, then looked back. Her face burned with the glow. "Wade . . ."

The body of Serpens was a thing of rods and hinges and wires—coiled and braided into the shape of an angled *S*. It gleamed of silver, tooled and delicately shaped and studded with diamonds of varying sizes and shapes. It shone like a constellation, its own impossible source of brilliant light.

"It's electric, Wade. Or, I don't know."

"It looks like it's moving," he whispered, feeling his fingers reaching for it, wanting to touch it.

"It's hot, and it's humming or something," she said. "And it *will* move after we connect it to the head," Lily breathed. "Oh, man, Wade. After all this, after the whole long journey, I can't believe we actually—"

There was a sudden dull whump from the square outside, a muffled blast, then yelling. This was followed by a distant spray of machine-gun fire. An engine revved noisily. Then another smaller blast, closer this time. Next came a rapid series of concussions. The floor shook beneath them.

"What in the world—" Wade started.

The square outside thundered with explosions and the rumbling of vehicles approaching the tomb swiftly. There was another blast. The walls shook, and a bright spear of light flashed across the room. Alarms sounded as a second entrance at the rear of the tomb swung in and closed quickly with a breath of frigid air.

Lily clamped down the lid of the box. "Wade, no, no, no—"

Before he could move, the room was filled with heavily armed soldiers dressed in black parkas and ski masks. The Brotherhood? FSB? He couldn't tell. They surrounded both of them. One who looked like he might be the leader grabbed the box from Lily and threw her into Wade. She yelled at the man.

"Shut up," he growled. "Get up the stairs. Both of you."

"Stairs?" Wade hadn't seen any.

The other men pushed both kids roughly to the back corner through a narrow hall to a set of marble stairs that led upward. They forced them to climb. Wade felt as if he and Lily were being led to their execution. She shook as she held on to his arm. "Omigod, Wade," she whispered. "What . . . what are they going to do?"

There was a door at the top of the steps. One of the men shot at the handle and kicked the door open. Snow swirled in at them. The air quaked to the sound of gunfire and the heavy rolling of military vehicles.

Wade didn't move, and he held Lily so tightly she couldn't, either.

"Go!" the officer said, and they were suddenly outside on one of the steps of the pyramid. It was a kind of reviewing platform overlooking the square. It had a marble wall about waist high. The square was a battleground. There were at least two military tanks now, several transports, some with military insignia, others unmarked. The army against the Brotherhood.

All at once, the air was different, full of pressure. Through the gunfire and the roar of the wind came a heavy thwack-thwack that overwhelmed every sound.

"A helicopter!" Lily cried.

A small black helicopter thundered out of the storm overhead. Snow flew around them as the chopper hovered a mere two feet from the roof of the top level. Wade clutched Lily to himself, each bracing the other to keep from being blown off, while both were locked in the vise-grip of several Brotherhood troops. They mounted the final steps to the roof itself.

The blades slowed. The door of the helicopter opened. Galina pounced out and calmly received the box from the officer who had taken it.

She turned to Wade. With a surprisingly penetrating voice over the sound of the battle below and the helicopter above, she said, "It turns out to be a good thing you two did not die in Vorkuta. You have found Serpens for me. And now that this relic will lead me to the next one, you have outlived your usefulness."

Galina slid the box lid off.

The object inside shone like a full moon on her face, flashing among the whirling snowflakes and beaming into her two-colored eyes like a spotlight, a laser. In that glow, Wade saw, Galina was more beautiful, if that was possible, than at the coal mine. Pale and pure in a strange way. Unless what he thought was beauty was something else. Electricity? A raw obsession? Hunger?

As if she *had to have* the relics? As if she *needed* the Eternity Machine?

As if there were another deadline that only *she* was under?

A very rare and almost unknown modality of cancer.

Galina drew in a very long, very slow breath. "The body of Serpens. I have recovered what Rubashov's father stole from the tomb of my . . . Grand Master . . . Albrecht von Hohenzollern. . . ."

Wade's chest was frozen. "How did you even know we were here?"

She raised her eyes from the relic. "Once I saw that you had survived Vorkuta, I knew that the good doctor had given you a clue. The Brotherhood followed you from the airport, partway, at least. Your friend Terence Ackroyd managed to set a little ruse for us, too. But I deduced the rest."

The square echoed with the rapid hammering of machine guns, then two unmarked transports exploded in flames. The lead officer stepped forward. "Miss Krause, the tide is turning against us."

Galina drew a gun on Wade and Lily. There was a strange, resigned look on her face. It was the end, Wade thought. They were out of time, unless . . .

All at once, he pushed Lily with all his might off

the edge of the roof. She disappeared over the side, swearing at the top of her lungs. He jumped after her, yelling "Dive-dive-dive!" as bullets flew, ricocheting off the marble walls of the platform below. Lily was on her feet, screaming along the passage, as machine-gun fire thudded the walls above and below them. She tumbled down the passage into the tomb, Wade at her heels. They raced down the stairs all the way to the subbasement just as an explosion thundered against the front wall of the tomb.

They stole out the same door they had used to enter.

Amid the chaos of automatic gunfire and vehicles and wailing sirens and whirling snow, Wade watched the helicopter ascend over the tomb, over the square, and move west across the city. "Galina has it! Lily, she has our relic!"

In the confusion of the final military assault on the Brotherhood, an unmarked car skidded to a stop at the rear corner of the tomb. Chief Inspector Yazinsky was behind the wheel. "In!" he ordered as Terence bolted from the backseat and dragged them both in with steely arms. "We need to leave Moscow right now!"

"What about the others?" Wade cried as he hit the floor with Lily. "Sara? Becca?"

"The city's riot forces are sealing off the square!" the

inspector said. "Not even I shall be able to pass!"

"But what about Sara?" Wade asked.

"There's no news!" said Terence. "We have to leave now."

The car tore away from the crisscrossing fire, racing past the Kremlin wall.

"But Sara," Lily cried. "Tell us!"

"We know nothing!" the inspector cried. "Nothing!"

CHAPTER SIXTY-ONE

Greywolf

Seven minutes to midnight became six minutes to midnight.

The machine—Kronos—shuddered as if it were alive. Darrell heard its clock ticking unceasingly. It had an open mechanism of fine gears and claws spinning rapidly, and hands of a sort that were turning counter-clockwise. The large wheel looked as if it was growing hot, and its barrel . . . was aimed directly at his mother's chest. The whole thing was counting down.

"Take my mother out of there!" he screamed at the man fiddling with the machine's knobs and levers. *"Get her out or I swear—"*

"I'm sorry," said the crazy man, having scooped up Marceline's gun before they could stop him. "I've never hurt anyone. But you see my time is nearly up. I haven't any left. I had a mother once, too, but I must . . . They want 1517, you know. This is unusual. I hope you see that. A master programmer who shoots people."

"He's crazy," Becca whispered to Darrell and his stepfather. "We have to get Sara out by ourselves."

Darrell edged slowly across the room, step by step with Becca and his stepfather, the pipe swinging in his hand like a pendulum. "I'm going to get her out."

"Stop where you are," squealed a voice behind them.

Ebner von Braun was standing by the door. He had a pistol in each hand, one aimed at Becca's forehead, the other at Darrell's chest just below the neck. He sneered. "Your mother is in the hands of Kronos now." His voice was hoarse, weary. "You are too late to do anything but watch her leave us."

Darrell's anger stuck like a knife in his throat. He wanted to tear the bent man limb from limb. But the guy was armed. He was *well* armed.

The machine went into another mode now. Its wheel began to turn quickly.

"Five minutes," Ebner said, his feet firmly planted on the floor. "Isn't it exciting?"

Roald was standing directly behind Darrell. Becca glared at Darrell, as if to get his attention. *I understand,* he thought. *The guy is an insane creep, and you're afraid.*

But that wasn't it. Becca flicked her glance down to the pocket of her jacket. The relic was there. So close to the German he could probably sniff it, if he wasn't such a demon-idiot-creep-troll. Then Becca raised three fingers so only Darrell could see them.

Three fingers! Three fingers mean . . . create a diversion!

Before he could devise anything, he heard a whimper. "Darrell, I love you."

It was his mother. Darrell swung around to see her lift up her pale face.

"I love you . . . ," she repeated.

Her faint voice exploded something inside him, and he knew what the diversion was. He jumped back and jerked the pipe around as far and as fast as he could. Into Helmut Bern's forehead. The man groaned and fell, dropping his gun. Ebner raised his suddenly, when Becca shrieked at the top of her lungs and Roald rammed him like an offensive tackle.

Becca then twirled impossibly and jumped with both feet on Ebner's right arm. His other gun went off. He screamed. His shoe had burst open and was smoking. He'd shot his own foot, the bullet going through and then grazing Marceline in the side. Darrell scrambled for the machine gun. He raised it to the cage lock. "Mom, look away—"

"Give it to me!" cried his stepfather. Taking it from him, he pressed the barrel to the cage lock. He pulled the trigger. The blast was deafening. The chain blew apart.

"Stand away from Kronos! Leave your mother inside!" Ebner had wobbled to his feet, his gun in his bleeding hand, and he had it pressed into Becca's throat. "Move and the girl dies. Then you die. Finish it, Bern. Finish Kronos!"

Bern staggered to his feet, bloody forehead and all, and resecured Sara in the cage. Darrell and the others were frozen where they stood. Bern jammed a quivering finger on the keyboard. "And the code begins to upload. Only three minutes now."

"No!" Darrell cried helplessly. "Please!"

The sound of the machine changed again, growing to a fever pitch. The giant wheel was spinning faster and faster, the barrel glowing with a white heat, while three jagged-edged brass cones located on the base of the machine began to rotate.

Becca couldn't think. As if the oxygen to her brain were shut off. The diversion hadn't worked. If there was a chance, any chance at all, she alone had it.

"Here," she said. "Here, take it."

Darrell turned. "Bec, no . . . no . . ."

Her hands shook. She thrust her fingers into her parka as Ebner stared at her.

"It? *It*?" he screamed.

She removed a small wrapped bundle, held it dangling in front of the bent German's face. "Take it. The head of Serpens. No more killing!"

The troll practically turned inside out, he looked so stunned. "Galina! I have it!" He thrust his hand at the relic, when Becca threw it as hard as she could out the door and down the stairs. "Fool!" he screamed, limping after it with his wounded foot. He was nearly out of the room when Marceline thrust her foot straight out. Ebner tripped out the door and back down the stairs. Everyone else ran toward the machine.

Darrell elbowed the programmer aside. He threw aside the chain, wrenched open the cage. "Mom!" he screamed. "Mom!" But the creep was all bone now, clawing at the controls. Just as Roald reached him, grabbing his fingers, Helmut Bern drove his hand at a blue lever on the console.

"Galina, I did it!" he shrieked. "Kronos is perfect!" Becca pounded his face and hands, then heard a final tick of the clock like a thunderous explosion, and Darrell screamed—*"Mom—Mom—Mom—Mom!"*—and Roald threw his hands toward Sara just as a blinding light flashed across Becca's eyes like a white razor, and then there was nothing.

Nothing but darkness and silence and nothing.

CHAPTER SIXTY-TWO

Bosporus Strait, Turkey
March 24
11:57 a.m.

The old steam-powered ferry rocked gently on the waves.

Galina Krause leaned on the starboard railing and watched in silence as ancient Istanbul shimmered before her eyes. A city of white and glistening gold, beckoning her to pause at the crossroads of Europe and Asia Minor before passing through the strait into the broad Sea of Marmara and beyond, to the Mediterranean.

"Miss Krause."

The voice was deep, icy. She turned. "Markus Wolff."

"You asked me to investigate the Somosierra incident."

"What have you discovered about the driver, Diego Vargas? The young student?"

"You will recall the theory that a time event establishes a hole in the past," Wolff said. "A hole that might linger some amount of time after the event before collapsing."

She trembled. "And?"

Wolff handed her a black-and-white photograph. "This image was taken by the war photographer Robert Capa in Somosierra. It dates from early September 1936. From the same sequence as Capa's famous portrait of the dying soldier."

This print showed a young boy, his jacket in tatters, his face worn by war—or something worse—staring, hollow-eyed, at the camera.

"The Copernicus Room's facial-recognition software has confirmed that this face is that of Fernando Salta, aged eleven years, four months, thirteen days," said Wolff.

"Fernando Salta?"

"The student stranded at Somosierra in 1808," said Wolff. "This photograph is proof that our student has traveled forward from 1808 to 1936. Fernando Salta is making his way back to the present."

Galina stared at the photograph. The boy's dark eyes burned with something. Desire to return? Certainly. But what else? Anger? Revenge? What manner of creature was eleven-year-old Fernando Salta becoming, during his passage through time? And where and when would he turn up next?

"What do you wish me to do now?" Wolff asked.

Galina removed the miniature Holbein portrait from her jacket pocket. She uttered a simple instruction. "London. Discover what can be discovered." Wolff pocketed the portrait and drifted away among the other passengers.

Galina turned to the sparkling cityscape, but her view of the many-towered mosques of the ancient metropolis blurred. Her fingers slipped into the same zipped pocket and removed Serpens's two sections. She connected them with an easy twist at the inner hinges.

The relic, complete for the first time in five centuries, lay in her palm for a moment, then twitched.

Tick . . . tick . . . tick . . .

The very breath was sucked out of her lungs. She felt dizzy, intoxicated by the hypnotic movement of the serpent sliding across her skin. Suddenly, as if it had stung her—cursed her—she unhooked the thing. Her thoughts flashed to Copernicus, disassembling his Legacy, distributing its relics.

Perhaps he'd known the horror of such power after all.

Ebner limped up behind her, a bruised fighter. She knew he was smiling despite his various wounds. "A momentous juncture," he said, leaning heavily on his cane. "On the one hand, the first relic, Vela, will soon be ours. A new effort is being mounted by the gentlemen from Marseille to retrieve it from the Morgan's vault in New York City. And with Serpens in our possession, we will soon locate the third Copernicus artifact. It is only a matter of time before the astrolabe is rebuilt, my dear."

"We are out front once more, Ebner, and sailing into the warm south."

He grinned. "I should tell you that the particle injection Kronos delivered to its passenger is working splendidly. Already our traveler has been located. Alas, not at the precise time and place we hoped—a thousand miles and six months off—but bizarrely close enough."

Galina felt her body flood with a strange glee. "Ebner, I want the Kaplans dead." She turned her eyes to him. "Kill them. All but the one, do you understand?"

Ebner laughed a subtle laugh. He tapped a few

buttons on his cell phone. "I am sending an alert to our man on the scene."

Galina knew that at that instant a message was delivered not only in Berlin, but also to a computer screen in a flat on faraway Foulden Road in London.

☑ Terminate immediately

"You have made Mr. Doyle very happy," he said.

"Collect my bags, Ebner; we are entering port."

As her doting physicist receded, scuffling across the deck on his cane, Galina leaned against the railing. She drew in lungful after lungful of sea air and lightly touched the scar on her neck. It was warm.

Once again, she had nearly died in Russia. She would never set foot there again, if she could help it, and thanks to the children, she would likely not have to. Not in this lifetime, at least.

CHAPTER SIXTY-THREE

London
March 27
9:27 a.m.

Wade Kaplan stared up at the exquisite vaulted ceilings of Westminster Abbey, but he wasn't seeing them. The thousands of footsteps that padded and clicked and scampered and slid over the marble floors of the enormous nave were no more than a blur of echoes, a soft whoosh of noise behind his twisting thoughts.

What happened?

How did it all happen?

Could we have done anything differently?

What do we do now?

Someone touched his shoulder. He looked to see Lily's slender fingers. He didn't want her to remove them. He needed something real to prove to him that they were actually there and that it had happened the way it did.

"You were good back there," she said. "In Russia. You were good. Me, too, of course, but you, too."

"We did what we could, right? There wasn't anything else we could have done, was there?"

"No . . . ," she said, as if maybe there was doubt. Then, more firmly, "No."

As tough as he thought they had become in New York at the beginning of the hunt for Serpens, they were tougher now. Tougher, harder, more steeled for the road ahead. It had been a horrifying week and a half of extremes—of bitter arctic cold, of danger and countless brushes with death—pushing each of them to the brink. It had exhausted every ounce of everything they'd had, but they'd come through it.

Mostly.

Lily and Darrell stood next to him, all three staring quietly into the shadows beneath the gallery of the north transept, where Wade's father leaned over the side of a wheelchair and hugged Sara as if he could lose her again at any minute, as if he were hugging her for the first time ever.

Sara Kaplan was alive and safe and with them again.

Wade recalled the frantic moment when they'd all met in the early morning at the airport in Moscow.

How Sara had wrapped her weak arms around Lily and Wade together and brought Darrell and everyone into it, crying their names over and over, not singling out her real son over anyone else, how soon they were all crying.

Then, on the flight to London, while the kids took turns filling her in about the search for Vela *and* Serpens, Sara was stunned and silent, until she threw herself on all the children, Darrell last and most, then completely lost it, shaking uncontrollably in his father's arms the rest of the long flight. She slept in the London hospital for a day and a half, where she was monitored and nourished. For three days they were in a kind of limbo, waiting on pins and needles until yesterday morning, when she woke up and it was suddenly over. "I want to see London," she said, and that was that.

Of course Sara was weak and she would, her doctors insisted, become exhausted despite herself. They urged Roald to make sure she used a wheelchair for another few days, but they were pleased to say that she would make a complete recovery. Sara's ordeal, everyone was happy to realize, was over.

Wade looked around himself like a panorama camera. "So where's Bec—"

Then there she was, still wrapped in her fur-lined parka, standing quietly to the side of them as if she'd been there the whole time. She wore a puzzled frown on her face, and her eyes were downcast nearly to her feet, while she rocked on the marble tiles as if to keep her balance.

At least since the Moscow airport, Becca had been so quiet—so *quiet*—and had barely spoken a word. He stepped over to her. "Hey. We lost you for a second."

"Lost?"

"I mean, how are you feeling? The headaches. Your fever? Were you crying?"

"What?" she said. "No. Why?" She lifted her hand, apparently surprised to find her cheeks wet and salty. Her puzzled look returned. "Oh. Maybe. It's . . . it's good to have Sara back."

He nodded over and over again, aware he was grinning like a fool but unable to stop. "Oh, yeah, it's good. I feel like crying, too."

Lost . . .

Becca had stood there immobile for many minutes,

her eyes throbbing, even in the abbey's diffused light. Her head felt as if it were being bisected by a battle-ax separating the hemispheres in a way that had, three times so far, preceded something like a blackout. The crossbow wound on her arm hurt like never before, too. It might have stung from the hospital antiseptic she'd received here in London, but it felt like it wasn't healing so much as deepening, getting worse.

Around Becca in every direction, the noise of the great stone room crashed into her ears like waves battering a deck in a storm. It brought back to mind scenes from *Moby-Dick*, which she had been reading just last week.

When she stepped after Wade to join his parents, who clung to each other like the lost loves reunited that they actually were, Becca was not aware of the words of her friends or the echo of their feet on the stones so much as the sudden terrible creaking of wood, and an odd forlorn voice in her ears crying, *I am lost . . . lost! Bring me home!*

Lily sidled up to Becca, joining arms with her. "You guys, we are never, *ever* splitting up again. I never want to make big decisions. Ever. Not without all of you there to back me up when I decide something brilliant." Lily held back her tears as well as she could, but she finally had to turn away and rub her cheeks dry. "I know I've said it a billion times since Russia, but I still sort of can't believe we had Serpens and lost it."

"It was worth it," Darrell said softly. "But yeah. We had it, and we gave it away."

The loss of both halves of Serpens was a gnawing ache to them all.

In the coming days, Lily knew, the weirdness of Kronos and Galina and the loss of Serpens and all of it would probably become less a kind of grief and more an alarm, goading them to keep up the hunt. It would force them into their next mission. They were Guardians of the Astrolabe of Copernicus. They were the *Novizhny*. If there had been the slightest doubt about that when they entered Russia, if they'd thought they were really only there to find Sara, there was no doubt now. After what had happened at Greywolf and Vorkuta and Red Square, there could never be any doubt.

Becca stayed mostly quiet about it, but Darrell had given them a stunning second-by-second account of the last moments before the device's clock struck midnight.

"After Ebner bolted for the jewels," Darrell had said, "Helmut Bern tried to keep us from getting Mom out of Kronos. But Becca punched—I'm telling you *punched*—the guy with, like, a movie punch. Bern looked like he'd just been insulted or something; then he fell back at the last second before midnight. Dad and I yanked Mom out of Kronos, the machine went all *ka-boom* on us, the lights and everything went out, and Dad dragged us all out of there, even Marceline, without looking back."

Lily couldn't get enough of the story, partly because she and Wade had had no idea what had happened before they got to the airport, nor that they had both recovered—then given up—their halves of Serpens. Neither Terence nor Inspector Yazinsky had had any news from Greywolf, either about Roald and Sara or about Darrell and Becca. Everyone had kept checking phones, but there had been no word.

Bright morning light streamed in the stained-glass windows of the nave, crisscrossing the floor in shapes of shadow and color. Darrell felt peaceful for the first time since his mother had been kidnapped.

"I keep thinking we should be holding Serpens right now," he said, gazing up at the brilliant gold altarpiece, then back at them. "We should have the relic right here in our hands. Cursed or not, I think we'd be able to deal with it. It's supposed to be ours. I mean . . . well . . . we should have it, end of story."

There wasn't much else to say. They all felt the same.

"I keep wondering if the umbrella man is out there somewhere," Wade said, scanning the vast nave of the abbey. "Not that we'd know it if he's in disguise."

"No problem," said Darrell. "Lily can spot a wig fifty feet away, right, Lil?"

She laughed. "Just one of my talents." Then she sighed. "I guess we go back to Texas now? Just like that?"

Wade grumbled. "No one wants to, but we don't know where to start searching for the next relic, do we? Only Galina does."

In a day or two, their London rest would be over. Lily's and Becca's parents were due to arrive to take them home. There would be all sorts of craziness trying to justify all they'd done, but Darrell knew that when the girls' parents saw his mother safe and heard how she wouldn't be there if not for the two girls' help, they'd realize that there had been no choice. They would all have to work out their individual returns to Austin, however, and even how safe that might be, given how the Order forced them from their homes. That was as big a question as anything else.

But then, only one thing *wasn't* a question.

They'd made a solemn oath, the four of them, that they were "totally and completely and absolutely" committed to the relic quest. And Darrell's mother and stepfather were just as committed. They had no real idea where to start looking for the third relic—a giant obstacle, but they'd overcome obstacles before.

Lots of them.

Wade was the first to see a familiar-looking boy trot across the marble stones to them.

"Thanks for meeting me," Julian Ackroyd said. "All safe and sound?"

"Neither," Darrell said, "but good enough. How's your dad?"

"Fine. He's tied up with the London foundation until tonight, but I've just gotten off the phone with him," Julian said. "Paul and Marceline are back in Paris and doing all right, but both will be out of action for a while. They reported that there's not a stitch of information on Galina Krause right now. When she disappeared from Red Square in the chopper, she might just as well have been swallowed up by the storm. Dad's people are searching, but you know . . ." He trailed off.

"She'll discover where the next relic is," Becca said, as if it pained her to talk. Her brow was furrowed again. "She'll do what she can to rebuild the Eternity Machine. She'll destroy the world."

"We might be able to help with that," Julian said. "Honestly, I've never seen Dad so into anything. Me, either, actually. He's dedicating a whole division of our foundation to stopping Galina Krause. We're not letting this go."

"Thanks for that," said Wade, watching Becca's expression darken as Roald wheeled Sara out of Poets' Corner and across the floor toward them.

"Which brings me to the real reason I wanted to meet you here in London," Julian said. He swiped his phone. "In addition to helping with the London activities of the Ackroyd Foundation, I've been doing some work. I believe you know this man?"

They leaned over the picture to see a tall, white-haired man in a long black leather coat standing by a river. He had close-cropped white hair and a stony expression.

"OMG, that's Markus Wolff!" Lily said. "He killed us in San Francisco! Well, almost!"

"He said he would finish the job if he ever saw us again," said Darrell.

"Markus Wolff," Julian said, "works exclusively for Galina Krause as a sort of personal archaeologist."

"And personal assassin," Lily added.

"There are boats behind him," Becca said. "Where

was this picture taken, and when?"

"This morning on the Thames, not two and a half miles from here," Julian said, closing his phone. "During the current renovations of the historic area, the remains of a trading barge from the early fifteen hundreds have been discovered. The question is, what's so interesting to Galina Krause about an old boat?"

"A boat . . . ," Becca murmured.

Wade stepped next to her. "A clue to another relic. A definite clue."

"You must be Julian!" Sara said softly, raising her hand to him as Wade's father wheeled her to a stop.

"I am!" Julian took her hand with a broad smile. "I'm happy to meet you, Sara Kaplan, and *so* happy to see you up and around."

"No way can you keep my mom down," Darrell said.

"And you won't," Sara said, her voice coming back to her. "Does anyone know where Galina's gone to? I have a score to settle with that . . . young woman."

Wade nearly laughed, then told her about Markus Wolff being seen at the riverside. "If Wolff is there, it has to mean something."

Sara nodded sharply. "All right then." She locked eyes with his father, then with each of the others. "We're going to the river. The hunt is on."

"Yes!" said Darrell, slapping Wade's shoulder and giving Lily a high five. "It's on, all right. It's on until it's done!"

Julian smiled. "My limo is just outside. "We can be there in ten minutes."

As they hurried across the marble floor of the abbey and out into the bustling noisy streets of London, the children knew there would nevermore be an atom of doubt.

They were on their quest once more.

They were the *Novizhny*.

They were Guardians.

EPILOGUE

North Sea
October 30, 1517
Evening

The whole thing was no more than a blur to Helmut Bern's fevered mind.

There'd been a flash, and something like a hundred-foot blade going through his chest, and he'd been sucked through an industrial-strength garbage disposal, ground down to nothing, and his bits reassembled. In the proper order, he hoped.

You there, sir . . .

476

But where in the world was he? His eyes ached when he glanced around.

You there, sir . . .

He appeared to be on the deck of an ancient sailing vessel. His stomach twisted. The ocean was stupid. As the ship tumbled up and down over ridiculous waves, he shivered under a filthy, mouse-ridden blanket of some kind. He was very cold. And also hot. His face felt like a frying pan. But why wasn't he at Greywolf? And where was the woman? And Kronos?

"You there . . . sir," a voice said in German.

Some tedious man bent over him. He was dressed in a variety of cloaks and sashes and belts as if it were Halloween. *Is that a sword at his waist? Good God!*

"You, there, Brother—"

"Yes? Yes? What's wrong with you?" Helmut snapped. "I hear you. Where the devil am I?"

"Where . . . Brother?"

"Where!" Bern snapped at the man. "As in *at what location*! And why do you keep calling me 'brother'?"

The ship rolled suddenly, lifted like a speedboat, then crashed into the waves again. Lord, the air stank. He tried to sit up but couldn't get his legs unstuck.

"You wear the cloak of a monk, sir," the man said.

Monk? An image flashed across his mind. Yes, yes. He *awoke* some hours ago surrounded by stone, didn't he? A church? Kronos! He saw it. Kronos was in a church. And he had stumbled out of the place and there was the shore, and a ship and . . . He must have blacked out after that, because suddenly he was here.

"What bloody year is this?" Helmut asked.

The Halloween man arched back as if the question were idiotic. He had intelligent, thoughtful eyes, creased with worry and study, perhaps. *A scholar,* Helmut thought. *But a swordsman, too.* The man was pleasantly bearded and tanned, well built, perhaps forty or forty-five, with a slouchy velvet hat perched on his head to complete the costume.

"The year of our Lord 1517, sir."

The gears in Helmut's brain stuttered. 1517? Copernicus had taken a sea journey from Cádiz in Spain in 1517. He himself had programmed the very coordinates into Kronos. But . . . no! It couldn't possibly be! Could it? Had he, Bern, actually done it? Had he actually managed to program Kronos I to send him back safe and sound into the past, with such absolute accuracy? He *was* a genius! Here was the bloody proof!

For the first time, Helmut peered closely at the man standing over him. The look of his face, as clear as it could be through blurry eyes, was as identical to the portraits as any face could be.

"Ha! Ha-ha! You are he!" he cried. "You are Nicolaus Copernicus!"

"Do I know you, sir?" he said. "You rather remind me of someone I once knew."

"When did we leave Cádiz? And where are we bound?"

"Cádiz, sir?" said the man he suspected to be Copernicus. "We did not leave Cádiz."

A cold knife blade of fear entered his spine. "Not Cádiz? But . . . then where is this bloody ship *going*?"

"Brother, we are en route to England."

"England? England!"

Crouching closer, the man set his palm over Helmut's forehead and eyes. "But there will be time for talking later, friend. You are unwell. . . ."

Helmut swatted the hand away and tried to rise, but the deck still refused to let him go. He looked down at the position of his legs. There was something wrong with them. And his fingers were curled, his wrists as weak as rope. He tried to examine them more closely, but seawater kept dripping over his eyes. The skin of his hands was dark red, as if he'd fallen asleep under a sunlamp. His cheeks were raw, and the salt spray stung him. Hot and cold again, both at the same time. "What in the world . . ."

"I know these sores," the man said. "My own brother . . ."

Was Copernicus speaking of his own brother?

The poor Andreas, who everyone knows died of . . . *leprosy*?

It came at Helmut with the force of a tsunami. The journey in Kronos had not only taken him to the wrong place and time, it had done something else to him. The particle injection! The radioisotope! It had sickened him!

Just then a shape moved behind the astronomer. Was this the legendary young assistant, Hans Novak, creeping behind his master?

But it was not Novak. It was not a boy at all. It was a girl. Long brown hair, wet, clinging to her face. A . . . parka . . . a modern parka; her cheeks wet, splashed by salt waves; bearing a crazed, puzzled expression; . . . and . . . *I* . . . *know her!*

"I know you!" Helmut screamed in English. "The American girl from Greywolf! They called you . . . Becca! What . . . what are you—"

Yet in that instant, just as she focused before his eyes, the girl vanished from the deck, as if the very air and waves had washed her into oblivion. Or back into the future from when she came.

"I am lost! Lost!" Helmut cried at the top of his lungs. "Bring me home!"

"Sir?"

"Bring me home! Bring me home! Bring me home!"

TO BE CONTINUED in *The Copernicus Archives: Becca and the Prisoner's Cross* . . . and *The Copernicus Legacy: The Golden Vendetta.*

AUTHOR'S NOTE

I've always been fascinated by the layering of imagined story and factual research in a novel and how the two finally become (or should become) indistinguishable.

The Serpent's Curse is of course a piece of fiction, though behind (and above and in between) that fiction was woven a good deal of reading, travel, conversation, code making and breaking, artwork, and a host of other oddments.

Of the books that have seeped into the present story, there are a good number; here are some of the main ones: Arthur Koestler's brilliant novel about a man's fight against inhumanity, *Darkness at Noon*, was a constant, not least for supplying me with the name *Rubashov*, but also for a certain sparkling bleakness of tone. Oh, and for the bit about pacing back and forth in a small cell that more than one character does here. *Gulag: A History*, by Anne Applebaum, and *The Gulag Archipelago: 1918–1956*, by Aleksandr Solzhenitsyn, along with *In Siberia*, by Colin Thubron, were the prime sources for the setting of the Siberian work camp. James H. Billington's *The Icon and the Axe* was useful as a starting place for study of the late-medieval period in Russia. Masha Gessen's *Words Will Break Cement* and *The Snowden Files*, by Luke Harding, were helpful with background color and because they recount current events. On the lighter side, I have to mention Daniel Silva's *Moscow Rules* and *The English Girl*, both delightful nightstand companions during the writing of this book.

ACKNOWLEDGMENTS

My thanks go first to my family. They are the foundation upon which I am blessed to be able to write at all. Heartfelt gratitude also goes to Andrew Freeburg for his close reading of the story's Russian pages, for his suggestions, and for correcting my more obvious mistakes in language and setting. Thanks to Patti Woods for her careful reading of the Venice episode; I do not, however, apologize for her subsequent desire to return there. To Kathryn Silsand and Karen Sherman, my copy editors, countless thanks (or rather, six hundred sixty thanks, based on the latest revision). To Karen, especially, who somehow read the story as deeply and fully as I wrote it, I send my best wishes and kindest thoughts and apologies for the length of the book. You are the best. As before and always, to Claudia Gabel, Melissa Miller, and Katherine Tegen, my good companions on this relic quest, my thanks beyond all thanks.

THE QUEST CONTINUES IN . . .

THE COPERNICUS ARCHIVES

A series of companion novellas,
each told from a different character's point of view!

THE
COPERNICUS
ARCHIVES

COLLECT
THEM ALL!

 KATHERINE TEGEN BOOKS
An Imprint of HarperCollinsPublishers

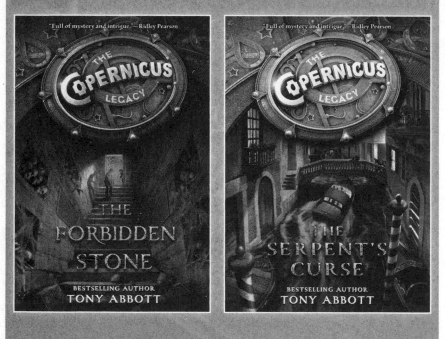

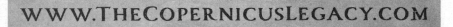

WWW.THECOPERNICUSLEGACY.COM

KATHERINE TEGEN BOOKS
An Imprint of HarperCollins Publishers